NULL STATES

ALSO BY MALKA OLDER

Infomocracy

NULL STATES

THE CENTENAL CYCLE, BOOK 2

MALKA OLDER

A TOM DOHERTY ASSOCIATES BOOK
NEW YORK

NULL STATES

Copyright © 2017 by Malka Older

Edited by Carl Engle-Laird

A Tor.com Book
Published by Tom Doherty Associates
175 Fifth Avenue
New York, NY 10010

www.tor-forge.com

Tor® is a registered trademark of Macmillan Publishing Group, LLC.

The Library of Congress Cataloging-in-Publication Data is available upon request.

ISBN 978-0-7653-9338-8 (hardcover)
ISBN 978-0-7653-9337-1 (ebook)

Our books may be purchased in bulk for promotional, educational, or business use. Please contact your local bookseller or the Macmillan Corporate and Premium Sales Department at 1-800-221-7945, extension 5442, or by email at MacmillanSpecialMarkets@macmillan.com.

First Edition: September 2017

Printed in the United States of America

0 9 8 7 6 5 4 3 2 1

FOR MY PARENTS
Dora Vázquez Older and Marc Louis Older
who make everything possible

ACKNOWLEDGMENTS

Thank you, as always, to my family: Lou and Calyx, my parents Dora and Marc, my brother, Daniel. I couldn't have done it without you.

There are so many people I need to thank from my time in Darfur that I cannot name them all. Thank you to the Sudanese staff of Mercy Corps Mukjar and Mercy Corps Um Dukhun, for your welcome, your kindness, your camaraderie, and everything you taught me. I know many of you may never see or hear about this, but I think about you often and with gratitude. Thank you to the expat and inpat staff of IMC and Save the Children Spain in Mukjar, and Oxfam, Triangle, and MSF Holland in Um Dukhun, and to the Zalingei, Nyala, and Khartoum Mercy Corps staff.

Thanks to everyone who made my time in Spain so wonderful, but most relevant to this book is the amazing Carbonería. In Switzerland, Jeannette Spuhler, Katharina Vögeli, Annahita de la Mare Michalsky and her family, and Jaqueline Latham. I traveled to Saigon alone, but have fond memories of the dance teachers in the park. In Singapore, Yibin Chu for his hospitality and for the introduction to Tiong Bahru. In China, Eric Sun, Wang Ming, Madoka Ono, Don Hayler, Lili Huang, PT Black. In Georgia, the Mercy Corps team and Carmen Crow Sheehan, who could also have been mentioned in the Darfur section, and her family.

Many thanks again to my doctoral advisor, Olivier Borraz,

for his patience as well as for his always interesting questions and insights about governance, democracy, and risk.

Thanks to NaNoWriMo: I wrote a good chunk of this book during November, and my years of NaNoWriMo experience made writing the rest of it easier.

I want to thank the Accountability Lab and Blair Glencorse for partnering with me on donations from *Infomocracy*; I know very well that periodic small donations of entirely unpredictable amounts is not the ideal way for a nonprofit to get funding. I so appreciate their willingness to work with that, and I am very proud of what they do with it.

Many many thanks to the wonderful team at Tor.com for all their support. Carl Engle-Laird's insight and patience has made my books far better. Mordicai Knode and Katharine Duckett have gone above and beyond in making sure that as many people as possible get to read the books. Wilhelm Staehle's amazing, complex covers have probably sold a lot of books for me, and they certainly make me very happy every time I look at them. Richard Shealy's care and flexibility saved me from many grammatical and spelling errors, and I particularly appreciate his attention to little-known place names on this book. Thanks also to David Gil, Thomas Wier, Rima Kohli, Catherine Galloway, Catherine Richard, Cynthia Rowe, and Sylivester Ernest for some last-minute language assistance. Any errors are entirely my own.

NULL STATES

CHAPTER 1

A huge tree branches high over the entrance to the compound. The shade would be welcome, because even in the rainy season the daytime temperatures are over 43 degrees, but a flock of large white birds is draped over it. Roz has to hope she'll get used to the smell, but getting in and out of the compound is going to be a literal crapshoot.

Information, projecting annotations and explanations over her vision, can tell her that the tree is an *Acacia auriculiformus* and that the birds are *Ciconia ciconia*, but Roz doesn't find out why they don't get rid of the birds until Amran's briefing. It's the first topic she covers, before the logistics of their meeting with the head of state or even the security guidelines.

"The birds weren't there when I signed the rental contract three months ago," Amran tells them, in a tone that says the cawing has already frayed her nerves. The owner of the compound, Halima, is pregnant, and it would be bad luck to disturb the birds and worse luck to cut down the tree. From the sound of it, Amran has mooted both possibilities.

Roz isn't going to judge her. Amran is the Information field lead for this centenal and will be here for years, while she and the rest of the SVAT team are only in Kas for a week, maybe two. She's more interested in the problem of how difficult it would have been to get that story from Information. Without the inside knowledge about the pregnancy you could ask about birds and trees all you liked without getting anywhere near the explanation. Roz starts doodling an algorithm.

"According to Information, the birds are seasonal migrants," Minzhe puts in hopefully.

"Halima says they will leave after the rainy season," Amran says, but she doesn't sound cheered. Roz switches on visuals of the local weather forecasts. This week: SUNNY, 47.8. SUNNY, 47.2. SUNNY, 46.1. SUNNY, 48.3. SUNNY, 48.2. SUNNY, 46.7. NEXT WEEK: SUNNY, 49.4. SUNNY, 48.5. SUNNY, 48.8. SUNNY, 48.4. SUNNY, 47.8. SUNNY, 46.1. SUNNY, 46.6. She flips further ahead: SUNNY, SUNNY, SUNNY.

Having explained the smell, Amran is getting into the protein of her presentation with a three-dimensional headshot of a thin, neatly bearded man with a wide smile and twinkling eyes rotating in the center of the room. A personal history tracks down the side of the image. "Abubakar Ahmed Yagoub, known by the identifier Al-Jabali because he was born in the Djabal refugee camp in what was then eastern Chad."

"And he became centenal governor here?" Charles's interjection is more disbelief than question, but Amran answers anyway.

"He moved here ten years ago and was one of the key activists pushing for the adoption of micro-democracy. Although of course it didn't happen until the Sudanese state had collapsed from within, Al-Jabali is credited with laying the groundwork for a smooth transition—and leveraging that into political success, both as centenal governor here and as head of state for the whole DarFur government."

Amran throws up a large projection of the area previously known as Darfur, now divided into 78 centenals of 100,000 people. Each is empowered to choose its own government from among the over two thousand worldwide, but in this isolated region most of them have stayed local. Thirty of those centenals are held by the DarFur government, led by Al-Jabali. It's a strong showing for a government competing in its first election, but Al-Jabali doesn't seem satisfied. The government's policy papers and rhetoric are rigorously, even stridently pacifist, but there have been troubling occurrences of nationalist talk and hints at expansionism. The most disturbing incident occurred a few weeks ago, when nineteen DarFuri citizens staged a rally in a centenal belonging to 888, a corporate government that originated in China. Al-Jabali has been courting the international stage, promoting the expansion of the Dar-Fur state to anyone who will listen. He hasn't gotten much play globally, but his rivals here are paying attention.

This is not a particularly sexy assignment—no knife-wielding fanatics ranting about people they hate just across the centenal line, no dicey border redrawings—but Roz can feel a jitter of excitement in the team anyway. For the past year and a half, SVAT agents, the elite of Information's global bureaucracy, have been cleaning up the mess left by the last election. Confusion, sabotage, recounts, and fraud sparked low-level conflicts in more than a hundred centenals worldwide. The first, urgent missions put SVAT agents and security officers up close and in the faces of swindled voters to explain what happened and why they shouldn't take out their frustration on their rivals, the ones they thought they had vanquished politically. Progress was slow and irregular, but the work was never boring, and less than two years later the handful of remaining battles have settled into a tense equilibrium. It isn't over, but this is their first job not directly related to the election fraud since it happened. Finally, they're back to classic SVAT work: a populace that, after a long history of propaganda exposure and conflict, is high-risk for nationalism and other pathologies, and a charismatic new government that doesn't yet understand the extent to which Information will call them on their exaggerations.

Amran is going through the locations of various episodes on the map, sometimes showing vid or zooming in for a quick auto-tour. "Al-Jabali has said he will address these problems, and there is no hint yet of open conflict, but given the history of this region, your team was requested as a precautionary measure." Roz notes the passive voice and wonders whether Amran opposed their deployment. She hasn't been here very long herself; she might have wanted a chance to work on things before the Specialized Voter Action Tactics experts swooped in to save the day.

"It's tough when people who have been the losers for so long finally get their chance, only to find the rules have changed," Maria comments. Roz is mildly surprised to hear that kind of empathy-based extrapolation from a pollster. Maria is the only member of the four-person team Roz hasn't worked with before, and Roz hasn't had time yet to form an opinion.

"Ten years must seem like a long time to wait for their next chance to expand," Charles agrees. Round-headed and forty-something, he's the oldest team member and the one Roz has worked with the most: solid, skilled at building rapport with local elites, and not in the least starry-eyed about Information. She wonders if he's making his feelings known about the latest controversy in the upper reaches of the bureaucracy. The director level at Information is concerned enough about cynicism and disengagement—and the competence of the new Policy1st Supermajority—that they're considering speeding up the election cycle, holding them every five years instead of every ten. For now, those discussions are both secret and hypothetical.

Amran's presentation is over, and they should get moving. "For today," Roz begins. "Let's focus on building the relationship with Al-Jabali, learning how he sees things. Reinforce election protocol in the background, but subtly. And listen for issues where we can work with Al-Jabali to make him—them—happy." She looks at Amran. "Is it time for our meeting?"

Amran blinks, probably glancing at the time in her personal, eyeball-level projection. "Uh, yes, we should head over there." She is twisting her hands in the front of her long skirt. "Actually, Al-Jabali may be a few minutes late. It seems he's traveling from another DarFur centenal." Unusual to make an Information team wait. Roz steels herself for an uncomfortable mission. "The visit was planned before I gave him the SVAT team's schedule," Amran adds, but Roz is still skeptical.

"Can you confirm his ETA?" Charles asks. They are sitting in a square brick room, one of two freestanding offices inside the compound. There is a wide-bladed fan shuffling air through the vent openings high in the walls, and the outside of the building is wrapped in heat reflectors, giving the interior the feel of a shaded courtyard. Even so, Roz can feel sweat dripping down her back. No one wants to stand out in the sun waiting for a dignitary any longer than necessary. Amran blinks rapidly, checking his location and trajectory on Information.

"Twenty-two minutes," she says. "But the rest of the government is already assembling at the arrival area, so we should go."

They take the exit under the bird-filled tree like a gauntlet, one by one, dodging between the white splatters on the sandy ground. Outside the brick wall of the compound, the packed-sand street runs straight between other similar walls, some of reed or sticks, others reaching the exalted level of concrete. A pair of children guiding a donkey with taps from a branch pass them at the cross street. There is little else to see, and everything is in shades of brown and beige. Information here is starved for complexity, for objects to identify and backstories to report on, and Roz gets a wealth of detail about everything she sees: the bricks were baked on the outskirts of town; the reeds are collected during the rainy season; the concrete comes in by truck over pitted dirt roads through the desert, their routes traced on maps that hover briefly before her eyes, 60% transparent. The children have no public Information showing, but the donkey is a Riffawi.

Despite the dullness of the colors and scarcity of input—no pop-out advids, even!—the newness of it all sparkles for Roz. She always enjoys this time at the beginning of a deployment, when all the Information is fresh and she can feel a composite understanding of the place building piece by piece in her mind.

She finds herself walking next to Minzhe. "How does it feel to be home?" she asks. Minzhe knows this area better than any of them. He grew up in Nyala, the largest nearby city, in what is now a centenal belonging to 888.

"Pretty good, actually. It's been a while." He stretches his shoulders back and exhales, as though the intense heat and burning glare of sun off sand are pleasant for him. All of them are wearing heat-reflective clothing except for Minzhe, who's wearing a flowing white jellabiya. Roz is sweltering despite the climate-control properties of her iridescent trousers, but Minzhe wears the thin cotton as though he belongs there. She doesn't even think he's sweating. "They almost didn't let me come, can you believe that?"

"Why?"

"Because of my mother. In the end, though, they decided it wouldn't be too much of a conflict."

Roz has no idea what he's talking about, and glances down so she can check with Information. If he sees the update flashing against her eye, he won't be offended: he gave her enough of a cue to search on without volunteering the intel himself, so looking it up is the most appropriate response.

In the meantime, she keeps up the small talk. "I don't know. I feel like I get sent on every African mission they get. And where I'm from is nothing like this place." Culturally, climactically, ethnically.

"I bet they've never sent you to your hometown, though, right?"

True. But her home is a special case. She sees that Minzhe's mother is now the governor of the centenal he grew up in. Roz can understand why that would give them pause. Information always tries to avoid letting its officers get too close to their jobs; that's why Amran, the field lead here, is Somali instead of Fur or Beri or anything else from this region. "Besides," Minzhe goes on, "it wouldn't go over so well if everyone on this mission looked more like me or Maria than like you and Charles."

Maria, chatting with Charles a few paces ahead of them, has already turned ruddy with the sun, giving her narrow, slightly puffy face a chafed look. She has a translucent blue scarf pulled loosely over her light brown hair, though Amran told them that foreigners don't need to cover their heads. The public Information that Roz sees projected next to her face gives her hometown as 5370293. It's unusual to identify where you're from with centenal number instead of municipal name. Roz wonders if it's because she comes from an impossibly rural place that no one has ever heard of, or if she is demonstrating some extreme commitment to the election system. Roz skips the mapping exercise of finding out exactly where 5370293 is and checks with her translator instead. Maria has been speaking Swedish.

The road leaves the residential compounds behind and enters rows of tents and shacks: a market zone. Roz has her Information configured to keep a small map at the bottom right of her vision, available for quick enlargement, but in the market she is also offered glowing signposts projected against her vision: IRONWORKERS down this row to the left, HAND PUMP to the right, POTTERY AND BASKETS beyond it. The flies and her nose tell her before the projections do when they approach the butchers' section: much worse than the guano back at the compound. The restaurant section is after that, which is probably logistically convenient but a bit too much for Roz's appetite. Minzhe, on the other hand, sniffs hungrily at the aroma of roasting meat. "Look at that." He points with his chin at a hefty haunch of geep turning on a spit, the juices dripping into the fire pit. "We're coming back here after the meeting."

"They *may* have planned a meal for us," Roz points out, amused.

"All right, later tonight, then! Best way to get to know a centenal is to have tea in the market."

Roz is about to murmur an agreement when she is distracted by something black and gleaming in the thicket of people moving along a cross street. She turns her head to look, and among the cloth of many colors, the baskets riding high on women's heads and the glare of the sun she sees it again, black and shiny and in the shape of an automatic rifle. The man holding it is wearing olive drab and moving away from her; a second later, he is completely blocked from view by other bodies.

Roz slips a hand into her satchel and activates the small personal Lumper she carries with her. Its range should just about reach the man with the gun, rendering the firearm inoperable if it wasn't already. It's hard to imagine that this place hasn't been thoroughly Lumpered over the past few years, and Roz supposes that properly Lumpered, harmless firearms may have kept some talismanic or status value here, where they held sway for so long. Probably what she saw is exactly that.

Which ought to put her mind at ease. But something about the gleam of light on the surface didn't look quite right. What if the gun isn't metal? Is it possible that the DarFur government, or some of its lower-level officials, countenance overt display of plastic weapons? It seems unlikely. Information, which has just identified the head of the market committee, sitting among his plastic wares with a couple of other men, has nothing to say on the subject, which makes it almost certain it isn't happening.

While she is craning her head after what is either a lethal weapon or a harmless anachronism, the rest of the procession bunches up in front of her. They have come up against a long, low wall running along the edge of the market and painted with an extended graphic news strip, each panel roughly the size of a market stall. "How brilliant!" laughs Maria. Roz squeezes into a place where she can read the section in front of them.

The first panel portrays the Mighty Vs: Vera Kubugli and Veena Rasmussen, the co-heads of state for the Supermajority government, Policy1st. Bas-relief headshots have been printed out and stuck above hand-painted bodies with a shared word bubble: *Corporations and the corporate governments they sponsor are separate*, it says (as Roz reads through her visual translator, Information agrees in a projected footnote that this is true, and offers citations for the legal basis). *Corporations should no longer be able to use their profits for corporate government election campaigns*. A separate bubble at the bottom editorializes: *Maybe they could use them to pay employees a little more instead!*

The next box shows Adaku Achike, the regional representative of 888, and Thaddeus Legressus, a spokesperson for PhilipMorris, rebutting with their own arguments about free speech, intertwined interests, and private property. The cartoonist has added a cigarette dangling from Thaddeus's mouth, even though he never smokes in public. The third panel is a cartoon of the Information building in Khartoum, which has a recognizable domed shape and is probably a familiar metonymic for the readers, with a hefty bit of text explaining the current statute and the timetable for reviewing the case. Information, as usual, attracts wordiness and boring illustrations.

That doesn't hold for the final panel, which is an exaggerated caricature of Vera Kubugli attempting to hunt a boa constrictor with a falcon. The raptor, labeled INFORMATION along its tail feathers, is too busy leafing through a huge tome. In the meantime the boa, a distension the shape of Africa in its middle, has wound the end of its tail around the leg of the Mighty V.

Pointed, almost over the top, but wobbling just this side of libel. Glancing down the wall, Roz sees that the next strip is an update on the legal processes against Heritage, the former Supermajority, and beyond that is a series of panels on a recent social capital pyramid scheme.

Strictly speaking, the cartoons are superfluous. All of this data is available on Information, to everyone. Functionally illiterate people can have their news read to them on Information, and accessibility for different levels of education has been a major objective, so there are options for various degrees of language comprehension. But someone—Information tells Roz it was the town council of sheikhs—thinks literacy is important, and the public comic strip seems to be getting people to read. There are a number of locals meandering up and down, taking it in, and farther along Roz sees what looks like a café set up so the customers can enjoy the view while they sip their glass cups of tea.

The meeting area is on the other side of the wall, about half a kilometer outside of town. There is only one species of shrub visible and very little else, so Roz has plenty of time to find out from Information that the reason for the remoteness is the traditional need for a landing strip for fixed-wing aircraft or helicopters. Even the more versatile modes of transportation tend to disembark at the same spot, at least on formal occasions. As they draw closer, she can see that a small stage has been arranged at one end of the dusty field, thankfully with a woven-reed roof tilted overhead. A small delegation is waiting for them: three men in flowing white robes, two with white turbans on top and the other wearing a cap, and three women in equally flowing but much more colorful attire. Roz is glad they kept the SVAT team down to four; after including Amran, they are still fewer than the centenal government group.

During the round of greetings, Roz keeps a close watch on Amran and Minzhe. Clasping of hands, long repetitions of similar phrases and occasional questions rendered meaningless by the lack of any follow-up or answer: *Welcome, God be with you, Praise God, Good to see you, And your family? In God's name, Are you well? God is merciful, God is great.* She follows the pattern as well as she can. When the flurry of introductions has settled and Amran has reported that the governor is only a few minutes out, Roz finds herself standing beside the deputy governor, the highest-ranking official present. It's not an accident; the Information bureaucracy downplays its hierarchy, but Roz is the team leader, and everyone here knows it.

The deputy governor is younger than she might have expected, but Al-Jabali is young and charismatic too, so maybe this is part of their brand. Roz has already forgotten all the names she just learned, but his public Information displays a graceful sweep of calligraphy beside his head. Her visual translator lets her appreciate it for a few seconds before resolving it into the Roman alphabet: Suleyman.

"Your first visit to this area?" he asks, when her eyes shift from the display to meet his.

"Yes," Roz says, and tries to think of something complimentary she can say about what she's seen over the past few hours. She's sure some people think of this place as beautiful, but deserts are not her idea of paradise.

"Very different from where you are from, perhaps?"

Roz catches a knowing amusement in his eyes and laughs. She's still thinking in diplo-speak, though, and asks a question rather than answering directly. "Do you get a lot of visitors?"

"We got very many in the time before the elections," the sheikh says. *Of course they did.* The eastern Sahel was one of the last entrants to micro-democracy before the vote; they must have been flooded with technicians, activists, campaigners. "And afterward some, I believe they called themselves 'adventure tourists'. They came to feel afraid here, where we live." He opens his hand, turns it up toward the sky in mystification. "Hard to understand. But recently that has dropped off."

"I see." Roz can't imagine coming here on purpose, without getting paid for it. Even if feeling afraid is your thing, there must be more thrilling places to do it. Not to mention cooler.

"And what are you here to do?"

Roz looks at him in surprise. "We were asked to support your new government in relations with neighboring centenals." Her words trail off and her face starts to heat. The sheikh's expression hasn't changed, but somehow she knows that he's not asking about the official job description. Of course he knows why they're here, and if he didn't, he wouldn't be admitting it.

"You are checking up on us? Policing us?" The question is hostile, but his tone is level, courteous even, and the warmth in his expression has not changed.

"We're here to provide support," Roz repeats. "You can request for us to leave if you don't want us here." This man really is extraordinarily attractive. His very dark skin is smooth and almost luminous, his features rounded and even. Roz is sure he knows that Information can overrule a request for a SVAT team to exit a centenal.

"Of course we won't ask you to leave. You are our guests. But we like to know what our guests are looking for here, so we can be sure that they are satisfied."

"Very hospitable," Roz says, trying to keep it as smooth as his comment. The sheikh offers a small bow, and she thinks she sees a smile on his lips.

The sun is still beating down on them. Roz glances at the horizon, hoping for some sign of the governor's transport. She sees nothing but sand, scrubs, and, over her right shoulder, Charles's face squinting into the distance.

"Imagine him making us wait out here," Charles mutters when she meets his eyes.

She tries to imagine Al-Jabali. Young, new at this, surrounded by rivals and enemies even more than most politicians. He chose to become a centenal governor as well as head of state, so he's ambitious. And yet the fact that he's not here attending to them suggests he's opposed to Information and confident enough to show it. Or maybe he's just not very good at this part of his job, Roz thinks. Maybe schedules get away from him. Maybe he's not anti-Information per se but trying to assert his independence. She glances at Amran, thinking they'll need a much more thorough rundown of local politics.

"The governor is very sorry to be late," Suleyman says on her left. Roz is almost certain he can't have heard Charles's comment unless he's using something to augment his hearing. "He will want to tell you himself, but there is still much work to do in our centenals. We had very little budget or autonomy before independence, and we are trying our level best to make up for lost time."

Roz smiles and nods. Rare for a politician to admit weakness like that; whatever they're hiding must be even more embarrassing than getting up to speed on basic governance. A minor insurgency? Some looming political crisis? She becomes aware of the faintest of hums against her eardrum, at first more a sensation than a sound. As it grows into a buzz the people around her shift, turning their gaze south, and a moment later, Roz makes out a dark smudge against the undifferentiated beige of the distance.

"He hopes your visit can be helpful in a number of ways," the deputy goes on.

"We also hope so," Roz answers. After a pause, she asks, "Are you from this centenal?"

"Yes," Suleyman says. "I was born here, and my parents never fled to Chad. Except for some small trips within the region, I've lived in Kas my whole life."

Roz wonders what that must be like. She's lived abroad since university, and she can never go home. Thinking of that, and because the deputy has turned his attention to the approaching vehicles, she glances down and taps out a message to her parents: **arrived safe. interesting place, it looks like what the rest of the world thinks of Africa.** They'll find that amusing. **talk soon.** She sends it and looks up again, hoping that wasn't too obvious.

Suleyman either didn't notice or is politely ignoring her inattention. She follows his gaze into the emptiness of the landscape. Roz thought she had gotten used to the desert from living in Doha, but this is different. There is no city to hold it off. This land feels unfinished and in-between, scrubby semi-aridity that has been pushing closer to absolute desert over the past century.

"Look at that," Charles murmurs. The smudge has gotten closer, and Roz can make out the tight formation of three tsubames. White cloth streams out behind each two-person craft, as if they were wearing the traditional jellabiyas. He clicks his tongue. "Why do these African leaders always have to make such a big deal of themselves? And why do we fall for it?"

"Oh, right," Roz says, glancing over at him. "European princelings *never* do pomp and circumstance."

Because she is turned toward him, she misses the moment of the explosion.

She sees the shock on his face at the same time as she hears the bang, louder than she would have thought possible, and a clattering smash that sounds like it will never end, so rushed and unstoppable that she jumps away from it, raising her arms as though the wreckage is about to crush her instead of smashing into the sand half a kilometer away. Through the explosion she hears, or feels, the abbreviated gasp from the man next to her, like a shout cut off by breathlessness.

It must all be on vid, Roz thinks as her head turns toward the sound. *Even out here, there must have been a feed trained on that.* She'll be able to see the explosion in detail and in slow motion as often as she wants. Probably many, many more times than she wants. Her eyes focus on the flicker of flame overhung by a spiraling column of dark smoke. There's definitely a feed on this receiving stand, so she'll be able to check reactions. Unable to stop herself, though she knows she's about to be too late again, she swings her head back around to the deputy governor, automatically her first suspect. His face shows shock, or a good imitation: mouth slightly open, eyes wild. Then he is down off the platform and plunging across the sand toward the scene of the crash. Roz leaps after him.

CHAPTER 2

Nougaz calls Roz within five minutes of the explosion.

Information presents itself to the world as an organization without a head, guided by (depending on the translation and the local connotation) a council, or board, or committee. In Roz's experience of organizations, though, there are always those who wield or are angling to wield more influence than others. Everyone with enough access and sense knows that Valerie Nougaz has been consolidating her position since before the last election. Even though she's not Roz's supervisor, Roz isn't entirely surprised to see her name on the call.

Besides that, Nougaz knows Roz personally. Unfortunately, the reasons for that overlap almost completely with the reasons why Roz is personally disinclined to talk to her these days.

In a crisis, though, it's all professionalism. "Does your team need to be evacuated?"

Roz is still breathing fast, not just from the run, and her heart is jumping. She should be scared—she *was* scared, for a moment or two—but evacuation from all this urgency is the last thing she wants. Still, she has to appreciate Nougaz prioritizing staff safety, and she shows it by thinking about the question for half a second. "Not at this time. No indication that the attack had anything to do with us." She's been playing this out in her head over the last five minutes. "It wouldn't have been that much more difficult to set an explosive device under the receiving platform—probably easier. I think for the moment we can assume that if this was an attack, it has achieved its aim."

"Are you sure he's dead?" Nougaz asks.

"Very sure." Roz is standing ten feet away from the wreckage of the tsubame, having stepped away to take the call. There's a scorched smell with multiple levels of unpleasantness. "On the assumption that Governor Yagoub was one of the passengers in this tsubame. Information shows him boarding, but since there are few feeds between the departure point and here, it is possible he got out at some point. Unlikely, though. The deputy governor has identified him, but the bodies aren't in great shape. We'll want it confirmed independently." Suleyman is kneeling beside the wreckage along with one of the other sheikhs, lips moving in what Roz assumes is prayer.

"Passengers? Bodies?"

"He was traveling with a bodyguard. There were minor injuries in one of the other tsubames that was hit by debris, but only the two in this one are dead."

A moment of consideration. "Is there any chance that this was not an attack, but an accident?"

"A chance." Roz sighs. "It was a pretty spectacular explosion." She watches as the deputy governor rises and walks back toward the platform. His body language has changed completely: he is striding straight-backed, fingers fluttering as he makes calls, his other hand gesturing to those still on the platform. The sheikh who was kneeling with him hurries to catch up.

"Okay," Nougaz says. "I want you to take the lead on the investigation—figure out if it was an assassination, and then find out who did it. I've—"

"Sorry," Roz says, and immediately wishes she hadn't. Even through the poor connection, she can see Nougaz's hatchet face sharpen. "Shouldn't that be the role of the DarFur government?"

"Probably," Nougaz replies crisply. "And if you find they're up to it, by all means leave it to them. But I have my doubts. And we can't be letting people assassinate our heads of state. We're having enough trouble on the Central Asian border; we can't look weak internally. I've already asked Malakal to join you. He should arrive from Juba in a few hours with the forensics team. In the meantime, you know better than I what will be useful. Ask for it."

Like someone with experience in criminal investigations? Roz thinks but does not say. Hopefully, it won't be too different from the data-crunching that she does when she's not on SVAT missions. True, there weren't many feeds in the desert between Djabal and here, but looking at the data from Djabal over the past day or two should let them pin down the saboteur pretty quickly.

"Your team will probably need to do some handholding during the transition, but that seems aligned with your original mission. And don't underestimate the risks of instability! Do not hesitate to request evacuation or security reinforcements if you feel any concern."

"Understood."

Almost immediately after Nougaz signs off, Roz gets another call. She sees that it's Maryam and cringes with a moment of irrational guilt before picking up.

"Hey. You okay?" Maryam's tone is perfunctory: as technical director for the Doha Information Hub, she is as wired into this as anyone in the world and already knows no one on the team was physically injured. "I heard the reinforcements are headed in, so I'm going to see what I can do to up bandwidth out there."

"That would be appreciated," Roz says, turning away from the scene of the crash. "Connectivity is pretty grim here even without data-intense work going on. Are you going to be able to tell us what the tsubame was processing before it blew up?"

"I've already started on a full analysis of the interface logs for the past week."

"Great, I'll work from here on external data." Roz sees a group of half a dozen people in dark blue uniforms jogging toward her from town. "Gotta go," she says. "Looks like the army's here." Or police? She didn't read up enough on that side of things, and checks with Information.

"Stay safe," says Maryam, and signs off.

Most governments this size would contract out their security functions to LesProfessionnels or YourArmy, but (as the Information commentary implies) DarFur government officials have had plenty of experience with foreign military on their soil, and decided to train up a police and militia force from scratch. Most members are either young and inexperienced or drawn from the guerilla groups that fought for independence over the past decades.

Roz blinks away the eye-level projection of that intel without high hopes for the approaching squad. She's pulling her shoulders back in preparation for managing them when Minzhe, trudging through the sand from the welcome platform, catches her eye with a half-nod. Roz gives him a warning look and motions toward the smoking crash site: *don't let them contaminate the scene.* He rolls his eyes, *duh,* and keeps walking toward the soldiers, a warm smile already strung across his face.

Roz turns to check on the rest of the team. Charles is still on the platform, apparently deep in conversation with one of the sheikhs, his hands clasped in front of him while the elderly Furi gestures and talks. Maria and Amran are gone. Glancing down, Roz finds a message waiting for her on the lower right of her vision. She focuses on it until it opens and the text flows in front of her eyes: Maria and Amran have gone back to the market to gather first-pass reaction data. Roz lets her initial annoyance dissipate; she couldn't have chosen anything better for them to do. Maybe she has the perfect team, no need to manage them at all. She snorts, but only inwardly, and starts walking back to the platform to get to work.

Amran is still shaking, and Maria wonders if she should casually lead her past the butcher's alley to give her an excuse to throw up if she needs to. She decides against it: the smell might be enough to make Maria vomit too, and she would rather not. She's been in a number of dodgy situations during her year working SVAT, but she hasn't gone through anything as loud and unexpected as that tsubame explosion. She nearly jumped off the platform. This is supposed to be a normal mission, laid back, up-close-and-personal Information dissemination for new citizens getting the hang of things, not a war zone. Or at least not an active war zone.

After the few seconds of shock, when everything seemed too close and scary, Maria realized that there was probably no immediate danger. She also saw that Amran, standing next to her, was about to lose it. That would not bode well for her professional relationships with the sheikhs grieving their leader and figuring out what to do next, nor for her long-term career at Information. So, Maria grabbed the girl—Amran doesn't look more than twenty-two, and Maria is nearer forty, so she feels justified in thinking of her that way—and pulled her toward the market.

Now they are hurrying along past a row of printer stalls festooned with the diverse products available for manufacture, the shopkeepers hovering by their machines, Amran's hand clammy and trembling in Maria's. The bustle and churn of the market are needling at Maria, and she jerks away from movement at her feet, but it's just a set of cheaply printed wind-up toys cavorting in front of a shop. Best to give her—both of them—something to do. Maria slows her pace, sets her voice to conversational. "What kind of surveys have you done here?"

Amran has to pull herself together to answer. "Not many. I know there were polls before the election, but few. Since I got here, we've been working more on qualitative and background details."

So, people here won't be inured to polling the way they are in the rest of micro-democracy. "We'll have to take it easy, then, but Information"—and presumably the DarFur government as well—"is going to want to figure out who did this and what happens next. Talking to these people is one of the best ways to find out."

Amran stops walking. "How would any of these people know who did this? They didn't see it. They might not even know it happened. Shouldn't we go back to the accident site?"

They might not know it happened? It's been twelve minutes since the explosion, and the vid has been available all that time. It was available live if anyone had known it was going to happen (Maria makes a mental note to check whether anyone was watching). Because there are so many feeds worldwide, most are unwatched at any given moment, but it's been *twelve minutes.* Plenty of time for an event of this magnitude to be filtered to the top of every news compiler in the region. Hell, the DarFur government should have sent out alerts by now (Maria checks; they haven't). Don't they have news compilers here? Do people not use news alerts?

Maria puts a hand on Amran's arm. "There will be plenty of experts there to look at the site. What we can do that no one else can is take a snapshot of what people here think of the head of state, their governor, and the government, right now. They might not have seen what happened fifteen minutes ago, but they know what's going on here much better than we do."

She can see Amran struggling with her pride for a moment,

wondering if this is a way of saying that she hasn't been doing her job, then she nods. "We should start over this way. There's a more open area in the center of the market for selling food-stuffs; people will be more leisurely and willing to talk."

Roz is tempted to shadow the deputy governor, who helped Minzhe keep the militia away from the crash site and is now conveying the same message to the growing crowd of onlook-ers that has trickled over from the town proper. He seems like the most interesting figure around here, as well as the one with the most obvious benefit from the governor's assassination.

But Minzhe is already out there and can keep an eye on him, and in any case, the deputy is clearly in public mode right now. He is managing the situation and interacting with the towns-people, and everything he does will be caught on vid. Charles is working on the other sheikhs, which is definitely within his com-parative advantage but also leaves a clear gap for Roz to address.

It takes some listening, a few minutes of respectful conver-sation, and a hint or two, but the three sheikhas eventually lead Roz out of the sun to a well-appointed compound on the edge of town. The compound belongs to the sheikha named Tho-raya, a sturdy woman in her thirties or forties whose cheek scars are thick as fingers. Her toub is a semi-translucent lavender, embroidered with light-up thread, the stitches flashing in se-quence like fairy lights. The two younger sheikhas, Khadija and Tahani, are wearing iridescent rose and canary yellow, respec-tively, and they are quiet, mostly deferring to Thoraya. As soon as they are all seated inside the hut, Thoraya covers her face with her hands. The other two sheikhas stare at their laps; Khadija is trembling. Roz waits. A child trots in, bringing a plate of desiccated dates, and Thoraya gathers herself, snaps out an order for tea as well, extra sugar.

"This is going to be very bad," she says softly as the child ducks out of the hut. "Just when it looked like we had things sorted out." She grimaces. "And there are plenty of factions, and people, who will be happy to take advantage of this."

"Like who?" Roz asks. She's not expecting any eye-expanding intel here; she can find the names of troublemakers on Information, probably faster than the sheikha will be able to pronounce them. But SVAT missions have taught her that human data can be almost as important as feeds and stats in finding solutions to problems. You may not learn everything you need to know to fix the problem through interviews alone, but often people only listen to your other data because you listened to them first.

Thoraya counts out potential threats on her fingers: "JusticeEquality, DarMasalit, *of course* the Sudanese would love to attack us any way they can, and the Chadians. Also 888. Then those who live here who are against the election system, and those who are against the governor—were, that is."

Roz takes advantage of the pause. "When you say 'the Sudanese,' 'the Chadians,' who are you talking about, exactly?"

Thoraya pushes the bowl of dates toward Roz, and she takes one reluctantly. "The Sudanese are the Sudanese," the sheikha answers. "They may be divided into different centenals now, but don't worry, they still know who they are."

"And 888," Roz sets this up with caution. "Do they have any specific grievance, or . . ." *Or do you think a global government and Supermajority hopeful would risk carrying out an assassination for one lousy centenal? Even thirty lousy centenals?*

"They campaigned hard here." Thoraya sucks the fibrous flesh off a date, spits the seed into the sand beside her rough-soled feet.

Now the most delicate part. "Those who opposed the governor . . . they were against him, not against the government? I mean, did anyone hate him personally?"

There is the clearing of a throat. Roz looks up to see a pair of feet in what appear to be—yes, Information confirms that they are—snakeskin shoes and the lower half of a white jellabiya in the open doorway. "Ladies?"

It takes Roz only a moment to recognize the voice: the deputy governor, Suleyman. Roz can picture that small smile, shy or sly, as he calls the greeting.

"Come on in, come on in," Thoraya calls out, sharing a quick smile with Roz: these men, so formal.

But Suleyman does not enter, does not even bend down. "I don't want to disturb you," he says, voice still warm with that unseen smile. "I wanted to inform our visitors that we will send the food prepared for the welcome lunch today to your compound." His tone shifts. "The funeral will be in Djabal, and we will be transporting the body once it is possible." Roz puzzles over that for a moment, then remembers the forensics team. "But the food should not go to waste. I will travel to Djabal, but I will be back late tomorrow, and then I will be happy to assist you in any way that I can."

Roz waits for a moment, wanting to resume her questioning, but the feet don't move, and Thoraya makes some hand motions that the gesture interpreter helpfully glosses as *a suggestion you exit*. Roz leans close to the sheikha to repeat her condolences, nods to the other two women, and then rises and ducks out under the hanging. Suleyman stands there, his white jellabiya spotless even after all the sweat, kneeling in the sand, and, presumably, grief. He is not smiling, and she wonders how she could have imagined he was. "How thoughtful of you to come in person," she says, falling into step beside him to leave the compound. He must have a million things do to. Maybe monitoring the Information intruders is still the top priority.

"It was . . . helpful for me to step away for a short while," he says, eyes on the ground, and then looks up. "But I should get back. I believe you can find your way to your compound from here?"

It is a question that is so old-fashioned that it is a pure formality: with Information, no one is ever lost. Unless the connection here is even worse than Roz thought. "Of course," she says, trying to match his tone. "I look forward to meeting you after your sad duty in Djabal."

"As will I," Suleyman replies, holding out his hand. He takes the tips of her fingers in his, bows over them slightly, and then turns to walk back toward the landing strip. Roz watches his back for a second, then turns toward the compound. She sends a message to her team to report in for the feast and speaks a quick message for Maryam: "Hey, all okay here so far. Can you coordinate with northeast Sahel team and start a scan for any suspicious communication, likely coded, that might relate to the explosion? Everyone here seems to think it was one of the traditional enemies from outside the government. I'll keep looking on inside. Thanks! I'll talk to you soon."

Still walking, she starts a search for images of the governor's tsubame in Djabal. There is a bit of a wait—she's probably not the only one intensely searching the feeds in this area—and when the results come up, they seem shockingly scant. Roz frowns, then adjusts her facial expression to nod a greeting to a couple of white-robed men who are staring at her as they walk past. She blinks the search file away from her vision to concentrate on what she's seeing: sandy dirt roads; stick and reed fences with the occasional conical roof visible behind them; in the distance down a crossroad, a tall and placid camel.

The sun pounds down, and Roz shakes her head. Why would anyone kill for this place?

CHAPTER 3

When Roz gets back to the compound, Halima's two servants have set up tables and chairs in the yard. They shuttle Roz into a corner to wash her hands with water poured from a plastic jar, then urge her to sit. Minzhe is waiting for the forensics team by the crash site—Roz spares him a thought of sympathy, but then considers that he will probably hit that barbecue in the market—but Maria, Amran, and Charles are already seated. As Roz walks over to the table, the women bring large metal platters piled high with gobbets of goat meat out from a kitchen area in the back.

Roz contents herself with an "everyone okay?" before digging in. Nobody else starts up the conversation: they are shocked and hungry. The smell of the guano has faded to a more muted level in her consciousness, only slightly affecting her enjoyment of the goat, which is pretty good, barbecued in several different ways and served with tiny cups of pounded red chili peppers moistened with lime. She's a bit distracted by the level of specific, illustrated data Information provides, unasked, when she looks at the meat: birth date, breeder/owner, age, date of slaughter (that morning). Roz could have done without the brief video of throat-slitting, although apparently that serves to prove the killing was halal. It feels like the Information stringers around here have too much time on their hands, and Roz glances at Amran, wondering again about her management abilities. On reflection, and with a few more calories in her, she decides it's not so different from the more

NULL STATES · 39

anodyne origin data Information usually provides in restaurants and supermarkets.

Roz registers a quiet thrum in the air and looks up to see a crow pulling in over the office. She gets up, holding her greasy fingers away from her clothes, and walks over as Malakal disembarks on the office roof, throws a rope ladder over the side, and eases his way down it.

"You're early," she says by way of greeting. "Have you eaten?"

"I didn't wait for the forensics team," Malakal answers as he reaches the ground. "And I had some energy chews on the way." In other words, he thought he might be parachuting into immediate danger. "Everyone's okay?"

"Seem to be," Roz says, not looking back at them. "We haven't debriefed yet." She waits. Malakal is not her boss, but he is certainly senior to her. Plus, she respects him, and his deep knowledge of this sub-region is born of long and dedicated experience.

"They can finish eating," he says. "Let's talk first." Charles looks up as they walk over to the office, but Roz motions him to stay, and he goes back to his food. "You saw it?"

"I was looking away," Roz says, as they step into the office. "And I haven't had a chance to watch the feeds yet. But I was there, for what it's worth."

"I've seen the feeds—well, the feed." Malakal is Nuer-dark and Nuer-tall, completely bald, with the rounded midsection of a thin man who has earned his girth with status and successes. "There was only one camera on the explosion, although there was another on the platform where all of you were." He half-sits on one of the tables, which has to be more comfortable for him than the small metal-frame chairs. "I didn't see anything useful, but I've only watched it a couple of times. Maybe there will be more in the analysis."

Only two feeds! But then, that landing platform is in the middle of nowhere. "I have to admit," Roz says, knowing this verges on the offensive, "I don't understand why people would fight over this desert."

Malakal looks amused. "Is it your experience that people fight over worthwhile things?"

A fair point.

"It's all they've got," he goes on, more seriously. "And if you're—I don't know, deputy governor of an obscure centenal in the middle of nowhere that just happens to be where you're from? Then the governorship is your next step, and that's what you're going to kill for, if you're the killing kind of person."

Roz finds this incredibly dispiriting. "So, you think it was the deputy?"

"No, I have no idea who it is. I was speaking hypothetically. I don't think I've met the deputy governor of this centenal. Why, do *you* think it was him?"

Roz shakes her head, relieved. "No, I don't think so, but he's on our radar. Anyway, we're talking about a governor, but also a head of state. If it is an internal power play, we could be looking at the whole government, not just this centenal." She hesitates. "Is there anything else I should know?" Roz is wondering why he got out here so fast, why he wanted to talk to her first.

"We're worried about this region," Malakal says, with a settling of his huge shoulders. "So few areas joined the election system last cycle, and there aren't many low-hanging fruits left."

"Sudan wasn't exactly low-hanging," Roz notes.

Malakal nods. "It's true; there may be other dictatorships that fall hard and unexpectedly. The question is whether they join micro-democracy or not afterward. We would love to have Darfur as a success story in our expansion efforts. There are a lot of eyes here at the moment."

"Surely, that's too oblique to be a motive for assassination?"

"I wasn't suggesting that, just that it is a motive for investigation. We're going to be throwing a lot of resources at this one. There's also the humanitarian risk, of course." He pauses. "I must admit, I feel some personal responsibility."

Roz looks up at him, surprised, and Malakal smiles, showing the gap between his front teeth. "I drew the centenal lines here, a few years ago."

Roz remembers now. That's why Malakal was mostly absent during the dramatic events of the last election: he was here, engineering their first election. "You know centenal borders are a puzzle without a solution. No one is ever totally happy with them, no matter how they fall."

"I didn't say it was rational." Malakal blinks. "The forensics team is on site."

"Good," Roz says. "Hopefully, they'll find something and Minzhe can get back here. I'd rather debrief with the full team."

Having assured himself that neither the militia commander nor the deputy governor will allow anyone to interfere with the scene of the crime—like Roz, he is convinced it's an assassination, not an accident—Minzhe lets a few of the soldiers drag him to the market for roasted geep and liberally sweetened tea. The meal is far from cheerful; the men around the table are stunned by the loss of their governor, even if, as the oldest man says, "he knew nothing about military tactics."

"So, you didn't know him well?"

There are headshakes around the booth, with shy smiles from the younger soldiers: why would they know the governor?

"And your commander?"

"Of course he knows him."

"He was appointed by him."

Minzhe lets a few minutes go by, concentrating on the sizable haunch he's holding. He's not sure what it is about the barbecue in this region, but he hasn't found anything like it anywhere else in the world. "I guess the deputy will be taking over now," he says, when he judges enough time has passed.

Shrugs and exchanges of questioning looks among the militia; they aren't clear on the legalities, but it seems to make sense.

"What's he like?"

Unlike when he asked about the governor, this unleashes a babble of conversation and anecdotes.

"He fought with us before independence."

"He helped me get my auntie to Nyala for hospital."

"Everyone knows him."

"He's my brother."

Minzhe focuses on that last one, a young guard named Yusuf. "How many siblings do you have?"

"Sixty-eight."

"He seems very young," Minzhe observes. What he is thinking is that the deputy can't possibly be the oldest of the siblings, no matter how many wives were involved, but they take it as a question about his leadership status instead.

"He's been a sheikh since he was twenty-three," reports the oldest soldier. "Born to it."

Minzhe blinks, both because of that assault on his democratic principles and because he's getting an update. "The forensics team just arrived," he tells the soldiers, swallowing the last of his tea in a stinging gulp. "Let's go take a look before I report in to my boss."

The forensics team includes two Dinka, a Luo, and another woman whose tribal affiliation is not noted in her public Information but who speaks Kiswahili by preference. Minzhe doesn't know any of them, and they all seem focused on business, so after introducing himself, he hangs back and watches them set up their tent. The militia take their afternoon prayer, two members waiting on guard and starting their ablutions only after the others have finished. Minzhe considers asking if he can help with the investigation, but he doesn't know anything about forensics and he should report in, so he heads back to the compound.

Not really much of a team yet, Roz thinks, watching them gather. Minzhe is excitedly briefing Charles about the culinary offerings he's scoped out at the market, and Charles is responding with praise of the movable feast he's just eaten, while Maria sits in the back, watching and waiting. Amran can't even bring herself to sit down and is twisting her hands in front of her skirt and glancing at Malakal looming against the wall by the door. Roz frowns at herself; she's going to have to resist the temptation to treat Amran as less than a full member of the team, even if she's not SVAT and quite possibly out of her depth.

"So. What happened?" Roz asks. They talk it through first: the sound, the spattering debris, the way people ran from the stage, what they saw at the scene. Only after they've gotten all their own impressions out does Roz project the feed; it tells them nothing new.

Except: "It looks like the tsubame slows a little before it explodes," Minzhe says. "Is that right?"

"It could be decelerating for arrival," Charles points out.

"Was it . . ." Maria hesitates before finishing her thought. "Is it possible that the explosion was triggered by a line-of-sight device?"

There is a moment of stunned silence. A line-of-sight trigger would put everyone who was on the platform squarely on the suspect list, and 5/11 of that group are sitting in this office.

Roz checks her messages, but neither Maryam nor the fo‑
rensics have checked in yet. "We'll find out," she says. "Hope‑
fully soon. All right. What happened afterward?"

Charles describes the shock of the elderly sheikhs he was
talking to on the platform. "Anger as well as shock," he says.
"They thought democracy would free them from political
violence."

A common misconception. "Suspects?"

"Sudan, mostly," Charles says. Sudan no longer exists;
they'll have to translate the accusation into the current admin‑
istrative terminology to figure out who it's pointing at. "The
surrounding centenals, 888 . . ."

"Any suspects not related to government?" Roz asks. She
doesn't want to dwell on the 888 suggestion with Minzhe in
the room.

"I asked about personal enemies, but he evaded."

"So, that's an assumed yes," Roz says. She looks at Amran,
but the field lead avoids her eye, and Roz decides to come back
to her later. "I had a similar impression talking to the sheikha;
she said something about—" Roz replays the conversation to
be sure. Most people don't record their every interaction—there
are fraught legal issues as well as storage concerns—but it is
standard procedure for SVAT teams in the field. For them, the
legal issues run the other way: they want protection against ac‑
cusations of Information manipulation and a digital witness in
case of violence. And storage is not a problem for Information.
"She said 'those who are against the governor' instead of
'against the party.' But I couldn't confirm either." Roz wonders
briefly about the timing of Suleyman's intervention but decides
that's paranoid; how could he have known what questions she
was asking? She turns to Maria. "Anything from the masses?"

Maria glances at Amran. "We talked to twenty-three re‑
spondents, of whom fifteen were women and all but one were

Fur, with an age spread of twenty-four to thirty-nine." Sounding very much like a pollster now, Roz notes, and smiles as a three-dimensional pie leaps up into the middle of the room, shiny and beveled with the latest textures. "As you can see from the results, while 35% felt shock and 12% felt grief, the most predominant emotion, at 44%, is anger. That does not bode well."

"It's a good reminder," Malakal says from the wall, "that our immediate mandate here is twofold: supporting the investigation and smoothing the transition to whatever is next. The *peaceful* transition."

There is a pause. "Minzhe?" Roz asks. "Anything to help us with either of those?"

"Well," Minzhe says, stretching out a little as he talks. "I got to chatting with some of the militia. Nothing like a long, boring wait to get friendly with people."

"Just a second," Roz raises her hand, updates flashing against her eyes. She meets Malakal's gaze, his nod. "The forensics team can confirm that the body is that of Abubakar Ahmed Yagoub, known as Al-Jabali; they're still working on the second body, presumed to be his bodyguard Adam Khaled Mohamed. They have 93% certainty the tsubame was sabotaged. We'll have more soon." She refocuses on Minzhe. "Sorry. Go ahead."

He nods, the swagger evaporated. "As expected, I suppose. Anyway. As I said, I had a long wait with the militia, and it turns out I know some of their relatives in Nyala, so I got the gossip." Probably all of it available on Information, if only they knew where to look. Or perhaps not. Roz looks at Amran again, wondering when she should call her on the appalling lack of intel. "To start, everyone thinks it was the Sudanese, or *just possibly*"—he's working back up into storytelling mode—"the Chadians, trying to get the Sudanese blamed for it. Same old stuff that's been going on for decades. I left that and kept them talking. Two things came up. First: Al-Jabali has—had—a wife in Djabal, but he kept a woman on the side here, too."

"Why didn't he just marry the second one?" Charles asks. "This government allows men to marry multiple wives, right?" He glances at Amran; her eyes are on her hands in her lap, but Information has confirmed at everyone's eye level before he finishes speaking.

"The militia guys had all sorts of theories, most of them inappropriate to this more polite setting," Minzhe says. "Basically their assumptions boil down to: his wife wouldn't let him."

"Meaning she probably wasn't resigned to the idea of a mistress, either," Charles nods.

"So, there's that. The other thing." He pauses for effect. "They said there have been skirmishes at the borders."

That gets the attention of everyone in the room.

"Skirmishes? What does that mean, actual battles?" Charles asks, as Malakal says, skeptically, "Skirmishes that Information doesn't know about?"

Roz is done giving Amran a pass. "Were you aware of this?"

Amran, startled into looking up, squirms. "There have been rumors of fighting, but nothing I could confirm." Roz bores into her with her eyes, but she doesn't say anything else, and Roz eventually turns back to Minzhe.

"The militia were quite proud that it hasn't shown up on Information—or at least gotten picked up. I suspect if we looked hard enough at feeds and satellite photos, and the conversations in certain plazas, we might see something. But you have to understand this region is not like . . . anywhere else you've been. Right now, where we are now, is probably the least observed any of you has been in your lives." He pauses to let that sink in, and to let them remember that he grew up out here, before it was even part of micro-democracy. "Information only started installing the feed infrastructure a couple of years ago, and given the extreme lack of population density, they haven't put in very many. There's not a lot of geopolitical linkage—almost all the governments here are tiny locals or megacorporate outposts." Like 888 and Heritage, which both have centenals nearby. "The only people who care what happens here are the people caught up in it, and they care passionately, insanely you might even say."

Roz blanks for a moment, caught up in an uncomfortable thought. If all this is true, then Minzhe must be the least documented person in the room. And he's caught up in it, isn't he?

". . . definitely battles," Minzhe is saying when she tunes back in. "But minor ones." He rolls his eyes up, checking his notes or replaying the conversation. "Seven killed in a fight last September. Three in an ambush in January. And five just last month." His gaze returns to the room. "Those numbers are only the casualties on the DarFur side; the militia don't know how many the other side lost."

"Who are the other side?" Maria asks. "And where are these battles taking place?"

Roz glances at Malakal. His eyes are heavy-lidded and darting back and forth: he is scanning as much recent intel as he can find about this place, she guesses, or looking for the right puzzle pieces to contextualize Minzhe's story.

"There have been a variety of adversaries: DarMasalit in September, NomadCowmen in January. They couldn't, or wouldn't, tell me who attacked in the latest incident; they said 'stateless people,' an old term, obviously, which I think we can take to mean 'not an official centenal force.' They said it derisively, which is how they talked about this whole issue. They either believe, or are pretending to believe for the sake of their pride, that this is nothing to be concerned about, that it's normal."

A brief, appalled silence. "Normal to have fighting between centenals?" Charles asks.

Minzhe nods urgently; the strain of trying to get them to understand what is so obvious to him is starting to show. "Low-level conflict has been going on here for decades. I'm not sure whether they think of it as conflict over territory, because they see the centenal borders as changeable"—out of the corner of her eye, Roz sees Malakal look up—"or whether they think of it as . . . something that just happens, not really to try to win land so much as to express their abilities, their loyalty."

"Doesn't sound like they have such great abilities if they're losing that many people each time," Charles points out. "How is it possible that we don't know about battles with so many casualties?" Twisting around in his chair to look at Malakal.

"Like I said before"—Minzhe grabs his attention back—"there just aren't that many feeds. It's not some big conspiracy. Let's not get caught up in the fact that we didn't know about this, and start thinking about the plan for addressing it."

"Did the militia think the assassination might be related to any of these . . . incidents?" Malakal asks.

Minzhe shakes his head. "As I said, they barely take them seriously—which is why they were willing to talk about them with me. But here's the thing: there are a lot of potential enemies here. Did you know, in one of his early speeches, Al-Jabali compared DarFur to the state of Israel when it was established?" He holds up his hands. More than fifteen years since Israel and Palestine acceded to the election system and ceased to exist as territorial entities, their history remains contentious. "I'm not saying it's a reasonable analogy, but that's how they see themselves. Anyone with an agenda could seize control of the narrative of this event to direct the resulting conflagration."

Roz bites her tongue not to ask Amran for a briefing on who might want to do that. She's remembering what Minzhe said: Amran has a lot less intel to work with than the field leads they're used to dealing with.

"Is the militia going to investigate the assassination?" she asks hopefully.

"I'm not sure they even have an investigative function," Minzhe says. "I asked, and they didn't seem to know what I meant. Mind you, these were, shall we say, beat cops. Their commander might know if it's in their charter; I would guess even if it is, they've never used it."

"The commander didn't come to the site of the assassination?" Charles asks.

"Oh, he was there, but he was dealing with the sheikhs and doing the brunt of the crowd control, so I couldn't talk to him beyond pleasantries."

"Minzhe," Roz starts. She's not sure if this has ever been done, but she needs a close link to the government. "How would you feel about embedding with the militia, or whoever they find to investigate this?"

"Sure thing, boss," Minzhe says, trying not to look thrilled.

"We'll need to clear it with the authorities first, of course. Amran?" Her head snaps up. "Who is in charge now? Is it the deputy governor?"

Fortunately, Amran doesn't have to pause to look that up. "Yes, according to the government code, the deputy governor automatically becomes centenal governor in a case like this. There will probably be a ceremony of some kind over the next few days, but technically, he's already empowered." She hesitates for a moment, then adds, "The more complicated situation is in the DarFur government as a whole. There's no statute for who becomes the new head of state. I guess . . . I guess they will have a new election."

Guessing is something that rarely happens in Roz's world. Elections, on the other hand . . . Roz represses a sigh. "We'll talk to the new governor tomorrow, then."

"He'll be at the funeral in Djabal," Charles points out.

"So will we," Roz answers. "That tsubame came from Djabal. Al-Jabali's wife is in Djabal. We need to check it out, and it is only appropriate to show our respect at the funeral." She's been thinking about this since the governor told her he was going. And it's ceremonial, so rank is important. "Malakal and I will handle that. Amran, I want you to prepare a new briefing file based on this event." She's letting her off easy, but now is not the time to get into it in front of everyone. "Maria, try to get a sense of the biggest threats to public equanimity— without exacerbating any of them, please!" Maria nods with what looks like offended dignity. "And Charles, start looking into these conflicts with the neighbors—*quietly*—and get to work on initial compilation and distribution. Keep it general and neutral to start, but let's remind people why they joined micro-democracy and why they were happy about it. Both of you, take into consideration DarFur's other centenals. Al-Jabali was the governor here, but he was also head of state for the whole government, and the assassination attempt may have its roots outside the centenal borders."

As the team files out, Roz taps Amran on the elbow, and the young woman startles, making Roz wonder if the light touch was inappropriate in some way. "Can you stay for a moment?" she asks her as courteously as she can. Malakal hangs back with them.

"Is something going on?" Roz asks, once the door has shut behind Charles, the last one out. "You seem upset, and I wanted to give you a chance to talk about it more privately."

Amran presses her palms to her face. "I should have known it," she whispers, chin bobbling. "I should have known this was coming!"

CHAPTER 4

The assassination of a head of state for a government holding thirty centenals, even a popular, photogenic one, is small news on the world scale. It makes some but not all of the global compilers, and where it does appear, it's a blip. No one has time to read *everything* that happens.

In her corner office at the Paris Hub, Nougaz dismisses the assassination as soon as she has signed off from the call with Roz. She hears Roz is quite competent, and Malakal is eminently capable of taking over if necessary. She has other things to worry about. Shepherding a new Supermajority into their role has been more challenging and time-consuming than she expected. Nougaz has already suggested instituting a longer handover period for any future Supermajority changes, but Policy1st is balking at announcing anything that will make them look bad, so it will have to wait until they are a little less sensitive. In any case, an extended handover was hardly feasible after the debacle of the last election, with the outgoing Supermajority under criminal investigation and the urgent need for stability and decision.

It is a cool autumn day in Paris, the leaves still green on the ancient chestnuts lining the avenues. The building where Nougaz works, the Paris Information Hub, is lovely if you like the city pieds-à-terre of an ancient aristocracy, but a little old and cramped for a twenty-first-century global oversight and transparency agency (the latest restyling of the Information mission). Nougaz has been toying with the idea of doing away with the mythical equality among hubs and opening a more centralized headquarters, maybe in a purpose-designed building like the one Policy1st has in Copenhagen.

Which reminds her of Veena Rasmussen. The lesser of the Mighty Vs has been pushing, loudly and insistently, for system-wide minimum environmental standards for all governments. Nougaz has explained to her, first through lower-level intermediaries and recently, repeatedly, in person, that micro-democracy exists precisely to allow for variation in how governments decide to address the substantial challenges of the late twenty-first century. Through elections and relatively free immigration policies, people vote in this marketplace of ideas and innovation.

"Leading to a race to the bottom," Veena always replies. "You already have minimum requirements for human rights. Why shouldn't you protect the environment that protects us all? These standards—not even requirements, *standards*—would be based on current practices, to prevent backsliding. They wouldn't necessitate action for compliance by any government." As if that were doing them a favor. She seems to think winning the Supermajority gives her government the right, the ability, maybe even the responsibility because that's just the kind of savior complex she has, to push its agenda for changes in the system, and she's unfortunately sharp at manipulating the news compilers. A pain in the ass.

Vera gets it, Nougaz is sure, but she seems unwilling or unable to control Veena. Nougaz hasn't wanted to probe into that partnership beyond what's available on public Information. It is important to draw a line in relationships, leave the other some privacy, especially in the early days.

She finds she is smiling, thinking of Vera, and she shifts her attention to other irritations: Heritage, with their stupid squirming to get out of the richly deserved punishments for their crimes;

PhilipMorris, pushing hard for the mantle tunnel approvals; 1China, with its deliberate provocations against nation-states along the frontiers of the micro-democracy system. There are growing suspicions about 1China's cozy relationship with China, the nation-state remnant of the PRC; Nougaz flips through the virtual pages of a report that appeared in her workstation just that morning on secret arms trading between the two.

The problem with Vera (as her attention drifts from the repetitive acronyms describing explosive materials and rocket launchers) is the shift to a five-year election cycle. Vera is adamantly against it, and from the perspective of her position she's completely correct. Policy1st needs more time to consolidate, figure out what they're doing, and produce visible successes if they're going to have any chance of retaining the Supermajority. But another five years could just as easily allow them to burrow deeper into a tangled mess, and Nougaz feels that they can't afford the risk. Besides, ten years is too long, regardless of who's in power. Voters lose interest, growing either complacent or frustrated. It lets incumbents get entrenched. Even those within Information who believe the bulk of power should rest with the governments are coming around to the idea. Nougaz can't consider that faction without a sniff. Buying into the fantasy that Information is a neutral, transparent facilitator is so naïve.

No, it will have to happen, sooner rather than later. It's true, it's unfair to Policy1st, but the system is larger than just one government.

Amran has high expectations for her own predictive ability. "No, no, nothing about assassination. Nothing about assassins. No, I haven't heard anything about anyone being particularly angry with the governor," she insists, still tearful. Roz and Malakal couldn't get anything coherent out of her until they started asking very specific questions.

"What, then?" asks Malakal, and Roz follows up quickly. "What did you hear?"

"Not . . . hear really, but there have been so many dramatic incidents lately." Amran looks up at them with big, pleading eyes. "I knew . . . I just knew it was leading up to something. But I wasn't sure whether it was over or if there would be something bigger . . ."

"Go on," Roz says, a suspicion growing.

A month ago, Amran tells them, there was a loud explosion in the town. "People went running, the smoke was dark and thick as the tree in front of the compound. It was a barrel of oil from the fuel merchant's stall in the market."

"They keep their oil in *barrels* here? In the market?" Roz can't believe it.

"It's not like someone can pick up a barrel and walk away with it," Malakal tells her. "They don't have the resources to dig underground tanks."

"No one was hurt that time," Amran continues. "But then, two weeks later, someone tossed an explosive at a truck coming from El-Geneina and blew it off the road. Then there was a haboob that blocked flights in for a day and a half." Dust storms are common here, but that, Amran tells them with a defensive note in her voice, was the longest anyone can remember. "Except maybe the oldest people." She looks down at her hands again. Doubtless, it sounds silly to her when she says it all out loud.

Roz wonders if Amran has ever been diagnosed. Or maybe she's trying to work up a narrative disorder that she doesn't actually have—that seems to have become fashionable lately. Either way, she could probably use some specialist help.

"You believe these were . . . portents?" Malakal asks, his

NULL STATES · 55

voice even deeper than usual, although Roz can't be sure whether it's from skepticism or unease.

"No, not . . . the way you mean. It just seemed to be . . . The tension was growing more and more . . . like something else had to happen."

"You couldn't have been expected to know exactly what was coming next," Roz says, hoping she sounds supportive. She hates having to baby a colleague, but Amran is not SVAT. Whoever assigned her here probably thought this was the perfect backwater for someone to learn the ropes quietly. They must not have seen the signs of a narrative disorder, or of the desire for one.

Roz isn't sure if Malakal has come to the same conclusion, although he glances at her with something meaningful in his expression before he turns back to Amran. "Can you write up those incidents?" The gentleness in his voice makes Roz think he's leaning toward *mentally unstable* rather than *wannabe intuitive genius*. She wonders if she can convince him to replace Amran but resigns herself to the fact that that idea is both unlikely and an overreaction.

They are halfway to Djabal, skimming over the scrubland and sands of West Darfur, when Maryam pings Roz. As soon as Roz is sure it's not a personal call, she puts Maryam on projection.

"Hi," she says. "I've got the report on the tsubame, are you ready?"

"As long as you keep in mind we're in a crow right now," Malakal answers. "Don't make it too gruesome." He grins at Roz, who didn't think it was a joke.

Maryam doesn't think so either. "You might want to walk after you hear this." She sends through her projection, and it auto-displays between them, a three-dimensional image of a tsubame hovering in front of the desert landscape speeding by on their monitor. The angle of view swings around to show it from all angles: a standard two-seater hovercraft, outfitted with those white drapes to give it a bit of drama and status but otherwise little changed from the factory model, either in hardware or software. "Which suggests," Maryam says, pointing that out, "that neither the governor nor his staff are very familiar with tsubame or crow mechanics."

"I would be surprised if they were," Malakal comments. "They're not used very often out here, even though they're well-suited to the terrain—mostly, that is," he adds as their own crow shifts up steeply to climb over one of the low, stony hill ranges common in this part of the territory.

Maryam's projection simulates the crash, then zooms in on the constituent pieces left scattered in the sand afterward. "No sign of any explosive trigger or other foreign material," she says. "Unless they—whoever it was—designed something that would disintegrate entirely."

"Couldn't they have packed the explosives someplace where the tsubame would trigger them itself, through its normal processes? It wouldn't take a very large amount of explosive to blow that thing," Roz says.

"It occurred to us," Maryam answers, "but there's the problem of the timing. It was close to landing when it exploded, no? A few minutes longer and they would have been out of danger. A bit risky. Still possible, but we found something much more compelling."

The projection shifts to zoom down lines of code: the tsubame's operating system log. Maryam slows it, searching, and stops. "Here!" From her office in Doha, she highlights a few lines.

"A remote command?" Roz asks. "That shouldn't be possible

with the standard package." For security reasons, there are strict regulations around remote aircraft. Permits are required to remove manufacturer safeguards, and while it's possible to hack it without going through that step, it's nontrivial. People who do set up illicit remote control on their own vehicle put high security controls on it themselves to prevent others from taking over from outside.

"And yet there it is," Maryam says.

Roz is reminded, with a shiver, of something else, something unnerving, something that made her feel this same kind of uncomfortable recently. Then she has it: the gleam of a gun, possibly metal, possibly plastic, in the Kas market. Relieved, she dismisses the thought as unrelated and focuses back in on Maryam.

"The remote command triggered the explosion by creating an interaction between the power cycle and the air pressurizers." The projection sprouts tubes and cylinders, the inner hardware of the aircraft.

"Have you traced the remote command?" Roz asks.

"We're working on it, but we're having trouble finding the source."

"Having trouble finding it?" Malakal asks.

"It doesn't seem to appear in Information, which means the signal's been masked, or bounced—made to look as though it's a command between two other points or made invisible in the records. Not an easy thing to do. We'll find it eventually, but it will take some time and it may not be very helpful."

"Is there any chance the remote command was via line-of-sight?" Roz puts in.

Maryam frowns. "If it was, that should have shown up in the logs. I suppose it's theoretically possible a line-of-sight command could be masked, but I've never heard of that happening. I'll look into it; thanks for the suggestion. Something else, though: whoever did this would have had to override the software failsafes. No big deal compared to initiating remote control. The thing is, there should have been a hardware failsafe as well." The three-dimensional blueprints zoom in on a small valve blocking the junction between two pipes.

"There was someone on the ground," Malakal says.

"Someone had to physically make the adjustment. Not terribly difficult; with the right instructions, any half-decent mechanic could have done it. And it could have been done at almost any time, because without the remote command, the removal of that valve would only lead to an explosion under very specific, very unlikely conditions. We might even consider it a factory error, if we didn't have full interior diagnostics from both the factory and the dealer. The change happened after this tsubame was bought, which fortunately was only six months ago."

Roz shakes her head. Six months full of time during which the tsubame was frequently moored and unwatched. "Naturally, you have the tsubame logs," she says drily.

"Naturally," Maryam said. "And we do have people here taking a look at them—al-Derbi put some of his staff on it. But I'll send our compilation and cross-referencing to you too if you want to take a look."

"Sure." Roz is notoriously good at data analysis; the more data the better. That doesn't mean she likes it, though. "Something else, too . . ." She hesitates, glancing sidelong at Malakal. "Could you send me the complete files for the full SVAT team? Just in case."

Maryam, a good friend, doesn't blink. "Sure, I'll get those to you. In the meantime, just in case, I've developed a patch for you and for DarFur's remaining tsubames." She uploads a bit of software to the crow. "That's designed to auto-shutdown at any remote control attempt. It should take you down to a soft landing before rebooting."

"'Should'?" Roz asks.

"I take it this hasn't been tested?" Malakal says.

"Not *physically* tested, no," Maryam answers. "But you've got my personal debugging and design test guarantee." She sounds snappy with confidence, the closest to pre-breakup Maryam that Roz has heard in months.

"In that case," Malakal responds soberly, "I suggest you consider a global distribution."

CHAPTER 5

Charles spends some time with Amran after the meeting. Yes, he could look up the friction with neighbors on Information, but he'd rather get as close to the source as he can. Besides, it's clear that Information here is not up to its usual standard. That's fine. Charles has worked in such data-straitened places before. It takes a little more legwork, but that keeps one on one's toes. As for Amran, she's flighty and inexperienced, but she means well. And she's not entirely clueless. Once he has calmed her down by ignoring all her sighs and dire hints (really ignoring, not just pretending; he couldn't repeat a single one of them if asked), she's able to give him a decent rundown of local intercentenal politics.

"Even though this government is called DarFur—house of the Fur—Al-Jabali took pains to ensure it isn't a nationalist government. There are plenty of citizens who are not Fur tribe."

"But wasn't part of Al-Jabali's vision the growth of the Fur nation?"

"Originally, it was. But he was smart," Amran says earnestly. "He saw what Information values: diversity, transparency. Citizenship based on something other than blood. He came from a different world, yes. He had been persecuted all his life, as had his parents and grandparents, for being Fur, and nothing makes nationalists so fast as persecution." Straight out of the Information handbook. "But he was the kind of politician who could merge different viewpoints into something new and exciting. More recently"—she starts searching for vid clips of speeches and throwing them to Charles—"he'd been talking about unity, about the project of a great nation, the nation of all oppressed people, not only the Fur . . ." Amran trails off, twisting her hands. "It still wasn't clear if he would be able to refine and transmit this vision, but it was interesting to watch."

"A great loss," Charles says, putting some warmth in his voice so that it resonates with Amran, but she doesn't look up. "And the surrounding governments?"

Amran nods. "JusticeEquality are hardliners. They're mostly ex-guerrilla, as you know, but I don't think they had realized how Al-Jabali was shifting. During the election, DarFur and JusticeEquality were fierce political rivals, but since the centenals were settled, they have been at least pretending to work together. DarMasalit . . . well, they would like to be doing the same as DarFur, strengthening their culture and growing into a political force, but there are far fewer of them: only seven centenals. But there's not much overlap, so while there is rivalry, it's not very strong."

"And the non-locals?" Charles asks.

"888 are very serious," Amran says. "I wasn't here during the election, but I heard they commissioned all kinds of pop-up advids and things that people here aren't very accustomed to. Even now, people are very aware of them, because there is constant trade between Kas and their centenal in Nyala. People go there for shopping when they can. 888 would like to have won DarFur's centenals."

"I'm sure they would," Charles agrees. "But why would they risk being sanctioned for an assassination for only thirty centenals?"

"That's thirty centenals closer to the Supermajority, no?"

Charles mutters something and his Information throws up a quick projection visualizing the top five governments in the world. "888 is nearly a thousand centenals away from the Supermajority."

"But Policy1st is likely to lose ground," Amran argues. "The way they're going?"

Charles decides to drop the cost-benefit argument. "How exactly would assassinating the head of state here help 888 to win this centenal in eight years?"

"Polling has shown that Al-Jabali's personality was very important in helping DarFur to win," Amran offers, but even she doesn't seem convinced. "Maybe they just hated him?" She looks down, twisting her hands again. "I heard . . . I don't know if this is true, but some of the government officials believe that 888 called in the SVAT visit."

Charles doesn't answer. He is too busy looking for evidence one way or the other. He doesn't find anything immediately, although he does hope that if that were the case, Minzhe wouldn't have been among those deployed.

Djabal is flanked with long columns of multistory apartment buildings in Chinese-style clusters of identical construction. Five white nine-story buildings; eight off-white twelve-story buildings; six desert-red eighteen-story buildings. Watching them glide past in depressing anonymity, Roz is reminded that DarFur only barely beat out 888 here, and that was only because 1China split the Han vote, coming in a not-so-distant third. It wasn't only the Chinese migrants voting for them either: a lot of the Fur who had been living in this camp for decades thought that a large foreign government had more of a future than one based on their own traditions. Roz wonders if that's why Al-Jabali decided to make his base in Kas, where there are still relatively few foreigners and DarFur won by a substantial margin.

Given the lack of appealing options for lodging, they decide to sleep in the crow. They moor it in a public lot near the market area and walk out to find some food. As uniform and blocky as the outskirts of town are, the market is low and patchy, preserving the feel of the refugee economic nexus that it originally was. Information's map shows Roz that Djabal proper is not very big, but faint overlays trace the common circuits extending out from the town in vast arcs, merchant routes linking the continent from Khartoum in one direction to Kano in the other.

"Been here before?" Roz asks. It is getting dark, but the shadows of the market are lit with torches, fires, and fluoron strings, some warped and colored to form shop signs. With evening the temperature has fallen, and Roz can feel herself relaxing, her forehead unknotting.

"Once or twice, during the centenal mapping," Malakal answers. They are close to the old Sudan-Chad border, and centenal designers tried to disrupt those lines when they could. "I think . . . hmm. If I remember right, there was a decent fish restaurant somewhere up here."

"Fish?" Roz asks, wrinkling her nose.

"River fish," Malakal says. "We're close to the water."

Roz shrugs, but the catfish, fried into satisfying crunchiness and served in a heaping pile on a metal tray with more of that chili and tiny limes, leaves her licking her fingers and wishing she dared order more.

The funeral is early the next morning, and they should go right to sleep, but when they get back to the crow, Malakal pulls out a bottle of sesame alcohol he brought from the south—every centenal for miles around here is dry—and they end up drinking it sitting on the floor of the cabin.

"I always feel weird working these kinds of missions," Roz admits.

"Assassinations?"

"No!" She chokes back an inappropriate laugh. "No, these

governments that are, you know . . ." He doesn't. "Ethnically based, or retro-nationalist. With their populist heads of state, pushing the dream for their people, and only theirs, to declare their greatness and difference from everyone else. I mean, it's so twentieth century, so the opposite of what Information is supposed to work for." Roz fidgets. "It's almost like we're working against ourselves by helping them."

"They were elected," Malakal reminds her.

"Just because it's democratic doesn't make it right," she shoots back at him; it's a quote from Valérie Nougaz during the turmoil around the establishment of Information twenty-five years earlier.

"They'll come around," he says, taking a drink. "We have to give them time to understand that the incentive structure, the whole political system they're a part of has changed."

"Or they won't," Roz counters, "because they've self-segregated into their own centenals and they don't have to interact with others or evolve."

Malakal puts up his hands, one still holding his cup. "Even if that's the case, we can't go second-guessing their decisions after we've told them that making decisions themselves is the most important thing, the basis for our system."

"I know," Roz sighs, and drinks.

"Micro-democracy is what we're trying now. If it doesn't work, then we'll come up with something else eventually, I guess. But I'll tell you, I can't think of a single case when telling people what they should want works out well."

"We don't tell people," Roz points out. "We offer them Information and pretend it's neutral. We help them choose, and tell them it's their choice." She hopes the sarcasm comes through; she's getting buzzed.

"We do," Malakal says, heavily. "As with, for example, centenal mapping." He takes another drink and changes the subject. "You think the team is okay after that explosion?"

"I'm pretty sure they've all seen worse," Roz says. "But most of them I don't know very well."

"They've all been screened, you know. Extensively."

Roz nods. "I know. I'm sure I won't find anything, but I want to cover every possibility. There might be something specific to this place that wouldn't have raised flags before." She can't help but think of Minzhe, his mother's powerful position, the ease with which he embedded himself into the militia group. "And Amran isn't SVAT. She hasn't gone through quite such a rigorous screening, or training."

Malakal sighs, and plays with his empty shot glass. "She does seem a bit out of her depth, doesn't she?" He reaches for the bottle and refills. "What did you make of her bit about the drama and the rising tension?"

"I don't know." Neither of them wants to say *narrative disorder*, so Roz decides to pretend they already have. "Do you think she's faking?" A pause while they consider the possibility. "She did seem very agitated," Roz points out, working against her worst impulses.

"She knew she'd messed up a couple of times that day, which could account for that," Malakal says. "Although . . . well, we'll just have to keep an eye on it. By the way . . ." he takes a swallow of the sesame drink, as though trying to put space between that topic and the next. "Have you heard from Mishima?"

Roz smiles into her cup. The lights in the cabin are set to a fire-like flicker. "Yeah, I talk to her pretty regularly. Should give her a call, actually; it's been a month or so."

"Is she doing all right?" Malakal asks.

"She's doing fine," Roz says, a little surprised. When is Mishima ever not doing fine? "You know, she's working on some interesting stuff, has a nice place . . ." She's not sure how close Mishima was with her erstwhile boss, and decides not to mention the significant other.

"That's good to hear," Malakal says, sighing himself a little lower into his slump against the wall. "I felt bad when she left, you know . . . Like I should have supported her better during the last election, all the crap that was going on. She didn't have to leave."

"I don't think that was the problem," Roz says. She's more awake now, shifting into reassurance mode, peering at Malakal with curiosity. First the centenal borders and now this. Who knew he had such a guilt complex? "She's never said anything to me about feeling unsupported—and, you know, she did all right on her own." Or not quite on her own, but without Malakal being actively involved. "I think she was ready for a change."

"I'm glad to hear that," Malakal says again. "I know I should write to her, or call, but I left it for a while and then it got harder to do."

"You should. I'm sure Mishima would be happy to hear from you." She thinks so, anyway. Mishima would certainly be pleased if he were calling to tell her that Information is falling apart without her. Roz almost laughs aloud, thinking of her friend.

"Well. We have to get up early tomorrow. I think I'll head to bed." Malakal raises his considerable bulk to standing. "You're okay here?"

"Of course." The crow has a relatively private cabin, which Malakal is using, and a main room with the controls and workspace, which also has a couple of bunks outfitted for visitors.

"Good night, then."

"Good night."

After Malakal retreats into his room, Roz finds she is too

wound up to sleep. Knowing she'll regret it, she opens her work inbox. She's barely been away for a day, and there's already a slew of messages. Roz can take care of most of them quickly, but she's working on a couple of highly sensitive matters for her boss, Nejime, and she wants to check on the updates. There is more back-and-forth on the idea of reducing the election cycle to five years. Nougaz is pushing hard for it, which Roz supposes has the added benefit of publicly demonstrating that she's not in Policy1st's pocket.

It's not that Roz doesn't like Policy1st. She voted for Save-Planet, but Policy1st would have been her second choice, especially after they merged with Earth1st. She probably would have voted for them if she'd thought they had a chance, and maybe the slightly bad taste they generate in her mouth is partly rooted in shame that she was so far off in her election predictions. Still, though. She's not thrilled with them as Supermajority, although they are better than Heritage, or at least bad in new and refreshing ways. They try too hard, design dense and clockwork-complicated schemes to make people care about policy, like trying to get kids to do their cerebral exercises by disguising them as games that aren't that fun and have to be played for seventy-five minutes every day. It's early yet; maybe they'll get better. Their rise was so sudden and unexpected, they must still be disbelieving and greedy about the power they won.

And then there's the fact that Nougaz dumped one of Roz's best friends in order to snuggle up with the Policy1st head of state. But Roz tries not to hold that against the whole government.

The best thing to come out of the Policy1st Supermajority as far as Roz is concerned is the spate of copycat policy-based governments. They are all small—none of them hold any centenals yet—but it's a good sign that they've started this early and will spend years in opposition, figuring out how they're different from existing governments. Some of them are whole-wheat hoagies—"healthy" policy on the outside, because it's trendy right now, greasy politics on the inside. There are a few, though, that show promise. Roz believes the system needs renewal. It needs young, idealistic parties. That's the reason she's reluctantly supportive of the five-year-cycle idea. That and the memory of the Heritage stranglehold on politics for the past twenty years.

Nejime has sent her notes from the meeting with Heritage earlier that day, the latest in a string of increasingly bitter negotiations as the former Supermajority tries to wriggle out of the sanctions imposed on it for election fraud and unauthorized construction of planetary import. Roz gets the sense that their approach is more and more precarious, but she ends up skimming through the notes when she sees a news alert at the bottom of her vision. There's been an escalation in the Kazakh-Kyrgyz conflict, a daring attack on Astana. Casualties and damage were low, and it seems to have been a one-off rather than the opening of another front, but it still marks a turning point in a war that until now has centered around the Bishkek-Almaty axis.

Information generally does not take this much interest in conflicts outside of its purview. But Democratic East Asia runs right up against the conflict, and many of the centenals on the edge are already feeling its effects in food shortages and fear.

Regional challenges add to the concern. More than a century of institutionalized, forced colonization has segued into a fragile democracy. 1China stuffs the ballots through continued migration and mobilization of existing partisans, while local Uyghur and Tibetan parties do their best to stave them off. The current border is a patchwork of governments, many of them balanced on a pichaq's edge, and there is growing concern that the Central Asian war could spill over and destabilize them, or force them to enter into armed conflict. Worse, many of the local governments in Democratic East Asia are poor, and they have either foregone a military contract or, at best, purchased a cut-rate defense package. If they are seriously threatened by the Kyrgyz or Kazakh armies, will the system somehow—through Information's budget, maybe, or a collection among other governments—fund their defense?

The Information powers-that-be claim that there has never been war between two governments participating in micro-democracy. Strictly speaking, that's true, although in her SVAT work over the past two years Roz has encountered a number of violent episodes that flirt with the quantitative threshold between "war" and "low-level conflict." Armed threat by an outside government is one of the outlier cases that nobody knows how to deal with yet.

This threat is so feared—collective defense is one of the big theoretical holes in micro-democracy—that there's been talk of Information stepping in as a negotiator to find an interest-based resolution to the conflict. There was a sense among Information officials, accustomed to the intricate cross-hatching of allegiances and rivalries among micro-democracy governments, that interstate conflict would be easy enough to fix. This has turned out not to be the case. Information does not cover residual nation-states like Kyrgyzstan and Kazakhstan, and intel is sketchy. Case in point: in addition to the official Kyrgyz military, several militias have splintered off with varying demands and leadership, and it's still unclear who is responsible for this latest attack.

Roz is both horrified and fascinated by the situation, and has been following it obsessively, in part because she finds nation-states so difficult to comprehend. She has never been able to get her head around why people and governments insist on clinging to the antiquated grab-as-much-territory-as-you-can philosophy. If they're splintering so rapidly that even a well-informed outsider like herself can't keep up, they might as well divide into centenals in an orderly way and be done with it. She can't understand why the Kyrgyz military or militia would attack Astana, when Almaty is a much more important city both in terms of population and economy. She realizes that the capitals of nation-states have some symbolic significance, but why didn't they make Almaty the capital in the first place?

Roz is a firm believer in democracy, but this war is enough to spur an illicit craving: that Information had the power to step in and make them stop, make them all citizens whether they want it or not. She learns all she can about the attack in Astana, and falls asleep late to troubled dreams.

CHAPTER 6

When they want to go out in public, Nougaz and Vera usually arrange a "chance" meeting in a café or restaurant or, occasionally, a museum, although those have an awful lot of cameras and open vid share policies. It's not that it's a secret; neither of them is hiding the relationship from their friends or colleagues. Nougaz has a long history, well-known in government circles, of pushing for a weaker Supermajority (and, implicitly but not incidentally, a stronger Information). She has no intention of changing that just because she's dating the head of state of the current Supermajority.

But announcing their entanglement for public consumption is an entirely different threshold, one neither of them is particularly eager to breach. There are plenty of vids of them together in leisure settings, but so far everyone seems willing to believe that these are informal meetings, or at most friendly networking. Indeed, that's how the relationship started, on one romantic rainy evening in Paris.

On this occasion, they meet in a tiny crêperie in the 6th with a student-heavy clientele. Nougaz is a public figure but, like most Information officials, not exactly a household face. Vera, with her distinctive hairstyle and plentiful press appearances, gets some glances and the occasional request for a joint vid (which she politely refuses) or autograph (to which she politely acquiesces). Once seated, though, they are rarely bothered.

"You look stressed," Vera comments, spooning up a dropped dollop of dulce de leche from her plate.

Nougaz, who calculates maximum utility like she breathes, selects the stress source that is most likely to lead to something else she wants. "There was an assassination yesterday," she says, an appropriate gravity to her voice as she lets her eyes trace the tabletop. "A head of state in East Africa."

Vera frowns, and blinks through recent headlines. "I did see something about that . . . Oh!" Nougaz watches her large eyes widen, flick back and forth as she reads. "Valérie, I think I knew him." A pause, then a decisive nod. "Yes, we met at an event for African heads of state last year. How terrible! We should put out a statement, draw attention to this." Her fingers twitch as she composes a memo. "I only spoke with him briefly, but he seemed like he was really trying to do something."

Nougaz twitches her shoulders affirmatively. "He was getting fairly good reviews. But it was still so early in his tenure. All that potential gone because of insufficient security."

She half-expects Vera to get angry that she's bringing this up again, but the Supermajority head of state fixes her with a sardonic look and replies mildly, "I'm following all the recommended protocols."

Vera's on-site security, in the form of two InfoSecs delegated to her detail, looms just outside the doors of the café as both warning and readiness. The more important element is off-site, where at least three layers envelop her every move, more in data-dense environments. One team monitors every feed on Vera at all times, looking for signs of illness as well as for external threats; the next watches every immediate approach; the third is at one additional remove—in this case, the streets around the café, the apartments above it, the airspace above that. Pretty soon, the earth's crust below it, if the mantle tunnel project moves ahead.

It should be enough. But the change of Supermajority created resentment, and Policy1st's insistence on putting policy wonks like Vera in visible positions instead of political spokes-models has not helped. Nougaz has seen the attacks in public and semipublic plazas, calling Vera (and, less frequently, her co–head of state Veena) ugly, stupid, unworthy of being broad-cast. Any literal incitements to violence are removed, but the more subtle dehumanizing content is only annotated. Nougaz is aware that not everyone takes annotation as seriously as they should.

"You can't control everything." Nougaz looks up from her thoughts to see Vera's smile and melts, but only on the inside.

"So I'm learning in Central Asia. Did you see the new of-fensive last night?" She clicks her tongue. "It's terribly frustrat-ing. A war between null states, and yet we keep being drawn into it one way or another."

"You shouldn't call them that," Vera chides. "It's derogatory."

"It's not, actually. Null states is a technical term, referring to the lack of data available for those areas." Nougaz realizes she's quoting her ex, and stops. "Perhaps it's worth investing in denser feed infrastructure there, if we can figure out a way to get it done. We're going to have to go global eventually."

"How about you keep the focus on the governments that pay your bills before offering Information to those that don't?" Vera cuts in. "Can you imagine how expensive it would be to put even a minimal coverage of feeds into those countries?" She shudders dramatically at the thought of the vast, cold steppes.

"Security and intelligence gathering are a benefit for the whole micro-democratic system. If not a necessity."

"I'd rather you kept your eye on Heritage," Vera says, tak-ing a sip of her chicory blend. "They're trying their best to wea-sel out of the consequences of their actions."

"That's not really your concern." Nougaz feels it come out too sharp. She can see herself in the mirror behind the bar: one eyebrow has gone up under her pale bangs, and the planes of her narrow face look beveled, like marble worn with use. She catches herself holding her breath for the comeback, but Vera shakes her head without anger.

"You'll see. These people, they don't get their own way, they're coming for the whole system."

Roz asked Malakal to accompany her on the trip to Djabal because of his rank and his knowledge of the area, but also so that they'd have representation at both of the gender-segregated gatherings of the funeral. They separate at the entrance to the compound, Malakal's tall figure towering over the other white-robed men as he heads to the right, while Roz is guided around a partial wall to a dusty courtyard. Her first impression is of the other foreigners, trying not to cluster together and yet still forming a clear group. It's not just their clothes and, in some cases, skin color that makes them stand out; unlike the locals, their public Information glows in the space beside their heads. Roz wishes she had thought to turn hers off. She sees representatives from ToujoursTchad, 1China, DarMasalit, and SahelLibre, all neighboring governments to at least one of DarFur's centenals, and she sees them clock her too, their eyes flickering as they murmur quick messages up the hierarchy, noting Information's presence and wondering why Al-Jabali merited their interest. *Mostly timing,* Roz thinks, going over to greet, and size up, the widow.

Al-Jabali's wife, Fatima, sits among silk cushions in the shadows of an unlit but well-appointed outbuilding, in the same style of concrete and roll-on linoleum as the main building. She looks genuinely grieved, or at the very least shocked, her large eyes sucking in the bits of light in the room, hovering above her defined cheekbones. Roz studied up the night before, muttering repeated bits of condolence phrases while she read about war in Central Asia. She's always had an ear for languages, and she's able to express her sympathy in Fur with a decent accent. Usually, the effort is appreciated, automatic interpreters notwithstanding.

After that, there's very little to do, ceremonially speaking. The temptation is to position herself somewhere with a good view of everyone, ideally not too close to any of the government representatives, and catch up on some content at eye level, or, more virtuously, get some work done. But Roz believes that there's still something to be said for in-person observation and interaction, and resolutely shuts off everything but the breaking news feed. Fortunately, there's a coffee station where a young woman is handing out tiny spiced cups. She hovers under the anemic mignonette tree in the middle of the courtyard near some of the better-dressed locals, sipping from her cup, but her eavesdropping gets her little besides tips on weaning toddlers and commentary on the dresses of other attendees. One woman does mutter something rude about the ToujoursTchad representative; Roz can't hear whether it's a personal criticism or political but decides that if there weren't political animosity, the stranger wouldn't be insulted. No one whispers anything about Al-Jabali's lover, although that kind of spectacularly bad taste is hardly to be expected, unless the widow were extremely unpopular. Nor does anyone within Roz's hearing speculate about the killer. She does catch two different people in separate conversations swearing off tsubame travel, although she doubts they have much opportunity to put that to the test.

Finally the food comes: platters of not only goat but what Information identifies in graphic detail as cow and camel, flanked by bowls of congealed porridge, brownish crêpes, and a gooey green semi-liquid that Information claims is vegetable in nature, although in that case it offers fewer specifics. Roz sets to without great enthusiasm but with some relief: it is custom here to serve women the leftovers of what the men have eaten, but once again, opulence is showing. There are no telltale finger scoops missing from the porridge bowls, and the meat couldn't be piled any higher on the trays.

As Roz is finishing her meal, she gets a call from Maria. She stands up, rubbing her greasy fingers together in the absence of any disinte-wipes, and steps off to the side of the hut, where she can mutter in something like privacy.

"How's it going?"

"All right," Maria answers. "And you?"

"It's going to be a long day," Roz answers, keeping a smile on her face. "What's going on?"

"It's unfortunate the funeral had to be held away from Kas," Maria says. "There's a rumor going around that it wasn't really Al-Jabali who was killed, and another saying the deputy was killed with him and nobody's in charge. We've circulated the forensics report and we're holding a community meeting in an hour and looking for other appropriate ways to get the word out."

"Try the mural," Roz suggests.

"It feels too soon, doesn't it?" Maria murmurs. "But I'll check with Amran and the locals and see what they say. Hang in there." She signs off.

Reminded, or given an excuse, Roz checks in with the rest of the team.

"The militia is handling things pretty much as I expected," Minzhe says, philosophically. "They haven't a clue where to start, even though my take is that they're genuinely upset about the assassination—once I convinced them that it was actually an assassination and not just a tragic tsubame malfunction. Commander Hamid is debriefing the other bodyguards as we speak. I have my doubts about their tactics, but I'll let you know if we come up with something."

Charles is having more difficulty. "I don't know how they get anything done here! There are so few feeds! None at all on eighty-seven percent of the border."

"Try talking to people," Roz offers.

"I am, I am," he grumbles. "But you know how much everyone loves talking to outsiders and especially Information."

"Good luck," she says. "And see if they have feeds on the other side of the border."

"I checked. Just as bereft. But I'll keep looking along likely routes, on both sides, to and from the sites of these alleged battles."

She decides she doesn't have to check in with Amran.

Instead, Roz figures it's as appropriate as it will ever be to approach the widow. She slips back into the room, edging past a tray laden with the remains of a meal. It's a few degrees cooler inside, or maybe it just feels that way because of the dimness, and Fatima is reclining on her bed with two other women. Roz eyes the entourage but decides that the bereaved woman is entitled to support. Besides, she's not planning on broaching anything too delicate.

"I'm sorry to bother you again," she begins, as softly as she can, "but as you know, we're trying to find out who did this. I was wondering if you had any thoughts on who might have wanted to harm your husband."

Fatima stirs, sits up straighter. "He was doing the right thing for our people: of course people wanted to harm him." She pauses. "Are you sure it was intentional?"

"Quite sure," Roz says. "Do you know why he was late to meet us that day?"

"Late?" She says it so quickly, Roz is sure it's genuine

surprise, but she pulls back into languor almost immediately. "I have no idea."

"He was coming from here to meet us in Kas. Do you know what he was doing before he left?"

"Some centenal business here, I don't know. A meeting with the sheikhs."

"Did you often ride in the tsubame yourself? Had you noticed any changes in it recently?"

"No. I'd only been in it once, when he first got it. No, wait, twice. We went to an event at an 888 centenal south of here about a month . . ." Her eyes flutter, looking it up. ". . . three weeks ago."

"Did you notice anything different the second time?" Roz asks. Fatima, after giving it thought, shakes her head. "Was anything bothering your husband over the last few weeks? Worrying him? Any new threats?"

Fatima doesn't answer immediately, just stares at Roz level-eyed, projecting as fierce a spirit as Roz has ever felt. But between her day job among the Information elite and SVAT episodes dealing with angry, violent, powerless people, Roz has a lot of practice with uncomfortable silences and accusatory glares, and she looks back without wavering. Finally, Fatima speaks: "No."

Roz raises her eyebrows. "Nothing?" She waits. "If you do think of anything, please let us know. You might be in danger too," she adds, although she doubts it's a high probability.

The widow's eyes lash out at her in the darkness. "Is that a threat?" she hisses.

"No!" Roz exclaims so loudly and quickly that she almost misses Fatima's next words, low and angry.

"If you or anyone in your organization harmed my husband, it is you who will be in danger!"

"No, of course not," Roz says again. "We had no reason or

desire to harm your husband." She would like to be able to say categorically that Information would never do such a thing, but she doesn't trust her employer enough for that. Or her colleagues, she supposes. But she's as certain as she can be without knowing firsthand.

Fatima subsides, but Roz can still feel her antagonism in the close space. "I'm sure you will find out the truth, then," she says, and Roz is left with no choice but to make as graceful an exit as she can manage.

Back in the hot sun, she blinks, first with annoyance, then to compose a message to Malakal. He's probably having a great time on the men's side, interrogating the interesting new Governor and all the local sheikhs, chilling however men do. She bullets out the little she learned ("widow suspicious of us") and sends it. Malakal doesn't answer right away, which probably means he's caught up in some sparkling conversation. Eventually, Roz gives in and starts working on the tsubame problem at a headache-inducing eyeball level. The vehicle went in for maintenance two months ago, but it was for a specific issue—a problem with the energy management—and it's not guaranteed that the mechanics would have noticed whether the valve was missing. Still, Roz decides to start from there. The first questions are about the mechanics themselves; it's an unlicensed shop, because there are no licensed shops within a hundred-mile radius, but at least it's back in Kas. She sends Charles a message to check it out.

"Salaam wa aleikum."

Roz looks up, blinking rapidly to dispel the table of locations and dates. The woman from ToujoursTchad has taken the plastic chair beside her, her fine toub a muted shimmer of purple and black.

"Hélène Ahmed," the woman says, holding out a black-gloved hand.

"Roz Kabwe." Knowing this woman must have come looking for something, Roz does not bother with small talk. "Did you know Governor Yagoub well?"

"Al-Jabali? We had met, of course. Information"—Hélène dips her head, simultaneously acknowledging that Roz is part of that vast organization and that she may not be aware of everything they are doing—"offered many incentives for the creation of coalitions and inter-centenal cooperation, so we were beginning to work together on some initiatives of this kind. Unfortunately, these projects were still in their infancy." She offers a deprecating moue. "We must hope that his successor will continue them."

"Let's hope so, indeed," Roz answers. "What kind of projects were they?"

"As I said, many of them were still in the *very* early stages of formulation. But obviously, Information infrastructure is a huge priority."

Roz frowns. A priority for Information, maybe, but it doesn't seem like it's been a priority for these governments. Not much has been done about it, anyway.

"And then economic stimulus, water purification . . . You've seen the evaporation processing plant in Kas? Anyway, as you can tell, there's a lot to be done."

"Most of the governments work well together?"

"We try," Hélène says, with some asperity. Her eyes flick up and down, assessing what she can get away with. "The Chinese, of course, they can be difficult. They just don't understand the culture here. And the Sudanese . . . Well, we don't actually work with any Sudanese."

"Do you think any of these frictions could have led to the explosion?" Roz motions at the surrounding funeral.

Hélène makes a show of thinking, although Roz imagines she came over with someone in mind to pin it on. "It could have been the Sudanese. Some of them have been very distressed about the fragmenting of their country. They blamed Al-Jabali as much as anyone."

More than they blamed Information? Roz thinks, and also: *"Their" country?*

"But, to be honest," Hélène sighs, "much as I would like for it to be the Sudanese—and I strongly recommend that you do not discount them—I suspect that there may have been outsiders at work."

"Why do you say that?" Roz asks, wondering if by "outsiders" she is again referring to ethnic Chinese who have, most probably, spent their entire lives in this desert.

"It's just not something we would do," Hélène says, waving her hand.

"Really." One of Roz's personal travel rules is never to fly with an African head of state, aircraft accidents being a traditional means of doing away with them. "I think I could name a few examples."

Hélène flutters her toub. "With the situation here, if one of us was to have designs against another, it would be very public. Many people still see conflict as the best way to win additional territory."

"Or start a costly feud, which could be avoided by secrecy or the appearance of an accident," Roz counters.

"On the contrary," Hélène says sweetly. "Feuds win support at home. My point is, there are elements of this disaster that suggest the involvement of foreigners. But you will be doing the investigation; I am sure you will find the truth. Surely, Information always does." She flounces to her feet. "No plans to visit ToujoursTchad while you're here?"

"I'm afraid we're very busy," Roz says, making a mental note to have someone schedule an unannounced visit as soon as possible.

CHAPTER 7

On the stretch of green between the arms of the avenue, people waltz to the strains of an audio-boosted ballroom dance projection. They dance every morning as Mishima slides by, a quick impression of couples twirling and a father-son team of instructors (Information provides an auto-link to their ads) making gentle corrections or beating time in the air. At the end of the avenue, she crosses the narrow park and skates back along the other side. Her soles taper to blade-edges, calibrated to be almost frictionless where they meet the pavement, with calculated patches of slight cling along the edges to target specific muscle groups, shifting according to her workout goals. A few blocks from her apartment, Mishima slows, then lets herself cruise, straightening up. When she's finally slid almost to a stop, she uses gesture control to gradually raise the friction to the level of clunky but adequate footwear. She steps cautiously, readjusting to her own weight and clumsiness as she transfers to a walk. She's breathing deeply, grateful every day for the decades of increasingly efficient atmospheric scrubbers in Saigon; the air is scintillating, far cleaner than Paris or Tokyo.

Mishima kicks off her shoes in the building entranceway and takes the five flights of stairs up to the apartment at a light, leaping run, the coda to her workout. She opens the door, drops the shoes, plops some foam from the dispenser in the entranceway, and runs it through her hair, along sweat-gathering areas, cleansing the exercise funk. She puts on some music, stretches against the wall and then on the floor. Looking up at the balcony railing reminds her she needs to water the plants. She leans into her stretch again, checks her diagnostics. She isn't stretching as far as yesterday, but her right adductor is a little tight, so she doesn't push it.

Cooldown over, Mishima moves to her workstation. She pulls over one of the balloon lights—thin layers of luminous fluoron wrapped around a sealed helium bubble that floats against the ceiling—and settles in to finish a report. Mishima is an entrepreneur now, selling her services to the highest bidder. It's a bracing change after spending years inside the world's largest bureaucracy, even if she did have a privileged position there. At the moment, she's working for an uptake accelerator specializing in political economy of marginalized groups, which seemed like an awesome match. They scour the world's centenals for successful policy innovations and then try to get more governments to notice and adopt those innovations. The first part is fun; the second part is both more difficult and less useful than it sounds. Almost always, a new context requires so much adaptation to make the initiative effective that it might as well be a completely new policy.

She doesn't have as much pull as a consultant as she did when she was veteran Information staff. Mishima finds it aggravating to have to provide a product to specifications that are often wrong, or at best inefficient. She has to tell herself, often, that her job is to give the client what they want, not tell the client what they should want. On the other hand, she finds it easier to detach from failure that way. Besides, her rate is high enough to cover a lot of aggravation.

Her last mission was to Nuwara Eliya, where a small, mildly Marxist government found a way to resolve the tension between tea's critical role in the economy and the exploitative economics of hand-picked tea production. The entire plantation labor force is provided through mandatory two-year stints for all youth, either before or after university, which their earnings help them to pay for. Mishima is trying to figure out the overlap between commodities that drive economies through low-paid manual work and the range of governments that would embrace a mandatory non-military service for youth. Maybe she can tweak the incentives so it's not absolutely mandatory?

She's toying with the labor-incentive-water numbers for cotton, and has just about decided that she's better off shifting the focus up the value chain to cheap textiles, when she gets a call.

"Hi! Roz! How are you?" Mishima gladly swivels away from her workstation.

"Tired, to be honest," answers Roz, safely alone at last in the workspace of the crow. Malakal is in the cabin with the door shut. She suspects the male side of the event was at least as exhausting; he has assured her it was just as boring. "Long, ceremonial day."

Mishima makes a sympathetic face. "Inauguration of some kind?" She scans newsfeeds as she says it to figure out what that might be.

"Funeral."

"What? Who?" Mishima has been consciously trying to reduce her addiction to news, and now all her disaster nerves spring alert, reaching out to find what went wrong and why she missed it and how she can fix it.

"No, no one you know," Roz says, and then hopes that's true. She can't remember if Mishima spent time in Darfur or Chad; she did work for Malakal, after all. "The head of state for the DarFur government was assassinated in front of our eyes."

"I missed that," Mishima says, still scanning.

"I'm sure it didn't make many global compilers. There's a lot going on in the world."

"There is," Mishima agrees, sounding distracted. She's wearing a sweaty tank top, and her auburn hair is pulled back into a messy bun: just back from exercising.

"How's the freelance life?" Roz asks, trying to bring her back.

"Oh, great, you know, busy, but I suppose I can always say no, so there's that. I keep telling you you should join me on this." She's still thinking about something else.

Roz casts around for another topic. She can see Mishima's apartment in the background as she wanders, and it doesn't look like anyone is there. She doesn't want to ask where Ken is; she can find out on Information without the potential awkwardness. She's been half-expecting that relationship to end ever since it began, watching as she would an inexpert tightrope walker, and she doesn't particularly want to see the crash. "By the way," she says instead, "I think the field lead here either has an undiagnosed narrative disorder or is trying to fake one."

"Oh?" Mishima's tone is more guarded than interested, and Roz wonders what she did wrong: the suggestion that someone might fake the disorder? Or would Mishima prefer Roz pretended she didn't know about her condition? Either way, she's in it now, so she goes on, keeping her tone light as she describes the scene with Amran the day before.

"Tricky," Mishima says, when Roz has laid it out. "I'm guessing you don't have too many mental health professionals out there, either."

Roz runs a quick check through Information. "None for five hundred kilometers in any direction."

Mishima ponders. "Let me see if I can find any resources that might help." She rouses herself. "Are you okay, though? You said this assassination happened right in front of you."

"It's not like I haven't seen worse."

"It's not like it doesn't hurt anyway."

"I hadn't met the guy, which helps." Roz shrugs. "We're okay. This is looking like an interesting one, though."

"In what way?"

"Well . . . there are obvious suspects for the assassination but—almost too obvious, you know? There's no trigger for why they would act now, and no one has claimed responsibility. So, there might be something else going on. Meanwhile, the fallout is going to be . . . complex."

Mishima chuckles. "So, you're still liking the SVAT work?"

Roz thinks to make sure she is. "What I really like," she says finally, "is the combination. A week or two out in the field, uncomfortable and slightly dangerous, dealing with real people; then back to a few months of heavy, brain-bending data analytics. Some thinking, some fear. It's a good balance."

"It sounds like it," Mishima says, and her tone is more wistful than Roz expected.

"What, you don't get enough fear in consulting?"

Mishima snorts. "Not enough thinking." Then she shifts topic. "Oh, Malakal is there," Mishima says, pulling intel from who knows what compiler or hack. "Say hi to him for me, please!"

"I will, but you should call him yourself," Roz tells her. "He's worried about you."

"Worried about me?" Mishima almost laughs. She has finally settled, and is sprawling on a chaise lounge on her balcony, the spotless sky behind her. "Why?"

"Because you left."

As a teenager and into early adulthood, Minzhe earned a substantial amount of side money as a gold farmer, and he is still up-to-date with the most recent and revelatory interactive series. When he was a small boy in Darfur, however, the connectivity wasn't good enough for interactive vid or even graphics, and his first gaming experiences were on old-fashioned text-only adventure games. His interior monologue still reverts to that mode whenever he's somewhere new:

> *You are standing in a small clearing in the city. Desperate grass clings to the sand in patches under the solitary acacia tree. To your right is the edge of the market, starting with a row of tailor stalls. In front of you, the ground slopes up to a rectangular one-story building of pockmarked concrete. Along the overhang that projects out above the doors, "Dar-Fur Militia: Kas Station" is written in Arabic, English, and Chinese characters. The building is painted dull turquoise up to shoulder height, desert yellow above that. From here you can make out five doors facing the front, and on the right, a small separate wing juts toward you. In the one small window on that wing you can see bars. A number of men are sitting in front of the building. It looks like they are playing cards.*
>
> *A single camel is grazing below the tree, a rope stretching from its long neck to the tree trunk.*

Definitely the camel. It's always that one detail that stands out that you need to do something with. He would type in every variation of **untie camel** he could think of (**free camel; release camel; help camel**) until it worked, and then ride it off into the market, maybe after winning a few rounds of cards to fill up his wallet. Minzhe grins, and walks up the slope toward the station.

Ken isn't in Saigon, because he is speaking in one of the smoke-stained, aged rooms of the former Fábrica de Tabaco, current University, of Sevilla. He's supposed to be trying life in the slow lane as a local government official, making a difference at the micro-level, but it's a lot more fun to jet around the world as a (reasonably) well-paid speaker when he can. In the last election cycle, Policy1st became the first government to topple a sitting Supermajority, and people who worked on the campaign became instant, sought-after experts. Most of them are unavailable, since they are currently working for Policy1st and are discouraged from sharing too many secrets, but Ken's former boss resigned just after the election and has become an almost inescapable pundit and commentator. When he's overbooked, he's started passing some of the (lower-profile) gigs Ken's way.

"That was a fascinating presentation! Tell me more about what you're doing now."

Right now? Hoping she doesn't notice he's checking his fantasy rugby stats at eyeball level. "I'm director of citizen engagement at Free2B." That's a slight exaggeration. Ken is only the director for citizen engagement of a single centenal, not the whole government, but since Free2B only has twelve centenals worldwide, he doesn't feel like it's such a big difference. "I do a lot of fun techie stuff, trying to figure out how to get people to participate more in both policy formation and implementation." It *is* fun. Last week, Ken rolled out "Policy Pub Trivia," which had a great response and allowed him to spend every night at a different bar. A few months ago, he developed a new algorithm for finding consensus that was written into the latest polling law. It is totally fun. It's just not as satisfying as saving the world.

He figures that calling in sick every so often so he can jet around the world and pretend to be an expert at campaign espionage is a small price for him or his employer to pay to feed his globetrotting addiction. Besides, he is building his network! Making new contacts! Learning about innovations in other centenals!

It's obvious to him that the woman he's talking to would like to be one of his new contacts. She is leaning so far on her elbow that her professionally shirred hair almost touches his shoulder, gazing as if she might fall through the floor if he broke eye contact. Ken can see that she's pretty—well, no, strike that. Her projected makeup shimmers every few seconds like headlights are rolling over her face, and he can't actually see through it to know whether or not she's pretty. But he can tell that a lot of people would think she's attractive, especially if she were telling them how amazing their work is. She's wearing next to nothing, which makes sense because it's forty degrees at eleven P.M., and also because she has a fairly good body. Ken is sure that sex with her would be fun, but he can't get remotely excited about the prospect. Either one of Mishima's eyebrows is more compelling than this woman's whole body.

Fortunately, there's a whole group of people from the lecture who convened for after-conference drinks at this bar in a cavernous old charcoal warehouse, now filled with long tables and wooden benches, talk, music, and the smell of wine and bodies. "Do you think Policy1st will be able to win again? Especially if the election is in only three years?" The woman who asks is sitting on Ken's other side and doesn't seem to be angling to sleep with him, so even though he hates the question, he turns to her eagerly.

"First of all, no one knows yet whether the term will be shortened—"

"Of course it will be," scoffs the scruffy-bearded man sitting across from them, who introduced himself as a freelance intel conglomerator. "Policy1st is not going to make it through ten years."

Whatever, guy who spends all his time trawling Information so he can sell repackaged facts. "Policy1st is doing great things, including not digging illegal tunnels into the planet. And—"

"Look, I live in a Policy1st centenal, and I love them, I really do." Although Ken notes he doesn't say he voted for them. Moved in once they became the Supermajority, hmm? "The evidence-based policy focus, it's refreshing, and sometimes even leads to positive outcomes. But as the Supermajority, they're out of their depth. After all, those illegal tunnels into the planet are getting built anyway, aren't they? Policy1st just won't get the benefit of them."

"It's not like they can control what all the other governments do." Ken twitches his fingers to pull up the original charter giving the Supermajority mandate and limitations, then stops himself. Using data-based projections is a sure sign the argument's getting away from him. "The Supermajority doesn't have as much power as people think." He forces himself to take a sip of his sangria and smile.

Scruffy-beard waves his hands, flapping the loose edges of his sideless drape top. "Heritage managed all right. But for the term limits, it doesn't matter anyway! Information lives off elections, and they're the ones making the decision. They need to hold elections more often to maintain their control, keep their status as kingmakers."

"I don't know," says the woman who's not leaning her leg against Ken's. She's wearing a sleeveless, mid-thigh-length jumpsuit that Ken has been eyeing enviously because it's a bit bulky and therefore almost certainly climate-controlled. "With the K-stan war and Russia acting up, some stability might be good for a while."

"Stability is overrated. Elections are so much more exciting, right?" The flirtatious woman's makeup sparkles as she leans toward Ken, aiming for conspiratorial.

He shifts away from her as his mouth obediently spouts forth something about how governing is more important than elections. Maybe it's her aggressive complicity, but suddenly, he can't ignore the fact that if he really felt that way, he would be in Saigon, governing.

It takes Charles some time to find the garage, partly because it's not labeled as a garage on the map but as GENERAL HARD-WARE AND REPAIR (he has to admit, when he finally gets there, that it's a more accurate description) but also because the map is out of date. It's only out of date by eleven days, but apparently the stalls in the market have shifted since then, and so when Charles was looking for a leather shop to make the right turn, he walked right past the tinware stand that had taken its place. It takes him longer than it should to figure it out because it is so inconceivable that a map could be wrong, and he huffs into the garage hot, irritated, and in the middle of composing a sharp message to Amran.

The shop is large enough for a vehicle to drive into, with buckets of wooden-handled shovels and rakes positioned around the door, the inside walls decorated with a pleasing metallic jumble of smaller sale items. A couple of skinny young men are lounging on a string bed in the rear of the space, and Charles asks one of them about the boss while shelving his message to Amran: she's stressed enough as it is. The lad takes him through the back, where the shop opens into a large courtyard. There, a prehistoric, or at least pre-Information, truck chassis is decomposing next to a more recent minibus tilted onto one axle.

The mechanic who stands up from his work does not tower over Charles, even though his public Information and the fine scar lines across his forehead announce he is a Dinka, from Abyei. "Hello, my brother," Charles greets him, giving the man time to read his own affiliation and background. "Could we speak for a few minutes?"

The mechanic, Paul, willingly leads him to a shaded corner. "I've been expecting you ever since that explosion," he says, as he wipes his hands. "It is true it was sabotage?"

"It was," Charles answers. "We have proof."

Paul nods, looks away. "I am so glad it wasn't me. That was the first tsubame I ever worked on, I was sure I did everything right, but still . . ." He looks back at Charles. ". . . I was worried somehow."

"Natural enough," Charles agrees. "But we are sure it was sabotage. Someone did this deliberately. What we do not know is who, or where, or when." He sees the mechanic understand: he was not at fault by negligence or error, but he may still be under suspicion of deliberate assassination.

"I'll tell you whatever I can," Paul says, then takes a deep breath and starts without waiting for any questions. "As I said, it was the first tsubame I ever worked on, so I was pretty happy when it was brought in."

"Who brought it?" Charles interrupts.

"In fact, I went to the mooring station by the governor's office to get it. The governor's secretary, Aisha, called me, told me there was a problem with the energy management system and asked me to look because the governor had some long trips coming up. I went there and they gave me a temporary access code to fly it back here."

"You take it for a spin?" Charles suggests.

Paul shakes his head. "Only after I finished working on it, when I wanted to test it. Flying back that first time, I was nervous. I had the auto-assist playing the whole time."

"Okay, and then?"

Paul shrugs. "I checked the whole thing, using the auto-assist—you can ask these boys here if you like," he said, waving toward the youths in the shop. They have stretched out their rugs and Charles can see their silhouettes rising and bending

in the afternoon prayer. "They were paying attention. They'd
never seen a tsubame before. I did a full and complete inspec-
tion, which was more than was asked, because I thought it was
my best opportunity to learn about these things."

"Not just the auto-diagnostic?"

"No, I told you, I wanted to learn. I checked everything by
hand. With the auto-assist, but visually, in real life."

"Did you find anything unusual at all?"

"No. Not a thing was out of place. The normal signs of use
were there but very minor. I changed the air pressurizer filters,
even though they weren't clouded, but it was the only thing I
could figure that would help reduce energy use. At the end of
the day, I never did figure out why the energy management was
giving that message. Maybe the governor accidentally programmed it wrong or something; it seemed to be working fine
when I saw it."

Charles doesn't want to do anything as obvious as finger-
twitching a note, so he gives the little crook of the head that he
has set to mark the timestamp in his recording. Then he pulls
up the schematics he's been given and focuses in on the fatal
valve. "Was this in place?"

Paul studies it. "Yes. That was there. There would have been
a warning if it wasn't."

Not if the diagnostic was hacked, Charles thinks. "Did you
verify it visually?"

"Yes. That section was open anyway because of the filters,
so it wasn't difficult to look at. I checked every part there
visually."

"How long was the vehicle here?" Charles asks, closing the
projection.

"Two days. It took too long to get it done in one."

"And was it open as you mentioned overnight?"

"Oh, no," Paul says. "Of course not. I couldn't have sand or dust getting into the mechanism. No, I closed it up and covered it. I was still nervous, though. It's silly, because who would steal the governor's property? You can't hide a tsubame anywhere. But I came in early the next morning, couldn't help feeling my heart pounding as I walked in, but of course it was still there."

"Nothing out of place?" Charles asks. He's noticed how vulnerable this place is: the walls around the inner courtyard come up to his shoulder, and there's no door closing it off from the shop either.

"No, nothing," Paul says. "I finished the check, took it for a little ride"—he chuckles at the memory—"and flew it back to the governor's office. Ran the auto-diagnostics three times on the way, too. Nothing."

CHAPTER 8

They arrive in Kas after dark. There are few lights in the town, and Malakal uses Information navigation to steer them to the compound, where he again moors directly over the roof of one of the offices instead of at the public mooring space near the centenal hall. They find Amran and Maria in the main office, working on a projected database. Around the table are three of Amran's stringers, identified in the public Information projected beside their heads: Mohamed Nour, twenty-three, a skinny man with thick eyebrows and reddish skin; Yagoub Mohamed, age not listed but probably late twenties, handsome and knows it; and Khadija Jibrail, a young matron of twenty-six with three children (names and ages listed, with tiny photos) and a winning smile.

"Welcome back," Maria says, leaning back and stretching her back.

"Thanks." Roz nods at the stringers, knowing they are reading the translated versions of her own public Information, or hearing it if they prefer that mode. "Where are the others?"

"Minzhe talked Charles into going to the market for dinner. They should be back soon." She looks from Roz to Malakal and back. "Did you find out anything?"

"Nothing to make us suspect anyone in Djabal," Malakal says. "Nothing to clear them either. I checked on Al-Jabali's delay in meeting us. He was meeting with the centenal governor and council of sheikhs right before he came here. I spoke with three of them, separately. All agreed that it was an important but not terribly urgent meeting. None had a satisfactory answer when I asked why it had been added to his schedule only three days before." Roughly when he would have heard the SVAT team was coming.

"What was the meeting on?"

"Centenal infrastructure: maintenance, and some new projects they are trying to work out. A piped water expansion, a bridge for the rainy season." Important but not urgent. "The sheikhs said that the meeting dragged and went over schedule, and that when Al-Jabali realized he was late, he hurried out as quickly as he could without being rude." A pause. "And you?"

Amran says, hurriedly, "I've prepared a file for you with some background and updates." She hurls it into their workspaces. "Our colleagues here are researching people that might be of interest; you will see them linked in the file."

"And I am updating on the battles," Khadija puts in, with that smile.

Odd choice, Roz thinks, and then sees a message from Maria in the corner of her vision: her husband is a local mercenary.

Maria waits for a beat before adding her own update. "There's growing concern about the assassination. People aren't used to a stable government, and they expect this to lead to chaos, if not armed conflict."

Malakal sighs, pulling out a chair for himself. "Do they like Suleyman?"

With a glance at Amran—Roz is impressed how hard Maria is working to include her—Maria throws up a pie chart projection. "Short answer? Yes. Sixty-eight percent approval for the governorship job, quite high. Amran has broken it down for us by sub-demographic . . ." Maria glances at Amran again, but the younger woman gives a tiny shake of her head, and Maria goes on. "You'll see it in the file, but basically his core constituency, um, based on clan, I guess you could say, they see him as completely legitimate. The others would prefer their own leader but in the absence of that are generally positive on Suleyman."

"Okay, so that shouldn't be a problem," Roz says.

"No. The problem is at the government level. No one knows who will replace Al-Jabali. There was no deputy; there was no plan for succession. The governing council announced twenty-seven minutes ago that they will hold a general election to choose the next governor, as Amran predicted yesterday."

"Okay," Roz says, settling into a chair herself. An election. The best and worst part of democracy. "Any candidates so far?"

"Only the former governor's wife." It is Yagoub who says this, projecting a short vid: the woman that Roz saw eight hours ago bereft and exhausted and angry. In the projection, her face is still solemn, but more thoroughly made up, and she speaks quietly and rapidly about the need to continue her husband's work.

There's a moment of silence. Roz is remembering her final exchange with the widow. If she wasn't in danger before, she very well may be now.

"Does that sew it up?" Malakal asks the room somewhere between Amran and Yagoub.

They look at each other noncommittally. "It depends who else runs," Amran says.

Yagoub nods. "She is popular in Djabal, maybe, but not so much here."

"Who *is* popular here?"

A pause, with a few more consultative glances running between the locals.

"Suleyman?" Malakal prompts.

"He would do very well here if he runs," Amran says. "But I doubt he will."

"He is not well known outside this centenal," Khadija puts

in. "And he will not want a job that takes him away from Kas very often."

"Why?" Roz asks. "Family?"

"His authority is here," Yagoub says, as if that explains it. "I don't think he wants to go somewhere else. He didn't run for head of state last time."

"All right, who else?" Malakal asks.

There is another silence.

"We can review potential candidates tomorrow night," Roz says. She sees no reason to force the local staff into speculating if they're not comfortable with it, and besides, she's exhausted. "Fatima's announcement will spur anyone else who's interested to get in the race quickly."

"Or to give up on it," Malakal mutters. He sighs and stretches. "Well, in that case, I'm off to bed. We'll see how things look in the morning."

Roz wants to follow, but everyone else is still working. Besides, she needs to push forward somehow on this investigation. She sets up a projection in the middle of the room, centering an image of Al-Jabali, then drawing connections. His wife. Suleyman. The local elite that Mohamed and Yagoub have been profiling, who are mostly sheikhs and sheikhas and a few business leaders. Rival governments. Roz has no precedent on how to investigate an assassination, but this is how she's always seen it done on interactive series and vids, and it seems like a good idea.

"Add Sheikh Abdul Gasig," Mohamed suggests. "He's a rival for power in Kas."

"He is well known beyond Kas as well," Amran adds. "He could indeed be a candidate for the head of state position."

Roz puts him in, with a double line showing a rivalry with Suleyman.

Charles and Minzhe come in, redolent with the smell of grilled meat and—Roz's nose twitches—possibly illegal alcohol. They certainly seem happy enough.

"Hey," Roz says. "How's it going?"

"Fine," Charles says with a wink. "Just checking on the local mood."

Seeing them reminds Roz of the report Charles sent her on the garage. She slaps up a picture of the mechanic, along with the unguarded, feedless courtyard where he works. Then she adds another projection: TIMELINE. "Since the mechanic found the valve in place, we can narrow the timeline. With the caveat that he could be lying, of course."

"It seems possible that the garage visit itself was, ahem, engineered," Charles says, smiling at his own pun. "Someone may have tweaked the energy management settings to make it appear that there was a problem."

Roz nods, feeling relieved: maybe this will be manageable after all. "So, we focus on the people who had access to the tsubame immediately before the garage visit?"

"I'll start with the governor's secretary, who arranged it," Charles agrees.

That leaves fifty-two blank days on the timeline, with another week before the garage visit for fiddling with the energy management. This is not helping as much as Roz had hoped. Staring at the relationship diagram, she has an idea.

"Minzhe, do you think the militia will be interviewing any of these people as part of their investigation?"

He studies the pictures. "I doubt it. And I'm not sure I'd want them to. Most of your suspects are sheikhs in this centenal, long-term power-holders. I'm not sure the militia can be objective regarding them, and even if they could, it would sabotage their ongoing relationship."

"I see," Roz says. She's still hoping that the government can do at least some of the investigative work. It's their job, not hers. "What about Fatima? She's not from this centenal."

"She could end up being head of state," Charles points out.

"She was the victim's wife. It's reasonable to interview her even if she's not a suspect. It doesn't have to be accusatory," Roz argues.

Minzhe nods. "I think it's possible. If they interview anyone."

"Do you think you can encourage it?" Roz asks.

"I guess I can try."

"Charles, can you keep pushing, gently, on the council of sheikhs? We're missing something in Al-Jabali's life. I don't know whether it's personal or political, but the local leadership should know something about it."

"One other thing," Maria says, as Charles nods. "Amran has a plan for starting the intensive SVAT work."

"Great," Roz says, happy to have something she can praise. "Tell me about it."

"Actually, we can show you," Maria says. "If you're up for a short walk."

Roz would far rather go to sleep, but it's only nine, and Amran seems eager, so she agrees. Minzhe begs off and heads to his hut, claiming exhaustion, but the rest of the team braves the rustle of sleeping birds in the dark mass of the tree and heads toward the market.

Everything feels different at night, darkness drawn like a shade over the glaring heat of day. The market is dim but for the occasional loop of fluoron over a shop door, dripping its yellowy light on the men sitting below it in quiet conversation. "Up here," Yagoub calls softly, motioning them on, and Roz sees more light creeping out from the flaps in a large tent. When they slip through the gap between the panels, Roz can see that the canvas was once white and has lettering.

Inside, she finds a bewildering onset of noise and moving colors. It takes her a moment to orient herself and realize that this is an old-fashioned mass projection theater, like they used to have before terrorism and technology made them obsolete. The flashing images, coordinated according to an old algorithm to give everyone the best seat in the house, jangle and compete, and the mass sound oscillates between too loud and incomprehensibly blurred, but no one seems to mind. There are so many people in the tent that their substantial group can huddle into the back without attracting anything but brief glances from those they jostle as they find their spots. Most of the viewers are boys and men between eight and twenty-eight, dressed in jellabiyas or long sweat-stained undershirts, but Roz counts enough females not to be worried about accidental cultural inappropriateness. She stares, fascinated, at the kids fascinated by this entertainment. In front of her, a young boy, head shaved close, sways in time with the fight scene, spindly arms twitching.

"They do this every night," Yagoub whispers. "Sometimes a sports match, sometimes a vid or a series."

"Do they pay to get in?" Maria asks. While Yagoub explains the pricing, Roz is looking up personal projector penetration in the DarFur government: a shockingly low 9.38 percent.

The vid has transitioned from fisticuffs to fucking, and Roz wants to move on. "So, you think—what, we do a talk here? Insert a public service newsreel at the beginning?"

"Maybe the latter," Maria says, observing with interest as some two hundred people watch three-dimensional simulated sex acts in close, if somewhat unaligned, proximity. "I'm not sure 'doing a talk' fits the ethos."

CHAPTER 9

Roz wakes up sweating and wrapped in damp sheets. Her bed is supposed to have climate control, but it must have shut itself off during the night to save power. The hut is round, with a circumference not much larger than the length of her bed, and a conical roof draped with cloth to catch any falling bits of thatch. It's dense with heat, like a warning, and Roz, still groggy, feels the pang of an old childhood fear: the Earth has been knocked off its orbit and is flying into the unlivable corona of the sun. She blinks, rubs her hand over her eyes and her wet brow. Maybe something much more prosaic has gone wrong: could the power be out? She remembers Amran's theory of escalating disasters and comes fully awake.

There is enough light in the room, seeping around the door edges and through the cloth-shaded window, to tell her it's after dawn; a blink tells her the exact time: 6:38. She rolls up off the bed and cracks the door to peer into the courtyard, unable to shake her unease. The air outside is marginally cooler, and so she ends up opening the door wide and leaving it that way as she slips into her sandals and tramps stiff-legged across the sandy compound to the latrine. Dawn has indeed broken, but only barely: the sky is still dim and faintly rosy. Even outside, even before she can see the sun, the heat presses down on her. A donkey hee-haws somewhere out in the town. Roz splashes water on her face and goes to figure out the electricity situation.

A woman that Roz guesses to be around fifty, wearing an oversized shirt and micro-crinkled skirt down to her ankles, is sweeping the tiny kitchen area behind the office. Her public Information lists her name as Maryam, and even with Roz's auto-interpreter, the two women end up communicating mostly by sign language, partly because Maryam apparently speaks an obscure dialect of Fur that the interpreter is not familiar with, and partly because she seems to expect foreigners not to understand her. Roz comes away from the conversation pretty sure that the electricity is shut off every night, although she's not clear on why.

Other than Maryam, no one else is up, but Roz feels restless in the compound. Glancing nervously up at the birds still dozing headless in the tree above her, she creaks open the gate and peers out. A donkey (an Etbai) jogs by with a child on its back and a jerry can over each shoulder; down the street, two women are talking as they lug full jerry cans in the other direction. Roz edges out the heavy door, careful to shut it behind her, and walks toward the market, contemplating a variation on her earlier algorithmic question: what would it take for Information to notice the relevant overlap and point out the proximity of a water pump?

Roz doesn't have any purpose for going to the market other than to sample its varied sights: a miniature city of stacked tin-pot skyscrapers; an ancient, blue-painted truck unloading twine-bound bales of cloth; a small cook fire wavering the air above it, making a coffeepot burble. She feels as though she's gone back in time.

Even without these stupid climate-controlled clothes—by now, even she can see how they make her look like a colonialist in some old film, and she fingers a toub on display as she passes—she wouldn't fit in. Roz's family considers itself Sukuma, and she has one Ethiopian and one Goan grandparent, on separate sides. Her brown skin is a few shades lighter than the average here, and her features are inflected by her Horn and

Subcontinent heritage, but it's not just that. The way she walks, the way she interacts with this world—she can't put her finger on it, but she sees how people glance at her: nothing unfriendly, but noting the differences. Every so often, she catches a word hissed at the edge of her hearing: "Khawaja!" She turns to see a boy in a dirty shift shooting a glance at her as he runs around a corner, or two women in conversation, their eyes darting at her outlandish clothes as they pass.

Then she turns a corner and wanders smack into the graffiti wall, the cartoon wall, the politics wall, and she's back in the real world. Or, at least, her real world. The first panel she sees is about the mantle tunnel proposal. The Mighty Vs are holding their hands up, palms out, telling everyone to hold up and slow down, while all around them cartoons of other major governments are urging, scientists are shrugging, businesspeople are offering bits, and in a tiny leftover corner, someone has already started digging—presumably a reference to the scandal from the last election, when then-Supermajority Heritage started a tunnel without approvals. Unless the cartoonist knows something Roz doesn't.

She wanders down the wall, soaking up the pictures, the commentary, the needling little jokes. There is a depiction of the odd, rivalrous collusion between 888 and 1China; a flowchart explaining the tax reporting process in DarFur centenals; something about a local cattle dispute she doesn't quite get; and, yes, a panel about the forensics report. Faceless Information techs stand around a tsubame, smoke twisting up off of it, along with the smoke images of Al-Jabali and his bodyguard, rising up toward heaven. Another panel shows the funeral, the male version of course, with Suleyman prominently in attendance. Nicely done, and in a soberly realist style except for the bit about the ascension. Much more effective than text, maybe even than vid.

Roz is so absorbed, she doesn't notice the café until she almost trips over a chair. It's one of the typical chairs around here, a metal frame strung with plastic twine, and after a moment's thought—no, she doesn't have to hurry back—Roz sits down in it. The café itself isn't much more than a shack, with a woven reed shade extended out from it over the tables and chairs, although the sun is still too low for that to matter. There's a sign above the door to the shack, the name of the place in a long, almost-unbroken line of squiggles, which the translator resolves for Roz as ZEINAB'S WORLD-FAMOUS COFFEE. An annotation informs her that there is no recorded evidence of Zeinab's coffee being known anywhere farther away than Khartoum, and Roz smiles to herself: people here still aren't used to Information debunking their every claim. The tiny tabletop in front of her appears to be—is, Information confirms—constructed from the chainring of a bicycle. She is still examining that bit of bricolage when a boy appears at her elbow and says something incomprehensible. Roz stares at him for a moment before she remembers that her translator is off. She must still be half-asleep. She mumbles "kahwa," which was one of the first words she picked up in Doha, and turns back to the mural.

Roz finds the mural compelling even though she, like everyone else, has instant access to all the intel through Information. She pulls out her handheld and starts doodling some ideas about how this characteristic, whatever it is, might be transferable and scalable. Digitizable, in short.

"Jambo! I didn't expect to see you here."

Roz looks up, surprised first by the tiny cup of coffee that has appeared on her table without her noticing, and then to see the deputy—well, now the actual governor, Sheikh Suleyman, standing in front of her, his white robe glowing against the dun and red behind him. And surprised again: her translator is still off, and she heard him speak Kiswahili. She twitches her hand by her ear, flicking her translator on, which is good because his next words are in Fur.

"I hope you slept well?" he asks, sounding a trifle worried, probably because she's been staring at him like an automaton working very slowly through its programming for the last half-minute.

Roz dredges up a smile for him. "Yes, although I woke up early from the heat. Will you sit?" And, when he has nodded and pushed his flowing robes forward to seat himself: "Where did you learn Kiswahili?" In Doha, Roz keeps her translator set to English, because although the working language is Arabic, many people still use English, and she likes to get her communications as directly as possible. When she's in the field somewhere without a lot of English speakers, she changes it back to Kiswahili.

"I've been to Kiswahili areas a few times," he answers, waving to the boy for his own coffee. Roz waits to sip hers, although now that she's aware of it, the smell is intense and seductive. "Once to Nairobi for a peace conference, once to Lokichoggio. It seemed useful. But I'm afraid my Kiswahili is still very rudimentary. I don't get much opportunity to practice."

"You're welcome to practice with me all you want." And even as Roz smiles, she wonders if it sounds inappropriate, too forward, as if there is something dangerously intimate about practicing one's native language with a foreign speaker. But he nods without comment, and takes a sip from his newly arrived coffee. It's probably only his physical attractiveness that makes her feel fumbling and flushed.

"I was also in Tanganyika once," he goes on. "Near Mwanza."

Roz studies him. "I'm from close to there," she says. "But you already know that."

"I am afraid I searched Information about you," he says, looking down. "I'm sorry."

"It's all public Information; there's nothing to be sorry about," Roz says, genuinely confused by the apology.

"But you probably don't want to talk about it."

She doesn't, but she's gotten used to it. "I wasn't there when it happened—I was already working far from home, in Durban at the time. And I didn't lose anyone close to me. So, I'm among the lucky ones."

"Al-hamdu lillāh," he responds.

She looks down at her hands. "Honestly, we're all lucky that we didn't lose more. We could have lost the whole lake." It is sectioned off now, with booms and filters and nets, but after several intensive cleaning efforts and the invention of new purification techniques, the bulk of Victoria survived.

"I cannot imagine what it's like not to be able to go home."

"Hasn't it happened to quite a few people here?"

"Many people here have been displaced. Al-Jabali's family, as you know, spent decades in Djabal. But those people always remained in the region, and they always hoped to return. For you, in a case where your home is no longer habitable . . ."

"It's terrible," Roz says. "But it's manageable. It's all in the mind games."

He raises his eyebrows; her gesture translator tells her this is interrogation, not affirmation.

"As I said, I was already an expatriate. I try to forget that now I'm an exile."

"An exile." Suleyman considers that. "And the other part of it? You must be so angry at the people who did this to your home, at the companies that profited off of it, at the government that allowed it."

Roz takes a deep breath, then finds she needs to take another. "Yes. I am."

Suleyman nods. He lets the moment pass. "I heard you were

at the funeral yesterday," he says. "Thank you; it was kind of you to attend."

"Kindness had nothing to do with it," Roz says. "As sorry as I am for your loss"—and she is, both because he seems legitimately sad and because of the terrible stresses it is placing on this government—"I was there in a professional capacity."

He nods. "I'm sure you will inform me when you can about the progress of your investigation."

"As you know, our staff will be working quite closely with your militia, so I'm sure you will hear of any breakthroughs in the field as soon as we do. As far as our forensics and other back-office functions, we will share with you as soon as we can."

"But the investigation isn't all you are doing. You arrived before the—explosion." The sheikh pauses, then raises his dark eyes to hers. "Why are you here?"

Roz considers which of her stock answers to use. "Micro-democracy is difficult," she begins. "Often, the availability of Information isn't enough to help voters participate in the system and keep it running smoothly. SVAT teams are highly trained—"

"I understand the theory," Suleyman interrupts gently. He places a fingertip on his eyelid, a gesture implying, in this context, that if he has looked up Roz, he has certainly done his research on her organization. "I'm asking why you were deployed here."

Roz remembers he asked her the same thing just before the explosion. "We informed the governor—the head of state—fully as to our mandate. If he didn't share it with you, I can forward you a copy." It's only appropriate, now that he's the governor. He nods, and she quickly sends it to him and goes on. "To put it briefly, there have been reports of tensions with some of the neighboring governments, and we prefer to smooth these problems before they become harder to deal with." He still doesn't respond. "Why was Al-Jabali late to meet us when we arrived?" Roz was not entirely convinced by Malakal's report from the sheikhs in Djabal.

"I don't know," Suleyman says. "I didn't interfere with governmental affairs beyond this centenal."

"But you were friends. You must have talked."

"Yes, sometimes he would mention details to me, but not about yesterday. But his schedule should be available; we can find out easily. We were friends, and I did know him well." And he doesn't know Roz at all. "Al-Jabali was a good man. He was ambitious, yes, but most of all, he wanted the best for his people."

All his people? Roz wonders. *Or only the Fur? Or only his clan? Or only the ones who voted for him?* Or maybe the problem is not exclusion but enthusiastic inclusion: *All the Fur, even those who live under other governments?* "That's all we want, too."

He studies her face. "If that's true, you will be the first foreigners to say that honestly."

Roz, who needs no one's help to nitpick absolute statements, is immediately plunged into an internal debate over whether it is really *all* Information wants here, or if her statement works better if the *we* is limited to the SVAT team members, and obviously *the best* for any group of people is an impossible concept. By the time she emerges, Suleyman has moved on.

"So, tell me. Now that you have spent a bit more time in our centenal, do you find it any more pleasing?"

Not wanting to obfuscate any more than she already has, Roz takes refuge in the truth right in front of her eyes. "I like *that*," she says, nodding at the mural since she can't be bothered to look up whether this is one of those cultures where pointing at any inanimate object is rude.

"It's quite impressive, isn't it?"

"Beyond impressive," Roz says, happy to have something

she can enthuse about. "I was thinking about hiring the artist to do some work for Information."

"Artists," he corrects her. "The panels are done by children and youths."

Roz leans back, takes another look. "You're telling me that all of these were done by kids? Different kids? No way." There's too much similarity in style, in sensibility.

"Well, they do all have the same teacher," the sheikh admits.

Roz jumps, as though the ground has shaken beneath her. A sudden sharp tingle runs through her fingertips, and her eyes water. The sensation is similar to a mild electric shock, but completely simulated. "Excuse me for a moment," she says, blinking rapidly. "I'm sorry; something urgent just came through that I need to check." Not waiting for his nod, she projects the five-alarm message from her boss at eye level: *HERITAGE THREATENING TO SECEDE.*

CHAPTER 10

They said *secede?*" Roz hastily excused herself from Suleyman at the café, and is now holding a whispered conversation with Nejime as she tries to walk herself back to the compound with one eye on projections and the other on the donkey- and pedestrian-filled road.

"They said 'secede,'" Nejime confirms. "Not just that. They made it clear that this is an attack against the system. Blackmail to get us to reduce the sanctions."

Roz is doing some rapid calculations. Even after their fall from grace, the former Supermajority is still the eighth largest government on the planet, holding—

"3,481 centenals worldwide," Nejime says, anticipating her. "Nearly five percent of the total. And extremely well dispersed, although there wouldn't be much impact in East Asia." Part of Heritage's sin—the root of it, in some ways—was their secret attempt to gouge a mantle tunnel from Tokyo to Taipei, an unapproved effort of engineering that many blame for the devastating Kanto earthquake two years ago.

Roz has made it through the market. On the less-busy stretch of road to the compound, she opens up a globe, still at eye level, and watches it spin, Heritage centenals dotted bright red. "It would be huge," she says at last.

Nejime's right. The number of centenals is bad enough, but this would open up holes all through micro-democratic territory. Information likes to present themselves and their system as beyond the confines of geography, but the unwieldy structure of thousands of governments is greased by the ease of traveling across neighboring centenals, the bedrock of common principles and minimal coexistence standards. If this many centenals end up next door to an openly hostile outsider, it will be a huge blow to morale and daily function, and a constant threat that Heritage can ratchet up, little by little or all at once, in any number of ways.

Roz has more questions. "What about their citizens? Are they going to vote for this?"

"I don't think it'll be put to a vote," Nejime says. "If they leave micro-democracy, they don't have to abide by our rules, either."

"What's the time frame?"

"One week."

"They're bluffing," Roz says, as strongly as she can. It's a gut reaction and she's not totally sure, but unless she sounds like she is, she's not going to convince anyone.

"It's a distinct possibility," Nejime says. "The question is, can we risk it?" There's a pause and Nejime's eyes unfocus, looking at something or someone else, then she comes back to Roz. "Mishima's calling in. I left a message for her earlier." Roz is about to offer to call again later (ideally after she's had the chance to use the bathroom and grab a jug of water), when Nejime says, "Would you stay on? I'd like to discuss this with both of you."

Roz barely has time to nod before Mishima's face appears beside Nejime's.

"This—oh, hi Roz, I'm glad you're here," Mishima says. She's got a mouth full of something to say and looks sharp as a ship's figurehead, cutting through the spray and the bullshit. Back on her game.

"We were just talking about the time frame"—Nejime

interrupts whatever Mishima was starting to say—"the potential impact, and likely reactions of their citizens. Any thoughts?"

"The time frame who? What? What are you talking about?"

"Didn't I explain it in my message?" Nejime blinks and shifts her eyes, looking through her sent folder to confirm.

"I didn't see any message," Mishima says. "I've been locked off, working. I was calling about—wait, this sounds really urgent. What time frame? What impact on what populations?"

Nejime runs through it, concisely. While she's talking, Roz slips into the compound. She makes it to her hut without seeing anyone, although she can hear the shower running.

"They're bluffing," Mishima says, her tone an almost exact echo of Roz's. Roz's and Nejime's eyes meet through their projections.

"Why?" Nejime asks.

"If they'd said three days, then they'd want us to miss the deadline so that they could go ahead with it. A week gives us time to accede to their demands; it also gives them time to figure out an alternative if we call their bluff."

"It could also give them time to prepare for the transition," Nejime points out. "Is it a bigger risk for us or for them?"

There is silence as they think about the question. No one arrives at a definitive or particularly hopeful answer.

"If Heritage leaves, other governments could follow." Roz breaks the silence. "Especially their main trading partners—and who doesn't import Heritage products?"

"It's a security threat as well," Mishima says. "One of the safeguards of micro-democracy has always been how dispersed we are, but if we end up with an enemy that's almost as diffuse, they could strategically harass our borders, distract us from other issues, or even grow their territory by taking over neighboring centenals by force—"

"Drawing us into war," Nejime finishes for her. "Mishima, we need eyes on Heritage, now. I want to embed you. We'll set it up for them to contract you for a project—we have someone in place who can accomplish that. Where are you?"

"Saigon," Mishima says. If she leaves now, she'll miss Ken getting back, which would be fine except for the timing. They both travel so much that it's hard to coordinate, and she doesn't want to miss this cycle.

"I'm going to recommend Geneva," Nejime says, as though she's already put some thought into it. "Most of the players you're going to want to get an angle on are there. But we can't wait to sort things out before you travel. Get on a plane now, and we'll backfill your cover story."

"Make it good," Mishima warns. Maybe Ken can meet her in Geneva. That would be more fun, anyway.

"Roz, I'm going to pull you out so you can be full-time on this."

Roz has been expecting as much: a global crisis definitely outweighs one odd assassination in a tiny government. She is already smiling, her lips opening for a crisp "Where to?" but she's cut off.

"Don't!" Mishima sputters, looking up from the bag she has already started to stuff clothes into. "That's why I called you." She pauses her packing long enough to send a projection to both of them. It's a timeline, short and scattered: deaths of the heads of small governments over the past five months. One in the highlands of Sri Lanka, killed in a car accident. One in Urumqi, heart attack. One in the Pacific Northwest of North America, drowning. One in Darfur, tsubame explosion.

"You think there's a pattern here," Nejime says, and frowns. "A bit thin, isn't it?"

"I'm not sure yet," Mishima says. "But I'm suspicious. It's not just the statistically significant cluster of deaths of political figures; there are similarities in the settings, too. All of these are leaders of new or relatively new governments representing traditionally marginalized groups. I think it's worth looking into."

"The one in Urumqi is particularly worrying, given its proximity to the K-stan front," Roz comments, her mind still running along geopolitical lines.

"True. But the one in Darfur breaks the pattern," Mishima says. "It's not an accident."

"It could have looked like one," Roz says. "Would we have investigated so closely if it hadn't happened in front of us?"

"Regardless," Nejime cuts in. "This is indeed suggestive. All right, Roz, stay where you are. Find out who killed the governor. But be warned: I may call you in to support on Heritage if we need it. I'm worried about a serial assassin," she tells Mishima, "but a threat to the entire micro-democratic system takes precedence."

Roz can't dispute that, but she gets a sudden shiver up her spine. A serial assassin seems like a pretty serious threat to the system to her.

Mishima keeps a few color wands in the bathroom for occasions such as these, and by the time she gets on the plane, her hair is shiny and uniform black. It's the best part of having a distinguishing characteristic: people use it as a shortcut for identifying you, and without it, they might miss you altogether.

She also has her new identity before she boards: Hirasawa Kei, following the trend of Japanese women removing the child signifier 子 from the ends of their names. Heritage will be in urgent need of data analysis as they plan their next move; both she and Kei are expert in that area. Mishima doesn't have the rest of the background story yet, but she knows that a team of specialized Information workers will be building it during her flight. It's almost impossible to lie in your public Information, the data displayed beside your face when you so choose, which makes a falsified profile all the more convincing. When you work for Information, it's possible; when you spy for Information, it's required. All Mishima has to do during the flight is lean her newly dark head back against the headrest, close her eyes, and silently repeat her new name to herself. Hirasawa Kei. Kei Hirasawa. Kei-chan! Hirasawa-san. Madame Hirasawa. Maybe Mademoiselle Hirasawa, if they're trying to flatter or diminish her. She wonders if Ken will recognize her with black hair. Ms. Hirasawa. Hirasawa-sama. Hirasawa Kei-san. Madame Kei, if they're confused about name order. Kei. Hirasawa. Kei.

CHAPTER 11

When Roz gets into the office, feeling mildly flustered by the morning's events, Malakal is already there, seated at a makeshift workstation with the chair adjusted as high as it can go and still looking cramped. "Good morning," he says, his high forehead furrowed. "I'm afraid I'm going to have to leave earlier than expected."

"Heritage?" Roz asks, trying not to feel like the ground is sinking farther and farther below her.

Malakal nods. "I haven't gotten the details yet, but I've been asked to babysit some centenals in Nairobi. I'm sorry. I'll try to back you up as much as I can from there. Did I miss anything last night?"

Trying not to feel envious—she has a sister and some good friends in Nairobi, and certainly the hotels are a lot nicer than a hut here—Roz takes him through the diagrams, which they update with his impressions of the sheikhs in Djabal and a newly announced candidate for DarFur leadership: a sheikh from a centenal in Jebel Marra. "Maria is in the market, doing surveys with Amran"—*training her*, she does not say—"and Charles is meeting with the council of sheikhs in a few hours to get their take on the assassination." Roz hesitates before telling him about Mishima's theory, but Malakal listens gravely.

"Worth checking into, if only because Mishima's intuition has an unsettlingly high success rate. We're going to need to understand the event here a lot better if we're going to fit it into a pattern, though."

Roz agrees, and after seeing Malakal off she settles in with the relationship diagram. She twists it back and forth along every axis and changes the design a few times, but she doesn't feel any closer to insight. She needs data. She starts setting up a table with everyone on the diagram, detailing their whereabouts over the past two months to look for intersections with Al-Jabali and, perhaps more importantly, his tsubame. It doesn't take her long to realize there are a frustrating number of gaps where trackers didn't work or feeds didn't exist. "There's so little data, it's like working in a bleeping null state here."

Charles looks up from the other side of the room to scoff. "Hardly."

Before Roz can respond, she gets a call from Maria. "Hey, could you come by the market? I think you'll want to be in on this interview."

Minzhe is, so far, not having great success in urging the interview with Fatima. His audience with the commander, Hamid Mohammed, was distinctly uncomfortable. The man was polite but laconic, rebutting any hint of the camaraderie Minzhe built so easily with the rest of the crew. Minzhe put out a couple of feelers about the interview, and the commander listened and said nothing. "Are we going to investigate the assassination?" Minzhe asked at last.

Commander Hamid looked legitimately surprised. "Should we?"

"Someone has to," Minzhe pointed out, feeling ridiculous.

The commander rose, a dismissal. "I'll speak to the new governor about it."

Minzhe was relieved to get out of there, and from the half-smiles a couple of the guys give him, they have a good idea how the meeting went.

NULL STATES · 119

As he found out on day one, the militiamen themselves are a friendly, jovial, mostly well-intentioned bunch, some more experienced than others. But for all their laughter and joshing around during the card games and at the teashop after work, Minzhe doesn't allow himself to forget that one of them could be the assassin. True, it seems unlikely in a few of the cases. Yusuf looks barely sixteen and grins sheepishly at everything, and AbdelKadir clearly idolized the dead governor. But some of the older men saw quite a bit of fighting during the dying throes of the nation-state that was Sudan, and Minzhe knows there may be invisible histories and animosities at work.

Besides, there's the matter of the skirmishes. Ongoing armed conflict is a serious issue, not just for their immediate mission in this government but for the whole region. While acting bored and downcast at not being able to learn much, he hacks into the militia's system and adds himself to the closed group receiving simultaneous broadcast of any deployments. Then he sets to infiltrating the closed circle of gossip.

That is how he learns that the camel tied in front of the barracks is impounded.

"It was a robbery," AbdelKadir explains. Five of them are sitting in a tight circle in a tea shack in the market, the same one where they waited for the forensics. "Three guys, they were trying to take a shipment of gold from the mines in Jebel Mara to Nyala."

There's nothing clandestine about the conversation, but they are sitting knee-to-knee because it is the only way for them to fit inside the tiny woven-reed shack.

"Only three men!" Yusuf jumps in. "For a whole load of gold!"

"Well, there were probably others waiting for them outside the town. They had five camels," AbdelKadir points out.

Minzhe is pretty sure everyone in town already knows this story. Everyone but the Information team.

"Those were for the gold," says Khaled. "Three men! Stupid. They must have thought that guns would load the gold and drive the camels for them."

"They had guns?" Minzhe asks, as though he were surprised.

Uneasy glances among the men, but they're talking about brigands, after all, and Yusuf is too oblivious to pick up on the vibe. "Big plastic guns!" he yells, opening his hands wide to demonstrate the size. "They crept up on the caravan just as they were trying to get out of the wadi, and *bang! bang! bang!*"

"There might have been more than three of them there," AbdelKadir says. "They were hiding."

"What happened?" Minzhe asks, unable to stop himself. Besides, appreciation for the tale is an important part of the active listening process; that's what they tell them at SVAT school.

"Well." AbdelKadir knows that drawing out the story is an important part of the active telling process, and didn't need to go to school to learn it. "The ground was too soft for the convoy to retreat quickly. The guards ducked under the wagons."

"They thought they were done, for sure," Mohamed mutters.

"Some bystanders on the town side of the wadi came running to the barracks," Khaled says.

"Meantime, one of the guards manages to creep up the bank, where it's kind of steep, see, and stab one of the attackers, right in the neck!" There is a moment of silent appreciation for this feat, knife against big plastic gun. "And he takes the gun," AbdelKadir goes on, "and starts shooting at the others!"

"Unfortunately," Jibrail puts in, "he didn't know how to use the weapon right, and he shot one of his comrades in the arm." They giggle about this, even Minzhe, guiltily.

"But the other guards ran up and grabbed another of the bandits."

"The last man only managed to set free the camels, and then he climbed up to ride away on them."

"Just then, the militia arrived!" Yusuf trumpets out a fanfare.

"A valiant soldier," AbdelKadir says, elbowing Khaled in the ribs, "grabbed the harness of the last camel in the line."

"Sadly," Khaled says modestly, "the robber was able to cut the line, so we were left with this one camel while he rode away with the other four."

"But no gold," Minzhe points out.

"No gold!" they agree.

"And we captured one robber," AbdelKadir adds.

"What happened to him?"

"He was extradited," Yusuf says, and then stops very suddenly. There's a weird quality to the silence. Minzhe looks it up surreptitiously on Information: yes, the gold mine is owned by 888.

Even if they had forgotten who he is for a moment, they remember now.

"And the camel?" he asks, as if he hadn't noticed.

"Impounded!" Mohamed says.

"You see, no one saw the third robber. But the camel knows him. So, if he comes back into town, or even tries to claim the camel . . ." AbdelKadir wags his finger.

"We've got him!" Yusuf cries.

Not the most subtle of strategies, Minzhe thinks, finishing off his tea, but the bizarreness of it appeals to him. Although they're probably going to run out of grass before the gold thief comes back. If the risk is being extradited to 888, Minzhe would keep running until he hit an ocean.

Roz hasn't given Al-Jabali's mistress much thought, except as a low-odds motive for, or agent of, murder. She first imagines her as a physical person on her hurried way to the market to meet her. Even then, it is a passive imagining, a conjuring to fill the blank in her mental rehearsal of the interview rather than a conscious consideration of what she looks like. The blurry figure wears too much lipstick, and is young and idle and either ashamed or aggressively determined not to be. This half-imagined set of stereotypes is nothing like the woman Roz meets when she catches up to Maria and Amran in a large brick building near the market hand pump.

They are sitting in a small office—concrete floor, a small plastic-rimmed mirror stuck on a nail on the wall, a plastic table, and four plastic chairs—that is sectioned off from the rest of the building, which Roz assumes is used for warehousing whatever commodity has made this woman wealthy. For she is clearly wealthy, at least by local standards. Her toub is a dusty rose silk, with woven patterns interspersed in broad stripes, and it is neatly arranged over a dark shirt. Her hands are hennaed with fading flowers and swirls, at least a week old by Roz's estimation, so from before the assassination. She is wearing makeup, but it is subtle, unlike her fingernails, which are long and painted a glossy copper. Her public Information gives her name as Amal Ishag Mohamed and her age as thirty-six, which is two years older than Al-Jabali was. Where Fatima is narrow, graceful, and steely, Amal is rounded, confident, full of authority.

Maria introduces Roz quickly when she walks in, and then continues with the conversation. "You were saying you don't know of any enemies?"

"Any specific enemies," Amal corrects her. "Of course he had enemies. He had power, so it is assured. But no one specific, nothing that was of concern right now." Roz notes sorrow in the woman's face, but her voice is composed.

"And there was nothing in particular bothering him recently?"

Amal hesitates briefly before shaking her head.

"No stress about the Information visit?" Roz asks.

"Not that he mentioned," Amal says evenly. "But I'm sure he saw it as an important event."

Maria takes the lead again. "Can you think who stands to benefit the most, either personally or politically?"

Amal considers this for some time. "I am sure there are people who would like his position, but no one could be certain enough that they would win it to make it worth the risk." *Not even the deputy?* Roz wonders. "Personally . . . again, I'm sure there are people in Kas who disliked him, but this was not a simple matter of an argument and knives. No, I believe this was someone from outside the centenal." She sighs, twitches at her toub. "I do think there were those in Djabal who would have preferred the seat of power, and his attention, to be there. I don't think there's enough anger there for an assassination, but it's the only possible motive within the DarFur government that I can think of. I believe the murderers are outsiders."

Maria gives Roz the nod, and Roz takes over. "Why *did* he establish the government here instead of in Djabal?"

Amal is pensive for a moment. "It seems like such a natural decision to me now," she says. "But you're right; it is a bit odd. He did have a life here, you know. He had been here for, what, five or six years before Sudan fell? So, it wasn't that he moved here and immediately ran for office." Information annotates this with a discourse on the history of carpetbaggers in various democracies, and Roz blinks it away. "But it's true: Djabal was his home. I could tell you he was here was because of me, and that may have been part of it but certainly not the main reason. What I think, and I'm not sure he would have recognized this himself or agreed, but I believe he was slightly— ashamed, maybe, of Djabal. He believed fervently in a resurgence of the Fur people as a nation, and he did not want that rebirth to be centered on the site of a refugee camp."

That, Roz reflects, tells her more about Al-Jabali than anything else she's heard or read since she got here. "You knew him so well," she says. "Can you tell me more about him?"

Amal takes a deep breath, leans back in her chair, and crosses her legs, and Roz sees that her low-heeled sandal is trimmed in lynx fur.

"What can I tell you about Abubakar?" she muses. "I am sure you've heard he was ambitious, but as I just said, he was far more ambitious for his people than for himself. Although I suppose it was hard to distinguish, at the end. He was a politician to the core. He loved meeting people, and remembered everyone, and he loved talking, both in person and making speeches. But he wanted to use his gifts for more than his personal glorification. He wanted to learn about innovations and try new things—that's why he was so happy to join micro-democracy. I know some people felt that Information was the unfortunate pill to swallow in exchange for being part of this system, but he was excited about the possibilities of Information, especially recently. He talked about learning from other states and getting assistance for development."

Amal pauses, thinking, and Roz risks a glance at Maria and Amran, wondering if their faces, like hers, are burning with the feeling of being an "unfortunate pill." *It's Amran's fault,* Roz thinks, knowing that it is unfair. Information is widely hated around the world, for any number of reasons: its power, its ubiquity, its terrifying and useful array of knowledge. Even so, the

Information representative here, where more data and inter-action are so desperately needed, should have been doing more to make their case.

"He was very caring," Amal says finally, her eyes meeting Roz's again. "He was a good man."

Roz decides, *Fuck it,* she doesn't need to be liked. "Why didn't he marry you?"

Amal smiles. "He didn't marry me because I wouldn't marry him." Roz imagines she detects a little *And they say these for-eign women are so liberal* smugness to the smile. "I never wanted to be a second wife. Sure, you are new and special for a while, but then maybe they go on to a third. No, it's first or fourth for me!" She laughs. "Or nothing." She becomes serious again. "But in truth, I was concerned that perhaps he wanted to marry me for my money. Unmarried, I felt I had a surer grip on his affections. And the arrangement suited both of us. I had no real wish to marry again, or need to. And while marrying me might have given him roots here, he did not really need that. And his wife preferred for me not to have official status with him, so"—she shrugs—"everyone was reasonably happy."

Amal most of all, it seems. The interview is starting to feel long, and that was a good note to end on, but Roz has one more question she wants to ask. "What was his relationship like with his deputy governor?"

"Suleyman?" Amal's smile warms again, fitting Roz with an unwarranted stab of annoyance. "They are very different. Suleyman is much more of Kas; he is rooted here. He believes in the Fur as a nation and supports it, but the well-being and survival of the people in this city is more immediate for him. He is focused on Kas, or at most West Darfur—what was once West Darfur."

"He wasn't jealous when Al-Jabali won the governorship instead?" Maria asks.

"I don't think so," Amal says. "He always seems content. And Abubakar was willing to let him take a big role in the areas he cares about." She pauses. "Suleyman is the natural leader here. By his family, his skills. Everyone knows him. But he does not like politics as a formal thing. He does not like running for election, or promoting himself among those who do not already know and respect him. So, in a way, it was the perfect partnership: Abubakar did the politicking, and Suleyman was in a position to do what needed to be done. He would have been doing much of it anyway, you understand," she adds after a moment. "Informally, as a leader in the community. But it would have been much harder if a foreign government had won."

A foreign government," Roz repeats, as they walk back through the market.

"Micro-democracy is still very recent," Maria says, adjusting her translucent scarf—magenta this time, shot through with gold—over her hair. "We know it takes time for people's allegiances to shift away from simple geographic proximity. We've seen that all over the world."

"So, she was a random survey participant?" Roz changes the subject, nodding back at the warehouse.

"Not only that, but she identified herself almost immediately as Al-Jabali's mistress and invited us to come into her office to talk." Maria glances at Amran, who nods.

An impressive woman, although of course being wealthy helps. Roz remembers that she never saw the inside of the warehouse. "What does she sell that she made so much money on?"

"Oil," Amran answers before Information provides the answer in a great deal more detail: Amal has been participating in a financial transparency program.

"So, that warehouse next to us was filled with barrels of oil?"

Roz shudders, and then stops, causing a chain reaction of collisions and giggles among the trail of children who are following them. "Amran! You mentioned an explosion before, an oil barrel exploding. Was it there?"

Maria looks from one to the other and starts searching Information for reference to a petrol explosion in Kas.

"Yes," Amran says, wary of what she might have missed this time. "Yes, that's where it happened."

Roz turns to Maria. "What if the explosion was not an accident? What if it was an assassination attempt? One that failed because it tried too hard to look like an accident?" She can see that Maria has found the data on the incident. "Was Al-Jabali there at the time?"

Maria's eyes scan back and forth, cross-referencing his locations. "It's—it's not certain, that would obviously have been a private visit, so it's not on his official schedule, but there's a gap at that time, and"—more blinking and scanning—"yes, it matches his routine."

"Can you check this out?" Roz asks.

"Amran could do it," Maria suggests.

"Of course she can." Roz immediately shifts her attention to the younger woman. "Amran, can you look into that incident? Find out if the governor was in danger, how he escaped—everything you can get about what happened." Still feeling guilty, Roz puts her hand on Amran's arm. "Maybe you were right about the buildup to the assassination."

Amran flutters, nods, glances quickly at Maria, and turns, flitting back toward the warehouse.

"What do you think?" Roz asks, watching her go.

"The interview as a whole? It didn't make me feel any more confident about the wife," Maria says as they turn and resume trudging through the heavy sand toward their compound.

Roz considers. She feels a heat headache coming on, and

there is an insistent smell in the air, some kind of pungent herb, sharp with burning. Roz doesn't have chemical tracers to check the source of the scent directly, but Information offers her a guess that it comes from talh wood and a recent dukhan. "She knew about the mistress and didn't want them getting married. Maybe Al-Jabali was pushing back on that, or simply spending more time here."

"She tries to kill them both, maybe, with the oil explosion," Maria says. "It fails, he confronts her when he gets home. Their argument makes him late to leave and she . . ."

"She would have to have planned it already," Roz points out. "To have made the hardware change. But let's say she did, as a contingency. Then the provocation, and when she snaps, all she has to do is . . ."

"A highly sophisticated software override?" Maria's voice holds all the skepticism Roz is feeling.

"It's not impossible," Roz says. "Let's comb her education and comms records, see if she might have those kinds of skills or be in touch with anyone who does. Hopefully, the militia will interview her and we can get a better sense for who she is."

"Ideally before she is elected to replace her murdered husband as head of state."

CHAPTER 12

When Heritage won the Supermajority in the first micro-democratic elections, they took over the old UN building in Geneva as their global headquarters. Theoretically, the grant of this building was connected to their status as Supermajority rather than to the Heritage government specifically, but the distinction was never codified. Twenty years later, when Policy1st finally toppled Heritage in the most recent, and messiest, election, there was some talk of shifting the building over to them, but even before it got to the point of finding out what Heritage would say about that, Vera Kubugli declined, more or less gracefully: "It's time for a fresh start." Veena Rasmussen, who was head of the eco-focused Earth1st spinoff of Policy1st before they reunited, contributed their headquarters, a completely energy-neutral building in Copenhagen, for the bulk of the back-office functions, although Policy1st tends to discourage the idea of a global headquarters and emphasize instead their flexible, networked structure.

Mishima hasn't been in Geneva in years, certainly not since the election, and she imagined the city as dusty and derelict since Heritage's fall. It was a silly assumption to make: Heritage holds only two centenals, with the UN building as a separate little bubble. There are four or five local Swiss governments in the greater Geneva area, some Francophone and some polyglot. Liberty, the disgraced corporate government that includes Nestlé, holds one centenal. Beyond the eastern edge of the urban area, separated by a ribbon of two-decade-old pines, the remaining Swiss nation-state clings to its territory, bitterly insular and anti-Information.

It's unsurprising, then, that the city is more or less unchanged, and as it turns out, even the Heritage centenal is humming. Mishima/Kei queues for security check in the middle of a line of tech law experts, sociologists, and economists flown in from Heritage centenals all over the world, dressed in fitted, multi-panel, long-sleeve T-shirts or furled skirts and chatting excitedly about per diems and the quirks of micro-democratic law. Mishima is already recording everything at a radius of one and a half times her earshot. She's not transmitting right now, because there are almost certainly comms scanners in this building, but when she does, there will be a team of Information grunts ready to disentangle the overlapping voices and transcribe the whole mess. She concentrates on getting herself through security.

It's not that difficult. Her stiletto is magnetized to her tablet and too thin to show up, so the long-distance body scan told them before she entered the building that she's not carrying any weapons. She's almost certain they won't find her recording devices, which are just slightly ahead of the public tech curve, and so should be ahead of the monitoring curve, too. They would have done the standard Information background check before she got here; the only reason there would be a problem with that now is if they waited to detain her within their jurisdiction, which is possible, but Mishima has a lot of confidence in the team that put her character together. The only tricky part, really, is the mental-emotional scan, supposedly pixelated for privacy unless they find any unusual spikes that suggest instability, extreme stress, or the intention to commit violence or espionage. Fortunately, Mishima has plenty of experience hiding her inner turmoil, and she isn't even worried enough to be relieved when the guard gives her the nod.

Her contact is waiting for her in the corridor on the other side of the checkpoint. Deepal Wanigaratne is a lifelong Heritage citizen who has been employed in their government bureaucracy since he completed his degree in micro-democratic public administration, and he still considers himself loyal to his government, but like many other Heritage supporters, he was shocked by the revelations of the last election. Since then, he's been providing unclassified intel and other low-level assistance to Information. "Sunlight is the best disinfectant, and all that," he says in the vid in his file. "We can be better and still win."

In this case, all Deepal had to do was hire Hirasawa Kei, a perfectly qualified unaffiliated consultant and Free2B citizen, for a legitimate job opening. He has complete, plausible deniability, so he shouldn't be worried, but Mishima can't help but notice how jittery he looks as they exchange formal cheek kisses and greetings. His file didn't say anything about nerves. Maybe he's amplifying the energy that pervades the building. Everyone is on their toes, speaking half a tone too high and two degrees too loud, playing with their cognitive calmers while they inhale espressos and blink through news alerts.

Heritage may be flush, and the UN might have been flush before them, but this building was built at a time when ideas about enabling productivity were very different. Deepal shares his windowless, low-ceilinged office with two other staff, Xandra and Loïc. They've squeezed in an extra workspace for Mishima in the corner. "As we discussed, we need an economic analysis of our government-wide viability independent of the rest of micro-democracy. It is, of course, completely hypothetical and aimed at finding vulnerabilities and opportunities in the trade balance," Deepal adds, a little too loudly.

"Interesting project," Mishima says. "I can't wait to get my teeth into it."

Deepal hovers for a moment as though he expects her to ask him for his security passcodes or the latest classified strategy documents, and then edges away. Kei gets to work, and so does Mishima.

It's an ideal setup in that the job they want her to do requires less than half her brain, and that without any Information help. Once she has laid the groundwork for what she needs to do, breaking it down into semi-repetitive tasks, she sets a program running so that it will seem that Kei is conducting these tasks at about half the speed it takes Mishima to actually do them. She uses the extra time to snoop.

To vary the leftover goat Maryam prepares for them in the compound, the SVAT team goes out for dinner at a restaurant Minzhe and Charles suggest. It's near the wadi, which is nothing but soft sand at the moment, but a thick screen of trees with actual green leaves suggests the power of the latent waterway. The one-room restaurant has brick walls painted blue, a big fluoron sign announcing itself as New Waves, and bustling waiters. Roz notes that the clientele is almost all male, although she does see one table with three women decked out in bright toubs and dark lipstick, deep in conversation with each other, ignoring and being largely ignored by the men around them. Another woman sits among a table of workers in blue coveralls with a logo on the back that Information identifies (slowly; bandwidth is not great here) as from the evaporation plant.

Minzhe pulls up the menu from Information and projects it above the middle of their table. It's decorated with photos of suspiciously well-lit and perfectly dressed burgers, fried eggs with yolks the color of marigolds, even one of laughing white people sharing a basket of popcorn termites. Of course, there are no burgers on the menu. Fried eggs and termites, yes, but the termites are stewed, not fried. Roz is confident they don't come with shiny happy white people. Absently, she marks up a citation for false advertising. Stock photos are illegal on Information, and New Waves will get twenty-four hours to respond to a warning before Information replaces them with any stills it can find of their actual food, unlikely to be flattering.

A boy, probably not yet twelve, hurries over to the table, but when Roz asks for the chicken kebab, he stares at her, motionless. Minzhe has to order for everyone in Arabic. The boy bounces a nod with a lightning grin and runs back toward the kitchen.

"Are you telling me," Roz asks no one in particular, "he doesn't have a translator?"

"Why would he need one?" Minzhe asks. "He's just a kid, and he probably doesn't run into foreigners that often."

"We met a couple of people without auto-interpreters while doing our surveys," Maria puts in.

Roz shakes her head and gets Minzhe to help her with her pronunciation of "thank you" in preparation for the arrival of the food. It comes promptly and, as expected, doesn't look anything like the photos on the menu, but it is delicious enough to silence the SVAT team while they eat. Her plate clean, Roz sips what remains of the particularly excellent mango juice, feeling far more at home in this desert than at any time since she arrived. Her feeling of well-being does not extend to progress on the case, however; so far, their investigations of Fatima have uncovered nothing to indicate she was capable of the remote attack. She leans across the table to Charles, who's deep in discussion with Minzhe about which of the sheikhs will run for head of state.

"How would you like to go to Djabal with me tomorrow?"

Roz uses the walk back to the compound to plot how she's going to use her own money to buy personal interpreters for everyone in Kas who needs one. Maybe she can bring a few friends in on it and cover the whole DarFur government.

By the time she gets to her hut, she's realized how quixotic that is. It's not just that translators, when she checks, cost a bit more than she expected. There's also the difficulty of identifying who doesn't have one, the logistical challenges in distributing them, and the potential problems that might arise from an Information employee making donations to citizens in one government and not in the neighboring one. Also, it occurs to her that the money, were she to donate it, could be better spent on something else (like streetlights, to pick the most obvious need she's facing at the moment). Finally, she resigns herself to the idea that Minzhe is right: a preteen in an isolated village might not have much need for an interpreter. Hating herself a little for giving in, she checks her messages.

There's the usual flood of mostly routine queries from the hub, but her eyes jump to the notification that Maryam called her two hours ago. Roz checks the time. Midnight in Kas, which means two in the morning in Doha. It would be reasonable to wait, but Roz knows it would just be an excuse for not calling because she's tired. She's talked to Maryam much later than this, and if she's asleep, she won't answer.

She answers immediately. "Roz! Thank you so much for calling me back."

"It's no problem," Roz replies, and immediately berates herself for the syrupy soothing tone that infects her voice, giving the lie to her words. "How are you doing?" That came out a little more naturally.

Maryam doesn't seem to notice. "Ahh," she says. She's pacing, one hand pushing back her hair, in her apartment in Doha. "Better, I think. Better than when I called you a couple of hours ago."

"But you can't sleep."

"I've been gaming. It's okay, I worked until almost midnight, I can go in late tomorrow."

"That sounds good," Roz says, stretching out on her own cot. "Be good to yourself. Do what you need to feel better." *For now,* she thinks. This is the mantra she's been repeating to Maryam at intervals over the last six months.

"It just . . . It still feels the same," Maryam says, her voice damp. "I can't stop thinking about her."

"Of course not," Roz says. "That's totally normal; you know that." She sighs. "You know you could . . . get a prescription for something to help you off of it."

There's a pause. "Have you ever used something like that?" Maryam asks. She sounds almost accusatory, but Roz knows her too well to take it that way.

"No, but you know, I haven't had a rough breakup like that in years"—*because I haven't had a long relationship in years*—"and back then, AmourOff wasn't around."

"No." Maryam is still pacing. "No, I hate pills. I got myself into this; I knew perfectly well that getting involved with her was a bad idea. Even if she wasn't my supervisor, she was the director of the hub—"

"Which you moved away from, risking your career," Roz puts in. Maryam doesn't answer immediately, and Roz wonders what part Maryam's unexpected ascendance in Doha had to do with Nougaz taking her back. Did she seem like a catch once she was the talked-about techie genius in someone else's hub?

"I knew I shouldn't get involved with her," Maryam says again.

Roz searches for something comforting. "It was part of your life, and in a month or two, you'll be able to see it that way." It's true, it's been a while for her, but Roz can still remember how this feels: the empty awful ache of waiting for another person that nothing else can make right. "You just have to give it time."

She repeats that mantra several more times before Maryam finally signs off, exhausted and effusive in her thanks. Roz strips to an undershirt and crawls into the climate control of her bed. As she's lying there, the day's events play through her mind, and she notices that she hasn't seen Suleyman since leaving him so precipitously that morning. She remembers Charles's description of the meeting with the sheikhs in the afternoon, which included noting that Suleyman was equanimous and utterly opaque. "Aloof, even," Charles had said.

Roz can't imagine any description less apt for the man, and she wonders where the difference came from. Could he be offended that she ditched him so quickly? She replays the scene from the morning, worrying whether she made it clear enough that the message was urgent. Maybe he has very distinct professional and personal sides. Either way, she thinks as she falls asleep, she should be sure to meet with him again soon to smooth over any uncertainty.

CHAPTER 13

I t is a few days before Roz manages to see Suleyman again. First is the trip to Djabal. The logistics of this are nontrivial. Going by road would take at least two days, so Roz asks Charles to look into flight options. "No problem," he says, looking briefly crafty. When he calls her out of the office several hours later, there is a tsubame neatly parked on the sandy ground of the compound.

"Is that . . ." She was expecting him to scramble a passing Information crow for them.

"Yep!" Charles answers. "I took the white streamers off."

"You took the—no one's used it since?"

"No one. The upside is, there was absolutely no conflict with us borrowing it. Hell, we could probably keep it here for contingencies."

"Let's try not to get any more entangled with local government assets than we have to," Roz says, walking slowly around the vehicle. It gleams. She sighs. "I suppose you checked the valve?"

"Personally," Charles says. "I installed the anti-remote patch, too."

"What about a general diagnostic?" The assassin could have used different approaches on different tsubames.

"Not a single irregularity."

"Did you have your friendly neighborhood mechanic handle it?"

"I did it personally, with the auto-assist."

"All right," Roz says, resigning herself to the lack of rational excuses. "Let's go."

Traveling by tsubame is not nearly as comfortable as flying in a crow, and Roz's legs are stiff by the time she clambers out of the vehicle in front of the Djabal centenal hall three hours later, but at least they made it in one piece. And at least it had climate control. After she steps out of that cool, cramped bubble, the sun feels even more aggressive, the heat more sweltering.

Inside the centenal hall is not much better. They arrived eighteen minutes early for the meeting that Charles arranged with the Djabal council of sheikhs, but fortunately they are able to go in almost ten minutes early, because in the stifling waiting room, Roz feels like she's melting. The conference room is only slightly better: there's a fan, augmented by a complicated breeze-amplifying vent system cut high into the wall. All in all, the hall is a more modern building than the one in Kas, cast in cleancrete in graceful lines; built with Information funds, Roz notes. The centenal divisions probably made Djabal more politically important than it had been.

The council of sheikhs is ever so slightly more modern too, one toubed woman staring impassively back at them at the end of the line of men in white jellabiyas. On the other hand, they are all *old*. As Charles introduces the Information mission, Roz realizes she was scanning the table for Suleyman or at least his equivalent. Instead, all the faces are worn and—is she reading this right?—scared. Or at least nervous. Roz sharpens up.

"Yes, indeed, we met with the President before his unfortunate accident." The leader of the council, and governor of the centenal, is an elderly man with a narrow, pendulous face and a white beard. "It was largely a routine meeting. We updated him on centenal business, talked through various infrastructure projects. When he realized he was late for the meeting with your team, he rushed out as quickly as he could."

"We understand he was normally quite punctual," Charles says.

"Yes, yes, generally," agrees the council leader. "My impression was that he had forgotten or mistaken the time of your arrival."

"Was there anything at all unusual about the meeting or his behavior?" Roz asks.

The council leader assumes an expression of exceeding blandness. "None, really, nothing at all."

"Are there records of the meeting?"

"Why, yes, of course." The aged sheikh gestures and the woman leans forward—*Oh, fuck,* Roz thinks, *they still use her as a secretary?*—and passes Roz a few sheets of paper. Roz stares at them.

"This is . . ."

"The minutes," the council leader explains.

"On *paper?*"

"Well, yes, we take notes by hand, usually."

"What about that?" Charles asks, gesturing at the autorecorder niched into the wall.

"Ah." The council leader, and indeed the whole council, turn to look at the recorder as though they're noticing it for the first time. "Yes. You see, the electricity was out."

In fact, Roz notices, the autorecorder is turned off now, even though the fan is turning. She starts composing a citation for lack of recording of government meetings but stops partway through. It's an important transparency point, but they may have further questions for these sheikhs, and considering that they will be notified as soon as the complaint is filed, she might as well take the time to check electricity status for the day in question and other mitigating factors fully before she sends it.

Mishima meant it when she said the job was interesting. No government remotely near this size has ever removed itself from micro-democracy, and trying to disentangle these tightly clinging economies is a fascinating challenge. Can far-flung Heritage centenals generate everything they need through intra-governmental trade? How might terms of trade change? Are sanctions likely, and if so, how will they affect the newly independent government? An added benefit to this job is that Mishima is in a position to skew the results, hopefully introducing a bit more worry into the minds of the decision-makers.

She doesn't let it distract her from her real mission. The main difficulty she has is zeroing in on her targets. This is such a big place that she could pretend to get lost in the corridors for days without stumbling on the right people for the intel she needs. Instead, she puts recorders in the canteen and listens to a lot of gossip, using an algorithm that shifts word timing and frequencies slightly to allow her to listen to multiple conversations at once.

"Do you think they gave her P-20 grade position?"

"They call that *authentic* mohinga?"

"No way! She should have at least fifteen years' seniority for that, and she only has, what, twelve?"

"Did you see *Boyling Point* last night?"

"Ooh, I love that necklace!"

"How fast can you finish that report? I need you working on advids for the secession."

"But why else would she take a posting way out there?"

"Thanks! I got it when I was in Cuzco last week."

"I didn't really buy the second act. She wouldn't have left Boyle like that."

"You should know by now not to eat anything they garnish with the label *authentic*."

"Unless the real reason comes out in an episode or two."

"Which target demographic?"

"Maybe she likes the work?"

"What, you think she's a spy?"

"888. We want them to stay open to trade with us—or, ideally, join us!"

Mishima snorts at that last one and covers it with a cough in case her officemates are listening. Information has analysts undercover in most of the major governments, and there are no signs that anyone else is thinking of joining the rupture for the moment. Besides, 888 are highly trade-focused, and micro-democracy has been good for them. If Heritage can make secession work, though, the balance could tip.

She sorts through everything she hears to find the loudest voices, the ones that say certain words most frequently, and then she follows them, casually, from a distance, turning into restrooms or stairwells, mapping the hierarchy of power. While staring at three-dimensional representations of economic networks projected ostentatiously overlarge in her workspace, she listens to conversations being recorded three floors away by tiny disks she has left clinging to doorjambs or under tables. By the end of day one, she has a pretty good grasp of the power ecosystem; by the time most people arrive at work on day two, she has bugged six conference rooms and three offices that she believes are likely to host high-level discussions about the secession.

That belief is reinforced when, scooting back down the hall after leaving a recorder, Mishima passes a whole entourage heading the other direction. In the middle of a gaggle of men in business-classic and women looking airbrushed, she catches a sidelong glimpse of Cynthia Halliday.

After the disgrace of the last election, Heritage's long-time head of state, William Pressman, resigned. He hasn't left Heritage territory since, and his extradition, along with the charges he may face, are one of the bargaining terms in the ongoing negotiations. He was replaced by Cynthia Halliday, one of those white women with shiny blown-dry hair and regular features who manages to convey youth and experience, competence and energy, in one fit, slightly underweight package. On the arm of her Ghanaian husband, a high-school sweetheart who grew up in the same Heritage centenal she did, she looked like the perfect breath of fresh air to bring Heritage back from its debacle.

Pressman was an actual head of state as well as a figurehead. He was backed up by a coterie of advisors and balanced with a council of mostly old white men like himself, but according to Information sources, he wielded a lot of power, usually with calculated suavity and consensus-building, but on occasion with a streak of ugly entitlement. Now, however, the situation is less clear. Information already has plenty of good intel from Heritage in the nearly two years since the election, and Mishima knows perfectly well that Halliday's role in decision-making at Heritage is limited. What they don't know is exactly who is in charge. Some say that Pressman is still pulling strings from the background, although there's been no evidence of this, and his movement is severely limited by the warrant out for his arrest. More plausible is that the old white dudes council has taken over the bulk of governing, possibly with a diminished role for the nominal head of state, or possibly with none at all. Since Halliday's normally based in London, the fact that she's here is significant. Is this decision epic enough that they need her buy-in? Or is she just being briefed for the press conferences?

Mishima is not a hacker, but skimming daily schedules off the intranet doesn't really count, even if they're confidential, protected, and encrypted. Within two hours, she's dropped additional recorders in every room that Halliday is scheduled to be in that day. The tricky part is that she has to pick all the recorders up at the end of every day. They're inconspicuous, but not so inconspicuous that a motivated cleaner won't find them, and she can't take the risk of tipping Heritage off to the surveillance, even if it doesn't get traced back to her.

W hat do you think?" Roz asks Charles. They are walking to Fatima's house. It is only 0.64 kilometers away, but Roz is already clammy inside her heat-reflective clothing and wishes she could have reasonably suggested they take the tsubame.

"I think they're not telling us everything," Charles says. "Something strange is going on there. It might not be related to the assassination, though."

"Or it might be," Roz says. She's skimming the minutes she was handed as they walk. They portray exactly what the council said they would: a normal-verging-on-boring meeting about infrastructure project updates. "How are we going to figure out what it is?" She's thinking about classic lie-detecting algorithms, not because she thinks they'll work but because that's just where her mind goes, but Charles has a better answer.

"I can stick around here if you want, try to suss it out."

"That would be great!" Roz says. "Do you want me to stay a few days to help?"

"I think one person will be less intimidating," Charles says. "I want to build relationships with the sheikhs, see what they'll tell me more informally."

"Look into these infrastructure projects, too," Roz says, passing him the papers. "Just in case the content of that meeting was more than a smokescreen."

Charles had messaged ahead to Fatima, but she still keeps them waiting. The main house is concrete and brick, the furniture relatively new and expensive for this context, although not what Roz would expect to see among her circle in Doha. Tired of sitting on the stain-resistant couch, she walks over to a window that looks out on an interior courtyard—the one where she endured the funeral, she realizes.

"You are back." Roz turns to see Fatima in the doorway. "What do you want this time?"

She's obviously addressing Roz. Charles answers instead. "Sorry to bother you again at this difficult and busy time, but we are still trying to find out who killed your husband."

Fatima does not move her gaze from Roz. "Prove to me that you and your colleagues did not kill him, and I'll happily prove for you that I did not."

Roz injects gentleness into her tone from some stored-up repository. "Why don't we, for the moment, assume that neither of us did so we can work together on finding justice?" She wants to kick herself for saying *justice*, but clearly there's no winning here.

"Promise me you'll investigate your own people," Fatima insists.

More gentleness, Roz tells herself, but it doesn't come out nearly as well this time. "I can look if you want, but I won't find anything."

Fatima's face turns dark with suppressed anger. "Are you so sure your colleagues are innocent?"

Not necessarily innocent, but certainly good enough not to leave evidence. "I will investigate," Roz says formally. "Now . . ." Direct, concrete questions. "Can you tell me where the tsubame was kept when your husband had it here?"

For a moment, she thinks Fatima isn't going to answer, but politeness or self-interest or some vestigial respect for Information or authority figures in general wins out, and she nods her head at the window. "Out there. In the courtyard."

Not terribly difficult to access. "Have there been any accidents or unusual incidents over the past few months?" Charles

NULL STATES · 145

asks, and Fatima finally looks at him. Her fury seems to drop off as she does, and she droops as if exhausted.

"No, none." She stops and thinks again. "No."

Fatima has nothing else to add. When they finish speaking with her, they interview her cook, Aisha. She confirms where the tsubame was kept and tells them she remembers nothing unusual about the twenty-four hours before the assassination. "He arrived the night before; they ate dinner. He seemed normal. I went home, and by the time I came back the next morning, he had already left."

"Do you still think it will be useful to stay?" Roz asks Charles when they finally trudge back to the tsubame. "Today hasn't been very productive."

"At least for a few days. It takes time to get people to trust you enough to tell you things." He winks. "I just hope I can find an accommodation without bedbugs."

"Send me an evacuation contingency plan tonight," Roz tells him as they reach the tsubame. She knows it's irrational, but Djabal feels so much more exposed and hostile than Kas. "And let me know if you need anything—or anyone—from Kas at any point."

She looks the tsubame over; nothing seems to have changed since they left it. She's tempted to crack it to make sure that valve is still there, but self-consciousness wins out over fear, and she says good-bye to Charles and climbs in.

Roz had been slightly dreading the lonely ride back, but she puts on some thematic music and about half an hour in, the arid, monochrome, unperturbed landscape starts getting to her. The late afternoon sunlight stretches across the sand, turning low hills ruddy and drawing giant shadows behind the scattered, knobby trees. Twice she catches the dark iridescent flashes of *Cinnyris osea*. She's almost sorry when she sees the evaporation plant that means she is nearing Kas.

CHAPTER 14

The Information liaison for Policy1st is Gerardo Vasconcielos. Born in a EuropeanUnion centenal in Santiago de Chile, he was able to move without migrating to Brussels, where EuropeanUnion still holds a number of centenals as well as its global headquarters. He worked for intergovernmental relations there for three years before signing on with Information. He has covered Policy1st for the past five years. Smooth and personable, he has good relationships with both the Mighty Vs while also maintaining a decent if somewhat Eurocentric roster of contacts at other levels in the hierarchy. His experience with bureaucracy proved helpful during the massive expansion Policy1st underwent after the last election. Guiding a new Supermajority has proven extremely challenging, however, and Nejime has projected in to accompany him for this meeting.

"Any update on the status of the corporate funding case?" Vera asks before they start.

"Not yet," Gerardo answers.

"PhilipMorris is ready to break ground on the mantle tunnel," Veena adds, coming over from the window. They are at the Policy1st headquarters, sleek and completely sustainable, in Copenhagen. "And now 888 have submitted plans for two of their own. They are carving up the planet. We should have more say in this."

"888's plans have not yet been approved, and as you know quite well the PhilipMorris tunnel goes from PhilipMorris centenal to PhilipMorris centenal," Nejime says. "There's no reason for anyone else to have input."

"They are digging through the mantle of the earth," Veena says. Long practice in politics has taught her to temper her environmental passion—passion for survival, she calls it—in public, but she sees no reason to do so in a closed room meeting with intelligent people. "It could affect the entire planet."

"And we are the Supermajority," Vera says.

They have been told a million times. "The Supermajority does not get to decide what everyone else does. They do not get approval on the infrastructure projects of other governments, even those that might affect the whole planet. This is a micro-democracy, not a representative dictatorship." It's true that Heritage managed to carve out more space for itself during their twenty-year tenure, but that was mainly through clever use of their unwritten power—trade, cultural status, economic might. It's possible that these subtle extensions of authority were given too much latitude, but since the transition, those at Information who believe in strong government autonomy have been united with those who would like to see a more powerful Information in pushing back against any repeat.

"If we don't, then who does?" Vera says. This is one of her tactics, pushing at the procedural questions and needling at the contradictions until she can force change. "Do you?"

Nejime lets Gerardo answer that, preferring to maintain her aura of ambiguous power.

"You know we don't," he says. His eyes dart to Nejime's projection while he does; Gerardo is a consummate bureaucrat and can't keep himself from calculating the interests of different parties, and the interest to himself in telling them what they want to hear. "But what we can do is better communicate the issues to make clear why 888's project should undergo a more thorough environmental study."

The Mighty Vs roll their eyes at each other.

"And what exactly," Vera asks, "is going on with Heritage?"

"What do you mean?" Gerardo asks, looking from one to the other. "Did they come up with some new reason to avoid handing over Pressman?"

Nejime keeps her mouth shut. She gives Vera a sharp look though, wondering if Nougaz has done the same. The rumor probably comes from someone else, she decides; this is too big to stay quiet for long. She changes the subject. "We need to discuss the K-stan war."

Veena immediately turns her suspicious gaze on Nejime but lets Vera answer.

"What do we need to discuss? Policy1st doesn't hold any centenals bordering on the conflict. A null-states war has nothing to do with us."

"The governments that are contiguous with the conflict are, for the most part, poor and at risk of democratic destabilization." Nejime minds her diction, letting that express implacability along with her flat tone. "If they fall, you will still have no centenals on the border, but if the second layer falls . . ." She opens up a map, zooms. "Your centenals 5290674 and 4803943 will be on the front line. Of course, such a progression is extremely unlikely, since the overrunning of the first centenals would already irrevocably destabilize the system from which you draw your power."

Both Vs are staring at her stonily now.

"Is this meant to be a threat?" Veena asks.

"It's meant to be realistic," Nejime says. "You have been privileged to be able to ignore foreign policy—"

"Ignore foreign policy?" Vera bursts in. "You mean get informed by Gerardo here that it's none of our business whenever we express concern about Heritage, or PhilipMorris, or any of the other governments that have been baying for our blood since we won?"

"By *foreign policy,* I'm referring to relations with states outside of micro-democracy," Nejime says. "Unfortunately, we do not exist in a vacuum."

"And there are places where even Information gathers no data," Veena put in with a grim satisfaction.

"What exactly are you asking for?" Vera asks, not sounding in the least inclined to give it.

"Support for defense of the front-line centenals and efforts to broker the peace."

"Support?"

"Financial support, technical support, data if you have any," Gerardo puts in. "We can be flexible. Let's work with your capacities to figure out what we can do."

"I hope you're requiring the same of Heritage," Vera says sourly as he projects out a worksheet.

Nejime doesn't share that they're in no position to require anything of Heritage right now. Behind her game face, she wonders which is the greater threat: the null states or the former Supermajority.

Mishima's strategic recorder placement pays off. She has only audio, and the five or six voices are anonymous to her, but she'll be able to run them through recognition later, hopefully once she has some good guesses to streamline the process.

"Any updates from the hive?" A snarky, but unoriginal, reference to Information. "Are they going to negotiate?"

"Nothing new. They're playing close to the chest. But they'll go for it. This is too big a hit for them to take."

"I'm almost hoping they don't agree. We have a lot of

momentum behind independence now, I don't think we should waste it."

"Are you crazy? How exactly do you think this is going to work? We'd lose our trading partners and tourist dollars immediately, and you can bet that those ivory-encased bastards"— another common epithet—"will find other ways to harass us. Besides, have you *seen* the economic projections?"

Five floors down, Mishima smiles and puts an extra flourish of pessimism on the latest analysis Kei is working on.

"You really think other governments are going to sanction our corporations just because Encyclopedia Boring tells them to?"

"You don't have to look any farther than Switzerland," someone else points out.

Scoffing. "Switzerland is one pathetic nation-state that wasn't even that integrated before the first election. We're talking about thousands of centenals, scattered all over the world, with virtually no trade barriers until now." Heritage has very loose border controls; as corporates, they make a lot of their revenue through exports and through luring visitors to buy on their territory. "You think all our neighbors, all over the world, are going to stop going to dinner in the restaurants they've used their whole lives, visiting the theme parks they went to as kids, buying the products they've always loved?"

"Even if the end state is something we can handle, it's going to be a shock, and shocks are never good for economies."

"It will be less of a shock for us than for them, thanks to our comms pipeline."

Mishima frowns and flags the reference to an unknown communications procedure.

"Not to mention the external inte—"

"That is not up for discussion!" The sharp voice is Halliday's, Mishima is almost positive, and she plants an urgent flag this time, wondering what Halliday is trying to hide. She doesn't have much time to think about it: the head of state is still talking.

"Leaving this speculation aside for a moment, I think we should consider our position if they come back with a negotiation, rather than an outright yes or no."

Silence for a moment as the conversation reorients.

"We don't even seem to be able to agree whether we want to push them toward a yes or a no."

"Let's aim for a yes. I think if we definitively want a no, it will be easy enough to get."

Again, a silence. Mishima has the sense that there is some unspoken agreement and everyone is deciding whether they want to be the first to put it into words, into recorded, immutable history. All the rooms in the headquarters are equipped with auto-stenos, and anyone or everyone in there might be recording the meeting.

"Do we think that amnesty for Pressman is a sticking point?" someone asks. "Because in my perspective, that sort of specific case is far less important than the systemic changes we need."

A murmur from people who agree but don't want to attach their names to the record.

"We need our corporate earnings to contribute to our campaigns; that's nonnegotiable."

"The five-year Supermajority term should be a deal-breaker."

"That could come back and bite us in the ass next time we win."

"I would hope we can make five years work for us, at this point. If not, we'll just change it back once we get in."

Roz puts an X through the projection of the sheikh from Mukjar who is running (far behind, according to their limited polls) for the head of state position: after a little footwork to fill in the gaps in the data, they have managed to confirm that he has never been in the same place as the flying murder weapon. "Sure, he could have hired someone," Maria admits, "but let's try to keep this simple."

"One down. How many suspects does that leave us?"

"Four candidates and 600,000 citizens from the six centenals the tsubame has stopped in over the past three months."

"But no one from Information." Roz has ruled out the entirety of Information staff, other than Amran and local stringers, by doing a similar search for geographic overlap between them and the tsubame over the past two months. She figures she's fulfilled her promise to Fatima with that alone, but for peace of mind, she pulled out the files on the SVAT team and went over them meticulously, sweating in the late-night heat of her hut. Nothing to tie any of them to Al-Jabali.

Amran is putting together the public service vid for tonight, Maria is doing background research and interviews with some of the head of state candidates, and Minzhe is at the militia station. Charles has checked in from Djabal: he's been meeting individually with the sheikhs on the council but so far hasn't gotten them to spill anything new, other than some salacious, unconfirmed rumors about Al-Jabali's mistress in Kas. He's going to visit the infrastructure projects over the next two days and then, unless anything else comes up, try to catch a ride back.

Roz spends another hour staring at the location cross-reference, hoping to knock off another suspect or two. But she is antsy. The Heritage deadline is drawing close, lending a seductively urgent lack of restraint to Information intranet discussions on the subject. Roz wishes she was working on that instead of staring at the gaps in this intel desert. The stale air in the office feels too hot to breathe, and she's tired of sitting still. After lunch, which is leftover goat with sorghum crêpes, Roz asks the local stringer Khadija to take her out to the sites of some of the battles.

Khadija is willing, especially when Roz volunteers the office SunCruiser. Solar charged and adapted for the sandy environment, the lightweight vehicle powers them out of town in a few minutes. The huts disappear and all they see is sand and scrub trees, reddish pebbles, the occasional low rocky hill range. It's still hot, but at least the movement generates a breeze. They cross the wadi, the SunCruiser skiffing over the ripples of soft sand, and climb up the other side. Khadija consults a locator. "Over there," she says, pointing, and Roz turns the wheel and accelerates.

They clamber out of the high vehicle at the spot Khadija indicated. Roz holds her hand above her eyes to block the headachy sun, but with or without it, she doesn't see anything special. What did she think she was going to find out here, clues?

"Where's the border, exactly?" she asks. She could look it up herself, but she wants to get a sense for how aware of it the locals are.

Not at all, as it turns out; Khadija has to check on the locator. These are new borders, written by Malakal and his team only two years ago.

"And this was a battle with . . ."

"The NomadCowmen." This, Khadija is sure of; the battles are already part of general knowledge, something she doesn't have to think about.

"Tell me about them," Roz says. She is still looking around, but all she sees are sand, soil, dry branches, and the huge sky, jagged at the edge where it meets one of the low hills. She knows there are no active feeds, but she catches herself looking for the telltale glint of a camera anyway. Nothing. No pop-up advids, no projections, no houses, no streets. Why would anyone fight over this place?

"They travel seasonally with their herds. Sometimes, they come into town to sell milk or cows. Of course, the shift to centenals has been hard on them."

How did they even win one? Roz wonders. "Do they hold that centenal there?" Pointing over the border.

"No," Khadija says, surprised that someone as educated and worldly as Roz wouldn't know this. "Their centenal is . . ." She pulls up a map projection from the locator, flicks it around, and points. "Over here." The border is a good thirty kilometers away, across a stretch of DarMasalit territory. Leaning over Khadija's shoulder to resize, Roz gets an idea of how the nomads won a centenal: their territory is huge and sprawling, curling around towns and cities to cover seemingly unoccupied area. *Solidly done, Malakal,* Roz thinks.

"Do they fight in DarMasalit territory, too?" she asks.

"I don't know," Khadija says. "If they did, we might not have heard."

Of course not. Roz walks over to one of the stunted shrubs, attracted by a discoloration where the trunk is blackened. *A flamethrower?* she wonders. She runs her fingers along its trunk and finds a splintery pitting big enough for two fingers to the first knuckle. "Do the NomadCowmen use plastic guns?" she asks, trying to look Khadija in the eye.

"I don't know," Khadija says, staring at the tree. Roz puts that down as a yes.

Roz and Khadija pass through the market on their way back to the compound, and as they trundle through the clothing section, Roz turns her head sharply. Yes, that is the straight-backed, turbaned figure of the new governor she sees walking away from them. "I'll walk back from here," she tells Khadija, opening the door to a furnace blast of air and swinging down. "I want to ask the governor about something."

Khadija nods without comment, and it is only when Roz has already taken a few steps that she realizes she doesn't actually have something specific to ask the governor. She has to make sure he wasn't offended when she left so quickly the other morning; that's why she had it in her head she wanted to see him. She glances back over her shoulder in time to see the Sun-Cruiser wobbling around the corner, and wonders if Khadija has ever learned to drive one. Seems unlikely, now that she's thinking about it, but SunCruisers are highly intuitive, auto-safetied up to their solar panels, and not very fast, so it's hard to actually hurt someone with them.

Roz hurries through the flux of white-robed and colorful figures, catching up with Suleyman at the next cross street. At least, she hopes it's really him—and yes, as she calls a polite "Salaam wa aleikum," he turns and she sees the governor's hovering smile.

"Aleikum salaam, and how nice to see you, I hope you are well," he replies, the translator smoothing the traditional barrage of greetings. "I hope your work is continuing without any difficulties? I've missed you at coffee in the mornings."

Perfect opening, thinks Roz. "We've been very busy with the election." He smiles obligingly. "And I wanted to tell you how sorry I was about leaving so quickly the other day; something urgent came up."

"Please," the governor says, hands spread gracefully. "Don't mention it." They are still standing where she stopped him, and though Roz tries to ignore it, she can feel the sun pressing down on her scalp, the heat like a persistent tickle of pain. She looks longingly at the thin band of shade his cloud-white turban leaves on his face and shifts her weight.

The governor notices. "Would you like to join me for a cup of tea?"

Roz hesitates. "I should get back."

"Please," he says, and she relents: after all, cultivating the elites is part of her job. Suleyman leads her down a side street to a lean-to teashop. There is no fan, not even a heat reflector, but at least there is shade. Suleyman settles into one of the chairs, woven string on a metal frame, with a wide recline angle, and tips a finger at a boy hovering in the back (*Are all waiters here underage?* Roz wonders). The kid darts away and is at their elbows seconds later with two small cups of reddish-brown, steaming tea, so intensely sweet she can smell the sugar.

"Thank you for taking the time," the governor says as they wait for the drink to cool enough to sip. "Actually, there is something I wanted to talk to you about." From the hesitation in his tone, Roz can guess that it's a topic that's not pleasant for him to speak about, and she leans forward, wondering if he's ready to confide something about the assassination.

"I understand . . ." His fingers are playing along the arm of his chair. "I have heard that you . . . cited Abdullah for lying?"

"Abdullah?" Roz races through recent faces, trying to attach that name to one of them.

He gestures directionally. "New Waves restaurant."

Roz is still drawing a blank.

"The menu?"

Oh, the stock photos. "Well, they *were* lying."

"But everyone knows that already. There was no need to . . ."

"If everyone knows, then no one will care when they see actual photos." Roz is puzzled. "It's one of four restaurants in town"—generously including Zeinab's café in the definition of *restaurant*—"I don't think anyone's making the decision to eat there based on the projections in the menu." Suleyman is still staring at her, like she's completely missed the point. "I'm saying, it's not going to affect their bottom line."

"It's not about the bottom line." She *has* completely missed the point. "Abdullah feels like he's been accused of something."

"I—It's not a big deal. We know it takes people time to get used to having Information everywhere." Now Roz feels accused. "And it's not public—I mean, of course it's there for anyone who looks, but it's not like I put a big projection up in front of the restaurant saying they lied. They change the photos, that's all."

Suleyman waits, then nods once. "I suppose he is being sensitive." He hesitates. "Maybe it feels too much like having the government back again."

"The government?"

"The Sudanese government, I mean."

During her career with Information Roz has heard the organization compared to a lot of uncomplimentary things, but this hurts. *Cultivating the elites,* she thinks grimly. "Is there any way I could smooth this over with—Abdullah? It truly isn't a personal criticism or even a remotely serious offense. It's just . . . part of the process."

Suleyman takes a considering sip of tea. "I will speak with him, insh'allah. And perhaps next time you go, you might say something."

"Of course," Roz says. Another difficult conversation to look forward to. She decides she should get something out of this one, at least. "We've been hearing reports of occasional fighting along your borders." His eyes, heavy-lidded, tell her nothing. "I wonder if any of those conflicts could have led to the assassination."

He sips again, thinks, sips, thinks some more. "It is not impossible," he says at last, "but I think it highly doubtful. Those small fights are about showing prowess and courage. The assassination was an act of cowardice."

If you say so. "Still, it seems that this centenal has enemies."

He smiles serenely. "How did you put it? 'It takes people time to get used to Information.'"

Right, like there were no conflicts here before Information showed up.

A sustained note from the mosque located a few streets over starts the call to prayer. Almost simultaneously, Roz hears a faint tinny echo; Suleyman must have the call piped into his earpiece in case he's out of earshot. "Excuse me for a moment, please," he says, and stands without waiting for her nod. Along with the proprietor and two other customers, he washes with a small jug of water by the entrance to the tea shop. They arrange themselves, Suleyman standing a few steps in front of the other three to lead the prayer. Roz watches as they rise and bend, her hands folded in what she hopes is a respectful manner. She feels itchy just sitting there, but leaving before they're finished seems rude. When the governor walks back to her, she stands to meet him.

"I should be getting back." She swallows what's left of her tea. "If you do think of anyone else who might have intel on the assassination, please let us know."

"Of course," he says, but Roz is not optimistic. "And sorry to keep you so long. But I hope to see you again one of these mornings. I usually take my coffee by the wall before work."

Roz looks up, surprised, and feels a flush of warmth entirely distinct from the climate as she meets his eyes. Is it possible he's flirting with her? No, she decides, it isn't. His expression is both sincere and utterly lacking in suggestiveness. Besides, why would he? It must be either hospitality or a desire to keep an eye on Information. Still, she smiles as she answers. "I'll see what I can do."

Kei makes a show of working late, and although Deepal seems nervous about leaving her alone, at seven thirty he gives in and wishes her good night. Mishima has already picked up five of her recorders during bathroom or coffee breaks, but she still has a dozen to reclaim, and the cleaners have already started their rounds. Their schedule was one of her snooping targets during the first evening she worked late, and so she can visualize the optimal pattern for the retrievals, as if she had the cheat sheet for an interactive in front of her. Hell, she could see it in front of her eyes if she wanted to take the time to put an interface on the data she's using.

It wouldn't make a bad game, Mishima thinks, as she takes the stairs silently up to the fifth floor, removes three recorders from offices in the south wing while the cleaners do the north, and then descends one flight to collect one from a large conference room between two departments. There's a time factor beyond the cleaning teams: the building lights remain on, with that eerie sense of well-lit emptiness, until eight, and then switch to motion-activated, which will give her away pretty quickly if anyone's watching. And there's always the extra risk of surprises, like the locked office door she picks open on the tenth floor, checking over her shoulder so often, she almost wishes the motion sensors were already on.

She is slipping down a corridor on the twelfth floor to pick up the last three recorders, all in rooms where Halliday had meetings during the day, seven minutes to go before lights-off, when the elevator doors open at the opposite end. Mishima dives through the first door she sees, which happens to be one of the rooms she bugged. She slides under the table, plucking off the disk on her way, and scoots to the far side of the room. A second later, she hears a door open, and her stiletto is in her hand before she realizes the sound came from one of her re- corders. It is followed by footsteps, echoing in her ears from somewhere down the hall.

"I was sure I left it here."

"Maybe in the other conference room?"

Mishima cautiously lifts her head up above the polished, ob- long conference table and immediately sees a pile of colorful cloth perched on the windowsill across from the door. She ducks down as the door of the room she is listening in on closes, and crawls to the middle of the table, which should be the spot least visible from the door, the windowsill, or anywhere on the path between them. She hears another creak, but the door of the room she's in stays closed.

". . . I *understand* what they meant," the first voice is saying. Cool, polished, just slightly petulant: Cynthia Halliday, no doubt. Without waiting for the cost-benefit analysis, Mishima scrambles out from under the table, her fingers finding the T-29 model recorder in her pocket and shoving it into the folds of cloth, jamming it into a gap in the thick weave. She dives back under the table, breathing deep to slow her pulse.

"Of course, *they* don't want to go through with it. They see everything as a bargaining chip, a little jockeying within the status quo. Just like Pressman."

Another idea: Mishima scrabbles in her pocket and pulls out a tiny vid recorder, arranges it on a chair arm where it should just cover the entrance. It's a risk, which is why she hasn't left vid recorders everywhere: though miniscule, the camera must necessarily be line-of-sight, and while the lens is treated with anti-reflectors, it may under the right conditions wink. She's counting on the late visitors to this room being distracted and hurried, and visual confirmation of their identities could be very useful.

"But they need to think bigger. They needed someone to think bigger for them. That's why . . ." The scarf still elusive, the door closes and the voices fade. Footsteps approach in the hall. As Mishima arranges herself in the deepest shadow of the table, the lights go out. Eight o'clock. A second later, the door opens.

The lights flick on again, and Mishima watches a doubled vision of the room: from her hiding place, she can see two pairs of legs from just above the knee; from her video feed, she sees the top halves of Cynthia Halliday and her aide Leticia. Halliday is talking and frowning, but her face lights up as soon as she sees the other side of the room. "—which is why I have to take drastic action. Look, there it is."

Mishima doesn't want to risk tracking her with her vid recorder, so she watches feet only as Halliday marches across the room and snaps the scarf from the windowsill. She does have a good view of Leticia's impassive face and brief glance at her (unnecessary, conspicuous, and doubtless Swiss) wristwatch. Then they leave, the door shutting behind them. "What kind of restaurant is it? No more fucking Swiss food, please. I can't take any more cheese and potatoes. It's so heavy. And that raclette last night gave me terrible gas." The voice whines on in Mishima's ear along with their footsteps, the elevator doors opening and closing, the quiet hum as they descend, the doors again. Louder footsteps on the polished lobby floor, then the outside doors, and wind. "Where's the fucking driver got to? Oh, there he is." The noises fade as the car drives out of simultaneous listening range, and Mishima lets her breath out. It was a silly gambit, really. The T-29 is the smallest recorder they have, the size of a ladybug egg, which is why its range is so short, but it is studded with burr-like micro-hooks that should keep it safely snagged in that scarf. Maybe she'll have a chance to collect the data someday if Halliday keeps wearing that scarf.

The lights in the conference room have gone off again. Mishima uncurls—blinking in the sudden illumination—and stashes her recorders. She hovers by the door. The lights in the corridor are out, so no cleaning crew on this wing yet. She slides the door open and slips out, triggering the lights, nips into two more rooms to pick up the last recorders, and makes for the stairs.

CHAPTER 15

Roz has been waking early every morning since she arrived in DarFur, the heat driving her from her bed around dawn, and the day after meeting Suleyman in the market, she makes a point of walking out to the café again. Always good to develop informal channels, she tells herself. Besides, she wants to see the latest cartoons; she's curious as to how much, if any, of this Heritage thing is leaking into public knowledge.

The governor isn't there when she walks up. She's pretty sure she's early, anyway. Coffee. Coffee and cartoons. She studies the latter while waiting for the former.

In the panel right in front of her, the recognizable shape of China is given the appendages and tweaks necessary to make it into a mother hen. Its wings prop up a dozen synecdochical 1China centenal-chicks around it, using them to block the shrapnel falling from the battle between two central-Asian soldiers, their helmets labeled KYRGYZ and KAZAKH. In the corner, the artist has sketched another mother hen, this one sheltering her chicks under her wing. A practice drawing? Or a depiction of the natural way of things to provide contrast?

Either way, the piece reminds her of the K-stan conflict, which she has almost completely ignored over the past few days. She pulls up some recent stories: the fighting has continued at a low level, but there is some interesting analysis of the impacts on Eurasian trade flows, and she starts to wonder how the war is interacting with the Heritage secession.

"Good morning."

Busy plotting the approach for an economic analysis, Roz hadn't even noticed the governor walk up. "Sabah al-khair," she manages in careful Arabic.

"That's very good," he says. "But you really should learn it in Fur."

"Tell me," she says, gesturing for him to sit. "And then, after you've polished off Kiswahili . . ." He looks at her questioningly. "You can start learning Sukuma."

Suleyman laughs fully, head back and eyes closed. "Yes! Enough with these colonialist languages that won the population game. Let us practice our small home languages."

So he is a revolutionary after all. Roz warms to him, but as SVAT team leader, she keeps testing. "That's what micro-democracy is all about," she tries. The governor gives her a steady look that makes her think he doesn't buy it. "What? Don't you know micro-democracy is there to protect the marginalized?"

He looks at her, serious now. "I believe," he says, "that you're doing the best you can." The plural *you*, according to her auto-interpreter. "And so that is what we will work with." He lets the smile creep back. "Now, try: Ef camo."

"Ef camo," Roz repeats. She has to admit, she has a weakness for tiny, endangered languages of limited usefulness. "It's amazing being here," she says, locating the feeling of strangeness that has been tickling at her all morning. "Just ignore that"—she nods over his shoulder at the low dome of the evaporation plant— "and there's no way of knowing we're even in this century."

"Remove Zeinab's and a few of the subtle details in the manufacturing of my clothes, and we could be any time in the past thousand years, two thousand maybe."

His response is so smooth, Roz imagines he must have heard her observation before, from other foreigners who have passed through without leaving a mark, but then he goes on, with an addition that seems tailored to her.

"You would have to remove the feed cameras as well, of course."

Roz can't stop herself from glancing around, although without knowing where the tiny cameras are she doesn't catch so much as a glimmer. Automatically, she blinks through the feeds, cycling across three different views that include their small table, but she flips through quickly; Roz hates watching herself.

"From your perspective, is it a good thing or a bad thing, this timelessness?" she asks. "It's interesting and exciting for me, but I don't have to live here."

Suleyman straightens slightly, not quite a wince, at *have to live here.* "You mean would I prefer progress or tradition?" he asks.

"Sure." It was a spontaneous question, but now Roz remembers Charles's report from Djabal. All of the infrastructure projects mentioned in Al-Jabali's final meeting are in more or less the stage of progress suggested in the minutes. What surprised her was the number and scope of the projects: a small solar farm; a manufacturing complex, with specialized printers and room for the related auxiliary workers; water purification; a sewage system, still in its infancy. They are definitely thinking about progress.

The sheikh leans back, arranges his ebony walking stick in his hands. "It is not either-or. Of course, if the question is *Do we build an evaporation plant?* then it is: either we do or we don't. But for our lives as a whole, we must answer yes to some types of progress, no to others, so that we can keep what we need and improve what we can."

"And how do you know where to draw the line?" Roz asks.

"In a micro-democracy, don't the people decide?"

Roz opens her mouth for a long-winded explanation of how each centenal determines its specific mode of micro-democracy, and while some use referendums on every important subject, many trust detailed decisions to the—and then she catches the teasing edge to his voice, and smiles instead. "I've been meaning to ask about the electricity. Why are there so many blackouts?"

"We get our electricity from the Sahara solar farm," he answers. "The problem is the connections. It is a long way to get here, with many suboptimal transfers along the way, and many branches to other small cities. And, I'm afraid, many opportunities for theft." That explains the plans for the solar farm in Djabal. She wonders if they're planning one here, too.

Suleyman pauses for a sip of coffee and continues. "And you?"

"And me?"

"Progress or tradition?"

Roz looks at her hands, arranged on the edge of the tiny table. It makes it easier that he already knows about it, no exposition necessary. "My room was on the third floor. My childhood room, I mean. The water came up above the second floor. We could row out there, careful not to splash any of the water on ourselves or into the boat, climb in through the window"—they had to break it, she remembers: a gloved hand wrapped in cotton cloth—"and remove all my old things, the ones I had left in my parents' house while I lived elsewhere. Of course, everything below the third floor was lost. The chemicals in the water ate away at the building. They put more chemicals in, to try to neutralize them, but it made it worse. The fish . . ." She stops, raises her eyes, and offers a grim smile. "I've seen how progress can have unintended consequences, so you can understand if in principle I come down firmly on the side of tradition. Although I have to admit that since being here I've learned I still enjoy a bit of progress and convenience." Climatization, for one thing, which uses energy. A wider variety of food, which requires transport.

"You'll get used to it," he says. "In any case, I find it interesting that you think of this as the past."

"What do you mean?"

Suleyman gestures, drawing her gaze over the shacks of

organic material, the sand-and-scrub wasteland, the distant evaporation plant, the images painted on brick that provide intel and entertainment. "This could just as easily be the future."

I can tell you the oil came from Abyei," Minzhe tells Amran, "which the militia naturally take to mean that the Sudanese were involved."

"How did you get this?" Amran asks, scanning the file he sent her. "I asked Commander Hamid for this report twice!"

"The trick is not to ask the commander," Minzhe says, and then glances around the tea shack, embarrassed he said that aloud. He's a little too proud that he managed to get that file, especially considering how little sneakiness it took. AbdelKadir shrugged and tossed it to him when he asked. After looking through it, Minzhe is less surprised about this: the militia's minimal investigation turned up very little besides the origin of the oil.

"The barrel could hardly be transported all the way from Abyei already rigged to blow up at the precise time the governor was nearby," Amran says, and then, because these professional SVAT agents seem to know about all kinds of tech she's never heard of, "Could it?"

"Seems unlikely," Minzhe says with that reassuring smile of his. Sometimes, when the angle is right, he looks just like Rajesh Kohli, one of her favorite Bollywood stars.

"Nothing on the trigger?" Amran asks.

"They found fragmentary materials that seem inconsistent with spontaneous combustion, but they might be foreign matter from the warehouse or the outside of the barrel. Nothing actually suspicious, you understand. And they don't have any testing facilities in the DarFur government, so they're languishing in an envelope in the extreme heat of the militia barracks storeroom."

"Could you have them sent to Information forensics? There's an associate lab in Nyala that might do, or if not then the Juba Hub."

"I'll see what I can do," Minzhe says, wondering how he's going to talk the commander into that.

"Nothing else?" Amran asks. She sighs. "If this were an interactive, there would be a clue there, waiting for us to see it."

Minzhe does his best to ignore that naïveté. "It might have been just an accident after all."

Amran is determined not to mess this one up. The love story of Al-Jabali and Amal, an assassination attempt foiled by Amal's competence: it's all just too romantic to be untrue.

The council of governors and ministers sets the debate to take place in Kas in seven days, which puts it in the middle of the campaigning period. As soon as it is announced, the candidates begin to converge. Sheikh Abdul Salim from the centenal in the south near Mukjar arrives in Kas, and another sheikh named Omar Ahmed is due in next week from Jebel Marra in the north. Fatima, Al-Jabali's widow, announces she will be leaving immediately for Kas, but whether from fear of more sabotage, because she no longer has access to government tsubame, or because of its folksy appeal, she is coming by road. She's following a caravan of traders so she can stop in every village along the way on its market day "to allow the people to pay their respects to my departed husband."

"And, incidentally, campaign like crazy," Minzhe translates. Polling is going slowly, and Maria is bringing in Information stringers from the more far-flung DarFur centenals for some training, but what data they do have puts Fatima in the lead, with the Kas sheikh Abdul Gasig in a close second. Al-Khadri has dropped out, citing health reasons, although Minzhe suggests it might have more to do with Fatima's influence, and the local stringers Yagoub and Mohamed agree. Hamid Mohamed, the Kas militia commander, has declared. A crowded field, but that's what happens when a leader dies suddenly with no clear successor. Charles hasn't been able to speak to Fatima again, but he is going from Djabal to Jebel Marra to interview Sheikh Omar Ahmed, so for the moment, Roz concentrates on the suspects in Kas.

Abdul Gasig is fat, wealthy, and unapologetically garrulous, an embroidered cylindrical cap on his head and a gold-tipped walking stick swinging by his side. No, he tells Roz, he didn't have any quarrel with Al-Jabali; they were united in their hopes for the resurgence of the Fur people. Yes, the government taxed his business, but within reason and for good purpose. Yes, he's running for governor now, but it was not something he would have killed for. He had barely considered it before this opportunity arose, and he's still not sure it's the best move for him. After all, his businesses keep him busy. Of course he's ridden in a tsubame before, but he doesn't own one of his own; he doesn't travel enough to make it worth it. Yes, he has ridden in the governor's tsubame, several times for various official functions in other centenals, but he has no way of knowing if he rode in the tsubame that exploded or a different one in the fleet. Anti-Information? He's pro anyone who will help his business interests, and so far, Information has been excellent for business. Roz is pretty sure he winks at her from behind his dark glasses.

Commander Hamid Mohamed is a far trickier proposition. Compact and dry, his face reminds Roz of movie stars from the 1930s, with wide cheekbones and a neatly trimmed mustache. Roz probes as gently as she can about the state-militia relationship but gets only monosyllables. She starts to push harder.

"Al-Jabali appointed you," she notes. "Were you close?"

"It was on the word of the deputy governor."

Naturally. Suleyman is everywhere in this investigation. "So, you didn't know him well?"

"We worked closely once he was governor. Before that, no."

"Why are you running for governor?"

"Because I don't like any of the other choices."

"You don't like Fatima?"

The commander frowns. "I don't know her well enough to like her or dislike her. Certainly not well enough," he adds in a lower voice, "to know whether she killed her husband."

"Did you like Al-Jabali?"

"Our relationship was not the kind for like or not like. He wasn't a bad governor."

Not exactly high praise. Although maybe it is for this guy. "Did he command you directly or through the deputy governor?"

"Directly, although if he was out of the centenal, the deputy governor often took over."

Roz feels like there's something he's avoiding, although she's not sure exactly what. "Did Al-Jabali know much about military tactics, security . . ."

The commander's expression is the equivalent of a shrug with no body movement. "He was involved in the independence fighting, but I don't think he saw much action."

"Did he listen to your advice?"

"Yes, usually."

"Do you have any idea who might have wanted to kill him?"

"Probably the Sudanese," the commander answers without hesitation. "Maybe the Chadians."

Roz changes the subject. "I hear there's been fighting on the borders."

The commander's expression doesn't change, but he is suddenly still, tense. "We defend ourselves," he answers.

"From whom?"

"There are those out there," he says, with admirable dryness, "who don't trust your rule of law."

Is he talking about the attackers or himself? "Why haven't you asked for help?"

That question, at least, seems to surprise him. "We don't need it," he answers, as if it were obvious.

If the interviews with suspects are not going well, at least at the staff meeting Amran has something to report back on the oil barrel explosion. "I was able to confirm that Al-Jabali was at the site when the explosion occurred. He and Amal were in a small room next to the office where we met her. The barrel that exploded was at the back of the warehouse, next to the wall of that room and also behind a lot of other barrels, which made it difficult to reach, so there was a high risk that the rest of the stock and the roof would catch fire."

"Eek," comments Maria. "Sounds like attempted assassination to me."

"Yes," Amran agrees. "It was a very dangerous situation. But Amal had prepared her warehouse staff for this sort of event, and they were very quick at putting out the fire."

"But why did the barrel explode?" Charles asks.

"I could not find out any definitive cause. . . ." Amran trails off, looking down at her hands, and then glances up at Minzhe, who shakes his head minutely.

"I wonder if Al-Jabali realized this was a threat as opposed to an accident," Roz muses. She is thinking aloud, trying to put herself in his position: the startling bang, the panic, heat, and sparks, the uncomfortably interrupted liaison.

"Actually . . ." Amran clears her throat. "Al-Jabali did a mental-emotional scan the day after the explosion."

Roz offers her an impressed nod and then, without a word, searches, finds the record of the scan, and uses her authorization and a link to the death certificate to open it. Mental-emotional scans are highly protected data, and it is with a shiver of taboo that Roz projects the scan into the middle of the office. The team studies it.

"I'd say he knew it was an attack," Maria says, pointing at the mountain of anger and only slightly smaller overlapping peak of fear.

"Not only that," Roz answers. She twitches her fingers, pulling a low curve of guilt into relief. "Look at this. I bet he thought he was responsible for it, somehow." She stares at the graph of a dead man's emotional state right after he realized someone was trying to kill him. "What did he do to make him think that?"

Roz calls Maryam that night before she goes to sleep. "How's it going?"

"Not too bad. Thanks so much for calling, Roz, I know I've been a pain over the past few months."

"It happens to all of us," Roz repeats.

"I wish I could just get past it, but I still feel . . ."

Roz waits, then tries to shift the conversation. "What are you working on these days?"

Maryam snorts. "I'm trying to crack the Heritage codes. We can't figure out how they've been communicating about the secession, so we're looking at new encryption, disguised discussions in public plazas, advids—anything that might provide government-wide communication on a difficult and detailed subject."

"Still in the office?" It's not really a question; Roz can see the familiar contours of Maryam's workspace in the background. It gives her an odd moment of homesickness.

"Yeah. Not much to go home for, really."

Hearing the droop in Maryam's tone, Roz asks, on the spur of the moment, "Hey, why don't you come out here for a few days? We could use your help, especially with the debate coming up."

"What—go to the field?" Maryam laughs. "Me? Tech director?"

"Sure! You can work on those codes just as well from here, and a change of scenery might be exactly what you need."

She can see Maryam chewing on it. "What kind of help do you need with the debate, exactly?"

As Roz describes the situation—the dire lack of Information infrastructure, the continual difficulties with connection, bandwidth, and basic services, the extreme remoteness, all coming into play with this unexpected election—she can feel her friend warming to the idea, but Maryam doesn't give her a direct answer immediately.

"I'll think about it" is as far as she'll go. "Now, I'm sick of always talking about myself. What about you?" Roz is ordering her impressions of the place and the team, but Maryam has a different topic in mind. "Tell me: is there anyone worth looking at there?"

Roz hesitates for a second, which is too long. Maryam pounces. "Aha!"

"No, it's nothing." She was thinking of that moment when the governor told her that he would work with them, because they were doing the best they could.

"Who is it?"

"No one." It seemed minimal at the time, another moment of their careful, friendly diplomatic dance, but it has kept returning to her all day, at odd moments.

"Come on, you might as well tell me."

"Well . . ." How should *he* know they were doing the best they could?

"Yeees?"

"I don't know if it's . . . I don't know what it is, but . . . I . . ."
Maryam waits.

"I don't know, there's maybe something . . . a little weird, a feeling . . ."

"With?"

"Maybe the centenal governor?" Roz cringes.

Maryam shrieks. "The centenal *governor*?"

"I know, I know, it's a bad idea."

"Terrible. But intriguing. What is he like?"

Roz struggles, then gives up. "I can't even begin to answer that."

"Never mind, I will find out myself."

Roz can see Maryam's fingers rushing as she starts a search. "Nooo, don't. It's nothing."

"Doesn't sound like nothing."

"It is. Anyway, if it was something, it would have to wait until this mission is over."

Maryam becomes serious. "Is he a suspect in the assassination?"

Roz sighs. "We can't definitively rule him out yet, but none of us thinks so. He's almost universally beloved here, and he's not even running for the head of state position, so unless there's something we're not seeing . . ."

"Are you worried he could be the next target?"

"What? No!" That hadn't even occurred to Roz, but it's true: they've been assuming that Al-Jabali was targeted because of the head of state position or because of something personal. It could have been because of something at the centenal governorship instead. Roz shivers, and pushes it away. "No. But even without all that, it's still very inappropriate."

"Yes," Maryam agrees. "But all the more fun."

CHAPTER 16

Mishima doesn't receive any transmissions from the T-29 she planted in the scarf, but nor does she hear any whiff of rumors about Halliday finding a recording device, so she figures that's a breakeven. Her other recorders have given her plenty to work with. She does some of the analysis herself, working late into the night in her carefully data-screened hotel room, but there's too much intel for one person, and tradecraft requires sharing as quickly as possible in case she is caught. Transmitting this kind of data—huge, voice-recognizable—is dangerous even outside of the Heritage headquarters. It's too easy for someone to watch her comms. Mishima transfers her intel through a series of in-person drops, once at the lakeshore and once in a hotel, but mostly at a number of pleasant outdoor cafés and bars. Setting the meets is easy; once she's established a code pattern, there is so much data on Information that it's easy to embed messages into prearranged plazas or trendy feedback sites. Mishima identifies her contacts visually and leaves her minidisks on the underside of tables or chairs or stuck to drink stems or once under a cloth napkin. Honestly, she's never been a fan of Geneva, but the weather this week is fabulous and they couldn't have picked a nicer spot for a bit of classic espionage.

If the setting is lovely, the content she finds is dire. Mishima is getting the sense that the idea of leaving micro-democracy has gotten away from the elites who started it as brinksmanship. It has grown in the imagining of the grunt workers, morale has unexpectedly waxed, and suddenly Heritage feels like a superpower again. If the higher-ups did intend this to be a bluff, they're going to have a hard time walking it back from the excited workers.

Of course, there are others, like Deepal, who are more worried than thrilled. On her fourth day, Deepal works up his gumption and quietly, almost under his breath, while looking at a projection over her shoulder, invites her to a small get-together at a bar after work. He throws in enough winking and nudging to convince her it's a meeting about resisting, or at least griping over, the planned secession. Mishima swings by the bar before the meet-up and leaves recorders under a couple of tables, but she doesn't stay. It will almost certainly be monitored, unless Heritage is too busy with all this craziness to even watch feeds. Besides, she has a date.

Roz didn't set an alarm, but she wakes as though she had: instantaneous, clear-eyed. She is up and dressed before she thinks about it, and it is only as she is walking toward the compound gate that her steps slow. She is going to get coffee at Zeinab's and look at the cartoons. That's what she does in the morning.

Really, she is going to meet Suleyman.

What a terrible idea.

Roz remembers talking about him with Maryam the night before and groans: the aftereffects of confiding something you shouldn't have, almost as bad as a hangover.

Not that she's worried about Maryam; even without her own experience with ill-advised liaisons, she's a good enough friend to be both circumspect and sympathetic. The problem is that in admitting her attraction to Maryam, Roz admitted it to herself.

Her feet are still moving; she is through the gate now and walking down the street, although not as fast as she would like.

She wants to see him. This is bad.

Roz believes in personal responsibility and making her own decisions, so she does not imagine that something tugged her out of bed, chose her favorite of the heat-reflective shirts, guided her steps around the guano splotches under the tree. She could stop, but she doesn't. There's no harm in having breakfast, she tells herself, even though she doesn't believe it.

Roz walks quickly through the market, and then stops, her heels digging into the soft sand, when she rounds Zeinab's shack and the governor comes into view. Suleyman is sitting at the usual table, turbaned head facing the cartoon wall. Is he waiting for her? No, Roz berates herself, of course not; she's the one intruding on his routine.

She walks up, making a show of studying the murals. There is a large central panel covering the groundbreaking ceremony for construction of the new mantle tunnel, with detailed maps tracing the proposed route between PhilipMorris centenals in Rome and Cairo. Roz frowns—she had forgotten that was supposed to happen last night. She turns to find Suleyman's eyes on her, and doesn't pretend to be surprised.

"Ef camo," she greets him.

"Wa misha kinehe?" he answers.

Roz laughs, which is more informality than she'd planned to allow today, but he says it so seriously and smoothly, she's sure he's been practicing. And those words sound like home. "Hot, and early," she says in Kiswahili.

The governor grins, which feels like another step too far. "Coffee, then?" he suggests, slipping back into his usual mix of Fur and Arabic.

"Actually," Roz says, panicking a little. "I have some things I should do, so I'm going to get back. I just wanted to . . ." She waves her hand at the murals.

"Of course," Suleyman says. There's no hint of surprise or

disappointment in his voice, and Roz berates herself again. He *can't* be flirting with her—really, why would he?—and if he's not interested, then her own silly little infatuation is all but harmless.

There's a pause, and Roz is about to say something leave-taking-ish when the governor adds, "Oh, there is one thing I wanted to mention to you." Roz nods, and puts on a professional listening face. "As you know, we will be hosting the debate here, with visitors from many other DarFur centenals. I am planning a feast after the debate for all the candidates, and I was hoping your team would join us."

That's easy enough. "That would be lovely," Roz agrees. "We'll have earned it if we get through the debate without any technological failures or security incidents."

Suleyman looks worried at that, so she smiles to reassure him, although she didn't mean it as a joke. And that reminds her . . . "By the way, I wanted to ask you something also. I was thinking I might like to . . ." She's oddly embarrassed. ". . . to buy a toub, you know, to wear while I'm here."

His smile widens immediately. "That's a wonderful idea! You would look very beautiful."

Roz coughs, wishing she had retreated while she had the chance. "I—well, I just thought I might like it. But you don't think people would be offended, or . . . think it was ridiculous?"

"No, no, no, not at all. In fact, I think it might help . . ." He trails off.

Roz reviews the conversation internally, decides that he didn't engineer this to get her to stay, sighs, and signals the boy standing by the lean-to for a coffee. "Help with . . . ?" Roz nods questioningly at the chair, and he immediately motions for her to sit down. "Is there resentment around our presence here?"

Roz already knows the answer; she would have been pretty

confident about the answer even before she arrived in Kas. The question is how widespread and how deep the grudge. She's surprised when he takes his time considering, long enough for her coffee to arrive.

"I'm not sure . . . *resentment?*—is the right word," he says finally. "Perhaps more *mistrust.*"

"And you think my wearing the local dress will help with that?"

"Yes," Suleyman says. "Not fix it, no. But people like to see that you are paying attention to what's around you, not simply . . . applying a template that you have used in a dozen other places."

Roz lets out a guffaw. "I don't think there's any template for this situation," she says, and then feels her face go hot, because that could be misinterpreted, couldn't it? She takes a quick sip from her cup, burning the tip of her tongue.

The governor doesn't seem to notice. "I believe that wearing a toub would show an openness to our culture."

"Well, if that's the case, then I'll go shopping." There's a pause after that, and then, worrying that he might think she's hoping he'll offer to help, she goes on. "Any further ideas about the assassination?" As she says it, she remembers the other unsettling part of the conversation with Maryam last night, and adds, "Have you considered that you might be in danger?"

His eyebrows go up in surprise or disbelief—the interpreter is ambiguous on this point—and then he laughs. "I'm accustomed to that."

K en finds Geneva pleasantly cool and autumnal after the south of Spain, but, unlike the latter, entirely lacking in beat. The city is already quiet at ten P.M. Maybe this centenal has some kind of noise-control policy?

Mishima leans out from the shadow of a doorway. "Hey," she says.

Ken looks up. It takes him a second to recognize her, but only a second, and not only because of her hair, though it is loose and inky dark around her face. She's wearing a wide-brimmed black hat, made from that new processed-kelp stuff that holds like felt but has a silky sheen. Her collarless trench, shaped seamlessly along her body, falls open just enough for him to guess that her matte black dress is strapless.

"Hey," he answers, catching his stride and swinging around toward her. He has nothing else to say: he's still too busy looking.

She steps out, puts her hands on his shoulders—she's wearing opera gloves too, he has got to get her somewhere he can get that coat off of her—and kisses his mouth like it's nothing, like that's how they always greet each other. Which it is. Then she falls into step with him. "What are we doing?"

Ken finds himself back on the train of thought he was following before he saw her. "Is it just me or is this town dead?"

"Pretty much," Mishima says. "RépubliqueLéman centenals are a bit better, and the EuroVision centenal supposedly has some amazing underground spots, but I haven't had the chance to find out where." Something else you can't ask Information: where the cool kids play.

"I hear there are nice hotels, though." Ken can't help himself.

She grins at him. "There are. Wanna see?"

It is fortunate that Minzhe didn't expect much excitement in the barracks, because he spends most of his days trying not to win too badly at cards and inventing improbable and occasionally pornographic text games to entertain himself. (**A gorgeous man stumbles into the barracks, his jellabiya torn to show his rippling muscles. "Help me," he whispers before passing out at your feet, a crumpled paper map clutched in his fist. What do you do?**)

Over the last three days, the only assignments they get are the removal of a dead donkey from one of the main streets; the brief imprisoning of a young man, brought to them by his father, who has broken his promise of engagement to a woman in the next town; and an accusation of petty theft by one of the shopkeepers, which is quickly traced to an outstanding quarrel that can be smoothed over. Abdul Gasig, the merchant candidate for head of state, has also called them twice about supposed break-ins to one of his businesses, but each time, they find nothing and spend more time drinking tea and chatting than they did searching.

For all the reasons that he's happy to be back in this region, he's also starting to remember why he left.

In the meantime, Roz is on him to find out why Commander Hamid suddenly decided to run for head of state after all. He has no idea how to do that, given that the commander shows little inclination to talk to him and the other guys generally avoid talking about the commander. Feeling useless, Minzhe eases up on the card games and shifts from text-based fantasies to eyeball-level hacking. When that proves less productive than he had hoped—their record-keeping is unsurprisingly poor—he starts snooping around the barracks instead. Sneaking into dark rooms when he hopes no one is watching gives him chills up his spine and makes him feel intrepid. Maybe he'll find something of use to Roz, and if not to her, then to someone else.

· · ·

Ken wakes slowly, and runs his insteps back and forth on the nano-smoothed sheets for the pleasure of it before he opens his eyes. Mishima is lying next to him in bed, eyes open but blank in the dimness. There are no projections playing on them, and no light for her to read by. Ken stares at her, enjoying the rare chance to watch her unawares, until he catches the tiny whisper of sound from her ear amp.

He smiles, and she turns to look at him. "Listening in on a meeting I'm recording," she says, muting one ear. "Sleep well?"

Ken stretches and moans in response. "So well. What time is it?"

"Just before midnight. You've barely slept an hour." She clicks the volume down a couple of notches on her ear amp. "Did I wake you?"

"Nah." Ken stretches again. "My subconscious probably didn't want me to miss out on the luxuriousness of this bed." Also he's happy, and nervous, and excited, and content. But nervous.

Mishima puts her hand on his chest. "You should go back to slee–" She freezes mid-sentence, her face electrified by shock. With a quick wiggle of her fingers, she switches the audio to exterior speakers—a sudden outrush of jangling static—and backs up ten seconds.

"—and just because they say that," a man's voice mutters urgently over the clink of silverware and glasses, "doesn't mea—" Then a cacophony, a bang a crash a shatter, the rushing sound of a burst of flame or sudden wind, and the sound chops into static.

"What the—" Ken finds he is sitting up in bed. He opens a news compiler projection just a fraction later than Mishima.

"Why, remind me again, why did I try to reduce my news alerts?" Mishima asks between her teeth. Ken assumes it's rhetorical, as the sound comes up on the compiler she's using.

Ken mutes his and sets it to text, and for a second, they are leaning shoulder to shoulder on the bed, watching the news:

"A bomb has detonated in a café in a RépubliqueLéman centenal of Geneva—"

Just like that, Mishima is out of the bed and pulling on clothes, dark pants and shirt, and a thick quilted jacket.

"I have to go," she says. "Our contact was at that café. They can't have found out about him, right?"

"It wouldn't make any sense," Ken answers, on automatic, and she nods with relief.

"It wouldn't. But then who—" And she stops, bent over to stick her heavy knife in her boot, struck with horror for the second time in five minutes. "Ken," she whispers. "I went by there before I met you. I set recorders there. I was sneaking around." She was careful, but probably not careful enough for a horde of amateur sleuths and news-compiler wannabes. "Everyone will be trying to figure out who set the bomb; they'll be scrutinizing every feed from that café from the last 24 hours. If they identify me, my cover is blown." And she's back in motion, wrapping a dark scarf around her neck, stuffing her hair under a knit hat. The perpetrator has to be found before someone points a finger at the mysterious woman who slid her hand under several of the tables some five hours before the explosion.

Ken is already at work on his tablet. "I'll go through the vids and let you know what I find." As usual, he catches himself just in time before saying "Be careful."

CHAPTER 17

Mishima jogs through the quiet streets of Geneva. She's far enough away from the café that there is no overt sign of disturbance except, there, the sound of sirens faint on the breeze. She slows to a walk and brings up her maps. There's not much point in going to the scene of the violence: emergency services and security must already be there, it's unlikely she'll find any clues that they won't, and she won't have any specialized access on-site unless she identifies herself as Information, which would blow her cover with Heritage.

A better bet is to head in the general direction and try to figure out where the assailant has gone. The bomber could have left the device hours ago, so the trail may be cold, but she examines the centenals around the strike in case it was an on-site attack. Presumably, the perp will want to leave RépubliqueLéman as quickly as possible; it's never a good idea to stay in a jurisdiction where you've committed a violent crime. Mishima slaps on an extradition treaty filter and sees only one of the contiguous centenals has a government that won't extradite to RépubliqueLéman: RepublicaHelvetiorum, to the east. The border isn't far from the café. She turns and heads in that direction, running again. If the bomber is holed up somewhere in that centenal, she might get back to bed before dawn.

. . .

It isn't until late morning that Roz has the breathing space to identify the trickle of unease she's been feeling all day. At this point in the day, she's able to dismiss the warmth of her feelings for the governor: a crush, nothing more. It helps that he's hopelessly unattainable. Roz hasn't looked beyond his public Information, which is mute on his relationship status, but it feels safe to assume he's married, possibly to more than one woman. Besides, he's so firmly rooted in this world completely unlike her own that anything serious would be impossible.

No, what's bothering her is the suggestion that Suleyman might be in danger. Roz was not impressed with his glib dismissal. It's not just her libido making that thought so disturbing: if the centenal is teetering after one assassination, another would destabilize it. Is that what the attacks are aiming for?

Nothing they've learned here has answered that question, and so Roz opens up the files Mishima sent about the other deaths she thought were similar. Roz was skeptical of the link when Mishima brought it up: Al-Jabali's assassination seemed linked to local or at most regional politics. Reading through the files, though, she has to admit that the similarities are unsettling.

While none of the deaths were ruled as murder, none of them could be conclusively proved to be natural causes. The drowning is the most suspicious: the victim was not a swimmer, no one knew what she would have been doing on the ocean, and there was no record of her boarding a boat of any kind. She disappeared right before an important centenal consortium meeting she had been working toward for months. The car accident in Sri Lanka occurred on a notorious stretch of curving mountain road, but one that the teetotaling victim knew well. The heart attack suffered by the Uyghur activist in Xinjiang was definitely a heart attack, but the victim was young with no previous or family history of heart problems, and any number of drugs could have caused it and disappeared before he was found four days later. Individually, none of the incidents raises flags; taken together, they start to feel eerie.

Roz finds she is even more convinced by the backgrounds of the different governments. These are tiny governments—DarFur, with thirty centenals, is the largest—and Roz has only the faintest recollection of their existence. Reading the details, though, Roz starts to transpose. She sees Al-Jabali in every assassinated leader, all of them charismatic, energetic, working tirelessly for a marginalized group that has never, until now, gotten a fair shot. Roz, whose family has had multiple tribal and geographic affiliations for at least three generations, finds the idea of *a people* hopelessly outdated—*aren't we all people?*—but reading through these, she can feel the pounding appeal for justice. More importantly, she begins to understand why everyone here keeps pointing to external actors. Before, she attributed it to circling the wagons or paranoia. Now, she's starting to give it credence.

K en is ten minutes behind everyone else searching for the bomber, but he has a couple of advantages.

1) Mishima has shared with him some of her lower-level access to Information. Not enough to see internal or classified documents, but enough to have an easier time opening every feed there is with a view of that café.
2) He knows he can ignore the mysterious woman who loitered there briefly five hours ago.
3) Ken has a high estimation of Mishima's powers of observation and he doesn't think she'd fail to notice a suspicious package, so he can set her pass-by as the outer

limit and concentrate on the period between then and when the café got busy.

He starts with the explosion itself. With five different vids catching it from different angles, it's not difficult to pinpoint the source. He opens a connection to Mishima using their encrypted communications code, relieved to have a reason for doing so. "Which table did you put the recorder on?"

She's breathing fast but easily. "I put one on every other table on the terrace, why?"

"The explosion happened under the second table from the right."

"Yes," Mishima says, and runs on.

Ken focuses on the table and tracks back from the explosion, but the crowd of Heritage workers jostling around three tables makes it hard to see who might be reaching underneath.

Which, now that Ken thinks of it, is another clue. If the attack is targeting this Heritage group, the bomber must have waited to place the device until the group was seated. He shifts back to the explosion again and works back from there with a larger visual frame and—

"Someone running from the café," Ken blurts, as soon as he sees it.

"Which way?"

"West. Hang on, I'm checking the next feeds . . . Got it! Dark coat and trousers, a cap with a brim. Continuing west— turning north—turning east. They doubled back. Heading toward the border with the RepublicaHelvetiorum centenal at a point north-north-east of the café."

"Already headed that way. Ref me the feeds you're looking at and I'll do the tracking. Stay on the compilers and see what they're saying."

Mishima opens the feed Ken has sent her and sees the dark

figure running toward its limit. She sets a parameter to open the next contiguous feed on a blink, and has the satisfaction of watching the person run into the field of view as expected. The suspect is already in the RepublicaHelvetiorum centenal and continuing east. Mishima checks on the map to see if she can find a faster route to the suspect to shave off some more time, but the path she's following is the most direct.

The person fleeing the café is still running, but not very fast, and Mishima is catching up. She recognizes the streets she is speeding down from the feeds she was watching—a dramatic red door here, a distinctive curve there. The figure on the feeds isn't hesitating at corners or crossroads and, after the initial misdirect out of the café, has kept on an almost straight trajectory. The route was probably planned in advance, which means that this person must have some plan for evading the feeds as well: a safe house or some other kind of cover. Mishima runs faster.

"Nothing but speculation yet on who did it," Ken reports. "Most of the compilers are still focused on . . . impacts." He finds himself unwilling to say *casualties*.

The suspect disappears off the edge of the feed. Mishima blinks it away and looks for the next one, but nothing comes up. She blinks again, still running along the last known trajectory, and brings up the map, but even as she does, she understands why there are no more cameras. In front of her she sees the dark wall of pines that marks the end of the Republica-Helvetiorum centenal, and of micro-democratic territory, and the beginning of the sovereign nation of Switzerland.

When the militia interview with Fatima finally happens, Minzhe almost misses it. He's out in front of the barracks, kicking a soccer ball around with Jibrail and Khaled and a couple of the other guys when Yusuf comes running down from the barracks and asks Jibrail to come see the commander. Yusuf tags in for him and the game doesn't stop, but Minzhe is curious. The commander rarely asks for anyone, and he notices the other guys are distracted, looking up at the barracks as he knees a shot through their erratic goalposts of the camel and its tree.

"Nice one," Mohamed says, and goes after the ball. Minzhe takes two steps toward the market, so they won't see what he's doing, and opens his hack into the militia's official vid recorder. Fake-coughing to cover his face, he sets it to eye-level in his non-dominant eye at 75% transparency to reduce reflection and flashes, volume turned down low in his ear, and turns back to the game.

At first, there is nothing to distract him from the football: the recorder is off. But in the midst of the next scuffle, clouds of fine sand following their desperate kicking after the ball, Commander Hamid's dry, flat voice speaks in his ear without so much as a crackle of static preamble. "Remote interview with candidate for the presidency, Fatima Adam Abdallah. Commander Hamid Mohamed, interviewer." Minzhe backs off from the game, coughing again and waving his hands as though defeated by the dust, as the commander drones through date, location, and context. He climbs the slope to where Abdel-Kadir is watching the football and occasionally glancing behind him into the shaded interior of the barracks.

"Hey," Minzhe says, and fidgets. He's pretty close to AbdelKadir, but he doesn't want to give away the hack. "Uh, the commander just called Jibrail up; is it for the thing?"

AbdelKadir stares at him a little too long before he answers. "The interview? Yeah, they finally got her to agree to do it, as long as it was remote so it wouldn't look like she was under suspicion."

"He doesn't want me in there," Minzhe says, dropping to a

squat next to AbdelKadir's chair so he can look him in the eye.
"It's fine; I understand that. But you have to tell the commander
he can't conduct the interview himself."

AbdelKadir laughs. "You want *me* to tell the commander
that? I thought you were the one telling him to do this in the
first place."

"Yeah, but that was before the commander announced he
was running! He can't interview her now; it will look . . ."

AbdelKadir glances back at the barracks again. "He knows.
That's why he called Jibrail."

Minzhe lets out his breath, settles to the ground next to
AbdelKadir's chair. "Good," he says, and proceeds to pretend
to watch the football while he listens to the recorder.

He can't help but worry that AbdelKadir is either wrong
or misinformed, and so he's relieved when he hears the
commander identify Jibrail as the primary interviewer. Jibrail
sounds nervous as he starts in with the standard questions,
asking Fatima where she was when the tsubame exploded and
how she heard about it. He's one of the younger militia soldiers,
only twenty-three, and Minzhe has to wonder why he was
picked for this.

Fatima, on the other hand, sounds strong but tense, her face
tight-lipped in the projection as though she's restraining some
powerful emotion: Anger? Frustration? Annoyance with having to relate this painful story again?

There's no real way to come at it subtly after all this time,
but Jibrail tries, asking in that too-high voice about Fatima's
familiarity with tsubames and when she decided to run for head
of state. Minzhe, leaning back into the slope behind him, wonders if the commander is feeding him the questions. He watches
as Khaled scores a goal and Mohamed disputes it. Abdel-
Kadir's fingers, hanging loosely off the arm of his chair, are

centimeters from Minzhe's knee, and he examines that distance clinically, wondering about its rationale.

"You killed my father!" Jibrail says, shaky. Minzhe jerks. AbdelKadir glances at him, and Minzhe slaps his ankle as though killing a mosquito. He focuses on the spot until he feels AbdelKadir look away again. Unfortunately, somewhere in that sequence, AbdelKadir readjusted his hands to his lap.

"I did not kill them!" Fatima is saying with cold fury. "I did not want to kill my husband. I *still* don't even understand how it was done! But I am sure it was Information that killed him. Talk to them!"

Minzhe is blinking up Information, wondering how he could possibly have missed that Jibrail is Al-Jabali's son, and blinks again in confusion when a different name comes up. Embarrassingly, it takes another two links for him to understand: Jibrail's father was Al-Jabali's bodyguard, and a militia soldier in his own right, killed with his charge in the explosion. Minzhe sighs.

"Everything okay?" AbdelKadir asks.

"Fine," Minzhe says shortly.

Fatima is still talking. "They come here; they spy on us. They decide who they want in charge, and then they control them. And if they can't be controlled"—she mimes a flamethrower's gush. "That's why it happened while they were here. I don't know if the whole organization killed him and those people are here to clean up, or if there is some division within them. Maybe they are spying on themselves and my husband was killed because of it. But you can be sure it was them."

"You really think so?" Jibrail asks, sounding younger than ever. "Why would Information kill him, though? Was he standing up to them?" He says it with a sort of admiration.

"I don't know; ask them!" Fatima hisses.

Minzhe hears a buzzing, probably as much as the recorder can pick up of the commander yelling into Jibrail's earpiece. "Do you have any evidence?" Jibrail squeaks.

"How could I have evidence?" Fatima spreads her palms. "I did not see the explosion, I have no experience with these machines, the body . . ." She breaks off into hoarse sobs and shuts off her vid.

Jibrail sputters his closing out as quickly as he can. "Thank you for speaking with us. We'll be in touch." And the recording is closed.

Minzhe blinks his vision clear and looks down at the soldiers scuffling and playing in the sand below him. He starts composing a careful message to Roz.

CHAPTER 18

Mishima steps into the shadow of the close-planted pines and lets her eyes make the adjustment from the well-lit streets of Geneva. If the bomber noticed her pursuit, he or she could be waiting under these trees to ambush her.

There's another reason to be cautious. Being a spy anywhere is risky, and Information will disavow any knowledge of her if it becomes politically expedient, but they have enough power that such a circumstance is unlikely. The weight of their authority provides her some protection anywhere in micro-democratic territory. In the null state on the other side of this line, she'll be entirely on her own, and from what she's heard, the Swiss are not welcoming to migrants who cross the border without permission.

She's not even sure she'll have access to Information or comms once she's over there. She pings Ken with her location, then steps into the woods.

Ken stares at the message from Mishima. *Switzerland? Really?* He glances at the clock: 12:38. If she hasn't contacted him by noon, he's going after her. In the meantime, he's going to do everything he can from here. He's already sent the feed reference of the runner to a couple of apex news compilers, and he goes back to track through the vids of the table again, searching for the moment when the bomb was placed.

• • •

Mishima steps carefully, knife in hand, glaring into the shadows behind each trunk she passes. Nobody leaps out at her, although the chills never stop creeping across her shoulders. Fortunately, the pine belt is brief; it is only a few minutes' walk before the darkness lightens and she sees the deep blue of sky ahead of her. A moment later she steps out from the trees. She is at the top of a steep slope covered in grass; at the base, maybe twenty feet below her, the curve of a road in the darkness. No streetlights; Switzerland has been hit hard by trade imbalances and is, as far as her intel goes, short on energy. If she had known she was coming here, she would have brought her knowledge of the country up to date a little. She checks and Information is still there, but she doesn't bother to look anything up now; she needs to focus on the physical and the present.

Mishima starts down the slope, wondering if anyone is watching her precarious descent. And if not, where has her quarry gone? Was there a car waiting? There is no sign of brake lights on the road in either direction, but with her slow progress through the woods, the bomber could have had quite a head start. She jogs down the last part of the hill and looks around. There might be Information, but there are no feeds, or at least none available to her. If she remembers correctly, the Swiss government does employ cameras, but their use is limited to police and government powers.

She blinks to look for them, thinking that maybe she can find a way to hack into the Swiss police vid monitoring system (how sophisticated can they really be? This is *Switzerland*), and Information isn't there. Between the top of the slope and here, she has fallen out of range. Mishima fights a rare moment of panic. It's like that first underwater breath in a dive, when you have to convince your body that the oxygenizer will keep you alive in this foreign element as long as you keep your teeth clamped on it. She wants to run back up the hill to find out everything she could possibly need, and maybe bring Ken in on a live comms link for a while. Instead, she breathes deep and easy, shutting off everything but her stored data to avoid the temptation to check every few seconds whether she's back in signal or not. She starts down the road, following the curve that takes her away from the border.

Geneva might have been sunny and pleasant during the day, but at night altitude tells, and the forsaken Swiss countryside Mishima is running through is bitingly cold. On the other hand, sound travels easily in the chilled air. Mishima hears the car long before she sees it. It's an old-fashioned motor, growling through the darkness with a steady thrum. She has to look hard for the source in the shadow and noir of the unlit countryside, and it is several minutes before she is sure that it is coming from behind her and not ahead. She realizes at the same time why she didn't see it: the car is running without lights, a darker patch crawling along the pitch-black tarmac. The only reason she can figure for driving without headlights on an unlit mountain road is pursuit. Mishima scurries over the shoulder and crouches out of sight. She listens to the throb of the engine get louder and more intricate, and risks a glance when she estimates it has just passed her. Yes, an old car, an ancient Renault or something of the sort, not moving much faster than she can run, the interior invisible in the night. She pulls her head back down and waits, but five seconds later, the sound of the engine slows, then shifts. The car is idling just down the road. Then a door clicks and swings open.

"You might as well come out." Even through her interpreter, the voice has a rustic twang; the French spoken here clings to forms and syntax popular several decades ago. "I've got you covered, and there's nowhere to go, anyway."

She should have figured that a car running without lights would have been refitted with infrared or sonar. Mishima considers her options. She is fairly certain she can outrun the guy, but it would mean leaving the road, and she could too easily get lost. She has no leads and no Information, and she doesn't have a lot of time if she's going to find the bomber and be back before Kei is missed.

She raises her hands above her head and stands as though it's part of a tai chi exercise to see how long one motion can take. She can see the figure now, dark beside the larger lump of the vehicle.

"Keep your hands up and come on over here." As she approaches, the man takes her wrists down and slaps elasties on them behind her back. His hands are small and uncallused but strong enough. He doesn't twist her shoulders any more than he has to, and the elastie is competently applied. *A cop*, she thinks; *a conscientious rural cop who doesn't see much action.* Once she is restrained, he removes her large knife from her boot. That's a blow, but of course he would have seen it on a body scanner. Her stiletto stays tucked against her skin, all but invisible any way you look. He guides her to the backseat of the car, a Renault as she guessed, something from the turn of the century or not long after, snaps on the clips for the protective crash web, shuts the door after her without ceremony, and walks unhurried around to the front.

"Now," he says, turning the key (an actual key!) in the ignition. "Sorry for the inconvenience, and we'll get this straightened out again as soon as possible if it's a mistake, but you were hiding from law enforcement and armed. And unless I'm much mistaken, you're not from around here." Mishima sees a flash of his eyes in the rearview mirror as he flicks on the headlights.

"I wouldn't do that if I were you," she says, keeping her voice low and on the calm side of conversational. She catches his frown as he glances in the mirror again. Confidence is everything here, and she feeds hers on the fact that he looks no more than twenty-five. Young males aren't normally her captors of choice, but given how polite and unaggressive this one has been so far, his inexperience may be a plus.

"And why is that?"

"Because the person you're looking for is still out there."

"And who would that be?" But he's switched the lights off again. On his dashboard she can see the corner of the monitor showing a combination of infrared and long-range scanner, mountains and trees in red, orange, and white.

"I assume you're looking for the person who bombed a café in Répub—in Geneva an hour ago. Feeds make it clear that person was heading for the border back there where the road curves." Although come to think of it, she has seen no actual evidence that this person crossed the border. She makes a mental note to go back to other surrounding feeds if this gambit doesn't work. If she ever gets back on Information. "I suppose the embassy asked you to take a look."

"That all sounds like something the bomber would have thought through very carefully," the cop says. He's keeping his voice conversational, too.

"If you've seen the vids, you know that I don't match the description of the suspect," Mishima goes on. "I don't mind spending some time tied up in the back of a cop car"—in fact, she can think of some distinct opportunities in this situation— "but"—and here she tweaks the admonishing factor in her voice up ever so slightly—"I will be upset if we miss out on capturing the actual perp because of it."

"We?" he asks, eyes meeting hers in the mirror again. He's still moving forward but just as slowly as when he was following her, and Mishima is itching to tell him to step on it; if the

bomber was met by someone in a vehicle, they are falling farther behind every second.

"I am, as it happens, in pursuit of the same fugitive, as so
empowered by Information."

In the mirror, his eyebrows tick upward a notch. He's probably never met an actual Information worker, and Mishima
wonders what kind of reputation they have here. It all depends
what interactive series, vids, and games have made it through
the trade barriers and gained popularity. She hopes for, say,
Cross-referencing the King, rather than something like *Datasift-
ers!* "Any way you can prove your affiliation?"

She lets her superiority tick up a notch. "What do you think,
we carry ID cards? If I can get on Information, I can prove it
easily enough." She hears the brassy edge to her voice: too close
to desperation, but hopefully he can't read her that well. She
pushes on to cover it. "Let me help you. Show me a map, and
we can try to figure out where he's gone."

"Maybe you're just trying to sell out your coconspirator,
make him the fall guy," the cop suggests. "Or maybe this is all
part of the plan, and you're leading me into an ambush."

She's going to have to lead him by the nose the whole way if
she's going to get anything done here. "Come on, kid, use your
brain. You've got me tied up back here; you lose nothing by
working with me. And if we catch this guy, you'll be able to
figure out whether he knows me or not."

Silence for a moment, then he pushes a button, and a map—
a hardwired map, not Information—appears in front of her.
Another button and a pulsing dot appears on it, presumably
their current location. "Well?"

Mishima looks at the map and unfocuses, tapping into her
distended sense for narrative and waiting for a pattern or a plot
to become apparent to her.

"You guys don't have an extradition treaty with RépubliqueLéman. Hell, you don't even like them. So, what are you doing tracking a criminal for them?" She answers herself before he can. "You like criminals even less, especially violent ones hiding in your territory, disturbing the order. That's why you're a party to international criminal and judicial information-sharing agreements. This escape has obviously been carefully planned, so the perp knows that, too. He came in here to get off camera for a while. A change of disguise, maybe a meeting with a sponsor or supervisor, and then back out again, probably in a different centenal with laxer security and less restrictive laws." The Swiss map is blank beyond the nation's borders, but at least it names the neighboring centenals. "My guess is ForzaItalia, the closer of the two. It won't take long to get to, and they're easy on those wanted elsewhere."

The cop grunts, and starts muttering into his earpiece, too low for her to parse. Then he steps on the gas without turning on the lights. Mishima doesn't quite relax, but she does let herself be soothed by the quiet shades of darkness speeding by with smooth alacrity.

About thirty minutes later, and roughly halfway to the border with the westernmost ForzaItalia centenal, the cop's earpiece chirps, and he lets out something like a guffaw or a cough, mutters into it, and then glances at the backseat, not using the mirror this time. "This car is armored, but better be ready to duck."

Mishima meets his gaze with one eyebrow up but gives him a nod. There is nothing for the next couple of miles, and she thinks the cop spoke too soon. They took too long and they've missed all the action. But then she hears pops, individual at first, and then booms, and then rapid-fire bangs. The cop swings the steering wheel and they bounce off the road, thumping through a meadow and a couple of fields toward the noise and the lights.

They haven't missed it. The Swiss cop, jawline twitching, takes them into the thick of the battle, right up to the front of the other police vehicles. His car has grenade launchers as well as armor, and there's enough rattling and exploding going on for Mishima to think about taking cover. She stays low but keeps her eyes open, fixed on what she can make out of the target through the smoke and afterimages. It's not a car but a concrete, pyramidal plinth of some kind—a monument, an old signpost—close against a sweep of rocky hillside, and the target appears to be tucked in between them. The Swiss cops—are they cops, she wonders, or some kind of military?—are playing it cautiously, laying down a heavy fire to both sides and announcing repeatedly over both analog and digital loudspeakers the moral and practical benefits of surrender. The fugitive is having none of it, and every thirty seconds or so, an explosive device shoots out from one side of the plinth or the other and bursts among the police circle. Based on the map still projected in the backseat, they are only a few kilometers away from the ForzaItalia border. It was a close thing; another half-hour and the bomber would have gotten away. He must have thought he was going to make it.

"What are you doing here?" Mishima asks when there's enough of a lull so that she doesn't have to yell.

"It's not clear to you?"

"The perp didn't *walk* here from the RépublicaHelvetiorum border. Someone dropped him. And that, son, is the person you want to talk to."

The cop twists around in his seat to look at her. "You're not used to being arrested, are you?"

Before Mishima can answer, the car jerks back in the midst of an enormous noise, rocking onto its side as a bomb explodes in its undercarriage. A whoosh of flame presses against the windows inches from Mishima's eyes and the car wobbles and collapses, the world swinging giddily upside-down. When Mishima regains coherent thought, the vehicle is still shaking back and forth, there is a roaring against the window, and she can hear the *tap-tap-tap-tap* of plastic bullets against the chassis, but the glass is uncracked and the armor seems to be holding.

"Do you have a problem with plastic firearms here?" she asks, wondering if this is a normal situation for them.

The cop grunts. "Not usually this bad." He looks around, moving only his eyes. "My fucking car." Both he and Mishima are in exactly the positions they were when the bomb hit, frozen in place by the sprung safety webs, but outside of the armored bubble of the passenger compartment, his car is shredded.

The casualties from the attack tick up to seven, and mortality tables for the centenal where it happened and the centenals of each of the victims pop up in Ken's vision. He appreciates how Information attaches the mortality probabilities so that everyone can see there is no change whatsoever in what you are most likely to die from. In RépubliqueLéman, the top cause of death is still cigarette-related illness; in the two Heritage centenals of Geneva (where most of the victims were from), it's still heart disease. Terrorism doesn't make the top ten list in any one of them, but Information is going to have its hands full annotating that data into every news update for the next week.

Being almost blown up seems to have created a rapport, and once they're extricated from the car, the cop cuts off Mishima's elasties, although he does seat her in the secure rear of an unharmed vehicle a little farther from the action, so she can't just walk away. A few minutes later, he comes back with a mug of something hot, a local herbal infusion, from the smell of it. Mishima takes a sniff but, in the absence of Information to identify it for her, uses it exclusively to warm her hands.

"What are those things, anyway?" she asks, to make conversation.

The cop looks around at the matching pyramids looming out of the night at regular intervals. Mishima is expecting something about ancient superstitions and ghostly rituals, but the cop's voice is prosaic, even if his answer is not. "Dragon's teeth," he says. "Supposed to stop tanks and airplanes from landing, that sort of thing. Odd for this one to be so close to the hill, but maybe that was tossed up in the earthquake of forty-five." There's another explosion, and they both duck instinctively. "I'll be back," he says, shutting the door before Mishima can get in a snarky remark about Swiss isolationism.

It has been clear to Mishima for a while that the bomber is determined to go out in a blaze of glory, and she can't figure out anything that will prevent that, so she lets herself half-doze in the backseat of the police car until it happens.

The door across from her opens, and the cop sits down next to her. Mishima thinks reflexively of her stiletto. She must be more worn out than she thought. She reminds herself that he's not her enemy, at least not yet.

"Done?" she asks.

"Done," he confirms. "In fact, looks like he was killed at least twenty minutes ago. He rigged it to keep tossing explosives at us after he couldn't anymore."

A bloody night, Mishima thinks. "Has anyone gone after the car that got him here? It's got a head start, but there can't be that many out on these roads this late at night. You guys do have some cameras on the road, right?"

"Already in process." A glance, possibly friendlier than previous ones. "Tell me again how I can confirm your story, or your identity, or any of it."

"Just get me close enough to the border to get on Information," Mishima says, feigning weariness. "Or get on yourself and look me up."

He harrumphs, but after a moment's consideration, he rolls down his window, reaches up, and, to Mishima's fascination, unfolds an antenna on the roof. "Try it now," he says.

She blinks and it's all there, everything the world knows about itself. She battens down her relief and only allows herself a quick glance at messages (Ken saying "WHAT?"; another from him with more details about the bombing; yet another saying he's got news compilers focused on the suspect and that no one is looking at her yet) before she gets down to business. She opens a verifier page, lets it scan her, and then whispers the projection up in front of the cop. He takes his time examining it. To plug any lingering doubts, and because the insouciance of her current persona seems to demand it, Mishima opens up some moderately classified intel about the Swiss police: this particular officer's name and complete file.

"So, you know that much, do you?" asks Donath Cashen. "I always figured." He shakes his head. "Must say I'm glad we're not a part of it."

Mishima lets her amusement show. "You don't know what you're missing. But while we're on the subject, let's keep some secrets, shall we?"

"You were never here?" Donath asks skeptically.

"Write me into your paperwork if you want," Mishima says. Especially if they use her real name; that won't make any difference to her current job. "Just keep me out of the press."

"And if I need to contact you for any reason?"

He's already pulled down the antenna, so Mishima line-of-sights him her details. "Can you give me a ride to where you picked me up?"

"I suppose that would be the hospitable thing to do."

He takes her right to the border, and goes so far as to return her knife to her, which shows a significant level of trust even given the barrier between the backseat and the front. "No sign of the vehicle?" she asks before she gets out, in case he's gotten an update he hasn't shared.

"We'll find it," Donath says. "It takes some time. We have to go through our vids and all. But we'll find it."

Mishima bites back an impulse to offer to help with the vids and all, given that her organization has a bit of experience with that. She gets out of the car and climbs the slope toward the pines. The black sky has turned blue. She has to be at work soon.

CHAPTER 19

Boarding the tsubame to intercept Fatima's convoy, Roz snaps at Amran. She is annoyed by her oversolicitousness and her inability to get her own work done, and, okay, she's still nervous about flying in these tsubames, but it's more than that. Once the hatch has closed her into relative privacy, she takes a deep breath, and then another. She doesn't want to sit there where everyone can see her so she starts up the air pressurizers. After she is out of Kas and unlikely to see any traffic for the next 150 kilometers or so, she turns her attention to herself.

The first feeling she identifies is anger: why aren't there more feeds in Kas, in Djabal, in this whole data-forsaken region? If she only had the intel, she would be able to solve this problem by finding the right vid or, in the worst case, with some slightly more sophisticated crunching. She could be sitting in the office, interspersing the quiet intensity of the search with quick inhalations of every bit of data she can find about the bombing in Geneva, trying to figure out how it will impact the Heritage secession. She wouldn't be flying out on this iffy conveyance for another useless interview with a woman who hates her. She realizes she's physically leaning away from the direction she's going.

That's why she's particularly short with Amran; not only does the woman rub her the wrong way, Roz also blames her for the lack of data. Which is probably unfair. She should look up the original data-collection agreements in the charter, but she's so stressed and gets so little time alone on this mission that she gives herself a break and watches an episode of *Starbright Warriors* instead.

Roz swoops in to land in the compound of Fatima's cousin, where the candidate will spend the night before covering the remaining distance to Kas the following day so as to arrive in time for the debate. Roz had only an imperfect aerial view of Garsila coming in, but this looked like the largest house in a small town. When she tells the first servant she sees that Fatima is expecting her, she is quickly shown into a large cement room tiled with laminate. If there are any lights, they haven't been turned on, and the room is shady and dim, which Roz welcomes after staring at semiarid scrublands for the last two hours.

Fatima grudgingly agreed to meet her, and Roz feels herself tense when she walks in the room, but Al-Jabali's widow looks more relaxed than Roz has ever seen her: Fatima has a smile resting on her face. It seems campaigning went well today, and indeed, when Roz checks, the numbers for her Garsila rally look strong. Fatima has removed her scarf and cap, and a servant is rubbing oil into her scalp; Roz notes with amusement that Fatima's hair is shaped into the diagonal oblong known as the Vera, after the Policy1st head of state who popularized it.

"I've investigated Information, as you requested," Roz announces, after the lengthy greetings. After Minzhe's report on the interview, she doubts that this is going to have any real impact on Fatima's belief that Information killed her husband, but it's a show of good faith and an excuse for coming to talk with her. She shows Fatima the geographical cross-ref she did on regional Information staff and the tsubame. She has prettied it up a little to make it easier to understand: unknotted her personal shorthand, added some explanatory headings. Fatima grasps the concept and doesn't seem to doubt the data, but she is stubbornly unconvinced. "What does this prove? Wasn't it a remote explosion?"

"Yes, but someone had to remove the physical failsafe," Roz says, and goes through the tsubame diagrams and timeline with her, step by step.

"You could be making this up," Fatima says as the other woman's hands run gently through her hair.

"Check it with any mechanic," Roz says, knowing how unlikely it is that she will be able to talk to one without communicating via Information.

"I mean the whole thing," Fatima says, with an impatient flick of her wrist. "The failsafe, all of it! It could all be a cover for an Information bomb."

Roz's anger spurts up again. "And how do I know *you* didn't kill him?" That militia interview was a joke, she thinks bitterly. If they had done their job, she could be back in the office, happily sorting what little data there is.

"I have no knowledge of how to do this thing," Fatima says, spreading her hands as if it were that obvious.

"You could have hired someone," Roz snaps. "*I* certainly don't have the ability to reprogram a tsubame for remote access"—well, she could probably manage if she tried hard enough and didn't mind leaving a trail of search terms—"and you still think I did it."

There is a silence, and then with a slight toss of her head, Fatima acknowledges, "Perhaps not you personally. But Information was involved. They are the ones who are able to attack someone this way, and the ones who would want to see him dead!"

How did it get to this, Roz wonders, that Information is not only hated but is the default bad guy, the one to blame for everything? "Why would we want him dead?" she asks, consciously aligning herself with the organization.

"Because you couldn't control him! He wouldn't do what you told him to do and you killed him!"

"Why would we care what he does?" Roz wonders how she can explain to Fatima just how little the rest of the world cares about DarFur without alienating her further.

"If you don't care, why do you need to record everything we do?" Fatima asks triumphantly.

"Did your husband feel the same way?" Roz asks, and is surprised when Fatima hesitates.

"He didn't, did he?" Fatima says finally. "He let you in. He took your deal. And then he grew angry at your incompetence." Roz blinks: *incompetence* isn't the usual complaint. "Angry about your rules, your insistence on surveillance above all else." That's more like it. "And so you killed him."

"Was he upset that my team was coming?"

Fatima hesitates again. At least she is thinking her answers through this time. "He was—startled. He wanted to make a good impression. In the months before you came, he was starting to believe in Information again." She wipes the corner of one eye and adds, furiously, "I don't know why!"

"Look," Roz says. She is weary of this conversation, this mission. "If you won't believe that Information wasn't involved, will you at least believe that my team and I weren't involved? That if someone from Information did this, it wasn't an official decision?"

"It's possible," Fatima admits after another disdainful twitch of her head. The woman working on her hair has finished and is lounging by her side.

"We really are trying to find out who did this, and to protect you," Roz says. "Please, if you think of anything that could help . . ."

"Yes, yes." Fatima waves her hand. "I will think again. But you, you must also look again on your side."

Roz promises and retreats. There is a light breeze in the courtyard, the sun is setting, and she feels almost pleased at the thought of the long solitary flight back.

Kei wears the best suit she has to work the next morning to counteract her pallor and lack of energy. The best appropriately sober suit she has, that is. The Heritage building is in mourning. Mishima couldn't bring herself to check until she got back to the hotel and had Ken's arm around her: only then did she open the news compilers. The numbers weren't as bad as she had braced herself for, but with seven people killed, there was far more data about each of them than there would have been for thirty. Mishima read, tears spilling, until she couldn't stand to know another detail of their lives. She had checked the names, fearing to find Deepal's among them, then felt bad about her relief: the pain she was saved belonged to someone else. She did find his name among the injured, but his wound is minor, and though he won't be at work today, he can be expected to return tomorrow.

Waiting in the security line, Mishima realizes she didn't have to worry about the shadows under her eyes. Everyone looks about the same or worse.

None of the news compilers characterized the group at the café as anything other than "Heritage headquarters staff," and Mishima is still wondering if they were targeted because of their opposition to the secession. She's convinced it was too well planned to be a random crime, and it seems like too much of a coincidence that an unrelated attack on Heritage would happen to strike the opposition group. Mishima decides that brings the bombing investigation under her purview. It's all she can think about right now anyway. She snoops on her recorders all morning, but conversations are muted and purposeless, and after lunch, she decides her time is better used by going home early, reporting in to HQ, and giving her narrative disorder space to breathe. Besides, Ken agreed to stay another day. Actually, he refused to leave.

I t's full dark by the time Roz gets back to the compound. She sees that Charles is back and Malakal has arrived for the debate tomorrow, and she should go into the office to see them and ideally do some after-work socializing, but she is tired and depressed, and goes straight to her hut. Where she finds a second bed.

She is still standing there, looking from one bed to the other, when the door opens again behind her. "You're back!"

Roz spins around. "You're here!" She throws her arms around Maryam.

"I wanted to surprise you," Maryam says, hugging her back. "I hope it's okay that I sleep in here? I can move . . ."

"It's fine," Roz says, wholeheartedly. Maryam doesn't count as socializing. "Just don't ask me to talk to anyone else tonight." She sits down on her bed, ungumming her boots.

"That bad?" Maryam asks, sitting down too.

"Just—so hard to get anything done here. Not enough data." Roz rubs her face with her hands, emerges. "What do you know about the Geneva bombing?"

Nobody knows much yet, but the two friends build up and tear down conjectures until Roz realizes how hungry she is. "I'm going to sneak out and see if there are any leftovers in the kitchen."

"Nah, I got something better." Maryam shuffles through the leather bag by her bed and pulls out a resealed coconut. She finds the fissure, works a fingernail in, and cracks it, releasing a savory fragrance.

"Is that from Medeterranée?" Roz asks, her mouth watering almost painfully.

"Garlic rice soup," Maryam confirms, prizing the laser-perforated spoon shape out of the top half of the coconut shell and handing it to Roz along with the bottom half.

"Shukran, shukran. Al hamdu'illah," Roz says fervently, sending Maryam into a fit of laughter.

"Wow. Five years living in Doha and it only takes two weeks in DarFur for you to start using Arabic."

"More useful here," Roz says around mouthfuls of soup. "Now I'm trying to learn Fur, though."

"From that very attractive governor?"

Roz sputters a few precious drops of the soup on her bed. "You met him?"

"I went along with Amran to a meeting this afternoon."

"What did you think?"

Maryam gives her the nod.

"Doesn't matter, anyway," Roz says, gloomy despite the growing warmth of the soup inside her. "Everyone here hates us; I'm sure he does too." It's a lie, though. Suleyman might not have been flirting with her, but she has a strong feeling, warmer than the soup, that he doesn't hate her.

Nougaz is given scant warning before Vera walks into her office.

"You knew about this Heritage idiocy for how long without telling us?" Vera does not yell, but the way her teeth are clenched might be the only thing stopping her. "A secession? And I find out about it from *The Newsest*?"

"It was closely guarded," Nougaz admits, stepping out from her workspace. "We didn't want to legitimize it." Or inspire copycats.

"And you didn't trust the Supermajority government to keep quiet about something this important? You're not going to sell me this bullshit about it not impacting us now. This is something we should have known."

Nougaz waits her out. "This is really something you need to talk to Gerardo about," she starts, but that only ignites Vera further.

"I did. He told me one of their demands, besides that worm Pressman getting amnesty, is a five-year term. Meaning *now*. Meaning changing our ten-year term *which we won* to a five-year term now."

Nougaz says nothing.

"Are you kidding me?" Vera is now yelling. "Do you know what will happen if you shift to the five-year term at this point in the cycle?"

"Everyone will start campaigning," Nougaz replies quietly.

"Everyone will start campaigning!" Vera repeats, not at all quietly. "Including us. Never mind that we will be judged on our first five years—our first four, really—when Heritage had ten to learn the ropes, and then another ten on top of that to cement their incumbency. Do you know how this has worked out historically?" Vera throws up a data-visualization projection. It was clearly prepared beforehand, and Nougaz wonders how long Vera has been expecting this conversation. "Japan 2009–2012. Mexico 2000–2012." She clearly has more prepared, but Nougaz cuts her off.

"We have limited options."

"You what? You have all the options! All the power you are keeping from the Supermajority, you maintain for yourselves!"

"Not so," Nougaz says. She has noted the plural and hopes more urgently than she would like to admit that this isn't personal, that it's not going to impact their cautious little personal relationship. "But please. Let's not get ahead of ourselves. No one is giving in to any demands yet."

Vera waits, arms folded and eyes narrow. When Nougaz does not continue, she asks, somewhat more calmly, "You are planning something?"

Nougaz shrugs. "It would set a poor precedent to give way to this sort of blackmail."

"Something invisible, then, a bit outside the rules, perhaps?" Vera chuckles. "Remind me never to get on the wrong side of your organization. Or at least not to underestimate you when I do." She draws in her breath suddenly, leans back. "Not the bombing?"

"Of course not," Nougaz says, disgusted.

Vera exhales in relief. "Good. Because the moment I find out you did something like that, we are done."

Nougaz exhales in relief but much more quietly and only when Vera has turned away.

Mishima's semi-virtuous plan of catching up on sleep and getting some distance from the problem only works for about half a day. When she wakes up groggy in the late evening, Ken is already asleep, and she is anxious to do something. She looks into what is known about the bombing (everything) and what is available on the Swiss component of last evening's excitement (nothing). The bomber, who has been identified as Andrej Xin Lanover, threw the bomb into the café without slowing his run and didn't stop until he crossed into Swiss territory. Every step of that run is meticulously documented; what happened after is a blank. No news compiler is even willing to confirm that he was killed in the null state, although there are rumors to that effect. Mishima wishes she'd insisted on seeing the body.

She tries following the data on Lanover into the past, but it turns out, unsurprisingly, that there are Swiss-based gaps there, too. Annoyed, she decides to hack into the Swiss vid system. How hard could it be? But she gives up three hours later, unsure whether it was the sophistication or the unfamiliarity of the encryption that defeated her, and no closer to understanding who ordered the hit on Heritage's anti-secession movement.

CHAPTER 20

Deepal is in the office when Kei gets there the next day, sitting at his workstation staring at a projection or at nothing. Mishima says good morning, quietly, and gets to work. An hour or so later, when she gets up to lay her bugs, she offers to get him a coffee, and he shakes his head, not moving his eyes. When she gets back, single coffee cup in hand, he's in the same position. His hands—one of them bandaged from a burn on the wrist—are shaking.

Mishima walks over. She wants to tell him that it's okay to be upset, that she's been there herself. Hell, she's still there sometimes. She wants to put her hand on his shoulder or maybe even offer him a hug. It's so hard to tell what will help someone and what will make it worse. But as she approaches, a cautious "hey" on her lips, he recoils.

"Stay away from me!" Deepal hisses, disgust and fear on his face.

Mishima nods and turns away, walking back to her workstation in as close to a normal pace as she can manage.

It's understandable. But she's going to have to get what she needs fast or find another access point. Her time is running out.

The debate is held in a massive pop-up tent brought out from the government warehouse and unfolded with some ceremony: a prized asset, apparently, not to be worn out in showings of projected vids every night. It is white, floppy, and so large that Roz is concerned they won't be able to fill it, and the debate will be lost in its emptiness; Maria's surveys haven't shown high levels of enthusiasm for the campaign. But perhaps she forgot to reckon with the lack of other entertainment in a place where most people still don't have personal projectors, or maybe democracy is still new enough to be valued sui generis, because on the afternoon of the debate, the people file in and keep filing. Roz feels fully justified in having asked Maryam to come out, solely for the tweaks she made to the sound system. She set up a rack of feeds algorithmically scattered throughout the tent to allow generous broadcasting (and recording) of each of the speakers, the moderator, and almost the entire audience. A thousand conversations are going on, in at least (Roz's struggling auto-interpreter tells her) four different dialects; without Maryam's system, it would be impossible to hear the debate.

Or so Roz thinks until the candidates file in from a cut in the back and settle themselves into chairs on the low wooden stage. The conversation level in the tent falls into a respectful hum.

Malakal offered to moderate the debate, but the Council opted for a low-intervention format and tapped Suleyman to manage it. Quite the vote of confidence in his impartiality, thinks Roz, studying his serene countenance from the back of the tent. Or maybe the powers-that-be want his opinion known. Either way, she's impressed by the mantle of gravitas he has gathered around himself. He emanates dignity. She wonders if this is what everybody means when they talk about his being born to lead.

Roz herself is very happy to be standing along the back wall of the tent, watching for reactions rather than working the annotation or moderating the debate (another possibility they had floated). Maria and Maryam are back at the compound, working together on the instant polling and crunching the reaction data while supervising Amran, who is managing the annotators. Charles and Minzhe are sitting up front, watching the debaters closely and liaising with Maria and her team.

Ken offers to stay for the rest of the assignment, but Mishima convinces him that he doesn't really want to lose his job at Free2B. She's fine, and having him there, while pleasant, would be a distraction she can't afford, so he flies back to Saigon after their second night. That afternoon, she gets an invitation from Switzerland. Not wanting to spend another night running through the wilderness (and to demonstrate the status she was lacking last time she crossed the border), Mishima borrows an Information crow to get there.

"After two days, I didn't think you were going to get him," she says as Donath escorts her down from the rooftop landing site. She wasn't sure she'd recognize him in the daylight, but she remembers the lines of his face well enough, even if she couldn't tell how blue his eyes were during that dark night. She's washed the black out of her hair, and she notes his surprise when he sees her, although she's pretty confident he will attribute the changed color to the earlier darkness. Mishima's surface reason for going through the difficulty of undyeing and redyeing her hair is to look as different from Kei as possible, to prevent problems in the very unlikely case that Kei and Donath should ever meet. She's also aware of a curious wish for Donath to see Mishima in all her intimidating and idiosyncratic reality. This is probably due to some sort of physical attraction, a by-product of all the excitement the other night.

"You can ride in the front this time, if you like," the cop says, opening the door for her with a flourish.

"Actually, I thought I'd drive," Mishima says.

The Swissman's eyebrows go up.

"It's a classic car," she says, gesturing at the vehicle: a peeling Peugeot this time. His Renault must still be out of commission. "We don't get much opportunity to practice shifting on our side of the border."

The cop shrugs, tosses her the keys. "Be my guest," he says gruffly.

Mishima had no intention of driving before he gave her the line about sitting in front, but now that she's behind the wheel, she's accomplished two things: she gets to drive this amazing car, and the ease with which he gave way quashed any interest she might have had in Donath.

"So, tell me about this suspect," Mishima says, pulling out onto the street and shifting into second. She doesn't even care if her clutch use is clunky. She hasn't done this in so long, it feels rare and exciting, like riding a horse down the streets of Tokyo. "How did you find him?"

"Her," Donath says, one hand gripping the dashboard. "Take the second right." They are in Martigny, some small city not too far from Geneva. It's strange to Mishima not to have to think about centenal borders. "It was simple, really. We used the vids of that road—we do have some, you know. There were few cars, and it was easy to eliminate most of them."

"Eliminate them how?" Mishima asks, wary of prejudices and preferences.

"By their routes, the times in between cameras," Donath explains.

Mishima makes the turn, sees a stretch of road without traffic lights, and upshifts.

"This is a school zone."

"It's Saturday." She takes them into fourth.

"This car doesn't actually go so fast," the cop says, frustrated.

"Maybe not, but the shifting is fun." She takes them down

into third. "What kind of times between cameras are we talking about?"

"The cameras are spaced approximately twenty kilometers apart."

Bleeping Switzerland. Anything could happen in that amount of time. "So, you picked up the suspect."

"We did. And she freely admitted to having given the perp a ride. Turn left up ahead."

"Let me guess," Mishima says, downshifting again. "Hitchhiker."

"No, indeed," Donath answers. "It was all planned beforehand. But he couldn't have been involved in that terrible bombing; he was the nicest man."

"She knew him?"

"The large building on the left. There is a parking lot entrance just before it. No, she said she didn't know him before she picked him up, so this is based on the conversation they had in the vehicle. She was so disturbed to hear he was dead. She's quite hostile toward us now."

Ah. "I'm the good cop?"

Donath winces. "I doubt either of those descriptors apply."

Touché. "The nicest man based on the conversation they had in the car and . . . the recommendation of whoever asked her to give him a ride?" Mishima pulls into a space, turns off the car.

"That is exactly the point we would like you to illuminate. Please remember to leave the car in the lowest gear when you turn it off."

". . . and continue my husband's legacy as only I know how to do," Fatima announces.

Roz darts a glance at Amal, whom she noticed earlier in the

rear of the tent, but her expression doesn't change from the small set smile she's been wearing all evening, and her hands are relaxed in her sunset-colored lap.

There is a brief pause after the last of the candidate statements. There was very little about policy beyond the vaguest platitudes, but Amran and the annotators did a good job of bulking it out with overlays reminding everyone of the stated policy positions, projected within the tent and in the marketplaces of this and every other DarFur centenal for anyone who doesn't have a personal projector. In Roz's professional opinion, the militia leader Hamid Mohamed gave the best performance, independent of policy: he was clear, matter-of-fact, and coherent, and he projected his authority clearly without being overbearing. The two sheikhs from the more remote centenals were obviously reading from notes at eyeball level, and Abdul Gasig's speech was informal and wandering. But it is Fatima who gets the biggest reaction, even though her presentation was quiet and almost self-effacing. Maybe that's what they want from a candidate, at least if that candidate is the widow of the former leader. Roz has long since given up on understanding why any given population will choose one person over another to be their leader.

On the stage, Suleyman stands, offers another brief invocation, and then invites questions.

Roz steps away from the post she had been leaning against, shifting into security mode. They did body scans at the entrance to the tent, but almost every adult male was wearing a knife, as Suleyman had predicted beforehand. The candidates had unanimously supported his petition that knives not be forbidden from the tent, and Malakal reluctantly agreed. Roz was more worried about the raised stage (why, when everyone else was sitting on the floor and they would have chairs? But apparently it was a necessary bit of pomp) and had it swept three times for explosives. She means to keep a close eye on any questioners who get agitated or aggressive.

Swiss holding cells are significantly nicer than Mishima's very low expectations. Maybe they have special accommodations for potential witnesses. Daisy Lepont, the woman sitting in the low, padded chair, is not quite what Mishima imagined from Donath's briefing. She is spare, dressed in a tasteful paneled sheath with a neat jacket, and her hair is pulled back into a harsh bun.

Mishima shakes out her own hair, unbuttons her jacket, and walks in. "Hi!" she says, holding out her hand. "I'm Jun"—one of the identities she uses for casual cover-ups, with the public Information to match. "I work for Information, and we've been asked to provide some outside oversight for this case."

The woman's eyes pop. "Information? I didn't think you had any jurisdiction here."

"We don't," Mishima says cheerfully. "But we're sometimes asked in as a third-party watchdog, to make sure there are no misunderstandings with the Swiss police. After all, one suspect has already died in this case." She wonders if Donath, still in the observation room, is cringing or nodding approval of her strategy.

"I'm—I'm not a suspect," Daisy says, one hand at her breastbone. *Suspect? Moi?* "Just a witness."

"Ah," Mishima says, making a show of blinking some intel up in front of her vision. "Is that what they told you? *Suspect in providing assistance, plotting violence, and impeding an investigation* is what I have here." She's grateful to the hub in Paris for providing, via Donath's nifty antenna, the correct legal terms under the Swiss system. It wouldn't have been a simple thing to look up.

"I didn't—" Daisy shakes her head. "I'm sure this will all be cleared up."

"No doubt," Mishima agrees. "And as you know, Information can help with that, especially if you give us some pointers on where to look. Now, how did you arrange to meet this passenger?"

"As I told them," Daisy starts, but her voice is already wavering, "it was on one of those anonymous ride-matching services."

Mishima shakes her head slowly. "That doesn't match our records." She has no intel on this; Swiss law, unfathomably, protects the data of those services, even from the police, and she doesn't have the time or inclination to hack through their robust security. But she doesn't see this buttoned-down, well-dressed woman taking that kind of risk for a paltry amount of money.

Daisy doesn't lose her composure as she takes the hook. She looks down for a moment, then meets Mishima's eyes. "I don't know who he was. And I *still* don't believe that young man had anything to do with the bombing in Geneva." But her voice falters again there—she is starting to believe, even if she doesn't want to. "My friend assured me that this was just a simple favor . . ." She lets it drift off before she loses it completely.

"Of course," Mishima says, soothingly. "That's hardly a punishable offense. And your friend probably didn't know any more about it than you did."

"I'm sure," Daisy says, struggling now not to cry. "I'm sure he wouldn't do anything illegal."

"He was probably misled," Mishima agrees. "And the person who did that to him, that's who we're after. The sooner we find that person, the sooner your friend will be out of danger."

"You think he could be in danger?" That startles her, and Mishima watches as her stunned brain slowly pieces together the links in the logic: if her friend is in danger for setting this up, then she could be too.

"Quite possibly," Mishima says. "Which is why it's imperative we get in touch with him as soon as possible."

Daisy is still reluctant, and repeatedly asks for assurances that he won't "get in trouble," but she does eventually cough up an address. A physical address in Aubonne. Mishima doesn't have access to Information, but she took a good look at the maps before crossing over again, and she can picture the town, to the north of what remains of Lac Léman. Big enough for a stranger not to be too conspicuous, close enough to Geneva to go back and forth. "No other contact details? How did you get in touch?"

"We would meet for drinks, lunches." Daisy lowers her eyes, and Mishima puts some effort into showing no reaction.

"You must have communicated to set the dates, though."

Daisy shook her head. "He was . . . He told me he was on a break from virtual interactions. When I wanted to see him, I would go by his place, and he would be working in the garden or painting. It was . . . refreshing."

Indeed. "Where did you meet, then?"

"At the lake," Daisy says; her voice and expression tell Mishima the encounter was suitably romantic. She can already picture the man scouting for a single person with a vehicle and the right attitude; the easily arranged chance of beach towels laid side by side on the grass.

"When was this?"

"Early summer," Daisy says, as if she doesn't remember the exact date and time. Mishima lets it go. Donath can get it out of her in the follow-up if he wants, but early summer is already enough to rearrange Mishima's assumptions about the case.

Excluding some lucky opportunism or an extraordinary level of contingency planning, early summer means this has been in the cards for months. Has the secession, and its opposition, been in play for that long? Or was there a different reason for the target?

Almost all of the debate questions are aggressive, starting with an old woman who pulls herself to her feet with a cane, offers a blessing, and then starts imprecating all of the candidates, together and individually, for not saying more about what they will do for children and the elderly. After their (for the most part still-vague) answers about school-building and hospitals, a minor sheikh stands up and asks about taxes and why he and his constituents have to pay them and why some have to pay more than others. Roz can almost feel Amran's panic as the annotations get longer and longer, and then Maria's calming influence as they start to sort themselves into a branching summary of the rationale, history, and political economy of taxation. Meanwhile, the candidates are dabbling in numbers or at least ranges of numbers, which is encouraging. A young man stands up and makes to talk for a long time about the assassination of Al-Jabali and what it means, but Suleyman cuts him off with unassailable politeness and tells him to come to a question. At which point he asks, still long-windedly, what the candidates will do to protect them from the pernicious elements that surround their wonderful government. The militia leader comes out best on that one as well, although Fatima plays gracefully on her bereavement before coming back with a rousing (if vague) proclamation of fierceness toward their enemies.

Apparently, these answers don't satisfy everyone. "What will you do about Information?"

The shout comes from the crowd, out of order, and Roz sees

Suleyman craning to identify the speaker as she runs the replay in front of her left eye, zooming in on that section of the audience. By her second replay, Maria's team has haloed and identified the speaker as one Omer Jibrail, and Suleyman has asked him, in the same courteous tone, to clarify his question.

"They make you spend all that tax money you just talked about on ways to watch us! And for what? So they can tell us what to do? How is that different from being under the Sudanese?"

Roz jerks forward in alarm. The audience turns restless, and as her view shifts through the marketplace projections in centenals around DarFur, she sees people standing and gesturing, and more voices join in across the linked feeds.

From Djabal: "Send them home!"

And from Garsila: "No need for Information here!"

"So, what I want to know," the original shouter goes on with some satisfaction, "is what all of you are going to do about it!" He is echoed by an approving murmur from the crowd.

Roz is balanced on her toes and considering evacuation logistics, but no one has reached for a knife yet (Maria's team will be watching closely for that), and Suleyman has nodded and turned to the candidates.

The sheikh from Jebel Marra tears into the question eagerly, expostulating about how he will kick out Information (by which Roz supposes he means withdraw from the micro-democratic system) and restore the independence, self-determination, and proud historic culture of DarFur, and how this will allow them to assert their traditional dominance and protect their borders and generally make everything better.

Roz knows that this kind of vague rhetorical gobbledygook can appeal to voters or incite violence, but she's glad he's saying it. Having a single, low-polling candidate come out strongly for an issue will provide great polling data, and she's very curious indeed to know more precisely how DarFuris feel about

Information. Also, unless she is badly misreading, the murmur in the debate tent has taken on a distinct tone of discomfort. People are wary of Information but none too eager for upheaval, either.

When Abdul Gasig gets the nod, he leans forward and shakes his finger at young Omer Jibrail directly. "You don't know what you're talking about! Information is our best opportunity to connect with the world and build our status. Their ways seem strange to you because they're new here, but most of the world is completely accustomed to them. Information is the way business is done! Do you want to turn us into a null state, backward and isolated? That is not the way to revive our heritage, not in today's world." He knocks his walking stick against the platform, and Roz startles even though she expects the hollow thunk. She glances at her crew. Malakal is impassive, Charles has a slight smile—if Abdul Gasig is supporting them, the wind must be blowing in their favor. Minzhe, however, is listening to the merchant's answer with an expression that looks like suspicion. Maybe that's his default debate face: when Abdul Gasig finishes speaking, he turns his intense gaze on the militia commander.

What do you think? Roz asks him in a quickly typed message. At first she thinks he's not going to look at it until the commander's answer is over, but then she gets the response: **He's no fan, but he hasn't kicked me off the force yet.**

Commander Hamid spins the question slightly off center by turning to defense. "It's what I know," he says, with an admirable humble-brag. "Information is useful for our security. We know more about what's going on around us. Attacks have gone down since we and our neighbors became part of the system. But if Information ever works against our security needs, at that point I believe we should abdicate from the system in an orderly manner." Roz wonders if this is a local framework, or if he's following the debate around intervention in the K-stan war.

Fatima waits for a long moment before speaking, and Roz feels the attention in the crowd draw taut. "I often feel as you do," she begins. It's the singular *you*; she too is speaking directly to Jibrail. "My husband was uncertain about the role Information would play, about what we give up to join with them. But as time went on, he came to see what we gain from them as well. He died believing that Information is the way forward for DarFur."

Died believing it, and maybe died because he believed it. Fatima meets Roz's eyes across the room, and Roz wonders if they are thinking the same thing.

"I hope he was right," Fatima continues, finally. "But I will not believe until I am sure. We must watch them as they watch us. We may try their way, and learn what we can. But as always in our history, we must be ready to survive alone when we have to."

CHAPTER 21

There are a few other, more anodyne questions, some projected in remotely from other centenals, and several more questionless comments that Suleyman parries before they can become too time-consuming or self-serving. The candidates are allowed one more statement, and then it's over. Roz lingers by the exit, listening to the conversations of audience members as they walk out (lively, excited, and largely substanceless—more or less what one hopes for after a debate). When the tent has emptied out, she hurries back to the compound and her hut, and pulls out the unwieldy length of her new toub, shimmering and soft. She feels vaguely exhilarated even though she has done practically nothing all evening. She wraps the cloth over her trousers and attempts various configurations for getting it over her shoulders and head, eventually turning to a tutorial vid on Information. More or less covered, although still uneasy about the anchoring of various folds, she heads out to the party.

The feast is held in the open area bounded by the militia barracks, the market, and two residential streets. The impounded camel has been moved behind the barracks for the occasion, and the VIP table, which is not a table but a woven mat, is settled on the close-cropped grass under the tree. The male VIP table, that is. Roz, still clinging to the loose end of her toub, is gestured over to a mat in the shadow of one of the compound walls; other mats with less-important women stretch out to either side of them, while the less-important men are across the way, nearer to the barracks.

She can't help shooting a glance toward the center: Minzhe, leaning his forearm on one knee, hand tilted up to protect the food curled inside, is listening to the militia commander hold forth. On the other side of the mat, Suleyman nods, with his eyes fixed on Malakal, who is gesturing expansively with his left hand; Abdul Gasig and Abdul Salim are eating side by side.

At least here with the women, she has a chance to talk to Fatima. The widow is flanked by two of her friends, or aides, and Roz settles in across the mat from them, beside the sheikha Thoraya and catty-corner to a woman in a jewel-green toub whom Information helpfully identifies as the wife of the militia commander, also named Fatima. Halima, Information's landlady, is at the other end of the mat, leaning on one arm as though to balance the weight of her pregnant body. Amal, Roz notices, is late or tactfully absent.

Probably she has better food at home, Roz thinks, examining the dishes arrayed on the circular platters in the middle of the mat. The usual five ways of preparing goat; three different vegetables, all stewed into something goopy; large bowls of the porridge, aseeda; plates of the sorghum crepes, kisra; and several stacks of flat, floury bread. Grabbing a piece of bread and using it to pinch morsels of goat, Roz engages Sheikha Thoraya in casual conversation, getting through the traditional greetings and the comments on the weather (still hot) and asking what she thought of the debate.

"Al-hamdu lillāh, it went very well," Thoraya answers, jovial with congratulations for the Information team's success. "There were many people there, and they listened!"

Roz, a little surprised by the sheikha's perspective, has a sudden inkling that she may have had something to do with the excellent attendance. "And you? Did you find it interesting?"

"Well . . . There wasn't much that was new," she says, apologetically. "After watching all of their position vids, I mean. Of course that fool from Jebel Marra made a fool of himself, but that was to be expected."

Unexpected frankness, or what she thinks Information wants to hear? Roz turns to include Fatima in the conversation. "Did you enjoy the debate?"

Fatima looks up from her meal. "Enjoy? Not really," she responds with a smile that balances between self-deprecating and shyly honest. "I don't particularly like speaking to crowds. But they seemed engaged, which is important. And I think it went well."

The perfect timbre of her answer sparks anger in Roz. All these politicians who pretend so well not to be politicians, these polished speakers who claim to hate speaking.

"But if you don't like speaking for crowds," she says, trying to sound genuinely puzzled, "why do you want to be head of state?"

"I don't want to be head of state," Fatima responds. "But I have an obligation to continue the work of my husband. He wanted a strong, independent Fur nation, and I will continue working toward that."

"What about what you want?"

Fatima's smile says this is a question she knows how to answer. "My husband wanted to live, I'm sure of that. This is not a situation where everyone gets what they want."

"Do you think you'll be a good head of state if you don't want the job?"

"The best leaders are the ones who don't want to be." She says it with certainty and, seeing that Roz is skeptical, leans forward. "It's not just about corruption, although that is an important reason. People who don't want the job can become corrupt too." She rolls her eyes as though this is obvious. The change in her personality is startling until it hits Roz that this may be the first time she has seen the woman not actively mourning. Maybe she was always like this before her husband was killed, suddenly and far away. "I have come to believe that the best leaders are those that are required to subvert some part of their personality to lead. They learn discipline, and in this way they are able to put others first."

"Didn't Al—didn't your husband want to be head of state?"

"He wanted independence and prosperity for the Fur people first." Fatima has shut off again, leaning back, eyes flattened.

"Why are you so convinced we killed him?" Roz whispers. "We came here to work with him. We had no reason to want him dead."

"He thought you did," Fatima says, voice low. Out of the corner of her eye Roz can see Sheikha Thoraya studiously focused on her plate.

"He did?" Roz asks. "Why?"

"I don't know," Fatima answers. Her voice crackles with frustration, and the woman next to her puts a hand on her arm. "He was nervous when he heard you were coming. He had been here in Kas and then had a trip to some of the other centenals, and he only got back the day before—but you know this, of course." She waves her hand, as if to lighten the bitterness in her voice.

"We can know where he went," Roz says, as gently as she can manage, "but not what he was feeling or what he said to you."

Fatima shakes her head. "He didn't tell me why. But he was unsettled, here and there, and then that urgent meeting with the sheikhs—he left straight from there." She looks down, places her hand above her eyes like a visor.

"I'm so sorry," Roz murmurs, and then turns away to engage Thoraya in conversation about the likelihood that the rainy season will arrive soon. She listens to the detailed response distractedly while she surreptitiously types her notes and revises her image of Fatima. She tries now to imagine her as the supportive wife, encouraging her husband in his first campaign, helping him strategize. And then sending him off to another centenal to dally with his mistress?

She doesn't have the cultural frame right yet. Her unthinking gaze strays to the tree, to the mat below it, to Suleyman, holding forth with the neat gestures of his hands, his deep voice muted by the distance and the murmur of the crowd.

The sun has disappeared behind the low rise in the west, and the air has cooled to the point where it is pleasant to be outside, sitting on a mat under the sky. The evening prayer has just finished when Roz hears a familiar voice and turns her head to see Amran coming toward her, followed by Maria, Maryam, and Khadija.

"We finished," Amran says, after she's done the round of greetings with the august women. "Any food left?"

On cue, a woman comes by with a fresh tray of meat, vegetables, and starches. The newcomers dig in. Roz, her appetite renewed by their enthusiasm, takes a scoop from the soupy bowl of yellow-green vegetable matter with her kisra. She grimaces at the sweet-sour taste: the vegetable is bourgette, a banana-zucchini cross that Roz still finds counterintuitive. Amran, young enough to have grown up with that ingredient as an established part of her world, is helping herself to more.

Roz has been working at eye level on and off since the conversation with Fatima. She checked for more mental-emotional scans by Al-Jabali, wondering if they can pinpoint the moment when he started feeling guilty or scared, but the scan he did after the oil barrel explosion is the only one on record. Not knowing where else to look, she goes back to the sheikh's meeting in Djabal and studies the infrastructure projects again. It is only after staring at the numbers in one eye while people eat and laugh around her that it occurs to her: where, she wonders, did DarFur get the money for all this?

Charles plops down next to her, breaking into her thoughts. He borrowed a gleaming jellabiya for the party and is sitting cross-legged, head tilted as he gauges the attention of others at the table. Whatever he wants to talk to her about is not classified, but private.

"Sorry to disturb," Charles says. "I wanted to tell you personally."

"What?"

"Nejime has asked me to go to Urumqi."

"What!"

"I'm sorry, Roz. I know there's still a lot to be done here, but with the debate over, some of the pressure will be off . . ." Charles trails off, looking sheepish, even though he really didn't have much of a choice.

"No, you're right. We can manage. But has the K-stan conflict really gotten that bad? Or . . ." She wonders for a moment whether he's being sent to investigate the other suspicious death Mishima noticed.

"You didn't see the latest?" Charles starts to blink it up into a projection, then stops, looking around again. It's public knowledge, but no need to advertise Information's weaknesses, especially not here. "Shells hit a 1China centenal along the border. They landed in a meadow, only killed a sheep or two, and our analysis shows they were misses, not deliberate targeting of that centenal. But 1China has officially requested assistance from Information, and China is holding military exercises."

"In case our military support isn't enough," Roz says, going cold. Because it won't be, not if either of the K-stans or, worse, both of them decide to attack in earnest. She feels a flicker of jealousy: it is going to be an important job, important and fascinating and global. "When are you leaving?"

"Tomorrow morning."

"Be careful."

"You too," Charles says, touching her shoulder as he gets up to go back to his place.

Roz glances around on the tail of a raucous peal of laughter from Thoraya's side of the table, and realizes that the party is thinning out. Most of the other mats have emptied, and centenal staff are already clearing dishes. Dark has fallen, and the night feels almost cool. Roz leans back on her hands and sighs. She wishes she could lean all the way back and lie flat, staring up at the stars. A flash of white catches her eye, and she looks up to see Suleyman standing at one end of the mat.

"Good evening, ladies," he says, and there's an immediate cheerful chorus of "good evening!" back from Thoraya and the other sheikhas. Roz notices Maryam trying to catch her eye, and avoids it. "A few of the gentlemen are joining me in my compound for tea, and I wondered if any of you would like to come along."

Roz looks up in surprise, but the sheikhas are already gathering themselves in happy agreement; this must not be untoward, or even so very unusual. Fatima and her companions decline, but then she is still grieving. Amran looks eager, Maria nonchalant. Roz finally meets Maryam's gaze, and they share a shrug and then scramble up from the mat.

Roz prepares herself, during the straggling group walk toward the centenal hall, for Suleyman's . . . house? Hut? Most importantly, for an imagined wife (or two?), perfect and pleasant and lovely, passing out the tea. His compound turns out to be a small one, practically adjoining the centenal hall (is it a centenal property, offered to the governor? Or did he buy it after he was elected?) and the woman who appears with the round tray of tiny, gilded glasses is a servant Roz recognizes from meetings at the centenal hall. She starts to relax into her seat, a wooden bed frame strung with twine, where she is pressed between Maryam on one side and Khadija on the other; similar seats are arranged in a rough circle, and the conversation flows with the ease of a successful day and a late night.

Roz does not hear how they get on the subject of the election blackout two years ago. The conversation finds its way to her awareness with Charles talking about working in the Lagos Hub, the disruption, the desperate attempts to figure out what happened, the waiting. "We were all trying to find things we could do to help. I remember people filming vids encouraging citizens to vote, to post once connection came back up, crunching whatever data we had every which way we could think of, doing old tasks that had been put aside for months. Huh! We even cleaned the office. Everyone wanted to be useful."

Minzhe was election-monitoring in a Liberty centenal outside of Harare. "Everyone was shocked at first—they definitely didn't know it was coming, nobody knew what was going on, there were all these crazy theories—but then, like twenty-four hours in, somebody woke up and they started showing all these vids and pop-ups *everywhere*. The thing was"—Minzhe shakes his head—"it happened so quickly. They had all those lies *ready*. They were meant for something else, but then someone realized that this was an opportunity and rolled them out. They weren't ready for that, but they were ready for something." There is nodding and head-shaking among the Information staff. The locals are listening politely: for them, Liberty is little more than a distant villain from an interactive, a character painted on the mural wall.

"Weren't you in Doha?" Charles asks Roz.

Maryam shifts in the seat next to her, remembering that time. "Yes," Roz says. "I was counting votes." There is a respectful silence after that, but she doesn't elaborate.

"I was in Juba," Malakal says. "It was very . . . frustrating." That pause speaks of the enormous effort it took to get the new centenals ready by Election Day, and the fury when those gains were threatened. Malakal raises his eyes to look at Suleyman. It's a question, and Roz wonders if any of the rest of them would have thought to ask the locals.

Suleyman coughs. "It was not such an important moment for us here. We're used to blackouts. We were worried about our votes, and worried that this system we had agreed to, invested in, was failing us." Roz has torn her gaze away from the governor to look at Malakal. He doesn't wince, but his face is frozen, eyes down. "But only in terms of votes, you understand, not . . ." Not the world-shattering episode it was for most of them, not a remember-exactly-where-you-were-the-moment-you-heard event. "Afterwards, when we learned more of the story, we were amazed," he says, as if to mollify those here who live and die with Information. "We wondered, too, how it might affect us."

There's a silence after that, as everyone present wonders the same.

Even though Roz and Maryam retire immediately after returning from the sheikh's afterparty (something which would have an entirely different meaning in Doha), they stay awake long into the night. They spend the first hour dissecting the debate and its associated events from every angle of their respective viewpoints, but once that is done, Maryam moves them on to Roz's crush.

"Come on," she says when Roz resists. "I would far rather talk about that than about how miserable I am." Roz is already crumbling when she adds, "And he is *very* cute."

How can she not give in? She takes Maryam through their recent encounters, which, spoken out loud, seem to amount to very little.

"It is impossible," she sighs finally. "I'm sure he's married at least once, maybe twice, maybe three times . . ."

Maryam pushes up onto her elbow to stare at her. "Are you kidding? He's not married at all."

"He's not married?"

"Didn't you even search him on Information?"

". . . No." She's thought about it many times, but always remembers how he apologized for searching her, and restrains herself. "Wait, you did?"

"Of course I did! I have to look out for my friends."

"Still," Roz says, busy digesting this new intel. How can he not be married? "Still. It's impossible; it really is. I don't even know why I like him. I mean, he's nice and he's hot and he's a leader here and people look up to him and he seems principled, and all those are things I like, but I don't know why I like him this much."

"We never do. We don't have the words for those things. That's why matchmaking algorithms are so hard to design well."

"Okay, but . . . I'm just waiting for him to say something that will make it impossible for me to think about him this way. You know, that women should be subservient to their husbands, or that unbelievers are going to hell, or . . ."

"That gay people deserve to die?" Maryam suggests.

"Yes, that would do it," Roz agrees, wishing she had used that example sooner.

"Or that political advancement is more important than love."

Maryam's tone sounds like she's trying to lighten the mood after that last comment, but she can't quite pull it off.

"That doesn't seem to be his particular problem," Roz says.

"Why not just ask him about his beliefs?"

"It's impossible anyway," Roz grumbles. "Let me just enjoy it a little longer?"

CHAPTER 22

Maryam leaves early the next morning, catching a ride on an Information crow traveling between Kinshasa and Baghdad and willing to drop her off in Doha. "Take care, habibti," she tells Roz during their long hug on at the landing area. "And thank you for inviting me. You were right; I think it helped."

From the airstrip it's only a short walk to Zeinab's; it would be a shame to go all the way back to the compound when there's better coffee on the way. Still, there's a shiver of the illicit as she walks to the café, and Roz reassures herself that there's nothing clandestine about these meetings. They are perfectly public. Anyone could walk by and see them, not to mention the constant, curious surveillance of Zeinab's various waiters and cooks. Who must also be some of the premier gossips in town, given their position.

Roz starts pulling up the various DarFur plaza discussions but manages to stop herself before she enters any potentially incriminating search terms. She doesn't know this context well enough to catch code words, and besides—glancing around at the camel lumbering past, the three women sitting by their market wares—most of the gossip here is probably analog.

Instead, she looks at what she knows: data. Yes, she reassures herself, it's perfectly visible, a handful of intersections between her timeline and his. The flat fact of it is comforting: nothing to see here, no one trying to hide anything. She tries to look at it impartially, from a distance: true, informal meetings are unusual but a distinct positive in building relationships with locals.

To know why it feels so wrong, you would have to see Suleyman, his beautiful face, his bearing of restrained power. Or see Roz trying so hard not to give anything away. You would have to feel the odd electricity that blossoms between them.

Their table at Zeinab's is empty. Roz drops into the chair and starts doodling an algorithm for rendering the unseen visible on Information. She doesn't for a second think that she can come up with a way to catch burgeoning attraction through surveillance and number crunching; she's just used to trying to design algorithms for impossible data collection problems. It's how she thinks through issues. Besides, this doesn't have to be about . . . her mind, dancing around the l-word, reverts to attraction. Stupid, irrational, short-term attraction. No, it could be about conspiracy, too.

She looks up from her reverie to see the boy waiter hovering, grin on his face. "Coffee," she says through her yawn, blinking away her doodles and turning to the cartoons. The debate obviously has pride of place. Looking at the panel in front of her, which shows the stage more or less as it looked yesterday, Roz can feel the excitement of the kid drawing it: the faces printed from Information are people who exist, here, in this world!

The coverage of the debate extends out in the panels to Roz's right, but to the left she sees that rumors of secession have finally reached the world. The panel in front of the café, which she has begun to think of as the front page, shows a caricature of Cynthia Halliday, ubiquitous Heritage head of state, straining to pull away from a jumble of other figures, Nougaz's Information-representing face prominent among them, all tied together by what looks like a bungee cord labeled

INFORMATION. Interesting, Roz thinks, that it's not called "micro-democracy," but she supposes Information makes a better bad guy. In the cartoon, Halliday has pulled out a pair of scissors.

She looks up to see Suleyman walking toward her (along the Heritage section, she notes, wondering whether he's already looked at the images of himself).

"Ah, good morning!" He raises his hand as he sees her. And that smile—everything the algorithm would miss is there. Roz can't help smiling back. "I'm glad you're here," Suleyman says, dropping into the chair beside her, her smile apparently invitation enough.

"Ef camo," Roz says automatically, although they have mostly dropped the language lessons. "Your party was a great success last night."

"It was only the secondary event. It was the debate that was the great success."

"It did go fairly well," Roz reflects. "No violence, good questions. All the candidates behaved." She smiles at him. "Not all elections are so decorous."

"Oh, yes," his smile fades. "That's what I wanted to talk to you about. I remembered something in the course of our conversation last night—"

"Conversation?" Roz is trying to remember if at any point she spoke to him alone the night before, or even spoke to him at all.

"About the Information blackout. What I said was true, for myself, but as I was thinking about it, I remembered. Al-Jabali was very upset about the blackout. I tried to calm him down. You know, not so many people here had individual connections to Information then, so most of the population hadn't even noticed. But he felt that it was a betrayal after he had thrown his political reputation behind Information." He falls silent, and Roz thinks that maybe this mission is a direct result of the election debacle after all.

"I hope we regained his confidence eventually," she says.

"Oh, yes, once the story came out and after some time had passed and we became accustomed to your ways. Yes, these past few months, he was very happy with the deal with Information." He stops. Roz is biting her tongue, remembering what Fatima said. "I wonder if . . ."

She waits.

"Perhaps while he was upset, perhaps he said something he shouldn't have?" Suleyman sounds unusually hesitant, almost as if he's afraid of offending her. And then Roz realizes what he's trying to ask.

"You think Information killed him because he was angry about the blackout?" She wants to laugh or cry. "I don't think so. First of all, there's no record of him confronting us or saying something he shouldn't have—that would have been in the file when we first came to meet him." The smile drops off her face as she remembers that this mission was not supposed to be a murder investigation. "If we killed everyone who criticized us . . . well. There would be a lot of people in line ahead of him. Even just from that particular episode, the heads of state of Heritage and Liberty certainly did much more egregious and damaging actions than he could have."

"You're right, of course," Suleyman says. "I'm sorry; I should not have suspected Information. But perhaps . . ." He pauses again, and Roz doesn't think he's formulating something new. He's still trying to explain what he wanted to tell her. "Perhaps he spoke hastily to someone else."

"Who?" Roz asks.

The governor shakes his head. "I don't know. But I thought you might."

"Me?" Roz asks.

"I thought Information knew everything."

Kei finds a reason to leave work early. It's not difficult: even if Deepal is no longer exactly on her side, he's too withdrawn to care. Mishima forges out into Geneva. She's considering whether one of the formal options open to her—Information, or LesProfessionnels, who are the official investigative body on the bombing—might be useful, but as she'd rather not reveal her identity until she has to, she decides to work a little further on her own first. She passes the lake with its jet d'eau, long since airscaped into a sleek spiral, the water corkscrewing up into the sky and then falling smoothly in the opposite helix, DNA as imagined by Escher, the tower of Babel as a transparent drill bit. Half an hour later, she is in a distinctly less salubrious neighborhood, where concrete apartment buildings in a Heritage centenal on the outskirts of the city lift higher and higher in proportion to population pressure. Mishima could have gotten there faster on a public crow, but it's much easier to search for faces on public transportation than on every possible pedestrian route. Besides, Kei hasn't had time to get much exercise.

The man that Daisy knew as Rolf from Aubonne has vanished, and the identity he gave her doesn't exist. A collaborative effort between the Swiss police and Information, embodied mainly by Mishima and Donath trading intel over a secure connection, was able to match Swiss vid of a man meeting his description with the identity of an ex-Heritage security officer, Vincent Salonika. He, too, is absent from any tracers Information can put out, but his financial records—traced with some difficulty by Hassan from Maryam's team in Doha—indicate Salonika's recent receipt of a staggeringly large sum and subsequent disbursement of a hefty portion of that sum in two tranches to the bomber, Lanover. The second transfer took place shortly after the bombing: probably, Mishima believes, when Lanover was confirmed to have reached Daisy's waiting car. The first tranche was transferred a week earlier while Salonika was in an apartment on the fifteenth floor of the building Mishima is staring up at.

The building's security is laughable, an eight-digit code to be punched in and a body scan that Mishima allows to observe her hunting knife and shuriken, since she already knows that it doesn't even connect to a recorder, much less a live security monitor. Always distrustful of elevators, and especially old ones with no hover capacity, she takes the stairs.

She is cresting the seventh floor when she starts to hear the murmur in her ear. It's so faint that she has to stop, wait for the echo of her footsteps to fall away, and steady her breathing before she can confirm there is actually a sound and not just a ringing in her ear. Yes, there it is. A voice, almost certainly, but she can make out no words. She climbs on, hand on the hilt of her knife.

By the tenth floor she's sure it's a voice, and there is a second one, fainter. Mishima estimates she should have enough definition for voice recognition by the twelfth, even if she still doesn't recognize it herself. But on the eleventh, something changes: a sudden overwhelming rustling and static, and then the voice is back, both closer and muffled. A sudden vision comes to Mishima: a scarf, wrapped around the lower part of a face to conceal it. Mishima starts to sprint. After a few steps, she hears a door open and close. She pounds up the stairs, trying to lengthen her breaths and hoping the elevators in this building are too old for anticipatory arrival, then comes to a shuddering halt. She can hear the shouting faintly in her earpiece and at the same time echoing from above her: a third person, calling attention to themselves in the hall.

"I've [. . .]ee [. . .]! You're [. . .] here [. . .]!"

The wearer of the scarf: "You haven't seen me. There is no proof. There is nothing you can do." The voice is contained, polite, supremely self-confident. Mishima no longer has any doubt: Head of State Halliday in a highly unlikely part of town and finally wearing the scarf with Mishima's planted recorder.

Mishima starts up again as the voices escalate, then, three steps above the fourteenth floor the elevator doors open and—Mishima teeters precariously for a moment—close again. Too winded to curse, she turns and races down again, letting gravity pull her and leaping the last three steps of every flight. Kei is getting more exercise than she planned. She collides—silently, a trick which requires long practice—with the ground-floor stairwell door just in time to hear the elevator door—opening? or closing? There's no feed in the lobby. Mishima presses her ear to the door, but it's the recorder in the scarf that gives her the footsteps across the lobby, along with sharp, mostly incomprehensible spurts of monologue. She waits until she hears the front door open, and then slips out of the stairwell and sprints across the empty, undecorated lobby to peer out of the glass doors.

The two figures are well wrapped, scarves—including one matching the scarf Mishima put the recorder into—around their faces, hats on their heads despite the mild chill, bulky jackets obscuring their bodies. Mishima only gets a quick glimpse, because they walk straight into an incongruous tour group, a milling mini-crowd of foreigners whose guide seems to have led them very far indeed off the beaten path of Geneva attractions. Even with three feeds covering different portions of the street scrolling in her vision, Mishima can't track the movements of the two people she's interested in, and when the tour group is bundled onto a waiting bus, she can't be sure if her suspects— Halliday and an accomplice, who is she kidding?—board the bus with them or make their way into surrounding streets. She scans a few of the neighboring feeds and considers requesting a track on the bus but decides it would be too obtrusive. She's looking for evidence, which if it is to be found at all, can be found by going through public feeds later. She doesn't need to follow these people home: she knows where they live.

Instead of leaving the building, Mishima turns back to the stairs, keeping the feed that covers the entrance of the building in her vision as she treks up the fifteen flights. She reaches the top without seeing anyone leave the building and makes her way down the hallway with caution.

The door she's looking for is almost closed and definitely not locked. Mishima eases it open with her palm, stiletto in hand. Inch by slow inch, a tiny apartment is revealed, one of those micro-lofts that were favored some years back as housing for the indigent: a single room with two floors squeezed into one. Standing room is only available in the area covered by the swing of the door and the curtained-off corner shower; the rest of the apartment offers the choice of sitting, crawling, or lying flat. Even for a micro-loft, this place looks particularly bereft. The faint light from the hallway shows a cluster of takeaway containers decomposing around a small cooker on the bottom level, and on the top a few layers of blankets, or maybe a sleeping bag, but no mattress. Mishima is pushing the door toward forty-five degrees when it stops against a soft resistance; she leans in, blinking against the dimness. A cloth over-the-shoulder bag, in muted colors, lies on the floor blocking the door from opening all the way.

Mishima slips inside in a crouch, closing the door quietly behind her.

Once her eyes have adjusted to the dim light—there seems to be at least one window on the far wall, but it is blocked by partitions and possibly curtains—Mishima slides back into the arc of the door to stand up. She couldn't see anyone on the lower level, although some of the view was blocked by the partitions, so she scans the loft space.

And sees movement far in the back corner.

After staring for a while, Mishima decides she is looking at someone on hands and knees, facing away from her and searching through . . . something. It makes sense; the upper level of a micro-loft is traditionally used for storage, as well as sleeping and some forms of recreation.

Silently, Mishima sinks down to a crouch again. She takes some twine from her pocket and strings the door handle to the cooker. It won't keep anyone from leaving, but it will delay them and make some noise. Then she crawls into the lower level, heading for the shower.

Roz is on her way back to the compound when she gets a call from Maryam. No way she can be in Doha yet. "Everything okay?"

"Yes, fine," Maryam says. "I was just going over my notes, and—it didn't occur to me until now, but don't you think it's odd how few feeds they have?"

"It's taken some getting used to," Roz says, in a welcome-to-my-world tone. Then she thinks about it. "It's to be expected, with the remoteness and low population density, right?"

"Perhaps," Maryam admits. "But even given all that, it seemed extreme to me. So, I just counted."

"You counted all the feeds in this centenal?"

"I set a program to count, yes. They're significantly short of the number they're supposed to have by now per contract."

"But why would they . . ." Roz stops, shakes her head. Everyone here has been telling her how suspicious they are of Information. But still, breaking the contract in their first two years? How did they manage it without someone noticing? "Can you count for the other centenals in this government?"

"Already in process."

Mishima rises slowly within the narrow cubicle of the shower, gathers her breath, and edges the curtain open. The figure is in the same position: crouched over, about five feet away. Mishima can now see the person from the side, but she still can't make out many details except their general shape and their fixation on the items being searched or sorted. "We should talk," she says without raising her voice.

The intruder's head shoots up, knocking against the ceiling.

"I'm not—" Mishima starts, but the intruder has already scrambled around to make for the door. Mishima ducks down to the lower level and scurries along the path she cleared on her way over, then stands against the door, stiletto out. "Easy there," she says, as the person she is chasing skids to a panicked halt in front of her. "Relax. I just want to chat."

They end up sitting against the door, where the extra space above their heads makes the micro-loft slightly less claustrophobic. It only takes Mishima a few moments to decide that she's not going to need her stiletto; she twirls it around her fingers for a minute or two to drive the point home, then slides it into the easily accessible sheath across her belly. The person she is talking to is androgynous, trim, young but not very young, perhaps thirty (and when did thirty start looking young?), hair cut in an oblong sloping to a point just behind the right earlobe, clothing that wouldn't look out of place in the Heritage offices: semiprofessional with an edge. In fact . . .

"Haven't I seen you at headquarters?" Mishima asks.

The person—Mishima is leaning toward female—blushes, splotches of color on a face that looks wan and distressed. "You mean the Heritage headquarters? Yes, I work there."

"What are you doing here?"

"I could ask you the same question." The person's resolve crumbles quickly. "Can I ask whose side you're on?"

Mishima wants to shake her/him, offer a warning. That's not a serious question; it's a plea for friendship, solidarity, and the sharing of confidences, all too easily taken advantage of. But she is here to take advantage, so she answers, "Not Halliday's; I'll tell you that." She's fairly sure that's true, although she doubts it's exactly what this person was asking.

Of course it works. Her counterpart breathes out with relief and sags against the wall. "It's a travesty, what she's doing," the person says, and then looks down as though that was the wrong word. "Tragedy, really" comes out in a lower voice, not far from tears.

"I know!" Mishima agrees, with more force than necessary to try to keep the conversation productive. "I'm sure she's breaking all sorts of laws. How did you find this place?"

The person sniffs, and rubs the back of a hand under her/his nose. Then s/he unmutes her/his public Information and holds out a hand. "Syl."

The public Information tells Mishima it's spelled with a *y*, and offers no clue as to sex or gender. Mishima decides the ambiguity is intentional and stops trying to figure it out. Because she is thinking in Japanese, she has little need for gendered pronouns in any case ("the person" sounds much more natural in that language), but figuratively speaking, she switches to the plural. "Kei," she tells them. "I'm a consultant." She lowers her voice and adds, "I was at the café the other night." True, if misleading.

Syl's eyes widen, then fill, and they look away until they're back under control. "I was supposed to be there. I should have been there, but I was late; I didn't—" They bury their head in their hands. Mishima bites the insides of her cheeks and then reluctantly reaches out to rub the young person's shoulders. She startles when she gets an alert from Lucien, the desk officer she's been working with in Paris, but has to admit relief: Syl has been crying for two and a half minutes.

"Sorry," she tells the weeping person by her side. "I have to take this." Not entirely true, since the alert wasn't marked urgent, but Mishima has always had difficulty with so-called emotional productivity. She manages to open the door enough to squeeze out into the hallway without disturbing Syl and calls Lucien back.

"What's going on?"

"We've made progress here," Lucien says. "We may have enough intel for what we need to do."

"Enough intel?" Mishima asks. It's not a concept she believes in. "What is it, exactly, that you need to do?"

"You can start wrapping up in Geneva," Lucien says, as if this is something Mishima will be happy about.

"I'm in the middle of something," Mishima says. "I'm going to need more time."

A hesitation on the line. Mishima knows that Lucien is primarily a coordinator, relaying data and decisions back and forth; he probably isn't used to pushback. "Umm . . . We were thinking by tomorrow?"

"End of the week," Mishima answers.

Another pause. "You see, mission priorities—"

"—are decided in the field," Mishima finishes. "There's more work to be done here."

Lucien tries again. "The funding for this mission—"

"Do you want me to move into a cheaper hotel?" Mishima

snaps. She's not used to dealing with budget line items, not from Information. "I'm in the middle of an operation. I'll be in touch with further details in a few hours." She switches off the call, takes a deep breath, and slips inside the micro-loft again.

Syl has gotten themselves under control, which allows Mishima to justify stepping out like that. *Maybe that was all they needed, a little time alone.* She settles herself in, waits a few moments for intimacy to reestablish. "What's going on?" she asks finally.

Syl, who has clearly been waiting for the opportunity to unload on someone, tells her. They tell her about Si and Nat, Heritage mid-level strategist and techie, respectively (Mishima immediately identifies these as Silas Massey and Natalia Avellanera, whose faces stare from her memory even before she pulls up their files: both killed in the bombing). They worked against Halliday during the campaign for a head of state to replace Pressman. After Halliday won, Si and Nat and their crew were initially soothed by promises of continuity. (This reminds Mishima that all these factions belong to a government she actively dislikes, but hey, that's what micro-democracy is for. To each her own.) Then Halliday started making her influence known. (Blinking behind her listening façade, Mishima pulls up data and cross-refs to confirm what she's being told.)

"That's when secession talk started," Syl goes on, gulping against their tears. "The council came up with it as a threat, but then people started to get excited about the idea. And Halliday—she didn't want Pressman regaining power anyway, and she was pushing hard for secession no matter what Information did." The word *Information* is bathed in a mild, unthinking scorn.

"So, the anti-Halliday movement became an anti-secession movement?" Mishima suggests, when the pause lengthens.

Syl nods. "But the bombing . . . we never thought she'd do something like that against her own, against Heritage citizens!" They raise their eyes to Kei's, pleading for equal outrage.

"How do you know it was Halliday?" Mishima asks, wary of assumptions from a traumatized survivor. Then again, Syl found this place. Mishima takes her eyes off her interlocutor to cast a quick glance around the depressing apartment.

"Nat." Syl has to pause to stifle another sob. Again, Mishima sees the smiling face frozen on the news compilers, and this time it fully hits her, blowing past her shield of urgency, and now she's biting her cheeks not out of impatience, but to push back the tingle behind her eyes. "Nat set up some tracking systems on the head of state."

Mishima blinks in surprise. "She must have been good."

"She was!" Syl sniffs. "Halliday was very, very careful to set up an alibi for the time of the bombing." Suggestive, Mishima thinks, but inconclusive. "We knew something was going on; we just never expected . . . So, I was supposed to follow her that night and figure it out before I met up with them." Syl looks up, fierce. "I saw her face when they gave her the news about the bombing." Probably when Syl found out about it too. Mishima can imagine her horror and fury. "She wasn't surprised. She just . . . waited for them to tell her exactly who the victims were. And then she gave a little smile."

The two are silent for a moment.

"Were you able to follow her communications?" Mishima asks when she estimates it's been a decent interval. She's worried the question sounds too pointed, but Syl brightens noticeably.

"Comms were my job," they say. "It didn't help much; Halliday is very disciplined with her protocols, and of course I couldn't monitor the Inner Channel—"

"Inner Channel?"

Syl blinks at Kei. "The Inner Channel. You know. The way they told your centenal about the secession plan?"

"Oh," Mishima says. Syl's expression is incredulity, which is usually the one right before suspicion. "Oh, we call it the Deep Vein." She cringes inwardly, but Syl seems to accept it.

"We never managed to crack that; it's a totally different system. But I figured out a way to at least track when Halliday received Inner Channel communications, and statistically they tend to strengthen her stance on secession, so we concluded"— Syl droops again—"that most centenals are in favor."

That seems doubtful. Mishima wonders if there's any way to ask for the data without giving herself away, but is wary after her faux pas. And what is this Inner Channel? She imagines Halliday leaning toward the dangerous surface of a magic mirror, conferring with centenal governors around the world, and shakes it off.

"So, how did you get here?" Mishima asks.

"I was sort of . . . Nat's backup. For the tracking systems. When I saw an unscheduled trip into the city, I followed her." Syl's eyes come up again. "I want proof."

"And you saw her," Mishima says, putting together the yelled conversation she heard from the stairs.

Syl slumps. "She said it doesn't matter. No one will believe me and there's nothing to tie her to anything. I don't even know what she was doing here, what this place has to do with the bombing."

Mishima could tell her. "You were looking for evidence. There." Mishima waves a hand back into the darkness of the loft.

"I thought there had to be some reason why she came here. It's such a risk. But I only caught them as they were going out. They either cleaned up the evidence already, or there was nothing useful in the first place."

Mishima spends the next hour crouched beside Syl, going through the detritus in the back of the apartment: disposable towels, a toothbrush, and traces of chemicals that can be combined in dangerous ways. Syl brought a DNA analysis kit: not as sophisticated as the one Mishima carries, but since she prefers not to explain where she got that, she reserves it for any inconclusive results on Syl's, and none of those appear.

As they work, Mishima puts together her theory: they expected the bomber to make it at least to ForzaItalia, maybe to safety. His death in Switzerland has left some questions; Switzerland may not have been forthcoming about the sequence of events, and they're worried enough to come here and make sure no evidence was left behind. Odd that Halliday would come herself, but "Rolf," the fixer, is already in the wind. Maybe she likes thinking of herself as a hands-on leader.

Mishima wishes Syl good luck, gives her Kei's contact details, and leaves before they can remember to ask any questions about her involvement in this. From the stairs (Syl is taking the elevator) Mishima calls the LesPro officer in charge of the bombing investigation to tip him off to the apartment. Maybe they'll find something she didn't.

She is just pushing through the lobby doors when an urgent message sparks her nerves. **Report to Paris at earliest convenience. Geneva Hub crow available for this purpose.** It has Nougaz's security signature, which means Mishima's convenience has nothing to do with it. The Geneva Hub is on the way, so she stops to pick up the crow and moors it on top of her hotel. The message said nothing about whether she would be returning to Geneva, and Mishima packs the few items that are not already in her valise and checks out of the hotel before starting the short flight to Paris.

CHAPTER 23

With the debate over and the campaign running as smoothly as can be expected—all the candidates have gone back to their home jurisdictions, and the first polls after the debate show Fatima firmly in the lead—Roz returns her attention to the murder investigation. She pulls budget data from Djabal to confirm her suspicion on the infrastructure projects, but there are blank cells and other discrepancies in the forms that obscure where the money came from. It's odd, because the technique is different for each of the budget lines she's interested in, making it hard to trace. Either these are legitimate errors, although they seem too strategic to be that, or the fraud is far more sophisticated than she would expect from a spanking new government with no experience writing Information budgets. Roz sends a message to Djabal's centenal governor asking for clarification and another to the Information desk officer in charge of financial support to the DarFur government.

While she's waiting for a response, Roz convinces Maria the campaign doesn't require hourly poll updates and dragoons her into combing through feeds and records instead. She tells her to look for any evidence of foreigners with a grudge in any of the centenals the tsubame visited. It's not a negligible number of people. Djabal, in particular, is something of a crossroads, and although it is earlier than their initial time frame, the period just after the election saw an influx of outsiders, looking both to migrate into the new system and to provide technical assistance of all kinds.

The biggest problem, however, is not the number of individuals—it's still very low by Roz's data-crunching standards—but the fact that they don't know what to look for.

"Anything," Roz tells Maria. "Anything strange. Anything that makes you pause. Anything at all." A little later: "And let's cross-ref through everything."

That gives Roz the idea to cross-reference with foreign visitors around the other suspicious deaths in Mishima's file. It takes some time to put together, and while the search eliminates immigrants and regional travelers, a surprising number of the consulting firms appear on at least two of the lists.

"I hadn't realized assisting new governments was such a tightly linked industry," Roz tells Maria.

Maria shrugs. "Data is money."

They spend another three hours trying to nail down full itineraries for all the consultants that visited at least two of the centenals. It's an impossible task, although for the opposite reason from most of the impossible tasks she's had to handle in her career. Usually, Roz's job is to find ways of searching through too much data; here, there is too little, and the whole proposition seems unformed and useless. How can she prove or disprove anything when so many places and times are invisible to them?

"I don't know how they manage here with so little Information infrastructure," Roz says.

"We do all right," Maria answers, a hint of deprecating dryness in her tone. As if she's referring to something Roz should know about.

It takes Roz a few moments to work it out. When she says *we*, she's not talking about herself and the other inhabitants of DarFur, so . . . Roz remembers the centenal number on Maria's public Information and looks it up, but in the infinitesimal slice of time it takes to find the data she wants, she makes the connection. "You're from Privacy=Freedom," she says, raising her eyes from the projection to focus back on Maria's waiting gaze.

"I thought you knew." Maria laughs, her pale face reddening. "I assume that's the first thing anyone learns about me."

Privacy=Freedom, a radical Luddite government that prohibits feeds and electronic monitoring systems within its borders, holds only two centenals, one in California and one, where Roz has just learned Maria grew up, in Thailand. Roz remembers hearing that there is a substantial colony of Swedes there.

No escaping the awkward now. "So, how do you do it? Not having any Information . . ." It's hard to imagine, although this experience in DarFur is starting to get her close.

"We do have journalists, you know," Maria says. She sounds amused. "Everyone thinks we're these extreme, anti-technology renegades. But we use all kinds of technology as long as it's not invasive, and there's nothing extreme about not wanting every moment of your life recorded from multiple angles." That's an exaggeration, but Roz keeps her mouth closed instead of saying so. "*And* it's not like we're not allowed to use content and Information from outside." That does make it sound different, if creepy: Privacy=Freedom citizens spying on the rest of the micro-democratic world without letting them peep back.

"Sure, but . . ." Roz thinks about everything she uses Information for, all the time. "If you're driving, and you come to an intersection, how do you know what vehicles might be approaching from either side?"

"Well, we try not to design blind intersections," Maria says. "And we use mirrors."

Mirrors! Ingenious. "You must have found it much easier than we did when Information went out during the elections,"

Roz says, trying to offer Maria's odd cult some credit. "If you even noticed, that is."

"Of course we noticed." Maria is frowning at the memory. "As I said, we do use Information from elsewhere, and we allow temporary feeds to be constructed during election periods, for vote monitoring. It was disturbing, although I suppose it didn't disrupt our daily lives as much as it did in most places."

"And what about stuff like this?" Roz asks. "Criminal investigations?"

"I guess you could say we do it the old-fashioned way? Ask around, look for physical evidence, um . . . I don't know, really. Not my area of expertise."

"Mine either," hmphs Roz, and gets back to work.

M ishima." Nougaz comes forward to greet her with bisous when Mishima walks into her office. "Nice to have you back in Paris." A reminder that Nougaz tried to recruit her for this hub, is probably still trying. "You did great work in Geneva."

"Am I done there, then?" Mishima asks. She decides to pretend this is another consultancy job: no reason for her to care. Just do what she's told.

"We got what we needed," Nougaz says. "Écoute: the secession is, or has become, a power play on the part of Halliday, right?"

She's pleased with herself, Mishima notes. "That's certainly what it is for Halliday. The others may have thought they were doing it for Pressman. A few may even have believed it was the best move for the government. But Halliday's not an ideologue."

"Yes, yes." Nougaz waves her hand dismissively. "Thanks to your intel, we were able to open private-side negotiations with Halliday. She will close off any discussion of secession."

Mishima waits, but clearly she's supposed to ask. "In exchange for?"

Nougaz smiles. "Power."

This time, Mishima waits as long as it takes.

"We will take the council off her hands," Nougaz says. "Including Pressman."

Interesting. "So, we get the criminals we wanted . . ."

"And Halliday gets free rein as the head of state she already is in name."

Very neat indeed. "What else?"

Nougaz's eyebrows go up but her smile widens: she's pleased that Mishima saw something was missing. "We've thrown in the five-year term for Supermajority."

"Policy1st isn't going to like that. Especially if they find out how it happened." Mishima is always careful not to sound like she's taking Policy1st's side, seeing as Ken used to work there, but Nougaz is even more exposed on that count.

Nougaz shrugs. "Ten years is too long between elections; people lose interest, forget what they're voting for, ignore politics." *Ignore us,* Mishima thinks. "It was inevitable. This way, we get something in exchange for what we were going to do eventually anyway. And while, yes, it would be nice to wait a bit longer, we're stretched too thin with the K-stan war. The secession threat is starting to leak, and we can't afford to be dealing with two global crises now."

"All that makes sense," Mishima says, because it does, whether or not she personally agrees with it. "I do have to bring up something that I've been working on."

"You've been working on something quietly?" Nougaz asks, but without anger; she likes initiative.

"I've been working on finding the bomber, per my mandate," Mishima answers. "What I've been quiet about is the direction the investigation is pointing, because it's unsubstantiated."

So far. "But I am now almost sure that it will lead to Head of State Halliday."

Nougaz's eyebrows go up. "She bombed her own people? Her own citizens, her own government staff?" They come down again. "Is this the evidence speaking or that narrative disorder of yours?"

Mishima has heard less-direct versions of this question too many times to bristle at it. At least Nougaz says what she's thinking. Still, she lets some of the weariness into her voice as she explains. "It's not *either* evidence *or* narrative disorder. The narrative disorder works from the evidence. As I said, I'm not yet willing to stake my reputation on Halliday as the culprit. But the data is highly suggestive." Nougaz turns to the window to consider, and Mishima goes on. "The very fact that Halliday would take that deal indicates a level of pathology—"

"It indicates a desire for power," Nougaz says. "A pathology all leaders share. Or almost all. And we're giving her what she wants."

"You think she won't find something new to want?"

"I think that knowing she's behind the bombing gives us the means to take away everything she has if we want to."

Mishima starts to pace. "So, you think you can control her. I'm saying I don't think she's entirely rational. She's not someone I would want as head of state."

"We didn't put her there," Nougaz points out. "She was elected through the representative mechanism of her government."

"But with this deal you're making her more powerful. And it means you're going to have to keep dealing with her."

"This is what we do. We deal with the dangerous, sociopathic, power-hungry individuals the people elect."

Mishima paces in silence for a few laps, strategizing.

"Did you ever figure out how Heritage communicated internally about the secession?"

Nougaz blinks, a substantial victory, and then flutters her hand dismissively. "The cryptographers and techies were working on it. I'm not sure what the status is, but I can check if you like."

"They're looking in the wrong place," Mishima says, battening down her uncertainty for battle. "It's not a code; it's some other method, an entirely different system. My most recent informant called it the Inner Channel, and there was mention in one of my recordings of a 'comms pipeline.'" Nougaz's interest sharpens visibly. "One which might include some clandestine intel."

"And Halliday was part of this discussion?"

"She shut it down," Mishima replies, gauging the older woman's reaction. "She wanted no talk about the comms and especially not of the intel, even in a high-level gathering that included open consideration of extraditing Pressman."

"I see," Nougaz says, and turns back to the window. Mishima looks for a reflection to get even a sense of what Nougaz's face is showing, but sees only slate rows of Parisian roofs. She decides to press her advantage.

"I'd like to stay in Geneva a little longer."

There is a pause, but Mishima is not sure whether it is a reaction to her statement or because Nougaz is still contemplating illicit intel streams. "I'm not sure what your usefulness is at this point . . ."

"At least until the deal is actually complete," Mishima says, knowing this will be a good pressure point. No one at Information wants to be left without an intelligence asset in place if something goes wrong. "Make sure she's managing the retreat from secession and getting the rest of the government on board with it. Dig further into this comms issue. And if I can prove her responsibility for the bombing, you'll have that in your arsenal."

Nougaz turns back to the room, lips pursed. "Isn't your contact already shaky? It seems to me you could follow the progress on the deal from here, or Saigon if you prefer."

It's a low blow, because Mishima would very much prefer Saigon. "Give me a few more days to see if I can find something concrete on Halliday"—because, Mishima is realizing, she's not just consulting on this one; she wants to nail that creep—"and I can monitor implementation of the deal at the same time."

Nougaz holds out one more moment. "Fine. But don't push too hard on your contact. In fact, leave the comms issue for the techies to deal with. Just get what you can on Halliday. You're right. We may need it."

What about," Roz says half an hour later, as if the conversation had never lapsed, "accidents?"

"You mean to assign blame?" Maria asks, still focused on her work.

"No, like situations where something happened, and it doesn't really matter, but you're not sure what you remember." Maria looks up from her eye-level projections, confused. "Like this: I was walking with an elderly acquaintance, in Durban, and he stumbled and fell. He was fine but a little banged up, and the more I thought about it, the less I could remember exactly what happened. Did I look away? Should I have been holding his arm? Was it my fault?"

"And you looked up the feed."

"All six of them, actually. It wasn't a big deal but . . . I just remember feeling sorry for people without Information."

"Only the ones with a conscience," Maria puts in drily. "But to your point." She arranges her thoughts. "We live the way we do because we believe in privacy, yes? But working outside, as I do, it leads one to develop a philosophy." Roz thinks how odd it is to refer to the entirety of the Informational world as "outside." "Can we state as a given that there is no single objective truth?" Maria asks. Roz nods easily: this is clear. "The problem with feeds, beyond all the obvious problems, I mean, is that they give us the illusion of a perfect truth, incontrovertible evidence, a flat, singular version of history. They are too easy to rely on, to believe in." She lightens her words with a smile and a half-shrug. "I practice sustaining my disbelief in objective, documentable truth."

Roz can think of many examples to counteract this—they are hoping, for one, to find incontrovertible evidence of murder, and maybe corruption, and she is not going to buy in to a universe where the bad guys both did and did not kill the governor—but she is intrigued by the larger point and disinclined to nitpick. Besides, it brings them to another question that Roz has been wanting to ask.

"What about when there is an injustice by someone in a position of authority?" Roz asks.

"That," Maria answers, "is an argument. But we have tried to arrange our system to give the benefit of the doubt to those who have less power. Besides, you and I know well enough that recording everything is not exactly a guarantee against abuses by people in authority."

True enough.

"And you like living there?" Roz still finds it hard to imagine.

"Yes. I like having my privacy. Besides, my family is there."

"You have family?"

"Yes, my partner and three children." Maria projects a quick succession of pictures. "One of the reasons I still vote for Privacy=Freedom is so that I can choose whom to show those pictures to."

264 · MALKA OLDER

Roz is still managing a slight but unmissable plunge in the gut. She finds herself estimating Maria's age, subtracting the guessed age of her oldest child: checking for data about a cutoff date.

"Tough to do this work with a family," she says, and changes the subject. "Why do you work for Information, anyway? If you believe in privacy, I mean, and no objective truth."

Maria flashes her a wink and a grin. "Guilty pleasure."

K ei stays out of Deepal's way as much as possible, prowling the halls and working in the canteen or in the various smaller coffee break areas around the building. It is closer to Mishima's preferred work style anyway and leaves her free to keep close tabs on the council and other upper leadership positions.

She also cultivates Syl. Having confirmed most of their story, she wants as much access to the Halliday-tracker as possible, and evaluates the best approach for getting it. Unfortunately, telling them the full truth is not an option. One would think it was obvious that Information would gather its intel in any way possible, including human sources, but for some reason, it's harder to accept a spy than a clandestine recorder (there have been extensive studies on the question). As such, the existence, even more than the identity, of Information's intelligence assets remains tightly embargoed.

So, Kei gives Syl a fictional version of the truth, hurriedly backed up by a team in Doha (Mishima has decided to get a little distance from Paris in this operation): she comes from a far-flung Heritage centenal (in Honiara, the farthest one they could find), dispatched by her colleagues out of concern for Halliday's decisions and to determine whether it would be wise to—Kei lowers her tone to a whisper—secede from the secession.

Mishima therefore receives two warnings when the grindstones finally begin to turn. Syl reaches out to her early one morning, telling her that Halliday has taken her crow on an unscheduled trip, headed east. Kei leaves an anodyne, previously agreed-upon message in one of the popular open-access plazas for Lucien to find, and haunts the upper reaches of the building where the council members are usually found, and so she almost immediately gets wind of their sudden excitement, flutterings from office to office, repeated update checks as they crisscross the corridors. The excitement seems to have a positive spin, which is a smart move on Halliday's part. Syl let her follow the progress of the state crow in real time, and Mishima estimates how she, were she in Halliday's duplicitous position, would time it. Mere seconds before the time she had marked, the agitation among the council reaches the boiling point, and they start to bubble toward the elevator, hair variously combed over or patted smooth, jackets adjusted, shirt panels centered.

Mishima, as usual, takes the stairs, wondering what pretense Halliday gave to get them out of the building. Unlike William Pressman, the council members are not (yet) wanted for arrest, and many of them regularly cross non-Heritage centenals every day, so they are not overly cautious. Once they are out of the building, it is only a few steps to the favored press conference location in front of the lake, with the jet d'eau picturesque in the background. They are still in Heritage territory, but the Heritage head of state has given permission, and Information security officers arrest them neatly: few struggles, no blood, and many loud, ineffectual protests. It will be on all the news compilers in seconds, and Mishima checks the crow: yes, it has landed in the Heritage centenal near Zurich, where William Pressman has been living for the past two years. She is not surprised that Halliday wanted to attend that arrest personally.

CHAPTER 24

With secession off the table, there's no need for Kei's report and no excuse for Mishima to stay in Geneva. She says a careful good-bye to Deepal, trying to thank him and convey that she understands his anger and is not offended by it without further upsetting him. She's not sure she manages it. Before she leaves, and then at greater length on the flight home, Mishima debates whether to send Syl the audio she recorded from the café. There are easy ways to scrub the identifying data; that's not what she's worried about. It seems like such a gift: to know what Syl's loved ones were laughing and arguing about in their last moments. But it might not work that way. It might exacerbate Syl's already-pounding survivor's guilt, obsess her further with the events of that night. Mishima lands in Saigon still unsure.

Ken is used to Mishima's post-deployment routine by now and is happy enough to spend every non-working, non-sleeping hour immersed in content with her. When she first arrives, she's too tired to even play through an interactive, so they watch old films and newer vids and get bánh mì and bánh xèo home-delivered. After six hours, she starts telling him bits and pieces about what happened; he listens carefully, knowing he'll need to remember the cast of characters for when she gets into the longer, more painful stories. By day two, she restarts her speedblading routine, and by that night, when he gets home from work (takeout in hand), she's ready for more active escapism. They spend the night playing through *TwinSpin*. Ken stumbles through work the next day, which fortunately is Friday, and that night, they take it easy again, curling up to rewatch the entire four-season run of *Nick Knack*. Saturday, they manage to get out for a walk before burrowing in again. Sunday is two weeks from when they met up in Geneva, and they sit together, Ken squirming and Mishima still, as Mishima runs her diagnostic.

The problem with the foreign consultants is that none of them have coincided with the tsubame during the period they're looking at. Roz wonders if they're going to have to reassess the mechanic's story or go back to investigating locals. She's considering calling each of the consultants personally, but there are a lot of them.

She takes a quick break to check in on the K-stan situation. Since Charles left, Roz has been monitoring it more closely. She had gotten inured to the sporadic reports of violence; having switched her settings to prioritize longitudinal animations, she can see the front creeping closer to the micro-democratic centenals. The confrontations have become both more frequent and deadlier. As an exercise, she applies the same visualizations to the fighting around Kas, but the data is too sparse to discern a pattern.

The Djabal centenal finance manager wrote back to her after a day's delay with many apologies for the mistakes in accounting, claiming something better would be sent to her soon. Roz is still waiting. The desk officer was equally contrite and unhelpful, baffled as to how he could have missed it or what could have gone wrong.

Here, at least, Roz has some idea where to look. She pulls the numbers for the Information assistance package on accession. It's tricky, because those budgets are government-wide, but she can crunch the line-item numbers for required Information infrastructure with the agreements by centenal and then subtract the cost of the feeds that actually exist. It doesn't come out to exactly the same number as the infrastructure costs minus the official budget, but it's pretty close. Roz leans back, tapping her fingers. Now she knows why that meeting in Djabal went long and Al-Jabali was late for their visit. The meeting was *about* their visit, about how to hide or at least distract from all this expensive infrastructure funded with Information money. Roz shakes her head. A SVAT mission isn't an audit; they probably wouldn't even have noticed.

What was funded here in Kas? she wonders. The evaporation plant is pre-Information era. Maybe they are planning to use the money on electricity?

Why hasn't Suleyman mentioned it in all their talk about Information and progress and trust?

Disgusted, Roz gets up and begins to pace.

She calls Maryam and sends her the data with the relevant numbers highlighted and crunched. Maryam stares at it for a while. "This wasn't a mistake. They deliberately moved the budget. How did we not catch this?"

"We weren't paying attention?" Roz suggests with a shrug. She tells Maryam about the desk officer.

"It's very strange," Maryam answers. "I'll see if I can find out anything about headquarters coverage of that area."

"While you're at it, see if you can find anything similar anywhere else. I'd start with ToujoursTchad."

Roz hangs up, and the numbers she had been working with reemerge on her workspace projection. It is satisfying to see them fit so neatly, but it tells her nothing about who killed Al-Jabali or why.

Mishima has been in Saigon long enough to begin to feel frustrated with her content binge, which means it's time to get back to work. That's when she gets a message (forwarded through Kei's contacts) from Syl: Deepal has disappeared.

"What do you mean, *disappeared*?" Mishima is stricken with guilt: if something has happened to Deepal, it is almost certainly her fault.

"I don't know. His officemate told me—"

"Xandra?"

"No, Loïc. He came into work as usual this morning and then . . . someone came to get him, around ten."

"Who?"

"Loïc didn't know. At first, he thought it was just someone calling him for an impromptu meeting. He said Deepal seemed surprised but not worried. But when Deepal didn't come back, he started to think maybe the guy was security. And then they came back for his workspace."

Oh, that is not a good sign. "And nothing from Deepal since?"

"Nothing. We've been calling, pinging. He's not logged on anywhere." Syl is gulping air, close to panic, and Mishima tries to make her tone comforting.

"No need to keep calling; he'll get in touch with you when he can." And no need to compromise yourself any more than you already have.

Deepal was close to breaking even before she left; they could tap him with a feather, threaten his parking privileges, and he'd give her up. Mishima paces, kneads her guilt, considers various courses of action, but before she can decide on anything, Syl calls her back.

"He messaged me!" If anything, they're hyperventilating more than before. "Deepal, he got in touch!"

"Is he all right?"

"I don't know. The message is for you."

Mishima's stops pacing, hands icy.

"The message says, 'Tell Kei she should go to the Governor's Ball ready.'"

Ready. That's not a problem. "But where is he? Where did he send the message from?"

"I don't know," Syl says, frustrated. "He hasn't been back to his office. The message came through the Inner Channel. What can it mean? Why would you go to the Governor's Ball?"

"It's a code we worked out before," Mishima says absently. "Don't worry. But . . ." She swallows her questions. She's still not ready to let Syl know she has no idea how this Inner Channel works. "Thank you, Syl. Keep your head down." Mishima signs off and calls Nejime. Four hours and one intense shopping session later, she's on a flight for Bamako, the site of this year's Governor's Ball.

CHAPTER 25

The Governor's Ball is a ceremony to honor centenal governors who have won awards for their achievements, but it's also a shiny gala that gets lots of attention from the news compilers. The heads of state from major governments typically attend, while those from smaller ones angle for invitations. Roz watches for the clothes and out of a twitch of professional curiosity about how world leaders use these partly social, largely performative events to further their goals. Seeing what groups people huddle into can be quite illuminating. But mainly, she watches for the clothes, and because she's slightly embarrassed about this, she holes up in her stifling hut to do so.

One of the first couples she sees is the last one she wants to be reminded of. Vera is wearing a blue-and-yellow dress printed with a traditional motif that, Information notes, is an adaptation of a popular pattern originating in a Policy1st centenal in what was formerly the Central African Republic, not far from Vera's birthplace in Kivu. Nougaz, thin and elongated in a way Roz has never found attractive, makes the most of it with a long, trailing black skirt, a strapless white top with a black bow at her breastbone, and a black drape flowing from one shoulder: a play on a tuxedo. She looks pretty great. Roz thinks she's going to gag.

Everyone in Roz's circle has known that Vera and Nougaz are together for at least three months, but this is the first time they've appeared together in public. Information grunts are working overtime to make sure to link every vid of them to the elaborate "Transparency Measures" document Nougaz has been circulating. It begins: "To protect against the appearance of impropriety . . ." and Roz actually did gag the first time she read it. She spends too much time trying to figure out whether she would be as angry about this if it didn't involve her friend getting dumped. Not *as* angry, obviously, but she's pretty sure she would still hate it. Most of the world seems to think they are the perfect power couple.

"She's too old for you," Roz says, and sends the message to Maryam. She would be worried about bringing it back up, but she's positive Maryam is watching the gala.

There's a buzz of excitement, and the projection cuts quickly to Jalyna Ness, a vedette and minor minister for StarLight, a celebrity-based government inexplicably in the top thirty. Her skimpy one-shoulder dress is a wrinkly patchwork of multicolored flesh swatches—no, it's completely made up of animatronic hands, gripping her breasts, rubbing her hips, tapping her ribs, stroking her thighs. Roz squints, unwillingly fascinated in her attempt to figure out whether the hands are attached at the wrists to some sort of shift or free-flowing under a minimum-coverage algorithm. Jalyna strikes a pose, the crowd applauds, and two tiny hands perched like wings on the clasped-finger shoulder strap clap along.

As the coverage continues, Roz sees the other glamorous global power couple: Halliday and her husband, whatshisname. Funny that they would show up so soon after Pressman's arrest—it looks a bit like gloating. Halliday must be trying to normalize the situation. It's close, but Roz decides she prefers Nougaz and Vera.

．　．　．

Mishima is both impressed by the party and disgusted by the amount of money Information must have spent on it. The venue is a spectacular new floating ballroom that flows past the city on the Niger, open to the warm air. Sheer white cotton curtains floating on graphene nanorods frame the views of a gently shaded sunset over the river and, as they continue downstream, the sand-colored skyscrapers of Bamako. There are two different bands at opposite corners of the barge, the music separated by some sophisticated air-current work that also cools the dance floors, and plates with yassa chicken, fried tilapia, and spicy vegetables pre-cut into bite-sized pieces are arranged on hovering tables.

A floating, open-air barge presents some difficulty for engineering adequate vid coverage. Mishima, linked in to the security network, plays through their feeds in front of her left eye, and they're pretty gappy. She dips her glass in the champagne fountain long enough to give the impression that she's been drinking, and scans the ballroom with her own eyes. She spots Johnny Fabré, the still-head of state for Liberty, hitting on some unfortunately impressionable young women in a corner; a cluster of photographers surrounding the StarLight representative, whose name Mishima refuses to learn; and Gerardo Vasconcielos chatting with Penelope Anoushiravani, the striking head of state for SavePlanet, wearing a dress sewn from fish scales and brilliant green breadfruit leaves.

The thickest crowd of hangers-on, though, is glomming around Valérie Nougaz and Vera Kubugli. The chusma is packed so densely that Mishima barely gets a glimpse of their contrasting dresses. She keeps her distance; Nougaz certainly has the clearance to know she's here if she looked, and has the cool not to blow her cover even if she didn't, but there's no sense in taking any chances. Mishima's not here for them.

Her target is not far away, and attracting a few limpets of her own, although not nearly as many as the Information-Policy1st power coupling. Cynthia Halliday is wearing something pink and froufy, which must appeal to some demographic that doesn't include Mishima, because she'd surely wear nothing that had not been vetted through at least five focus groups. For the moment, she is standing quietly with her husband and a few Heritage governors, but as Mishima watches, she and her husband step away from them and begin to mingle.

Roz is reading Maryam's response, "Even Vera's not old enough for her," when she hears a knock on the door. Hurriedly she shuts down her projection, the sudden quiet seeming loud after the chatter of the party, and stands up to open it.

"Sorry to bother you," Maria says, peering into her hut in confusion. "I thought . . . I heard you watching the gala, and since I was watching it in my hut, I thought, well, it's much more fun to watch together . . ."

By that point, Roz has ushered her in and popped the projection back up.

Halliday has moved into a cluster that includes both Mighty Vs, Nougaz (another V, now that Mishima thinks about it), a couple of governors (from Bolivia and Sarawak, according to their public Information), and a mid-level Information administrator who was one of the judges this year. Veena Rasmussen has a micro-garden grown on her shaved scalp, trailing vines and flowers over her bare shoulders and down her back. Seems like a lot of work for a global-level politician to manage, but Mishima supposes it speaks to her environmental commitment. Beside her, her husband has a single marigold growing out above his ear.

Mishima positions herself next to a dessert island that puts Vera's headdress between her and Halliday, where she can observe most of Halliday's face without being completely visible herself. For further cover, she selects and starts eating a choux cream, very slowly. She is suddenly distracted by something beyond her targets: a face in the crowd, lighting up with recognition. Malakal, and he's turning to move toward her. Even before she can arrange her face to warn him off, he stops, considers her posture, her solitude in the midst of a ballroom. She shoots him the briefest look of glowering eyebrows, and before her expression has softened back into blandness, he has already turned away to make conversation with the person next to him.

Mishima also turns, though more subtly in case anyone has noticed their exchange of glances. She refocuses on the group she is observing. Why is Halliday here? Is she trying to renegotiate with Nougaz? She catches a look Nougaz gives Vera; it's the warmest expression Mishima's ever seen on the older woman's face. Mishima has a somewhat more nuanced reaction to Nougaz's affair with Vera Kubugli than Roz does. Mishima herself initiated a relationship with a government operative while she worked for Information; she can hardly complain that someone else does. Still, both Mishima and Ken quit their jobs pretty soon after hooking up. She imagines this must get awkward sometimes.

Case in point: Halliday is burbling on about one of the honorees and manages to bring the conversation around to the new five-year Supermajority limit. "I'm sure we would have supported it even when we were in charge," she gushes, turning to her husband for agreement. "Elections bring such energy into politics."

Mishima can't see Vera's face, but she imagines she's enough of a politician to keep it unreadable. Halliday's not done, though. "You know," she says, turning to the Bolivian, "they're making it out in the press that we demanded that, but"—with a coquettish glance at Nougaz—"it's what Information wanted. They get so much relevance from elections. We just gave them a convenient excuse." She bats her patterned eyelashes, built by a new crystal-forming mascara that knits a swatch of black lace above each eye.

What is she doing? Mishima wonders. Nougaz is excellent at muting her reactions, but Mishima is very close to her, and that dress isn't doing her any favors, either. The contrast with the white top makes the flush of red more noticeable as it spreads up her thin chest to her throat. *Why would she antagonize Nougaz?*

"Of course," Halliday goes on. "It's only right." A wobbly laugh as though she's drunk, although Mishima doesn't think she is. "It should be a short term. It's unbelievable that you people won it! Only in a perfect storm."

The governors pull back, faces frozen in the shock and mortification of watching a social situation go badly wrong. Nougaz looks like she's searching for words; she must be out of practice with street fights. Vera is unfazed. "A perfect storm of criminal corruption," she says without ire.

Halliday throws back her head and laughs, reaches across Nougaz to clap Vera on the shoulder, the furbelows on her dress swinging dangerously close to Nougaz's drink and appalled face. "Nice one," she says, still chuckling. "Anyway"—moving back to include the rest of the group—"you can see why I might not trust Information."

Something is about to happen. Mishima steps into the outer orbit of the elite group, standing just behind the gap between Halliday and Nougaz, and waits.

. . .

Within an hour, Amran and Minzhe are sitting on the floor of Roz's hut along with Maria, Maryam has given up on the messaging and projected in herself, and the other Maryam, Halima's servant, is standing in the doorway, refusing all requests to come in and get comfortable. When the assassination attempt occurs, none of them notice a thing.

Even Mishima, who is waiting for it, almost misses it.

"Oh, sorry!" Halliday jostles half the champagne out of a glass while taking two from the waiter. "How terribly clumsy of me!"

Mishima's eyes narrow: apologies and self-deprecation seem out of character.

"Here, take this one." She puts the half-empty flute back on the tray, reaches around for another one with her left, nearly dipping herself in the glass in her right hand in the process. "Here you go!" Halliday beams, handing the two flutes to Vera and Nougaz.

It's ridiculous, a farce. Doesn't every woman learn never to drink from something they've been handed by anyone they don't trust with their life? But Vera and Nougaz are exchanging amused glances. Maybe they're drunk already? Lulled by the setting?

They didn't see what Mishima saw: a bit of unidentifiable frippery from Halliday's dress, a lacy drawstring or decorative bow, dissolving into a champagne glass.

She is no longer sure which glass it was, although she suspects the one now approaching Nougaz's mouth. No time for a replay. Mishima steps in authoritatively, says, "Thank you so much," as she takes the champagne flutes from the startled luminaries, and walks away to outraged clacking.

Nougaz's measured tones cut across them: "I'm sure it's

standard procedure for something. Come on, Vera, let's get another drink."

Mishima walks quickly, ready to toss a glass in Halliday's face if she grabs her from behind, keeping the flutes as even as she can, watching the level so they don't spill over, watching the stems in case they start to disintegrate on her, watching her path for obstacles and tipsy partygoers.

She walks straight to Malakal, puts the glasses into his outstretched hands. "Thorough analysis. Probably poison, or acid." Or she has just made a fool of herself for nothing.

She turns without waiting for his response and walks back, faster this time. The two governors are sharing an uncomfortable laugh, the Information administrator is blinking frantically in an effort to figure out what went wrong, Veena and her husband have taken the hint and wandered off. Mishima scans rapidly, spinning a quarter-circle, and finds Nougaz and Vera, drinkless, in another tight group; as she looks, Nougaz's cold eyes rise to meet Mishima's and then return to Vera. Mishima turns, turns again. She doesn't see Halliday anywhere.

But wait—something catches her attention. Not what she was looking for, but—she snaps her head back and sees it, him: Halliday's husband, talking to yet another small group, this one mostly adoring governors from small governments. Mishima edges toward him, taps him on the shoulder.

"Excuse me, I have an urgent message for the Heritage Head of State," Mishima tells him. "Do you know where she went?"

"Restroom," he says amiably, nodding his head at a narrow corridor along the back of the boat. Mishima sprints through the crowd, dodging trays and outflung elbows, and speeds down the row of doors, pulling open the unlocked ones and tapping at those that are locked.

"Have any vehicles of any kind left the barge?" she asks the air.

A brief pause that suggests an unwelcome answer, and then: "A tsubame took off sixty-three seconds ago."

"I thought the airspace was closed above this thing!"

"It was, but . . ." Fumbling, then the security commander cuts in over the switchboard.

"We were focused on security threats from outside," he reports. "We didn't have a protocol for vessels leaving from within the cordon. As far as we knew, guests could leave any time they wanted."

Mishima privately concedes that's a fair point. "So, she had the tsubame stashed somewhere on the barge? Are you tracking it?"

"Working on that right now," the commander says shortly. Mishima shakes her head, then stops, remembering something. She calls Syl, only to learn that the tracker died five minutes earlier. "It's tied into her head-of-state identity," Syl tells her. "It looks like she severed all connection with that and is working with her personal passwords."

Mishima goes back to the party to interrogate the husband. Looks like he got ditched, so she's not hoping for much. It will be an annoying interview, if not outright infuriating. She looks forward to catching up with Malakal, because that's going to be the best part of this ridiculous gala.

CHAPTER 26

Mishima is scheduled onto one of the new long-haul public transportation crows for her return to Saigon. There has been a push to use the same principles as public transportation—algorithmic optimization of pickups and drop-offs—for distance travel, but it turns out the algorithms are much trickier to make commercially viable. The crow, even kitted for twenty-five passengers, is more comfortable than economy class on an airplane; but then, it has to be, because it's substantially slower. There are other disadvantages, too. When Nejime decides she wants to see Mishima in Doha before she goes home, she can convince the pilot to drop her off there at minimal inconvenience to the other passengers (who look daggers at Mishima nonetheless).

"Deepal was released," Mishima says as soon as she gets in the room with Nejime, not even waiting for the door to close. "Do you have any news on his status?" She hasn't wanted to contact him directly. He would be perfectly justified in blaming her.

"He's fine," Nejime says. "I don't think they did much to him, but he certainly wasn't happy. However, you should know that he denied sending you any message while he was being held."

"He denied it?" *It didn't happen?* Just for a moment, Mishima questions her memory; it does seem terribly unlikely, that cryptic message from an unwilling operative. Could she have invented it out of guilt and narrative need? But no, she has the recording of the conversation with Syl. "Do you think my informant invented the message?"

"Either that or it was sent by somebody else, somebody close to Halliday who disagreed with her more drastic methods." An image of Halliday's impeccable aide Leticia flashes into Mishima's mind, emotional backstory already weaving itself, but she pushes it away. She doesn't want to jump to any narratives right now. "We are trying to find out, but so far, no one will admit to knowing about this comms pipeline. For the moment, we're trying to crack it from the outside."

Mishima nods, still trying to quiet the whirling proto-plots in her head.

"And thank you for what you did in Bamako." It's odd, being thanked for doing her job in a way that happened to save someone's life. "She should never have been able to get that close."

"Was it poison?"

"Yes."

"Traceable?"

"Borderline. We probably would have noticed it wasn't a natural death, but could she have known we have that technology? Unclear." Was Halliday trying to kill someone and get away with it, or was she always planning to disappear?

"Did you figure out whose glass it was?"

"The poison was meant for Valérie," Nejime says. "I do wonder what it was that made her, particularly, the target of Halliday's fury." Her face is unreadable. Mishima had always imagined that Nougaz and Nejime's mild rivalry at work carried through to the rest of their lives, respectfully disagreeing from a distance, but maybe they are closer than she thought. "Unfortunately, and through no fault of yours," Nejime goes on, "we don't know where Halliday is."

"Dangerous," Mishima agrees.

"Heritage is floundering."

282 • MALKA OLDER

"Not my problem." Mishima is very sure about that. If entitled former Supermajority governments elect punk-ass self-serving sociopaths as their leaders, picking up the pieces is not Mishima's job.

Nejime smiles indulgently. "I suppose not. We do have something else for you if you're up for it."

Mishima wonders if that last clause is a reference to her current condition. She wouldn't put it past them to have sniffed that out.

"The war in central Asia is getting out of hand," Nejime goes on, and Mishima focuses. *Dealing with war, now that's a job.* "We need to get China to align with us on it—China the sovereign nation, not 1China centenals."

"I understand." 1China is commercially powerful and popular enough to be consistently among the top ten global governments, but scattered and unsophisticated in geopolitical thinking beyond its own borders (within its borders, the government has a very sharp analysis indeed). They also haven't invested much in military might, with China the country to back them up. The nation, while smaller than it used to be, is entrenched, secretive, mighty, and jealously guarded.

"We'd like to broker a deal with them. Ideally, this would include their assistance in ending the war without—and this is paramount—without any harm to the centenals that lie between China and the combatants."

Mishima nods again; the worst-case scenario that has been floating around in the Information plazas has China, Kyrgyzstan, and Kazakhstan battling it out on top of the microdemocracy territory that is currently a buffer zone.

"There's also a less-immediate goal, although we think that now is the best time for it, with that war as a reminder of our . . . interconnectedness. We'd like to initiate greater mutual engagement with null states, starting with China." Nejime runs through a sketch of the current ideas for improving the standing treaties with China. "Of course, all of this is just a draft until we have a better idea what their interests and thresholds are." Weighty pause. "Unfortunately, we have a dearth of intel from China right now."

Uh-oh.

"Our operative there was sent to the northwestern border to monitor fighting, and was killed in a mortar attack."

"Kazakhstan shelled China?" Mishima is sure she would have noticed if that happened.

"He was in Kazakhstan at the time, on some kind of diplomatic mission." Even Nejime, famously cold-blooded, looks grim.

"It was a setup."

"We don't have any evidence one way or another, but the assignment does seem unusual, given his profile."

"So, his cover may or may not have been blown." Nejime nods. "If it was, will China guess that we're likely to send in another agent?"

"It's possible. Although I have to say"—holding Mishima's gaze—"if they knew, it's unlikely they would have let him be killed without getting everything they could out of him first."

Mishima shuts that away from her mind. "And there was no evidence of that?"

"None. But we have no conclusive evidence he wasn't tortured. The body was . . . not in a condition to be examined."

"And if I go"—who is she kidding? They both know she's hooked—"you need me to find out everything I can and then negotiate a deal? I start as a spy and turn into a diplomat? You think they'll listen to me at that point?"

"We think they will if you're saying what they want to hear. But use your judgment: if you don't think they'll buy it, get out."

They're talking as if it's already decided. "Why me?"

Mishima asks. "You must have people who have been immersed in this situation for months. Why bring me in suddenly?"

"Three reasons. You were, although admittedly tangentially, involved with the negotiations with Heritage. You have a sense for the directions the system is moving and what our governments need from it. Secondly, you've spent time in a null state recently and even interacted with their government."

"Switzerland is hardly China. What's the third reason?"

"There is a position open in the central government for a narrative design consultant. It is a position uniquely suited to better understanding their perspective and goals, and one for which you—"

But Mishima is already shaking her head, her ears cloudy as if she just lost atmospheric pressure. "You told them?" She wants to double over to retch or to get her breath back, but she forces herself to stay upright, palms rubbing hard against her thighs.

"Your backstory—"

"You told them?!"

"Your cover identity has a *mild* narrative disorder, combined with years of experience in a major content factory in Singapore."

"Which one?" Mishima asks automatically. She is something of an expert in content factories; it is one of the side effects.

"Moliner Productions."

Mishima nods, reluctantly. It is one of her preferred studios; she knows their catalog backward and forward. "Working for Poppy Chung?"

"You will work for her, for a few days, while you inhabit your cover."

She sighs, lets herself cover her face with her hands. "You realize . . . if they suspect me, they'll be able to use the disorder against me." Plant narrative clues that turn her in the wrong direction, shape her perception of trends and trajectories, confuse her until they uncover her secrets . . .

There is a silence long enough for Mishima to raise her head and meet Nejime's steady gaze. "I've been watching you," the older woman says. "I know you can handle it. You'll be able to distinguish the narrative from the real."

That's the difference between Nejime and Nougaz, Mishima reflects: Nougaz would have just given her that steely look and asked if she was ready to go. Any reassurance in Nejime's approach is undermined by the fact that Mishima has long understood that the narrative *is* the real. At least for her.

Restless and unable to sleep, Roz climbs up to the roof of the office and stares out over the city. The birds hover on the tree, giving it a faint ghostly glow in the darkness. She imagines slipping out of the compound . . . and then what? Finding her way to Suleyman's unmarked compound among all the other unmarked compounds near the hall? And if she did? She tries to picture herself moving soundless among those huts, finding the one where he is sleeping . . .

The fantasy stops there. She can only imagine shock across his features: this crazy foreign woman, essentially breaking into his home.

What if he came here? If, somehow, no one could hear them in the compound below, and they were alone and exposed to the sky . . .

She's not even sure he wants her.

He does whispers from inside her.

But maybe that's just her own desire speaking.

Even if he does, it would be insane. It would be counterproductive. Trust, impartiality, her career; it would threaten them all.

286 · MALKA OLDER

But these rationalizations, these hard outlines in the night make no difference, and she paces the roof, unwilling to climb back down into the real world.

It is not until Mishima's on the flight to Singapore, with too much time to think and to wish she was flying instead to Saigon and Ken, that it occurs to her that it might be a trap. Why would they throw her in on such short notice? Maybe Nougaz is angry at her (For saving her life? No. For showing her up) and planned this whole thing out. Maybe this is how Information manages an unmanageable operative.

Mishima turns on the onboard immersive content. She should have stayed a consultant.

Roz has just convinced herself that it really is time to climb down from the roof and go to bed when she hears a noise from the side of the office, the quick shuffling of someone coming up the rope ladder. She walks to the edge, more curious than alarmed, and sees the top of Minzhe's head barreling toward her so quickly, she has to take a step back as he swings over the parapet.

Minzhe doesn't ask what she's doing there. "Something's about to happen," he says, and walks to the western edge of the roof.

Now Roz is alarmed. She follows him. "What? What do you mean?"

Before he can answer, there is a deep boom, felt more than heard. The night is velvet black and quiet for about fifteen long seconds, and then another explosion goes off, a flash of light to the west. Roz blinks, and Information gives her a range of options for how far away the detonations are, depending on their size. The best guess is about a kilometer and a half, which doesn't seem very far at all. She glances at Minzhe, but his face is tense and absent, and she guesses he's listening to something through his earpiece. She looks down at the compound. There's an almost-full moon, which seems like either a good or a bad time to mount an attack. The light casts faint shadows from the huts and the blocky offices and the ragged, stork-strewn tree. Nobody else seems to be up. Another flash, and Roz flinches.

"What's going on?" she asks Minzhe, feeling herself poised for the emergency.

When he turns, she sees the projection playing against one of his eyes: something with a lot of movement. "It's an attack," he says, his voice disjointed, as though he were sight-translating into a foreign language. "By the 'stateless people,' whatever that means."

Roz gapes; whatever she was expecting, it was not that. "Are they attacking the town?"

"I think so. This is far closer than they've ever gotten. All the other skirmishes were on the outskirts, near the centenal borders."

Before he's finished the first sentence, Roz is requesting emergency security assistance, with a possible evac of up to ten (the four of the SVAT team, the four on Amran's team, and a strategic rounding error). She knows as she sends, though, that it will take any security team at least an hour to get here, and that may well be too late.

There's a particularly loud explosion, and they both jump. "Are you linked in to the militia feed?" Roz asks.

Minzhe nods. "I'm seeing exactly what whoever's broadcasting sees. I think it's . . ." He squints, probably trying to figure out who he's not seeing. "Yusuf, maybe? Or they might have left him behind . . ."

"Are they requesting that you join them in battle?" Roz asks. She's not planning to allow it, but she wants to know.

"No. The link to the feed is automatic for anyone on the list. No one's asked me to go in. No one's talked to me at all." His voice drops. "I think they've forgotten I'm here."

Another distant bang, and Roz shivers. Then she can see, out there where the bangs were—there are not enough lights in Kas to give a good referent for where the town ends— headlamps. A trail of them, at least five or six, and behind them a string of unpaired, less disciplined glimmers: men on foot or, by the speed they are moving, horseback. She can see the headlamps, she realizes, because the vehicles are heading toward town.

"How are we doing?" she asks Minzhe, hoping her voice sounds steady. She has been close to violence before, but never with security so far away. Never as the one in charge.

"Seems about even so far." Roz sees his Adam's apple rise and fall as he swallows. He's frightened too. She should go wake everyone up. But to do what? Be frightened with her? If they can sleep through this, better to let them rest. She'll get them up when she has a firm ETA on evac.

It feels like Minzhe has been silent for too long. "Tell me," Roz says.

"It's not easy to see what's going on," Minzhe answers a little defensively. "It's dark, and whoever's broadcasting the feed doesn't have night vision. It looks like a sort of caravan, a group in a long formation, and they've got grenade launchers and . . . and some other explosives."

"And the militia?" Talking about it seems to calm him, and it's definitely helping her.

"Same kind of equipment," he says quickly. "Ummm . . . not everyone is out there yet, but we had fifteen men on duty, and the rest are arriving as they can—there's another small group coming in now. . . . It looks like they're heading for the centenal hall."

Roz flinches.

"Right now, we're ranged along the mural wall, taking potshots when we can. I don't think they'll get by, the way it's going. . . . The governor is out there too, I just saw him."

Roz bites the insides of her cheeks, furious at herself for the urge to suggest that Minzhe go fight after all. "Do you think they do this all the time?" she asks.

"The fighting? Probably. But I haven't heard any stories about defending the town. And I think I would have. They can't just run away this time if they're losing. Wow," he adds. "The governor."

Roz waits, alone and blind on the rooftop while Minzhe watches the action a kilometer away.

"Wow," Minzhe says again. "He's completely in this. No wonder they love him."

There's a louder boom, and Roz ducks, though she knows it is too far away to reach them. But if the fighting gets closer, they are unprotected. What if the attackers are coming for them? Why would they suddenly attack if not because Information is here?

"Who are these stateless people?" She checks for a response from the security team. What is taking them so long? "Nomads who didn't get a centenal?"

"My sense is more like mercenaries," Minzhe says. Roz finally gets the response: security team has departed El Fasher, ETA eighty-three minutes. Maybe soon enough to save the compound. Maybe. Too late for the men defending the wall. She sets a countdown in the corner of her vision. "I'm not sure whether they are literally stateless, as in not having citizenship in any centenal, or if that's sort of a euphemism for men who sell their violence."

290 · MALKA OLDER

"Sell to whom?" Roz wonders.

"I don't know," Minzhe says. He sounds frustrated, and she should stop asking, but she can't. "I hear the militia talking about Sudanese, Chadians, sometimes JusticeEquality, but I can't tell if these are their eternal boogeymen or if they really are an imminent threat."

"What's happening now?" Roz asks, hugging herself.

"The reinforcements have arrived, at least some of them. Our reinforcements, I mean."

There's a flash out where the fighting is, and then a bang. Roz blinks, and when she opens her eyes, she thinks some of the headlights have gone out. "What was that?"

"A grenade," Minzhe says. He is grinning. "We got one of their trucks." A pause, and then: "They're over the wall," he says, and before she can gasp, "We! I mean we're over the wall. Going after them with flamethrowers."

"Is it working?"

"Look!" Minzhe points into the night, and she sees the wavering glimmer of the torches scattering in disarray. "It's like they're not used to fighting flamethrowers," Minzhe says, wonderingly. "The horses hate it."

"I hate it too," Roz says. She stretches her arms out, trying to get some of the tension out of her shoulders. "So, we're winning?"

"For the moment." Minzhe stretches too, shakes his neck out. "It's not over yet. The horsemen are coming around for another pass." There's a quick series of bangs, and Roz catches her breath. She can't imagine how she'll feel if Suleyman is killed. She barely knows the man, nothing seems real about him. "They're rallying, and we've retreated back to this side of the wall."

"Casualties?" Roz asks, her mouth bitter.

Minzhe shakes his head, *no* or *I don't know*. "Wait—the

vehicles have turned around." Peering out at the night, Roz catches the last pair of headlights sweeping into obliqueness, then disappearing. "Aha! We've won!" Minzhe throws his fist in the air. "That last charge was to cover their retreat! They're running away!"

Roz lets out her breath and sits down on the roof. She leans her arms on the parapet and her head down on her arms so she looks more sleepy and less like she's trying to hide her shaking. She updates her security request with a notation that the crisis has passed and waits. Normal protocol would be for the security team to finish the trip out anyway, debrief, and do a physical tour of the site, but there's some discretion. Given the hour of the night and the fact that they're only ten minutes out of their base in Fasher, maybe they'll go home and do a virtual debrief tomorrow. Frankly, Roz can't see how they could secure this compound short of digging a bunker. Right now she feels nauseous and tired and wants to go to bed and pretend for a few hours that this never happened. But if they tell her they're coming, she'll stay awake and wait, because that's what team leaders do. "What's going on out there?" she asks Minzhe.

"Ahhhh. Ummmm," Minzhe is saying. "It's all still very confused. But the commander is calling them together now, so we'll soon know." A pause. Kneeling on the edge of a roof on a hot night, muscles weak as the adrenaline seeps out of them, she watches Minzhe's handsome face in the darkness, projections playing against his eyes, lips moving slightly as though he's trying to sound out a difficult passage. Sorting out a jumble of voices maybe, or making notes on the visuals.

"He's telling everyone good work, thanking them for their courage. They're going to leave five soldiers on patrol tonight. Oh, shit . . . oh, shit."

"What? What?" Roz is on her feet again.

"Two injuries . . . shit. Khaled's gone. Damn it!" He turns and walks away from her, going to the other side of the roof, and after a moment, Roz hears his voice: he's calling someone. She slides back down to her knees, looking out over the parapet to give him as much privacy as she can. A message comes up from the security team, asking whether she wants reinforcements tonight. Roz replies in the negative, then fiddles with her handheld, wondering if there's anything else she can do right now. Start the incident report; that would be good. She realizes her underarms are dark with sweat. She's auto-entered her name, position, and mission number when she gets the reply from security: **Copy. Returning to Fasher Base. Debrief tomorrow 0800. Consider any possible security improvements.** Roz snorts and goes back to her report. When she's finished, she stands. Minzhe is still on the other side of the roof, but he's not talking anymore. She goes over and touches his shoulder.

"I'm so sorry," she says.

"Thanks," he says. "I should have expected something like this after hearing about all the other battles."

"Expecting it wouldn't make it any better," Roz says. "Is there anything I can do?"

He shakes his head, then hesitates. "Maybe. I'll talk to them tomorrow, see if I can convince them to take some assistance from us. But I don't know. They are . . . wary of outsiders."

Roz was expecting him to say *proud*. She remembers Commander Hamid's apparent bafflement when she suggested he request help. "And for us? Anything we can do here?"

Minzhe looks around the roof. "I don't think they were after us. But yeah, keeping a crow here for evacuations would be a good idea. Just in case."

CHAPTER 27

R oz doesn't expect to see Suleyman at the café the morning after the battle, but she goes anyway, hoping, and drinks her coffee alone. She keeps remembering that Minzhe said there were two injuries as well as the man killed in action. He would have mentioned if one of them were the governor, wouldn't he? There's nothing about the attack on Information. It's an eerie feeling, as if it didn't happen and she only dreamed it. After her coffee, Roz walks the entire mural wall, possibly hoping to find Suleyman arriving late, and there's no mention of the fighting there, either. She doesn't understand how an event like that can disappear so completely. What about the death certificate? Medical records?

Roz hasn't had many direct dealings with Amran recently. The field lead rubs her the wrong way, and since Maria manages her so much better, she has let her deal with the kid. Today, though, she calls her over immediately after staff debrief. It was a difficult meeting anyway, since she had to tell them about the attack the night before. Minzhe was conspicuously absent, having gone in to the barracks early. Amran looked disturbed and Maria surprised ("I was watching crappy vids in my hut while *this* was going on?"), but they agree that she did the right thing by telling the security team not to come.

"It was not an attack on us," Amran says.

"We don't know that," Roz points out.

"If it was an attack on us, they would have gotten us," Amran says, and Maria nods in agreement.

So Amran is already looking a bit shaky when Roz sits down with her. "I don't understand how it's possible that these battles don't make it onto Information," Roz says. "Can you find out for me?"

Amran twitches. "It's—There aren't many feeds outside of town, because nothing happens there, and—"

"It's not just the feeds," Roz says, although it does remind her she needs to figure out what they're using the feed money for. "What about death certificates? What about equipment loss? There should be some kind of record that something happened last night. Can you check into it? It's not your fault," she adds belatedly, and a little disingenuously. She does think Amran should have done something about this by now, but Amran brightens so obviously at the reassurance that Roz starts to hope it's true. She sends the younger woman off with a smile and literal pat on the back, and then focuses on her lists of foreigners.

Mishima's entry point is through 888. Someone there—or maybe the whole government, who knows?—owes Information a favor or has decided that this particular exploit is of mutual interest. It's a useful angle. In its pre-governmental form, 888's private sector leaders were commercial and economic threats to China's political class. Now they are one of its best conduits to the outside world. Unlike 1China, 888 aren't controlled by the sovereign nation of China, but their shared roots and shared interests mean the micro-democratic government and the null state are often aligned. This uneasy relationship is perfect for Mishima's purposes: an 888 citizen has a relatively easy time getting into China and being accepted there, but is not expected to know much about the country. More important, 888 aren't expected to hand over intel about her.

Mishima's cover identity, Chen Jun, is given citizenship in an 888 centenal in Singapore, a city Mishima knows well enough to describe as her hometown. She spends an intense three days there, brushing up on centenal specifics, 888 and Peranakan culture, and the details of her job at Moliner Productions. It's a pretty sweet setup, actually. Moliner is one of those businesses that see extravagant success as a reason to keep bucking the status quo, in the cosseting of staff if nothing else. Their offices are in Tiong Bahru, in a repurposed water treatment plant. Despite the high quality of the working spaces and free treats in the break rooms, most of the staff spend their days keeping the surrounding cafés, bookstores, and bookstore cafés afloat, brainstorming over lattes and char siu bao.

Moliner is known for breaking content taboos, and Mishima wonders why China would have selected them, out of all the production companies in the world, for a contract (unless it's a trap). At least during these days before going off to her doom, Mishima gets to fangirl over all her favorite content producers. Since she's pretending to work there—and most of the staff believe she *does* work there, brought in to headquarters after years of off-site consulting—she even gets to make suggestions. Before she leaves, she feels comfortable enough to pitch Poppy Chen, the visionary founder and CEO, her idea for a series about a character with narrative disorder, very meta-meta. The weather is good, her borrowed apartment is lovely, and the food is stellar. During those days, Mishima twice catches herself pretending this is her actual life.

Roz is still wrestling with the problem of the consultants. Even if she hasn't found a link to the assassination yet, the industry that has grown up around ushering new governments into micro-democracy seems like an area ripe for corruption. The consultants arrived with a baffling array of specializations: Data Management in Fledgling Democracies; Capacity Building for Bureaucratic Staff; Highly Participatory Election Monitoring Techniques; Gender Equivalence in Micro-Democracy; Micro-Accountability. Her eyes start to glaze over before she gets halfway down the list, but her insight on the feeds question has given her an idea. She shifts her view of the database to something she understands: budgets.

After reading for half an hour, Roz is convinced she understands budgets better than these consultants do. She has to stop herself from marking up the errors and inaccuracies: even if that were her job, these projects are already done and paid for. Paid for by Information, for the most part; accession to micro-democracy includes substantial assistance in areas that are believed to support successful integration. Highly participatory monitoring and gender equivalence, apparently. In another section of her workspace she flips open an Information budget cube and finds the line for technical support to the DarFur government, then sets up a cross-ref between that and the consultant proposals.

And there it is, what she's been looking for all this time: a discrepancy.

Roz jumps, tingling with shock. Minzhe is calling her, on urgent. Roz blinks him through. "What—"

He interrupts her, panting and desperate. "They've come for me, I'm not sure what—" In the background of his projection she can see colors, people's faces, someone shouting. He's running. He's running through the market.

"Who?" she asks.

"The militia, they're trying to arrest me—" He can't get more than a few words out. He's leaping and dodging his way through crowds, and now Roz is sure the shouting is aimed at him. She's on her feet already.

"I'm coming," she says.

The heat outside the building is dazzling, but she doesn't stop to get her hat. As she crosses the courtyard, Roz slips her hand into her satchel, finds the personal Lumper, presses it almost talismanically: the first thing you do, always, on your way into battle.

"They're saying—" The rest is unintelligible, blurred out by yelling and ambient noise and Minzhe's panting breaths. Roz moves faster, barely hearing the splat of guano falling behind her as she runs through the compound entrance and swings herself toward the market in a full sprint. She blinks to call in help from Doha, to locate Minzhe on her map, when the call goes dead.

"Maria, where are you?" Roz says as she plunges through the fringe of vendors around the market proper. She heads toward the hand pump; she thought she recognized the muddy clearing behind Minzhe. Doha comes back telling her there are too few feed cameras; they are analyzing vids from the last few minutes and have caught Minzhe on a few of them, but they can't pinpoint his current location. Cursing, Roz tries to reconnect with him, but he's not answering. She's heading toward the militia barracks as she hears Maria's voice.

"I'm at the barbecue. Some militia just ran by, and there's a crowd gathering."

"Careful!" Roz warns. "They may be—not acting rationally." Otherwise, why would they be after Minzhe? Last she heard—she weaves around a trio of slow-swaying women with wide tin trays of potatoes and onions on their heads—he and the militiamen were best of buddies.

She whips around a corner and sees the crowd, a thicket of twisting, shoving bodies all aiming to get closer or farther away. Roz strains her neck, blinking against the glare, and catches a glimpse of Maria's light hair under that shiny translucent scarf.

"Maria! I'm coming around from your right," she yells, starting to work her way around. "Can you see anything?"

"No," Maria says, short of breath or maybe crying. "But I thought I heard shots."

The glimmer of light on metal or plastic.

Roz blasts a message out to Malakal, Nejime, and Nougaz. "Any security backup in range of us, please direct to Kas immediately!"

Malakal responds before she makes it to Maria's side: "InfoSec en route from Abyei, ETA ninety-three minutes."

Roz grabs Maria's arm, and Maria jumps around, a Zippo-sized flamethrower in her hand. "Easy," Roz yells, trying to back into the jostling crowd. "Put that away and let's get out of here."

"But—you think Minzhe's in that?" Maria nods toward the densest part of the crowd.

"I don't know, but this is delicate and we don't need to make it worse." *Or get ourselves killed*, Roz thinks. "We can't do anything for him from here."

Maria hesitates. Roz takes her arm again. "Come on, at least we can pull back out of the crowd."

They edge away, and Roz leads them down a mostly empty alley between padlocked warehouses. She keeps going straight, figuring to get out of the market and work back around the edges instead of trying to find their way through the midst of the shops and risk getting caught up in the mob again. She blasts out a security alert to all staff in Kas, including the stringers: *Shelter in place at Information compound or home, avoid the market and maintain comms.* She is speaking through a message to update Malakal when a call comes in from Amran. Annoyed that she didn't just talk on the secure channel or send a message, Roz accepts it.

"I'm at the militia station," Amran says, and Roz can make

out the pitted concrete building in the background. "They say they've arrested Minzhe and are bringing him back here."

Roz exhales with sudden relief. "They've arrested him," she tells Maria. "So, presumably he's alive." Her imagination had Minzhe crushed in that mess or shot dead. Back to Amran: "Is he all right?"

"No report on his condition," Amran says. "From the way they are talking, I'm pretty sure they beat him up. Or they will."

"Stay there—I'm headed over," Roz tells her. "Have they said what he's charged with?"

"You have to understand: they haven't said *anything* formally," Amran says. "But what I'm hearing is espionage."

There's a curious combination of shock and confirmation. "Okay, I'll be there in"—Roz glances at her map projection—"two and a half minutes. Stay there, and if you see Minzhe, try to keep eyes on him if at all possible." She signs off and sends a new message for the Information higher-ups. *Urgently requesting legal support conversant in laws of the DarFur government!* She turns to Maria. "Go back, eat, sleep if you can. We're going to need to have witnesses with him nonstop."

R oz stays at the militia station all night. They won't let her in to meet with Minzhe, but she can sit outside his door, which has a tiny barred window. It's too dark to see inside, but when the night is very still, she can hear his breathing, and twice he whimpers in his sleep. Amran sits next to her, refusing to leave even though Roz tells her they're going to need to do this in shifts. Except for one guard, who's young and twitchy and won't meet her eyes, the militiamen are all at the other end of the barracks. Roz is glad because she doesn't think she can stand to look at them right now.

At some point in the night, Amran tells her that one of the

men has been locked in an office on the other side of the barracks.

"Locked in an office? Why?" The urgency has faded and Roz feels bleary, ineffective, and old.

"He tried to help Minzhe," Amran says, not sounding too sprightly herself. "He told them the accusations weren't true, but they didn't believe him. They beat him too and locked him in the office because there's only one cell."

Roz has nothing to say to that, although she would kiss this militiaman if it weren't a totally inappropriate thing to do in this context.

"I don't think they will prosecute him, though," Amran goes on. "I think most of them like Minzhe, and they understand someone doesn't want to believe he's—that he did something wrong. They locked him up to make sure he's not—that he won't help Minzhe escape or something."

Something finally sinks in. "How do you know all this?"

Amran dithers. "I was asking, I was talking to them. Before you got here. A few of the—of the militia guys. I—I know them from our outreach efforts."

"That's good," Roz says, leaning her head back and closing her eyes, just for a moment. "That's excellent work. You have informants."

Amran says nothing, and Roz wishes she could see her face, whether she's happy, but she's too tired to look.

Later, she wonders if Minzhe might have overheard them.

At dawn, they are relieved by Maria, who shows up, quiet and serious, with the first installment of legal support, a natty, petite young man from El Fasher. Roz sends Amran home—she appreciates her help today, but Roz is frayed to the point of exhaustion and can't stand to be in her company any longer.

Once she is sure no one is watching to see which way she goes, Roz heads over to the mural. She finds the wall before it intersects with the market, where it is still blank, and walks along it toward the café. The drawings begin with bits of sporadic graffiti, messages and doodles, sketches, then full, well-thought out panels. She was hoping to catch the children painting, but they must do it in the middle of the night, because she sees no one working on it. She gets to the café and keeps going, her feet heavy in the uneven sand, until the drawings peter out on the other side. Nothing on yesterday's excitement in the market. Nothing about Minzhe. Nothing about a spy

CHAPTER 28

From Singapore Mishima flies to an 888 centenal outside of Chengdu. The job will be in China's capital, Xi'an, but according to her 888 liaisons, the immigration process is much stricter at the capital airport than at the land borders. Moliner informed the Chinese contractor that some time in the hinterlands would be helpful for narrative refinement purposes.

It's helpful for Mishima's other purposes, too. Although Chengdu is still some two thousand kilometers from the K-stan war, they're empty kilometers by Chinese standards. The city shows distinct signs of nervousness: soaring prices and supply gaps for basic items, going out of business signs, harried expressions. She soaks it in over a few hours of walking and one extremely spicy meal, then heads for the border.

When Roz gets back to the compound, Malakal is there, drinking coffee with Halima and three InfoSecs, newly arrived. There is a gleam of metal prosthetics from under the plastic table; Roz nods at Simone Dumitrache, who used to run security at the Doha Hub and lost her legs to an explosion outside Caracas a year ago. She doesn't stop to chat on her way to the latrine, though. She didn't even want to see the bathroom options at the militia station.

While she's in there, she sends Malakal a message, since it's crowded in the courtyard and she's too tired to do a dance to get him in private: *Did you contact Minzhe's mother?*

When she comes out of the latrine, he's waiting for her by the entrance to her hut; tiredly, she gestures him in. "It's not standard practice to inform family at the time of an arrest," Malakal says without preamble. He's standing just inside the doorway without moving; he has to hunch his tall frame against the curving roof.

"I would call this more of a kidnapping than an arrest," Roz says.

"It's an arrest under their laws."

"She's only a couple of centenals away."

"Exactly!" Malakal pauses, calms himself. "You know perfectly well that if the governor of an 888 centenal finds out that her son is being held 'only a couple of centenals away' under suspicion of espionage—which is, by the way, a capital crime in this government—this will quickly escalate into a major intergovernmental incident."

"And if she finds out without us telling her?" Roz puts it there, then waves her hands at him. "Out! I'm going to sleep for a few hours. Go to the militia station if you can."

Lying in bed, Roz still can't sleep. The hut lets in a lot of light in the daytime, and she stares at the ceiling through a linen-colored haze, wondering where her exhaustion went. Minzhe seemed to have a great rapport with those militia guys. Amran said they liked him. What could he have said or done to make them that furious? What did they find that made them suspicious?

Maybe it's true. Roz remembers at least two occasions when Minzhe found reasons to stay at the compound in the evenings while the rest of them went out, despite his professed love of the village and the market. Was that so he could transmit intel to his mother? But how could he get it to them without being spotted? Especially in this low-data environment. Anything unusual that he sent over Information would be instantly noticeable.

Bringing in a spy is a nightmare scenario. Information is supposed to be impartial; much of its power rests on that reputation, and yet its whole purpose—intel-gathering—suggests espionage hiding on the flip side of the coin. Information staff go through a rigorous vetting process, and they're supposed to undergo mental-emotional scans every quarter, but Roz knows from personal experience how often that gets pushed back by supervisors who are trusting, understanding, or busy.

She wants to trust her team. Right now her *job* is to trust her team so that she can give Minzhe all the support he needs. If they did find something really damning, it will come out, but while the government is against him, she has to back him up.

She can't help wondering, though.

The border station is at the entrance to Huanhuaxi Park, presumably so that visitors' first experience of China is greenery, tea pavilions, and fishponds rather than industrial wasteland. There's no line, and after presenting her visa, Mishima is quickly ushered through the impressive door into a courtyard holding area. The path along the walls to the exit gate goes through three stations: a more thorough check of her visa; a standard body scan; and then finally a Sherlock scan, analyzing minute particles from her hair and clothes to track her recent movements. Anticipating this, both Bamako and Geneva were built into her cover story (narrative production work at the gala and a vacation). Her handlers hope the scan won't go any further back than that. At least it's been a long time since she's been to Tokyo, Mishima thinks, eyeing the exit gate. It's an arch, apparently open although she's sure some kind of barrier would crash down if she tried to rush it. The top is all pagodaed out, and the lintel and sides are ornate with curlicuing designs in green, blue, and red, tiny mirrors winking out from the curves.

Mishima blinks, replaying what she just saw in slow motion, zooms in on the mirror that shifted.

She looks back at the two uniformed immigration officers hunched over the readout from her scan. Is that entire arch inlaid with cameras?

Mishima has spent almost all of her adult life, certainly any of it that occurred in the public sphere, in front of cameras. You get used to it; you count on the improbability that anyone could be watching your particular feed at any moment (unless something newsworthy happens, in which case they're guaranteed to be watching the recordings).

But the density of cameras in that arch . . . She blinks again, risking another replay. Yes, there's another movement. And another. If all of those mirrors are cameras, what could be the purpose of having so many? What can they learn with all that overlapping data that Information misses with only a few feeds directed at any one point?

Did the compound image show her blink? Does it allow them to analyze the image projected against her cornea? Will she give herself away if she doesn't react to it?

Will she give herself away if she does?

Mishima doesn't let herself show biometric signs of stress. She wraps the knowledge up, locks it away, shoves it in the back of her consciousness to think about later, leaving only the reminder: no camera can read your mind.

The officer in front of her looks up, meeting her eyes.

Maybe people can.

But no, he is line-of-sighting her the visa stamp from his station. Mishima bows slightly in thanks, and then asks with a tilt of head and hands whether she should proceed. He nods, waves her on; the two officers step out of her way with bows. Mishima follows the path to the elaborate archway and steps through.

B y the time Roz wakes up, Minzhe's mother has discovered his arrest. She did not come to Kas personally; that would have been unworthy of her dignity and would have weakened her position by looking too much like an emotional, personal plea, too much like begging. She has sent, instead, a phalanx of representatives: lawyers, security officers, diplomats; some ethnic Han, some high-ranking Fur, some sent from the regional 888 headquarters to show that this issue goes way beyond a personal, centenal-to-centenal squabble. The entire weight of the third-largest government in the world is behind it.

When Roz gets back to the militia station, she finds herself hovering on the margins. Minzhe's cell is witnessed to the barred gills, and the militia commander will be having long, meticulous discussions for the foreseeable future. Roz is surprised not to see Suleyman there; she wonders if that was part of why she came, knowing as she did that she wouldn't be needed. She almost bursts into the station when she sees the image the 888 lawyers have been allowed to take of Minzhe: his face is almost unrecognizable, purple and swollen. The lawyers talk her out of it, reminding her that this is their game now and a show of anger from her would be counterproductive, and reassuring her that none of the injuries are expected to have lasting effects.

Back in the office, she puts her worry and sneaking doubts about Minzhe resolutely to one side. She has work to do. The excitement creeps back to her as she reopens her workspace to the files she was looking at yesterday. Yes, finally, an outlier.

A consultant group that didn't get paid. That seems terribly unlikely.

Immersed again, Roz is triple-checking the project proposal against Information's budget and doesn't hear Malakal until the second time he says her name. When she finally looks up, he is smiling, if tiredly. "Did you find something?"

"Maybe—I think so—I need to . . ." How can she confirm this? "I need to talk to someone in the centenal government, I think." She blinks at him. "What's going on?"

"Do you have a minute?"

Roz disengages from her workspace and walks over to where he's sitting. The office is empty; a blink gives her the message board, which tells her that Amran is at the militia barracks, probably trying to wring more intel out of her informants. Maria is there as well, compiling polling data while she provides an Information presence.

Malakal rubs his eyes and leans with his elbows on his knees. "The security team is here because of an anonymous tip about plastic guns."

"I thought they were here because of Minzhe," Roz says. She had been a party to all the back-and-forth messages about the logistics of the security visit the night before, but it hadn't occurred to her that they were coming for any reason other than the arrest.

"That pushed the departure forward, obviously, but the team was already prepped, planning to come in today. It's not in the deployment message for obvious reasons, but you can see it in some of the later documents."

Roz grimaces, makes the universal gesture for *inbox full*. "I thought I saw a plastic gun here, once, when we first arrived, but I couldn't be sure." Malakal is silent. "Wait—was Minzhe the source of the tip? Is that why they arrested him?"

"I don't know," Malakal says, heavily. "It was anonymous."

Information has a heavily veiled anonymity mechanism for staff wishing to pass along confidential intel. They say it's impossible to break short of massive force, but Roz suspects someone has a back door into it. "The DarFur government hasn't announced any charges—according to their laws, they have seventy-two hours—"

"Seventy-two?"

"Yes, it's long. But with the 888 reinforcements, I'm confident we'll get him out before then, at least temporarily." He pauses. "You should know that it was 888 that requested the initial SVAT team involvement. Specifically, the 888 centenal in Nyala."

"What?!"

"It's not unusual for governments to suggest a SVAT intervention may be necessary for their neighbors."

Roz knows that. "But still, given the uneasy relationships, and 888's relative . . . sophistication compared to a new government . . ."

"I know," Malakal says. "But SVAT teams are not supposed to be punitive, or even investigative! They don't come in and look for wrongdoing or—or guns, for that matter!"

Roz has to think back to the beginning of the conversation. "The guns."

"Yes." Malakal clears his throat. "It's a major stash."

"In the barracks?"

He nods. "There will be investigation as to whether they were used entirely in self-defense, which would lighten the penalty, but in the meantime, the security team is going to melt them."

"That's not going to help government-Information relations here," Roz observes. She takes in Malakal's expression. "Wait— you don't expect me to be the one to tell them about it, do you?"

"No, no—the governor has already been informed. They

know they weren't supposed to have them in the first place." He shakes his head. "I made it clear, again and again and again during the run-up to integration. I went over the procedures for requesting security subsidies. I told them . . ."

Roz puts her hand on his arm. "You did a good job. You did!" when he shakes his head. "I can see it here. The way you designed the centenal for the nomads, the knowledge people have about Information . . ." She trails off, trying to think of other examples. "It takes time."

"Sure," Malakal says. "Let's just hope they don't give up on us." A pause. "Have you thought about wrapping up here after the election?"

"And the assassination?" Roz asks, trying not to show her dismay.

"A lot of that will be remote work now. You're pretty convinced they weren't locals, right? Amran can handle any legwork, with higher-level visits as needed."

"Makes sense." Roz nods, telling herself that it does.

The centenal hall is a high one-story, concrete-columned building doing its best to look imposing. It's pretty much the last place Roz wants to be right now. She still feels the insistent magnet tugging her toward Suleyman, the faint and fluttering eagerness to see him, but this does not promise to be a pleasant conversation. But Roz can't figure out any other way to move ahead on her investigation. She has already tried contacting Mishima to talk her theory through with her, but she's unavailable, completely absent from the system, which makes Roz queasily nervous about what could be happening in the rest of the world. So, she's here to check the intel against the ground by asking the people who were really there.

She finds Suleyman outside the hall, under a woven screen

suspended over the front door that provides shade and depletes the intimidation factor of the building. He is sitting with a few other white-robed men, and when she walks up, he stands to take her hands with his usual warmth. He seems happy to see her, Roz thinks, as they rattle through the greetings, or at least not angry or suspicious. She keeps an eye on the other old men sitting on the stoop and nodding.

The governor's office is even worse than the building's façade: thick rugs, maroon drapes, stuffed falcons. *Well. He probably didn't choose the décor himself.* Despite that public show of support out front, Roz is not sure what to expect from Suleyman. She's already seen how dramatically he shifts between personal and professional; with all that's happened, she's expecting something significantly chillier than professional, but his smile as he turns to her is still warm.

"How are you? Is everything okay? What can I do for you?"

"Fine, and you?" Roz answers automatically. She wonders if he expects a petition for Minzhe's release, a harangue about the illegal weapons. He looks tired, and she remembers that two nights ago, he was fighting for his city. She wishes she could see that vid. "It's about the assassination. I've been looking at the lists of groups and individuals from outside the government that could have come in contact with the governor's tsubame." She throws up the projections. "There are quite a few of them, even over the last three months, which is the period we're focusing on."

"The head of state believed in getting as much assistance as possible with the challenges we're facing," Suleyman says, the statement modulated almost into a question.

"Right. Can you tell me anything about this group?" Roz highlights a name: IntelliStream.

Suleyman frowns, thinking. "I believe those were the fellows working on transformative nano-resilience? No, no, wait, those were these other ones." His forefinger hovers over another name. He thinks some more. "IntelliStream must be the people who came to work on criminal justice. Is that right?"

Roz has a flash of the militia cell where Minzhe is being held. "Did you talk with them at all?"

"I don't think I even met them. That was something Abubakar wanted to work on. It was government-wide. I saw some specific plans for this centenal, but I wasn't really involved in the design. Do you think they might have sabotaged the tsubame?"

"I'm not sure yet, but I find it odd that they weren't paid."

"They weren't paid?" If he's faking his surprise, he's doing a good job at it: not shock, but a mild befuddlement. This makes no sense to him, but he's also not sure why it's important.

"There's no record of it, neither from here nor from Information."

"Let's check with finances." They walk down the hall and into a significantly more cramped office, where a very young woman in a brightly patterned silk headscarf and eyeglasses is hunched over a tiny projected calculation sheet.

Suleyman shows her the name and asks their question, and she frowns, then brightens. "Oh, yes, I remember. They said there was no payment because they're a nonprofit consultancy."

"But the other nonprofit consultancies were paid for their time and expenses, usually through a voucher that Information made good on," Roz points out. She's fascinated by the woman's eyeglasses, trying to gauge the distortion of the lenses to figure out whether they're retro-fashion or actually corrective. AISHA is etched into the bright red frames; she must have had them custom-printed, which argues for fashion, but they do seem to be magnifying.

"Yes, that's true. I figured this group was self-funded or something." Of course, she wasn't going to argue with someone asking not to be paid.

"Did you meet them while they were here?" Is it possible they don't have corrective eye surgery here? Surely, in Nyala at least . . .

"Oh, I rarely meet anyone. Everything is done through messages or calls. So, I really do appreciate you coming by." She gives Roz a grin. "It's nice to see someone in person."

"Did the calls use vid?" Roz asks, last-ditch.

She flutters. "I never use vid. It seems so wasteful."

"Thank you," Suleyman says to the puzzled accountant, and makes to leave, but Roz raises her hand.

"Sorry, there's one other thing I wanted to ask you about." She has been trying to figure out how to phrase this question. "What did you do with the excess money from the feeds that weren't installed?"

Aisha—assuming that is her name, and not a romantic gesture or something—looks confused at first, and Roz thinks she's going to have to push further or maybe project the agreements and budgets, but then she looks up with a smile. "You're talking about the emergency fund!"

"Emergency fund?" Roz asks.

"There was a moderate harvest failure last year," Suleyman says. "We used the funds for that."

"The emergency fund," Roz repeats.

"Yes." Aisha's slightly magnified eyes are darting back and forth now between her boss and this stranger from the most powerful organization in the world. "Of course, the money was supposed to be for more feeds, but the governor—sorry, the previous governor—he explained that there was a margin of leeway for emergencies."

"Of course," Roz says, nodding with as much reassurance as she can summon.

"We wanted to use it for something more productive in the long term," Suleyman adds. "But the situation at the time was too urgent. Abubakar said he would look for ways to share out funds from other centenals or find new sources elsewhere."

"Of course," Roz says again, mechanically; this may be the least matter-of-course thing she's ever heard. "Thank you again," she tells Aisha, and they turn back to Suleyman's office. Roz stops outside; she's desperate to get back to the hunt.

"These consultants. They did it?" Suleyman asks, his fingers tight on the head of his ebony walking stick.

"We don't know yet," she cautions, and seeing the tension in his face, presses on. "There's no evidence that they did anything other than volunteer their time. We don't know that they came in contact with the tsubame, or that they had any reason to harm Al-Jabali."

"But it is suspicious," Suleyman insists. "No one has seen them; no one knows what they did. I don't know what they did."

"It is still tenuous," Roz repeats, although what she really wants to do is touch his hand, smile at him. "I'm going to look at feeds and see what I can find out."

"You will tell me?"

"What's going on with Minzhe?"

He has the grace not to turn away or go cold. "We are looking at the evidence."

"So are we. I guess we'll talk when we can."

CHAPTER 29

Roz avoids the melting of the plastic guns. She's been to a few of those in her time, and they're both smelly and boring. Back in the office, she finds Maria working alone and recruits her to help run down the lead on the assassins. ("Leave my mess of depressing statistics to catch a murderer? Sure!") Roz cross-refs for the possibility that the same group participated in the other suspicious deaths Mishima highlighted, but looking for Intelli-Stream doesn't garner any hits, so she goes through the other sites more carefully, looking for instances of "nonprofit" consultants that weren't paid or approved. In the meantime, Maria is checking vids to get visual identification of these guys.

"When did you say they arrived?" Maria asks, scanning. "I don't see *anything* at the landing ground that day."

"Check Information—look, here are the dates." Roz pauses, pulls up the cross-reference. "It's the same day the tsubame was in the garage!"

"Very suspicious," Maria agrees.

They pore over the vid from that day together. "Maybe they landed somewhere else, the way we do," Roz suggests. "Check the meeting with the governor at the centenal hall instead." She goes back to her lists of foreign organizations while Maria speeds through feeds of the centenal hall entrance.

"There's nothing," Maria says at last, between frustrated and mystified. "Did these guys even show up?"

"Let me see." Roz leans over and they run through the footage again. "Is it possible they met with the governor elsewhere?"

Maria checks. "No, he was definitely in the building. But according to his schedule, he left for a constituent visit at two P.M."

"Could that meeting be with them?"

"Maybe . . . but look, I'm not seeing him leaving, either." They run through the vids again.

"There must be another exit," Roz says.

"Without a feed on it?"

"Such outrage from the woman whose home has no feeds," Roz jabs. She's relieved, actually; the elusiveness of these consultants was starting to get creepy. *No feeds* is a preferable explanation to *ninjas*. "Where else can we look? Check the garage."

"I thought the garage didn't have a feed?"

"No, but we can check the feeds around it. Otherwise, we go through every feed in town over these days." Not as daunting a prospect as it should be; there just aren't that many feeds to go through.

Roz goes back to her list of consultants. The other suspicious death locations must have better Information coverage than Kas; maybe she can find some visuals there. She keeps glancing over Maria's shoulder at the vids she's scanning, but she's deep in an explanation of improving service provision in the Sri Lankan highlands when Maria nudges her. "Look at this."

Roz leans over to watch as Maria replays the segment, showing an intersection in the market. Roz can make out tinwares on one side, a clothing shop on the other. "Where are we?"

"The garage is half a block down this way. Look here."

Roz follows Maria's finger: blue cloth, the side of a sleeve from elbow to mid-forearm, passing along the corner of the feed. "Okay . . ."

"No, look at this." Maria replays it again, directing Roz's attention higher, and she sees it: a flash of brown hair.

Roz reaches in to pause it, replays it again. "A foreigner."

Maria nods. "I just checked. There's no mention of any other non-African foreigners in town during this period."

"As we've learned, that doesn't mean there aren't any." Roz is thinking, arms folded. "And we don't know they were headed to the garage. The tsubame could have been sabotaged at any time. Whoever this is could have been going for lunch or shopping."

"No, this is him. Or them," Maria says. "Look at the map. He had to walk all the way over here to be out of the feed. He's probably tripping over pots outside this shop."

"They're avoiding the feeds. That's why we don't see them at the centenal hall."

"That's why they don't land at the airfield."

"Shit."

"Do you think the governor was complicit somehow?" Maria asks.

"In his own assassination?"

"Or . . . someone else in his office?"

Roz thinks of Suleyman and wishes she hadn't. "I talked to the governor—Sheikh Suleyman, I mean—and the finance person today. Both told me, convincingly, that they'd never met these people." She pauses. "Someone must have met them. They're not ghosts. We'll have to do further interviews tomorrow." She checks the time: past eight.

"I want to know," Maria says.

They spend most of the night looking through every feed in town, trying to catch a glimpse of the consultant-assassins.

For once, Roz does not wake up at dawn. Maybe her schedule has been thrown off by the night spent at the barracks and the late night of research, but she senses some other change in the air. Her hut is hot, yes, glowing with absorbed energy from the sun, but not quite as hot as it was yesterday. She stretches, gets up, and steps outside. Yes, something is definitely different. A stork squawks from the tree, and Roz looks up.

The sky is clouded over.

She finds another difference after she uses the latrine: there's a security officer stationed by the gate. It's not surprising, and Roz nods to him before going around back to the breakfast table. Amran is there with Yagoub and Mohammed, the stringers, already deep in discussion this early in the morning. Simone Dumitrache is there too, and Roz sits next to her with her coffee and oatmeal.

The metal door to the compound flies open and Suleyman bursts in with such energy that a small sub-flock of storks takes off and then resettles. The security guy, no slouch, puts his palm out to Suleyman's chest, but the governor brushes it away like a fly and keeps walking. Simone is up, but Roz has a hand on her arm and gestures with the other to the guard at the door, who reluctantly puts away his baton. The sheikh is burning with anger, his white robe whipping around his ankles as he crackles across the courtyard. Roz strides out to head him off, heart pounding with urgency and a flash of fear: what if it's about her? About them? Someone saw them at the café, read her face—that's all it takes in a place like this; the secret is out. She wrestles down her shame, because the only way to fight this is with dignity and statuesque blankness.

But that's not what it is.

"We've been attacked by 888," he snaps out, voice like metal. "Men have died on the border. Did you make this happen?"

Dignity and blankness will serve for this too, although Roz lets a little anger creep into her too. She's going to need it not to wilt in the face of his fury. "I didn't even know it happened until now."

"Don't give me that!" His eyes burn into her. "You are Information; you know everything!"

"It wouldn't be the first battle here that Information didn't know about." Out of the corner of her eye, Roz can see Amran blinking quickly, hopefully getting the update from Khadija.

He dismisses this with a flick of his wrist. "Now you know. They have attacked our people, our home, our land, our . . . our centenal, if that's what you care about! 888, these people who don't even belong here! What are you doing about it?"

"What do you want us to do about it? We aren't your army."

"You've got security right there!"

"They're here because you have arrested one of our people!"

"We arrested him because he broke our laws!"

She can feel the heat coming off of him; his eyes are bright, wide.

"We have no evidence that it is anything but a trumped-up charge."

"So, you have your allies attack us?"

"Information has no governmental allies."

"No? No? You don't play favorites? You don't coddle the powerful and the wealthy?" He throws up his hands. "You melted down our guns! You melted down our guns so we could not defend ourselves, and that very night, they attack us. This is a coincidence?" He is hoarse with frustration.

"Did 888 use guns to attack you?" He can't answer that, his lips pressing together to avoid letting out either truth or lie. "No. Because they don't have any. Because they are *illegal*. So, removing your illegal guns did not give them an advantage."

"No?" Suleyman is back on the attack, stepping closer. "A government with a highly trained army funded and resourced from thousands of centenals worldwide, against our tiny militia? And they don't have an advantage?"

"I didn't say—"

"They attack us when we are without a head of state, in the midst of an election, and you say that is fair?"

"I *didn't* say that it was fair, nor that they don't have an advantage. I said we didn't *give* them one by melting your illegal, dangerous, provocative guns."

"Provocative? Are you saying this was our fault?"

"Are you requesting our assistance?"

He stops. Roz feels like she's standing on a precipice, at the height of some arc of stone. She presses forward, building her walkway as she goes. "It's not our job to police your borders," she says, putting her own steel into it. "Use your militia properly or send in a request for military training and support." She snaps her fingers, and the appropriate form appears, projected into the air between them before she disintegrates it into sparks, fast and angry.

"It is your job to judge infractions and illegality by sovereign governments." Suleyman is still angry, but he's starting to cool down.

"*After* the fact. And this will be judged." She pauses the appropriate amount of time. "I suggest you pursue that judgment with more deliberation than you are showing now." Roz wonders if she overdid it, if that's going to set him fuming again, but instead, the tension loosens. She sees him inhale deeply.

"I will pursue that judgment," he says, in something approximating his normal tone. "And in the meantime . . ." This is harder. ". . . I can't let my centenal be so exposed. We will be calling in assistance from other DarFur centenals, but in the meantime, I would like some . . . some support from any source possible."

Roz nods. She realizes Simone is standing behind her right shoulder, and wonders when that happened.

Suleyman lowers his voice, speaking for her now. "Whoever

did this should understand: it makes it much more difficult for me to release the man accused of spying."

"I don't see why the use of physical force should have any bearing on the justice of the case," Roz answers. She turns her head slightly without taking her eyes off him. "Simone, can you do anything for this centenal's security?"

"I'll be happy to take a look," Simone answers smartly, and gestures toward the gate. "Lead on, sir."

Suleyman holds Roz's eyes for a long moment, and then sweeps away in a swirl of white, and they are gone.

The security guard on duty lets his breath out and then repositions himself outside the gate.

Roz walks back to the breakfast table. "What did you find out?"

Amran's eyes are wide, and she keeps them on Roz while she answers, not double-checking her notes for once. "According to Khadija, there was a battle last night. Far from town, on the southern border." In the direction of Nyala. "At least one casualty, possibly more. But she can't confirm the aggressor."

Roz drops into a seat. "Ugh," she says, all her energy draining away. She probes gently at the residual discomfort: did the fragile attraction shatter? Did he say something she can't forgive? Did she?

"Nice graphics," Yagoub says next to her.

Roz feels compelled to give him a grin. "SVAT work includes a lot of flash. For persuasive purposes only, of course." Hooked, she can see it in his eyes. Another ready recruit. She's going to have to remember to talk him out of it.

Appetite drowned out by the adrenaline, Roz goes into the office. Maria is already in there, working on some tangle in the polling data. It's only five days until the election, and it occurs to Roz that she should ask the InfoSecs if they're willing to stay until then. She wonders how Simone is doing with the governor, whether he mentioned taking part in the fighting, what she thinks of him.

She confirms DarFur's story about the emergency fund: there was indeed a food shortage and distributions of rations bought from Nyala and Khartoum. Roz finds it hard to focus, though. The population of the compound has doubled in the last twenty-four hours, and people keep walking in and out, throwing up projections, talking about guns and punitive fines and sampling errors. Roz turns on her music and even considers projecting up some walls, but she doesn't want to seem antisocial, or for people to think she's upset about what happened earlier.

Roz gets up and edges her way through the team of stringers—swollen to five now in preparation for the vote—who are meeting with Amran and Maria. Outside, she stands in the narrow triangle of shade that falls from the building, and flexes her fingers. She needs some space. She needs to walk back and forth, and she doesn't want to do that in front of everyone. She wants to go for a walk—to the market, to the barracks, anywhere—but the morning's clouds are gone and the heat is more intense than ever. She makes it three steps out of the shadow and then gives up, scurries around to the shaded kitchen area, and makes some tea before going back inside the heat-shielded office.

She's not used to being on SVAT missions long enough to feel like she's running in place.

That reminds her that they're going to leave at some point.

Before she worries too much about how dismal that makes her feel, Amran is standing in front of her, twisting her hands in her skirt. She looks so young. "Yes?"

"You had asked, about the fighting," Amran says.

Roz has no idea what she's talking about.

"About why we don't know about it," Amran prompts. "About not just the feeds but the other intel . . ."

"Oh, yes." Roz remembers, and takes a sip of her tea to cover her confusion, scalding her tongue. "You found something?" Amran is again exceeding her expectations, especially considering all the disruption over the past few days.

"Just, I mean, not so much, but"—Amran passes a file into Roz's workspace—"mainly, some blanks in what people are reporting. Not many lies."

Roz opens the file, starts flipping through it. She has no desire to report doctors for marking *cause of death unknown* for bodies with bullets in them, especially understanding the context here. Still, if someone had said something earlier, maybe DarFur would have gotten the help it needed with security and there would have been fewer bodies. She remembers that soldiers died last night, and frowns, her headache worsening.

"It takes time," she mutters.

"What?" Amran asks. "What takes time?"

"Nothing," Roz says. "Thank you for this; great job." She wonders if it will be very noticeable if she goes back to her hut and takes a nap. Although it's probably too hot to sleep in there.

"It does seem like . . ." Amran hesitates.

"You noticed something else?" Roz asks reluctantly. Working alone with quiet music is the next best thing to sleeping.

"I don't know; maybe I'm just being dramatic." That clicks something in Roz's aching head, and she remembers that it might be a good idea to listen when Amran is feeling dramatic. "But it's almost like . . . some of the intel isn't coming to us?" Amran sounds as puzzled saying that as Roz is hearing it.

"What do you mean?"

Amran's hands grip each other in the folds of her skirt. "Some things that . . . it seems they should have been recorded but . . . I haven't seen them; I haven't been able to find them. We don't have them."

"*Seems* they should have been recorded?"

"Remember the oil barrel explosion? You asked me to check if Al-Jabali was there? I remember when it happened. I heard it. I went running. I didn't get into the building—there was a crowd—but I saw it, you know? I reported on it, and I examined the data. At the time, I mean. Then when you asked me, I went back and checked again. I saw his schedule, with a gap there. I asked Amal, and she told me he was there. But there was no data."

Roz thinks about this. Information always misses some data, and here, for reasons that she's getting very tired of listing, it misses more. "I mean, I can see why people wouldn't want to publicize that the governor was visiting his mistress in the reports on the explosion. What should have been recorded?"

"At a minimum, the governor's handheld should have recorded the noise and the high temperature. And there are feeds he should have passed on the way there. None of that was in the data I got; none of it is in Information now. I checked."

There's a stir outside, voices, something going on. "Can you keep looking into that?" Roz remembers to add "good work" as she gets up and hurries toward the door.

Malakal comes in before she gets there, closing the door behind him. "It's okay," he tells the room. "Minzhe's back."

"He's here?" Roz asks, walking with Malakal to an unoccupied corner. "Not at the clinic?"

"We took him there first to get cleaned up, but the injuries aren't serious. He's resting in his hut. Better not to bother him for now." Malakal looks exhausted. "DarFur has dropped the arrest."

"What?" Roz had assumed he was out on some kind of bail. "He's free to leave the centenal, and he's here?"

Malakal rubs his huge hands over his face. "He refused to go. Said his mother agrees. I don't know; some blabla about wanting to finish what he started." He removes his hands, meets Roz's eyes. "I did everything short of ordering him to go. Told him we've gotten reinforcements, we don't need him, it won't affect his career . . ." He shrugs.

"He wants to show that he's not a spy," Roz says.

"Or . . ." He doesn't have to finish the thought. *Or he is a spy.*

Roz shakes her head. "Even if he was . . ." She doesn't want to say it either. "How did he get the intel out?" There are ways of transmitting illicit data, of course. But when a potential spy has been identified, finding the transmission usually isn't difficult.

"We've been looking," Malakal says heavily. He doesn't like checking up on one of their own any more than Roz does. "Nothing yet."

"Maybe he didn't do it," Roz answers.

Malakal doesn't answer.

Simone comes back after lunch—an unsettled meal with too many people and too few chairs—and Roz, deciding that she needs to get out of the office anyway, invites her to go out for coffee.

"It's a model designed specifically for soft sand," Simone tells Roz when she notices her eyeing the bases of her prostheses as they walk through the market. She lifts a leg to show the bottom of the foot, angled and vented. "You'll probably have boots with soles like this in a year or two."

Roz is heading for Zeinab's, but when they get there, Simone wants to walk the whole mural wall. "I got a glimpse of it earlier while we were going over the lay of the land, but I didn't get to read many of them." They walk it both ways, Simone occasionally chuckling or exclaiming over a cartoon. Roz is achy with the sun and the tension, but she's oddly proud to see Simone appreciating the murals.

"So, how did it look?" All she really wants to ask is what Simone thought of Suleyman, whether he is really as fascinating and dedicated and brilliant as Roz imagines he is, but she has some interest in the security situation as well.

"Not too bad." They pick a table in the spotty shade. Roz motions for coffee. "The governor has some sense when he's not erupting—nice job standing up to him this morning, by the way. You defused the situation without giving in; super. He handed me off to the militia commander, who took me through their routine and concerns."

That's good enough for Roz to feel momentarily satisfied.

"I mean, you can only do so much to guard an entire centenal," Simone goes on, "but they seem to be doing the best they can with their limited resources. I can't imagine attacks like the one they had last night are commonplace."

"They did tell you about the other skirmishes, though?" Roz notices her language. *Skirmishes.* Downplaying it.

"They mentioned something earlier this week but said it normally only happens once a month or so."

"That's still too often," Roz says. "They need . . . something. An inter-government consortium, a regional police force— something to keep the peace in the long term."

"Definitely," Simone agrees. She pours her coffee into its tiny ceramic cup, takes a sip, shivers. "Whoo! Good stuff. Reminds me of Doha."

"Were you able to ask around about the other thing?" After Simone left the compound with Suleyman, Roz sent her a file with all the data they have on the elusive IntelliStream consultants.

"I did ask." She sends Roz a file, which Roz opens discreetly at eyeball level. It's a survey graph, very professional. "No one admitted to meeting or knowing of this group. I spoke with 72% of the salaried staff at the centenal office and, incidentally, six members of the militia."

"I'm sure they were happy to talk to you." Roz says, and hears her own voice overly acid.

"I can't be sure everyone was telling the truth," Simone answers, "but everyone was polite. Wary, maybe. The militia seems split; there were definitely some of them who were avoiding me, and a few dirty looks. But the ones who spoke to me seemed relieved."

"Relieved that Minzhe was released and they're unlikely to have to go to war with 888?"

Simone snorts. "Ha! No. Relieved that someone else, someone from the big leagues who knows what they're doing, is taking charge of things."

That's a little scary but an interesting perspective nonetheless. "Speaking of which. Is there enough evidence to sanction 888?"

"Not 100% yet, but I think we'll manage." Simone shakes her head. "Can you imagine? Pulling something like that?"

"If she thought Minzhe might be executed?" Roz reminds her.

"Still."

"Yeah. By the way," Roz goes on, taking a sip of her own coffee, "I was wondering if you or one of your staff could stay through the election, just in case . . ." But Simone is already shaking her head.

"Not that I don't think it's a good idea, but there's no way we can do it. Everyone is on standby for Xinjiang."

"Everyone?"

"The front has shifted almost two hundred kilometers east

over the past week. China is getting nervous. I'll be shocked if we're not redeployed there within forty-eight hours."

With Minzhe back safe and security people in town, the team is going to go out that night and celebrate. Malakal has been quietly encouraging this, and the InfoSec team is eager to see what limited nightlife there is. Roz is grateful Malakal is here so she doesn't feel obliged to go and keep up morale herself. She is shut into her hut before they even leave, a cool cloth on her forehead, trying not to think.

She might have fallen asleep; she certainly has no idea what time it is when she hears the knock on the door. At least she feels a little better. She swings her legs off the bed and goes to the door, running a hand through her hair.

Suleyman stands there. His usual turban has been swapped for a simple white cap, and his robes glow in the darkness of the compound. He smiles at her surprise. "May I come in?"

Roz's brain jerks through conflicting impulses: *of course not, that's not allowed here; of course, he knows better than she does what's acceptable; yes, right now.* She steps aside, and he steps in.

Roz closes the door and turns to him. "What are you doing here?" The compound is full of people, inordinately suspicious strangers. Is there still a guard on the door?

"I came to apologize."

"You didn't do anything wrong."

"No," he agrees. "I didn't. But when I am emotional, people sometimes find it . . . frightening."

"Did I look frightened?"

"No." That smile. "In fact, you may have scared me a little."

Oh, a man who can admit he was scared. Roz smiles at him,

with reassurance or relief, and gets caught in his eyes. She can't look away.

"I should go," Suleyman says, but his fingers have somehow found hers.

Just in time, Roz remembers to turn off her recorder. "Stay." It comes out low and unmistakably urgent.

He takes a rough breath. "Every night," he whispers, "I dream of nothing else." He presses his lips to her palm, and then he is gone.

Roz forces herself not to follow him to the gate, not to stand in the doorway of her hut and watch him go. She locks the door behind him and starts to pace. She walks the hut from one side to the other, tracing every possible diameter not blocked by her bed or her suitcase.

Finally, she gives in and calls Maryam.

"Habibti." Maryam's voice is rough with sleep, her face lit only by the glow of Roz's lights projected through her hand-held.

"I woke you, I'm sorry, I'll call you back."

"No no no, what are you talking about?" Maryam is sitting up, tapping on a bedside lamp, smiling. "Now. How are you? What is going on?"

Roz lets it all out in a rush: Minzhe, the strange face-off that morning, this sudden visit, although she elides the last exchange.

"Oh, wow," Maryam sighs. "This is amazing."

Despite herself, Roz relaxes. They gush over Suleyman for a while. When the conversation smoothes into more mundane issues, Roz remembers she had a question for Maryam. "Did you ever get a chance to follow up on the low-intel infrastructure? Have you found it anywhere else?"

"I'm sorry, we've been working nonstop on the war; I just haven't had a chance to do anything else."

"You too." It's unnerving that they no longer need to iden-tify it by location. *The war.* Roz shivers.

"I'll put someone on it tomorrow," Maryam is saying.

"No!" Roz says, without thinking. "No, I'd rather you did it yourself."

There's a long pause. "You think someone in Information might be involved."

Roz remembers what Amran said about intel vanishing. "I'm not sure," she says. "But I don't want to take the chance."

CHAPTER 30

Roz replays the touch, the words, all night, slipping into a dreaming half-sleep at some point before dawn. She is not entirely upset when she wakes up too late to go to Zeinab's before work. What would they do, hold hands under the table? What would she say? She's sick of feeling like a teenager in *luv*, mooning around after this man with his minimalist expressions of affection and his impossibility. She has real work to do. She has responsibilities.

This morning, those responsibilities begin with seeing off the security team, returning to Abyei with almost certain redeployment to Xinjiang. She waits until the crow has faded into the distance, then climbs down from the roof, wondering if it's too late to catch Suleyman at the café. She might not have many more opportunities to feel that glow. And they should talk about what happened last night, shouldn't they?

Instead, she sleepwalks into the office. Where she jerks awake with a pseudo-shock: an urgent call. She walks out again as she answers, expecting Nejime with some new bombshell: Heritage has collapsed completely, or Policy1st is fighting the five-year term with a secession plan of their own.

It's Nougaz, and she doesn't waste time on small talk. "Roz. The Asian frontier is wobbling. I want you on a SVAT team in Urumqi immediately."

Roz opens her mouth, expecting the thrill of pleasant adrenaline for a sudden, urgent, potentially world-saving deployment, and doesn't find it. "I'm neck-deep in the investigation into the DarFur assassination," she says. "If there's anyone else available . . ."

"There isn't!" Nougaz snaps. "We're sending teams to six different centenals just to start, and we need people with your experience there immediately!"

"All right, I'll start handover to my team . . ." Roz is already sorting files by what Maria doesn't have or hasn't read, but Nougaz cuts her off.

"They're going too. Didn't you hear me? Six different centenals, and we may need to expand to more! We should have more people there already; the complexity of dealing with null states has held us back far too long. What you're doing in DarFur isn't a SVAT matter anymore. You can talk to Nejime about a non-SVAT replacement; I'm sure she'll authorize it. So, pack up. I'm sending you a briefing packet now. Be ready; this is far more serious than we'd realized."

Roz stands there, stunned, until the heat prickles down into her scalp and wakes her. She turns to the door of the office, sticks her head in. "We're about to be redeployed to Xinjiang," she tells Maria, who looks up, startled. "You'll be getting a call."

She ducks back out before Maria can ask her anything, goes to her hut, and starts packing her bags. She stops again, half-packed. It's going to take time to get someone out here, so the replacement request has to be the priority. She checks to see if Mishima is online, more for her input than because she thinks she would agree to take the job, but she's nowhere to be found. Again Roz feels a shiver of unease. The next three people that come to mind have already been deployed to Xinjiang.

Roz is suddenly filled with despair, as though this is a climactic and hopeless battle where all the soldiers of Information are preparing to meet their ends. But of course not: Information needs its SVAT teams, its best and brightest. If it's a choice between losing them or losing a few centenals, they'll be evacuated. And then she feels guilty, because losing centenals doesn't mean a clean transfer of ownership. It's not the status of micro-democracy they're talking about; it's hundreds of thousands of people subjected to war. Which makes her both miserable and terrified all over again, because will Information really know when to pull them out? She wants to throw up, thinks about going to the latrine to do so, but she's a professional, and besides, fuck it. If this is how she's going to go out, well, she doesn't have any other plans. Feeling pathetic is better than feeling terrified and guilty, so she sticks with it. Now she has to figure out how to say good-bye to Suleyman.

Ken is in Saigon when Roz reaches him. He always feels strange being there when Mishima is away. This is by far the nicest apartment he's ever lived in: airy, with huge windows, recovered hardwood floors, balloon lights, fine furniture but not enough for clutter, strange bits of useful art on the walls, and on the master drive the largest collection of narrative content he's ever seen. With Mishima, it feels like home, an exotic, luxurious home, but still home. Without Mishima, it feels empty but also exciting, unfamiliar, slightly illicit, like he's a teenager who's snuck into his best friend's apartment while they're away. He wants to jump on the beds, play projections at top volume, invite all his friends to come stay so they can see what a nice place he's got now.

Ken hasn't heard much from Roz since the election, but they message every now and then with short updates. That's more or less what he's expecting when she calls.

"Hey, how are you? Long ti—"

"Ken, can you come to DarFur right now to take over

for me on a complicated election-monitoring assassination-investigation mission?"

What's he going to say to that? "Sure! I'll, um . . ."

"I'll have Nejime contact you with the details, but if I were you, I'd start packing. I'll send you my files." And she's gone.

Ken has to sit on the couch for a moment after that. Then he starts packing. He's already finished when the contract and travel authority comes through, a scant half-hour later, from the Doha Information Hub. It's real. He has to call his boss.

He dithers for a while, considering another round of sick days, but that tactic is getting old. Besides, this is not a silly speaking engagement about what he used to do. This is working for Information!

Phuong is grumpy about it. He *has* missed a lot of days recently, and Free2B is launching a new initiative to boost referendum participation with auto-personalized messages he's supposed to be working on. Mentioning Information helps, but when he offers to take unpaid leave, she negotiates him into clocking in at least a few hours on the auto-personalization while he's away. "I suppose it's a skills-building experience," she says finally. "From now on, tell me when you've got something like this going on!"

Four hours later (oh, the efficiency! Nothing like working for Policy1st), Ken is on a flight for Juba.

It takes Roz a lot less than four hours to depart for Urumqi. SVAT administrative processes are highly streamlined, and it helps to have a dedicated crow, which zooms in from Bangui, already loaded with three SVAT members who were deployed there. The planned departure is delayed only briefly, and then they are skimming toward the steppe. The flight is long and tense; Roz turns up her music and tries not to think about the last few weeks, the last few days, or especially the last few hours.

She almost didn't say goodbye to Suleyman. It had crossed her mind that she could leave without seeing him, blame the urgency, and send him a message from six thousand kilometers away: *nice knowing you.* Just thinking about it gives her a sense of detachment, like frost forming on a window— something, it occurs to her, that Suleyman has probably never seen. But she couldn't do it. And so, with her bags packed, files sent to Ken, and handover notes maybe one-tenth done, she marched over to the centenal hall.

He wasn't there, not sitting out front, and not in his office. Roz checked the timing: eighteen minutes until the crow would arrive. She walked back out to the market, scanning the alleys and byways. She started to feel ridiculous, and twitched her fingers to open up a call with him, only to realize that she had never called him, always depending on chance, unspoken agreement, or initiative to meet. Once leaving without seeing him seemed inevitable, it suddenly seemed intolerable. She was searching her files for his contact details when she heard her name called.

She had returned almost to the door of the centenal hall, and it was from there that Suleyman was calling her. When she didn't immediately move, he hurried forward to greet her.

"Roz! Is this true what I've heard? You—your team is leaving?"

Roz nodded, unable to speak with the relief of seeing him.

"You are leaving?"

"Yes," Roz managed finally. "I'm sorry."

He lowered his voice. "Is it because of yesterday, yesterday evening? Or"—an afterthought, with a ghost of his usual smile—"yesterday morning?"

Roz, suddenly aware of how exposed they were in the middle

of a market street, shook her head. "No, of course not! It's for work; we've all been redeployed." It doesn't feel like enough. "I had no choice."

Suleyman said nothing to that, but Roz heard herself instead. How many times, coolly debating international diplomacy or organizational politics, had she derided the telling fallacy of that phrase? "I'm sorry," she said again. The numbers blinked against her vision: three minutes left. She wasn't going to make it back to the compound in time. "I have to go," she said. "We're leaving now."

"What about Al-Jabali?" Suleyman asked. "Will you find his assassins?"

"We will. Someone will," Roz said, knowing it sounded weak. "We haven't given up on this. There's a war."

He leaned toward her, just a little, and for a moment she thought, *This is it*, the impossible kiss. But in DarFur, you cannot kiss in the street, or even hold hands. Instead, he whispered: "I didn't think—I don't know if it had anything to do with his assassination. But Al-Jabali wanted—he was hoping to win more autonomy."

"What?" It made no sense. Governments *are* autonomous under micro-democracy, almost entirely. "I don't understand. What did he do?"

Suleyman shook his head. "Those consultants. I've been thinking. I think I know which ones you mean. I knew there was something odd about them, what they were doing, because I never met them, never approved anything, never heard any reports about their work. But Al-Jabali always let me get away with not knowing what I did not want to know."

"The consultants were helping him work for . . . autonomy?" Roz was still confused. "But why . . ."

There was a hum, and they both looked up to see the crow passing to their north on its way to the compound.

"I have to go," Roz said. She couldn't keep them waiting; this couldn't be the reason she kept them waiting.

"I knew you would leave, but I thought we had more time." Roz had expected Suleyman to be his usual unshakable self. She wasn't ready for this: the tremble of his smile, the emotion in his voice. "I thought I had more time."

"I'm sorry," she said, and turned. Their hands brushed; she doesn't know now, thinking back on it, whether she let her hand sweep out on purpose or whether he reached. Maybe both. But she didn't look back. After that was the breathless rush to get to the compound, Amran's unexpected tears as she said good-bye, climbing the ladder into the press of her peers, all of whom understand: you go somewhere, you stay a while, then you leave.

Sometimes it happens this way, Roz tells herself, eyes closed and face turned against the wall so no one will talk to her. *Sometimes it's harder. But it will pass.* And she lives again and again the moment when he leaned in toward her, and each time that brings her back to the question: autonomy?

CHAPTER 31

The SVAT crow stops twice in Kurla to drop the team members from Bangui at various locations and again at one of the rural centenals, where Maria and the last of the other team gets off, and then continues to Urumqi, where Roz will be stationed. The first thing Roz does is buy a huge down parka; the days are still hot, but the nights drop to near freezing, and she's not confident enough in the electricity grid surviving a war to want to depend on a heated jacket. It's autumn in the northern hemisphere, and western Asia is smoky and chilled, street corners gleaming orange with persimmons or pale yellow with sultanas against the brown-grey of impending war.

Roz is teamed up with two SVAT members. Laurent, an ex-LesProfessionnels, was with her on the Kashmir job, the first after the election, and greets her with a hug. She's only worked with Nerol on one other assignment and doesn't know her nearly as well, but she doesn't have to worry about figuring out her motivations or weaknesses. It's not her job this time: Laurent is the team lead. Roz doesn't care, doesn't want to. She is still numb from DarFur, still wondering if Minzhe is actually a spy and who killed Al-Jabali and whether she fucked everything up. No, not whether: how badly.

To take her mind off of self-blame and unsolved mysteries, she focuses on the distractingly dire situation at hand. Information has finally caved and coughed up the money to deploy an initial detachment of LesProfessionnels. They are part of a coalition of soldiers from the top eight governments, the first joint mission ever. This includes contingents from 888 and 1China, which not only bulks up the numbers but, it is hoped, may act as a deterrent to China from stomping over them to reach the K-stans. There seem to be armed soldiers on every street corner. Which is nice and all, knowing that they are here to protect her, but Roz has spent a lot of time with soldiers over the past two years. Even by military standards, these don't look happy. Just beyond the centenal borders, two huge armies are pounding each other. It's like watching two school bullies fight, wondering when one or the other of them is going to realize how much easier it would be to just take your lunch money. And on the other side, only a few layers of centenals to the east, waits the massive military of the remaining PRC. Roz imagines both sides like steamrollers, flattening everything before them. Getting caught in the middle is not an attractive prospect.

The day after she arrives, Kyrgyzstan takes Ili from Ka-zakhstan. By the next morning, the refugees are pouring into the centenals. The SVAT teams have their hands full support-ing humanitarian logistics and working with locals to prevent backlash. If Karamay falls, it will get worse.

Still, it's some relief to be in a place where everyone under-stands the stakes, where everyone agrees on Information's role, and the very grimness of the outlook spurs truth-telling and the camaraderie of arms.

The SVAT members work in a small office in the centenal hall and take turns making themselves available at rotating public locations to answer questions and allay fears. They sleep in a small shared apartment, bare floors and sparse fake-wood furniture. At night, they go up to the roof of the apartment building, thirty-some stories of dubious concrete in a forest of similar-sized steles, and watch the flashing across the border. They are too far away to hear the explosions, but when the clouds are right the light bounces off them in staccato leaps. They try to guess, from the rhythms, who is attacking whom.

"Watching destruction from rooftops is a time-honored responder tradition," Laurent says, drinking.

"As is drinking," Roz says, drinking.

Later, lying in the spinning darkness with Nerol's soft snores coming from the next bed, Roz thinks that the worst part is not her doubts about Minzhe or her failure to manage her feelings for Suleyman, but the lingering sense that it isn't over, that she missed something with consequences into the future. Someone could be assassinated at any moment! She conjures up a government-filter globe the size of her fist and spins it in the darkness, looking for small, populist, new governments at risk of losing their heads of state. She gets nowhere but dizzy before she falls asleep.

In Juba Ken meets Malakal, who has agreed to accompany him to Kas and stay for a night or two while he gets settled.

"So, you're the guy Mishima left Information for, huh?" Malakal asks Ken as soon as they've taken off.

"Um," says Ken. Malakal is at least a foot and a half taller than he is, and now that he thinks about it, he's pretty sure he used to be Mishima's boss. "I think she was already leaning toward leaving. And," he adds hopefully, "it seems like now she's joined again!"

Malakal glowers. Ken shuts up and looks back at the screens showing the land below them.

The handover notes failed to prepare him for the remoteness of this place. They cruise above kilometers and kilometers

of empty land, and every minute of flight makes him feel farther and farther from anything he's ever known.

They land directly on the office, a one-story building in the
middle of a small compound ringed with brick walls. As they
climb down the ladder, Ken is struck again by the wildness of
it all. From this small height he can see where the city's buildings fade into the emptiness, and the office building he expected
is decomposed into cement cubes and cylindrical huts. He is
pulsing with excitement, waiting for the challenges and difficult decisions to arise. Malakal points Ken toward his hut and
then, once he's put his bags down, takes him into the office to
update his access and show him around the file system. After
an hour or so, Malakal slaps Ken on the shoulder, probably not
unnecessarily hard. "Lunch should be ready soon. Why don't
you go start? I'm going to finish up a few things here."

In the courtyard, Ken looks around. He doesn't see any
lunch, and he's itching to get out of the compound, check out
the market and town. He's edging toward the gate when Minzhe
wanders out of his hut.

Ken jumps. "Man! What happened to you?" As usual, Ken
has skimped on the background reading.

"I got mistaken for an 888 spy," Minzhe says, rubbing his jaw.

"Really?" Ken examines his face. "Funny story, the same
thing happened to me once. Although looking at you, I'm
starting to think I got off easy." Ken proceeds to tell some
crazy story based in Beirut during the Information blackout
of the last election, but Minzhe doesn't seem to find it very
funny.

"You know most 888 spies are not Chinese."

"I know, I know . . ." Ken catches the tone and, a second
later, the fact that Minzhe said *spies*, not *staff*. "Well. Glad you're
okay."

Minzhe glares. Ken retreats to the hut he's been told is his.

· · ·

The next morning, tired but sober, Roz takes a more rational approach to the problem. She sets up a list of governments that fit the pattern of assassinations and studies it at eye level whenever there is a lull in her official duties. It's a long list; she needs more criteria.

She does find one possible additional case: a deputy head of state who died in an unsolved mugging in Tegucigalpa six months ago. Roz can't be sure if Mishima missed it or dismissed it as irrelevant, because she still can't contact Mishima, and she doesn't have time to sort through the case details herself. She sends it to Maryam to take a closer look.

While she's at it, she asks Maryam to do a geographic analysis of the feeds in Kas to see if there's any pattern to places that weren't covered. She also sends some detailed instructions to Ken; being up on the roof last night gave her an idea for how Minzhe might have transmitted his intel if he was a spy.

Information is staffing a refugee fair to match the newcomers with micro-democratic governments. Some of the governments have restrictions, requiring documentation on criminal backgrounds or trades and skills, but for the most part, refugees are recognized as a good bargain. Treat them well, and they will vote for you more loyally than citizens who were born in your centenal.

The fair is set up with "booths"—in fact, spaces separated by waist-high, half-transparent projected walls—for governments to make their cases. 888 offers those who stop by a bamboo basket of helpful coalition company products (a travel tea thermos, silicone cooking pots, personal translators), while 1China soldiers do regular parade maneuvers to attract visitors to their display. Heritage sent troops as part of the coalition, but with all the recent disruptions in their government, they didn't manage to send a promotional team, and few refugees are choosing to immigrate there. PhilipMorris has their usual free cigarette cart drawing people in to see the slick projections of their most appealing centenals. Policy1st has deployed personnel to offer individualized counseling on which centenal to move to, and—in a nice, practical, policy-based move that probably does more for them than anything else—offers child care for people exploring the fair, no strings attached.

China has its own booth. They have long been aware of the power of population, and although they require strict screenings, their lusciously produced vid projection gives refugees the hard sell for joining the Middle Kingdom. However, these people have heard horror stories about the giant to their east all their lives, and few of them sign on.

While the sorting process continues, the refugees still have humanitarian needs, and Laurent's team is helping the centenal government organize the inflatable shelters and volunteer kitchens. In between the rushes of work, Roz's mind drifts back to DarFur. She wonders what Suleyman thinks of her now. She wonders if she's right about how Minzhe communicated his findings without being noticed by Information if he was a spy. She spins the geographic analysis in front of her eyes whenever she has a chance, overlaying it with different data patterns. And she goes back to the four—or five—suspicious death cases and looks for more similarities to add to her algorithm, wondering how much time she has left.

CHAPTER 32

Given the sensitivities around spies within Information, Roz was hesitant about getting Ken to check her theory, but she decided she trusts him. Also, she didn't think he would figure out why she was asking him to look for repeaters. In this, as it turns out, she underestimated him.

"Wait until you're sure no one else is around," she cautioned him, and it's not difficult. Malakal is already gone. Minzhe hangs around the courtyard until ten or so and then shuts himself in his hut, and Amran and the locals are already in bed by then. As instructed, Ken climbs up to the roof of the office. There's no rope ladder there now, but Roz told him where to find an actual ladder, and it's easy enough to set up, if louder than he expected. Standing on the roof, he pulls out his handheld and takes a long, slow turn. He's looking for a line-of-sight repeater, so he starts by pointing at one of the low hill ranges he can see out of town, the one to the south, because Roz suggested a general southeasterly direction. Nothing. Maybe he is holding the handheld at the wrong angle. When people set up a repeater, they usually program their handheld or tablet with the coordinates, so it can automatically guide the alignment. Ken keeps pinging, moving his handheld up and down in each direction before shifting minutely to his left and trying again.

At thirty-one degrees from where he started, his ping bounces back to him. He's so startled, he jumps and has to align all over again, but he finds it, logs the coordinates, sends them

344 · MALKA OLDER

to Roz. He's sitting on the low wall along the edge of the roof, waiting for further instructions, when his antennae twitch for the first time since he's gotten to this low-stimulus environment. The miniscule cameras that watch Ken's back have caught an anomaly and sent vibrations along the microfilaments that run down the nape of his neck to alert him. Ken turns to see Minzhe's head come up over the ladder.

"Hey, man," Ken says, getting up quickly and moving into the middle of the roof, as far away from any of the edges as he can get. "What's up?"

Minzhe climbs the rest of the way up, slings a backpack off and lays it along the low wall, then walks over to stand beside Ken. "I guess you found the repeater?" he asks, looking out at the horizon.

Ken almost denies it, but Minzhe looks both certain and, with his overlay of bruises, scary. "I was doing what Roz told me. I have no idea what's going on."

"I know the DarFur militia have been scouring the hills for it," Minzhe says, still looking away. "Poor guys. They're amazing, you know; they just have nothing to work with."

"Yeah," Ken agrees, thinking: *If you like them so much, why did you sell them out?* "So, um." He edges toward the ladder.

"The repeaters were already here, you know," Minzhe goes on. "They've been there for decades. They were old walkie-talkie repeaters, if you can believe it. My mother just repurposed them for line-of-sight. She moved some of them too, I guess. Anyway. When I was deployed here, she suggested we use them to communicate. Not to spy, really, just to talk."

"Of course," Ken says, still trying to get himself to the side of the roof with an exit route. "Makes total sense."

Minzhe is in confession mode. "Then . . . when I saw the guns, I was shocked. Worried. You have to understand I didn't just see them sitting around somewhere. I saw them being used in battle." He stops, replaying the images.

Despite himself, Ken is interested. "You were in a battle? Here?"

"I hacked into their closed feed and watched."

Ken is almost as impressed by that.

"I was worried about my mother and her whole centenal. Not that my mother had any plans of attacking these guys, but what do I know? They could have wanted to get her or her people. Her land, right? As if land meant anything anymore. Guys with guns get crazy. And there are lots of people who still don't want people who look like us here. So I told her, just to warn her." He lowers his head. "I should have guessed she'd go to Information with it. She's always been a stickler for the rules."

"If she hadn't, somebody else would have," Ken says, trying to sound reassuring and reasonable. "We would have seen it eventually."

"I guess," Minzhe says. "I feel terrible about it. Not because I got beat up; I feel bad for the guys in the militia. They're really good guys. Most of them. And they're just trying to defend their territory."

"Do they really think their territory's at risk?" Ken asks. "I mean, all their neighbors belong to the election system." With the news compilers constantly pounding on about Xinjiang and Russia, it's hard to take any conflict that doesn't include null states seriously.

"Of course it is! You don't think the borders shift with every battle, in ways that don't show up on Information? This hill, that tree, changing hands over and over. We might think it's silly, but to them, territory still means something." Minzhe shakes his head, although Ken can't tell whether it's over the hopelessly outdated idea of geographical size or the micro-democratic world's scorn. "But I should have said their people. That battle I was talking about—it was right out there." He points into the darkness. "At that point they weren't fighting for some empty plot of land, they were fighting to protect noncombatants. I'm pretty sure we—the Information team—would have been in danger if they hadn't had the guns."

"Yeah, but . . . guns." Ken's been on the wrong side of them often enough to want them all eliminated.

"Yeah, I know." Minzhe deflates again. "There are plenty of legal weapons they could have used. And the more they use them, the more the others are going to think they need them, the more they're going to use them here. That's why I . . ." He still doesn't want to say *ratted them out* and can't seem to find any softer synonyms.

Ken's starting to get more concerned about Minzhe throwing himself off the roof than for his own safety. "Look, man," he says. Minzhe turns toward him, throwing a hand up in irritation—*Why are you bugging me about feeling crappy about this?*—and Ken takes a cautious step back and around toward the ladder. "Easy," Ken says. "I'm on your side." Ken's not actually sure about that, but it seems like a good thing to say.

"What?" Minzhe's eyes widen, and then he laughs. "What? Are you actually worried?" He laughs louder and relaxes into it. "Look, I'm going to lose my job, okay? I can live with that. I would have told Roz where the repeater was if she had just asked me."

"I don't think she wanted to believe it was you," Ken says, a little more relaxed himself but still staying away from the edge of the roof.

Minzhe shrugs. "It doesn't matter."

"And, if it makes you feel any better . . ." Ken is frowning. ". . . I don't think it was your mother who turned them in."

Minzhe laughs, although not as happily this time. "She wouldn't hesitate for a second."

"She might if it would put you in danger," Ken suggests, but Minzhe is still shaking his head. "In any case, if she had, she would have used her name, right?"

Minzhe thinks about that. "Probably. Unless there was something to gain from doing it anonymously. But I think the domestic benefit of having her name on it would outweigh anything else."

"And if she had put her name on it, Roz would have known that it was you. But she didn't. She wasn't sure. That's why she asked me to check."

"I thought she just wanted the technical specs," Minzhe says with something like a laugh. "So, you think someone else knew about it? And talked?" He thinks. "It's true; it wasn't exactly a locked-down secret. Hey, you want a drink?" Minzhe opens his backpack to pull out a couple of sealed plastic sachets of clear liquid.

"Isn't that illegal here?" Ken asks, wary of some kind of trap.

"Technically, but lots of people drink. Besides, this is an Information compound; shouldn't it count as an embassy or something?"

Ken shrugs and sits down too, although it isn't long before they're both lying on their backs, looking up at the thick field of stars above them. "You see why this place is so great?" Minzhe asks dreamily.

Ken isn't sure he can completely agree, but lying on this warm roof in the dark is pleasant enough. "You know what we should do?" he says. "We should find the assassin. For Roz." And for Mishima, really, because, as he can admit when he's drunk enough, everything he does is to impress Mishima.

"We should find the assassin for the widow," Minzhe says.

"And for the governor, and for all the citizens." He drinks. "But yeah, also for Roz. She was pretty great, you know? I didn't really thank her properly."

Despite a mild hangover the next morning, Ken is still enthusiastic enough about finding the assassin to call Roz and ask where he should start looking.

"Never mind that for now," Roz tells him. She is stuffing her face with bread and goat—more goat!—on a brief and late lunch break. "Focus on the election, it's"—when is it? She's lost track of days—"the day after tomorrow, right?"

"Don't worry; we've got everything under control," Ken says, exchanging a glance with Amran, who gives him a determined nod. "If you've got any ideas where to look for the assassin, we can put some time into it."

Roz hmphs but sends him her work file: the data on the feeds from Maryam, and all the permutations she's tried on it. "But don't get too distracted! The election is the important thing right now."

"Of course," Ken says, thinking privately that finding the assassin would go a long way toward raising confidence in the election. He clears his throat. "How are you?" Ken isn't sure what to say that will be sufficiently awed, supportive, and not jealous. The news compilers are going nuts over what they're calling the standoff in Xinjiang, and he can't help wishing he were there.

"A little desperate," Roz says. She manages to make it sound ironic and jaded, but even so, Ken is alarmed. He remembers how calm and flat-toned Roz was during the election fiasco. "Call me during the election, okay? As soon as you know how it's going?" She cuts the call, shovels the last of the meat and puffy bread into her mouth, and nods to Nerol, who pays.

Roz completely missed Ken's envy. She is not following the news compilers, because she can't bear their breathless excitement about what is the tragic and dreary reality of her daily life. They have no real recourse if the armies turn against them, and as they wait to be overrun or evacuated, they are supporting recent arrivals, striving to calm the population, and then spending the long nights smoothing data management wherever they can before repairing to a bar or a roof to drink. When their desultory talk touches on the current situation, it is almost always to ask what China will do.

CHAPTER 33

Mishima had expected that an autocratic nation-state outside the realm of Information and surrounded by micro-democratic centenals would lie outright to its citizens to keep them happy. What she finds is far more subtle and more familiar. China has its own version of Information, 见闻网. It is more top-down than Information while also oddly gossipy. Yes, there are topics that don't show up at all or deviate from the more broadly accepted definition (looking up *micro-democracy,* for example, triggers an impressively academic barrage of snark and shade). Advertisements are all but unregulated; Mishima stares for thirty seconds at an advertisement selling 'rejuvenating' face cream, wondering how it is possible, until she remembers it doesn't have to be. But most of the world's knowledge is there. Current events are somewhat distorted (reminding her, with uncomfortable déjà vu, of the Information blackout two years ago), but what she misses more are external communications.

If she can ignore how much she wants to talk to Ken and her yen for up-to-date intel, the day-to-day of her fake job is not bad. Granted, it's not Singapore. The skies are gray with some mix of clouds or pollution (air quality readings are one of those taboo topics), and the weather is trending toward a cold winter, with Siberian winds chapping her fingers and blowing in sand from the Gobi. Her apartment is tiny and mostly made of plastic (synthetic fiber rugs, silicon dishware, slotted plastic bed and chairs), but—and she's sure this is an incredible privilege offered to visiting elite—it is in a wonderful neighborhood.

She's not in the city center—most of that is heavily restricted—but between the first and second ring roads, not far from the Giant Wild Goose Pagoda and the Tang Paradise park. She walks to work every day on a road lined with adorable one- and two-story shops with sloping roofs, offering the wealthy everything from old-fashioned leather-bound notebooks (she buys one for Ken, who has something of a pen-and-paper fetish) to wicker furniture to charcoal braziers (now strictly decorative, as charcoal is illegal) to tai-shaped pancakes filled with chocolate (which Mishima eats for breakfast for a week before getting sick of them). At night, usually very late at night, on the way back, she stops for dinner, different establishments every night, nearly all of them delicious.

It's also not Switzerland. China maintains conduits to micro-democracy and its rich trade through 1China and 888; Mishima doesn't see any classic cars like the Swiss cop's. What is different is the public transportation: China strongly discourages private crows and tsubames, and doesn't use public service crows either, relying instead on the massive infrastructure investments of the first half of the century. On Mishima's scarce time off, she rides the maglev out to the end of every line and back, to get a sense for what she's missing by living among the wealthy. She sees fields of towering tenements, clothes hung to dry on every balcony, and unrefurbished industrial estates with dirt roads and low concrete factories. The government is very vocal about the fact that the city is powered by a solar sail in the Gobi, and as far as Mishima can tell that is true at least for the center, but out on the edges she sees smokestacks, and once the endless dragon fire of what she believes is a refinery. Back in her neighborhood for the evening, she strolls a street of tiny art galleries, buying a few modest pieces to take back to Ken, then gets a massage. Thinking how much he would enjoy this makes her miss Ken more.

Even the work situation is, if not enjoyable exactly, not un-pleasant. The first difference she notices is that everyone works a lot. The offices are regularly buzzing until eleven or twelve at night, and nobody seems to take more than one day off over weekends. The second thing is that there are plenty of content designers here. These two pieces of data, put together, would send her into a panic if Mishima had such a mode; certainly, they suggest that they didn't need an outsider to produce content. Fortunately, the projects the Chinese are manufacturing are fascinating enough to distract her from the uneasy sense of ground falling away beneath her feet.

The massive floor where Mishima works is open-plan, and project teams are encouraged to set up projections with slices of their work as partitions. Naturally, this became competitive. Finding her workspace means walking through a mutable labyrinth of glowing, humming, leaping plot points, expressed through cartoons, actors, the faceless avatars of storyboards, or scrolling ideographs, with images of their radicals shimmering behind them. It's narrative disorder heaven, if somewhat risky for her sense of focus, and gives her a chance to peek at a lot of other projects.

The largest is the virtual warriors project, for which ten thousand individual life stories are being scripted in tribute to the current head of state (whom they refer to as "determined leader"), as a modern take on the terra cotta army. Ten thousand people who never existed, imagined through every detail of their life: dazzling. Beyond that are a plethora of smaller endeavors: detailed reimaginings and re-reimaginings of every glorious period in Chinese history, which form the basis for an entire category of interactive series and vids; the backstories and shenanigans of the celebrities who star in these and the more modern dramas, all of which are entirely fictional; the more subtle (in plot; the production is still extravagant) opposition stories: the narratives that allow the resentful, the disen-franchised, the young to believe themselves part of a daring or devoted or punk-influenced resistance to the ruling powers. While picking up the premises and plot points of these is part of her mission, Mishima is careful not to look too closely at the technical details of the politically shaded projects: it is too easy to fall into that habit, and she doesn't want the temptation when she's back in her real life.

Her own project area has shortcut images of China's great-ness all along the partitions: light shimmering off of rich brocade, ancient brick fortifications, young and attractive ex-ecutives in paneled suits. On the inside, the projected walls are a deep indigo, blank until they are figuratively papered with ideas, to-do notes, storyboards, icons, and calendars. Mostly, though, the dark walls are used to screen bits of narrative.

All of the story beads have already been constructed: epi-sodes projecting China's commercial greatness and hinting that no foreign company can consider itself a success until it has broken in here; sunny residential fantasies urging migration; action-adventures that masquerade as crowd entertainment while hinting at the insurmountable military power of the na-tion. There are narratives slated and ready to be shopped to Information-based news compilers if China joins in the K-stan conflict on the Kyrgyzstan side; if China joins on the Kazakh-stan side; if China obliterates both of them; if China mediates a peace deal; if China stays aloof.

Mishima's job is to help them put the content blocks together in the ways that will be most effective for a foreign audience. How many beats between this twist and the dénouement? Is this surprising enough? Too surprising? Does the heroic sweep here work? And, occasionally, the detail work: will this joke be funny or offensive?

It only takes a few days working in that hive, the glassy

domed roof arching high above, for Mishima to understand that her position might not be a spy trap. Yes, China has plenty of content designers, but they are almost all Chinese content designers. Mishima is working on content for the outside world. That also explains why they went to Moliner. They might be risqué, but they have a reputation for ushering blockbusters across a wide range of different markets. Taking an algorithm from their procedures, Mishima suggests planning in minor tweaks for as many sub-markets as they can afford (in terms of time; money is almost as abundant here as at Information). It will mean hiring at least one more foreign content designer, and she lobbies for that, too: it will give her more time to address her other responsibilities, but also she wants her team to have another narrative designer on hand in case she has to suddenly disappear or is equally suddenly arrested for espionage.

Because, despite the long days of work and the constant danger, Mishima has conceived an unusual affection for her team. The ten narrative developers assigned to her are young, hard-working, and curious about the world beyond their borders. Their questions start with a cautious patter of raindrops and build to a storm front: What place is she from? Has she been to many centenals? How many? Really? How does trade work? When two centenals disagree, who decides? Does Information really know everything? How do people choose whom to vote for?

Mishima does her best to answer from the perspective of Chen Jun, less worldly than Mishima but much more experienced than these kids, and believing herself the last word in sophisticated. She tries to draw her examples from vids and series as much as possible, ideally from Moliner but occasionally from their competitors, and feels pleased that all the hours she has spent immersed in content finally have a use in the real world.

After the second week, they send the most gregarious, Chu

Lifen, to invite her out for drinks with them. They go not to one of the hyper-cool bars she has found along the walk home but to a restaurant with spill-proofed tables and prices a tenth of what Mishima has been paying. They eat bullfrog sautéed on an iron plate and a Sichuan-style fish not quite as good as the one Mishima had a week ago in Chengdu, and start with water chestnut juice before quickly moving on to hard alcohol. The questions get sillier and riskier.

"Is it true that centenals are a way for people to segregate?" one shy young man asks halfway through the fourth bottle.

"No . . ." Jun has no particular reason to want to defend Information, but she would probably feel some pride in her system. "No, most centenals are based on policy preferences or cultural practices, and almost all of them"—a slight exaggeration—"allow free immigration."

"I heard there are centenals that don't allow black people," another young man adds.

"And others that don't allow white people."

"Or Chinese people."

"There might be some places that end up like that." Jun would probably be uncomfortable talking about this and proceed cautiously, so Mishima does too. "But if it's an urban area, they're going to come in contact with people from other centenals anyway."

"What do you do if you're in the minority and the government you want isn't elected for your centenal?"

"You can always move," Mishima points out, and offers them a pre-cooked story about how she moved a few blocks over when she got her job with Moliner to switch citizenship to a centenal with a more favorable tax structure. That garners her a few moments of stupefied silence.

Mishima knows they are watching her. She is watching them, too. When they ordered the first bottle of baijiu, she excused herself to the rather smelly bathroom and inserted her alcohol neutralizer. She stays sober enough to remember everything but cultivates a sympathy buzz strong enough to enjoy joining in the impromptu singing of one of their flagship vid series' theme songs.

All of which is to say it's not a bad gig, being a fêted foreign content designer in the capital of China. Not a bad gig, and tons of intel. Mishima could happily hover there in stealth mode for another two weeks if it were up to her. But the war in Central Asia is getting worse and closer to the centenals lying between it and China; she has to move on to diplomacy soon if this mission's going to do any good. She starts asking around, subtly but not too subtly, about who in the narrative studios has connections to the ruling party.

CHAPTER 34

Roz is working the refugee fair when the electricity goes out. Most of the government delegations have backup power storage, so after the lights go out the projections hyping cheap domestic goods and exotic locales keep running; in a breath, the space goes from the bland vulgarity of a voter rally to the eeriness of an abandoned amusement park. In the flicker of the projections the assorted soldiers can be seen raising their weapons, finding formation, and then, as communications come through, filing out into the city, leaving the refugees and staff alone in the pavilion.

Roz takes a deep breath. Some of the refugees are, sensibly enough, under tables already, but her first adrenalized thought was not *mortar shelling* but *assassination attempt*. Information is unaffected as long as they have the backup power to access it and keep the relays running; she checks the grid status and sees that the whole city and part of the surrounding countryside are out. It's not centenal-specific, then.

"Roz, you okay?" Laurent's voice over her earbud, calling in from the temporary campsite.

"Sure," she says, pleased she doesn't sound quaky. "Some traumatic flashbacks going on here, though—we're going to need to project an explanation fast." She's already working on the beginnings of it, a big friendly NO IMMEDIATE THREAT sign. "Do you have a cause yet?"

"Not yet, but we can confirm that there is no direct shelling going on, no artillery close enough to hit us."

It takes forty-six minutes to confirm that a mortar hit the lines connecting to a hydropower station a hundred and fifty kilometers west in the mountains. Although data coming out of the null states is sketchy, analysts believe it was an error rather than a deliberate attack on the power grid of Urumqi.

The situation calms quickly when explosions fail to materialize, but with governments reluctant to continue to use limited backup power on projections, the fair is shut down for the time being. Roz goes to help Laurent at the camp, but the work there has slowed down too. Shelter inflaters use too much power to be run off of backup electricity, so Laurent has been organizing a temporary common space for those who haven't been assigned shelters yet. Fortunately there haven't been many newcomers today, so it's manageable, and Laurent tells her to go home and get some rest.

Roz is briefly tempted to go back to the apartment and lie on the thin mattress with light streaming through the ineffectual curtains. Instead, she turns toward the nearest maglev station. The urban coalition apparently thinks the train is important enough to run on backup power, at least for now, and as she boards, Roz remembers a story she heard from some other city—Kunming?—that lost power after China's breakup and pulled its trains along with a massive magnet on an oxcart. This train goes much faster than that, and after three stops, Roz gets off two centenals from where she started and walks a kilometer and a half, sweating under the sun, to the address in the file Mishima sent her.

Ilya Turani was thirty and unmarried when he died, and the apartment Roz is visiting belongs to his mother and sister. When she explains who she is, they invite her in, although not without some sidelong glances that Roz doesn't know whether to attribute to antagonism or grief. The apartment is cramped, although more due to a profusion of carpets and bric-a-brac than because of the size, and dim without artificial lighting. There is a faint smell of worry. Two printed plastic canvas bags sag in the hallway, unpacked but ready, and on the wall a projection set to energy-saver shows the latest updates from the front.

"We would offer you tea," his sister Patigul says, "but with the power outage . . ."

"It's fine," Roz says. "I am so sorry to bother you again, but I wanted to ask a few questions about your brother."

They array their faces expectantly.

"How did he feel about Information?"

The mother's eyes slide away, but Patigul answers haltingly. "He did not *like* Information much. To begin with. But later, before he died . . . I believe he was starting to feel more positively toward it."

Roz feels the knell of familiarity in her bones, but she still doesn't understand. "What didn't he like about Information?"

Patigul shrugs. "The surveillance, the superior attitude. The attempt to control us."

"It took four days for you to find his body!" The accusation bursts from Ilya's mother. "How is that possible when you know everything?"

How, indeed? Roz has read the file; the presumption is that Ilya skirted around the edges of the feeds on his way to the unvidded alley where he collapsed. She feels a shiver, remembering the invisible consultant-assassins. She can imagine them leading or marching the young man along the edges of the streets, circling the invisible borders of the feeds. It's a silly image, though. It's not that hard to avoid feeds: you just have to watch them yourself to note where the coverage ends. Ilya could have easily done it alone if he had a reason to. "The investigators thought he might have been on his way to meet someone? A friend, perhaps?"

"Not possible!" his mother cries. Roz has her eyes on the sister, but she too shakes her head.

"Ilya was very focused," she says. "And if he did have a girl-friend, there was no reason to hide it."

Roz can imagine someone saying that about her and flashes back to turning off her recorder alone in her hut with Suleyman—but there's no point in pushing. She asks if there's anything else they remember about the time before his death, offers her condolences again, and leaves.

Yes, Roz told Ken to focus on the election, but Amran has assured him that she has it under control, and he does want to find the assassin for her. He and Minzhe pore over the feed files, looking for any kind of pattern.

Of course, it is Amran who spots it.

"That's odd," she says, looking at the projected map of Kas, turquoise dots showing the locations of feed cameras.

"What?"

"Look how few feeds there are in this part of the market." The market is the area of Kas where the feeds are densest, if still not anywhere approaching standard levels. "And over here, too."

"Is it random?" Minzhe asks.

Amran fidgets her hands in her skirt. "I don't know if it's random, but it's odd. You know I've been looking at the financial holdings of head of state candidates? Those areas are around Abdul Gasig's warehouses."

"Could be just chance," Ken says; the feed cameras aren't very thick on the ground anywhere; easy enough for them to miss someone.

Minzhe frowns. "It reminds me, though. After the assassination, Abdul Gasig kept calling the militia to check his house for intruders that never materialized."

"You think he was trying to point you in the wrong direction?" Ken asks. He doesn't know who Abdul Gasig is, and is rapidly blinking to find out.

"He was scared," Amran says, her tone unusually declarative. "He was afraid whoever came for Al-Jabali was coming for him."

Minzhe leans forward and starts developing a quick filter, then expands it to all DarFur centenals. "Look," he says, flipping through the maps on the projection. "No feeds cover the entrances to his warehouses or shops here, his business in Zalingei, or his trucking company in Djabal."

"There are a lot of businesses without feeds on them," Ken objects.

"Still," Minzhe says. "When he has so many, it's a pretty big coincidence." He cross-references the top ten business owners in DarFur; all the others have at least one feed on public space near one of their businesses. Minzhe can check, if he wishes, who has entered and exited, stood and chatted, glanced at the entrance, over the past year and a half. None of them are under comprehensive surveillance, but to have no intel at all for Abdul Gasig stands out. "Worth a chat at least."

"Yeah," Ken says. "Definitely." He stands up, looks at Minzhe again, more meaningfully.

"Oh, no," Minzhe says, raising his hands. "I can't leave the compound, remember? Security risk." Ken's glance strays toward Amran, but Minzhe cuts him off there, too. "She has to work here long-term. Abdul Gasig could become head of state. Don't put her in that position, not when you're here to do it instead."

Amran, meanwhile, is pointing at the election events timeline, which, unlike the assassination timeline, is blooming with color and notations. "Abdul Gasig has a rally in Mukjar this afternoon." She blinks. "He and his staff are out at the landing site, you could probably still catch them."

"Go on," Minzhe says encouragingly. "Remember, you have the full force of Information behind you."

It occurs to Ken during the walk to the landing site that Minzhe might be setting him up. You don't live with Mishima without becoming at least a little paranoid. Or maybe it's just incipient heatstroke. Ken has a heat-reflective hat, but it looks silly and definitely doesn't project the full force of Information, so he left it at the office. Grumbling to himself, Ken vaults over the mural wall (you don't live with Mishima without becoming at least a little fitter) and holds up his hand to shade his eyes as he walks toward the landing site.

There are a few young people in sharp haircuts crowded around a tsubame. One of them is draping it with an ABDUL GASIG FOR HEAD OF STATE banner, trying to cover the label from a vehicle rental company in Kampala. The others are standing around looking important, or watching the legs in mechanic's coveralls that protrude from under the vehicle. Ken recognizes Abdul Gasig from his file but would have picked him out easily; he is standing a little ways away in the shade of the covered platform, tapping his cane with impatience. When he sees Ken approaching him, he jumps.

"Good morning," Ken says, planning on a formal introduction despite the public Information beside his face.

Abdul Gasig cuts him off. "Who are you?" he asks, stepping back and bringing up his cane like an ungainly rapier. "What do you want?"

"We," Ken says, with dignity and the full force of Information, "had a few questions." The cane is trembling a little in front of him, but then, Abdul Gasig is old. With his wide mouth and his eyes hidden behind those round dark glasses, he reminds Ken of a frog. "We wanted to ask you about the Information feeds around your businesses."

"Is this a threat?" the sheikh asks, jabbing with the cane,

and then, without waiting for an answer, turns to the group by the tsubame. "Never mind!" he yells. "Pack it up; we're not going. Younis! Call Mukjar to cancel my appearance. They can hold the rally without me."

Not entirely displeased with the effect he's had, Ken pushes ahead. "Can we talk here?"

Abdul Gasig turns back to him, cane still raised and shaking more now. "I won't tolerate threats, you understand? I won't have it!"

"There is no threat, sir," Ken says as soothingly as he can. "We just wanted to talk about the feeds."

Abdul Gasig leans in, not very close because everyone else is out of earshot, but still to an unpleasant proximity. "Are you *really* from Information?" he hisses. "The *real* Information?"

Ken draws himself up. "Just because I'm a temporary consultant doesn't mean I am not part of the official organization," he starts, but again Abdul Gasig doesn't let him finish.

"Are you trying to sabotage my candidacy?" the sheikh asks, voice tilting upward now toward outrage.

"Not at all," Ken says, "we just—"

"I don't know anything about the feeds," he says. "Not my job, not my problem. But if you try to use this against me, you'll be sorry!" With a final shake of the stick, he scurries over to his waiting entourage and heads toward town, leaving Ken and the mechanic standing there looking after them. Without taking his eyes off them, Ken calls back into the office.

"I think this is worth more investigation."

If Mishima had known she would be tied to a chair less than twenty-four hours after starting to make noise, she would have waited a little longer.

It is Chu Lifen who turns on her, setting up a private booth, enclosed in projections for them to watch a vid. Mishima has a flicker of warning as Chu Lifen moves behind her, but fighting her off with any efficiency would destroy her cover. Before she can change her mind, Lifen has strung her hands together and slapped a gag on. She doesn't seem angry or resentful, just pushes Mishima down into a chair, elasties her ankles and elbows to it, and slips out of the booth.

Her politeness seems like a good sign to Mishima, as does the fact that she's at work and not in a dark alley or her tiny apartment, but as the hours go on, she begins to doubt. The vids that play on a loop on the partitions don't help: Mishima can close her eyes, but the sound of a knife slicing across the skin of a stretched throat is hard to disassociate from the image once it has been seen. If Mishima could get up, she could walk right through the projections that hide her from the colleagues presumably hard at work all around her, but no one is going to barge in; the convention of projections as walls is so accepted as to be unbreakable. And so she waits, wondering if the studio after-hours is really any better than a dark alley.

When Roz calculates her route back from the Turanis' apartment building, she sees that the city has decided to shut off the maglev to conserve energy, and she turns toward the guesthouse on foot. Information tells her that a squad of LesPros accompanied by local electricians and engineers is en route to the site of the power break, but the repairs are nontrivial, requiring significant hardware, and there is no estimate yet for when power will be back up. It doesn't help that there are few feeds in that area, a rural tract near the border with Kazakhstan.

Roz skirts around an outdoor game of pool and buys a skewer of lamb from a charcoal brazier beside it. People imagine a sharp border between the world of Information—dazzling, rational, replete—and the supposedly bereft null states, but she can feel absences pushing in toward them, giant blank spaces in the countryside fingering into smaller fragments in the cities, all those slivers of unwatched space around the feeds. She finishes her meat and tosses the bamboo skewer into a kindling collection point for the poor before calling Maryam.

Her friend answers right away. "Tough break with the power cut."

"Yeah," Roz answers, absently checking their electricity reserves. Information has, as usual, stored more than anyone would have expected to need, so they'll be fine for four days at current usage levels. The city might be in trouble in a day or two. "Hey, did you ever check whether the feeds in Toujours-Tchad matched their agreement?"

"I did! And they are in fact short. Funny regional trend, that. I wonder who came up with the idea. Considering how much they say they hate each other, it's interesting how fast a local innovation like that can spread."

"Can you check the centenal I'm in now?" Roz is tired and headachy, and Maryam already has code written to do this.

There is a brief pause as she runs it. "Yes, low," she says. "Not as dramatically as the others, only by 14.2 percent."

"Still significant," Roz says, rubbing her forehead. But maybe not enough by itself. "Have you heard anything about data . . . not showing up? Data we should have disappearing?" She feels silly even saying it, but Maryam, a techie who's unsurprised by any kind of bug in the system, takes it seriously.

"I haven't heard anything about that, and I'm not sure how it would work, but I can try to figure out some diagnostics." She's frowning, already thinking through the problem.

"Is there any simple way to search for other centenals with a feed gap?" Roz asks. Maybe that will be quicker.

366 · MALKA OLDER

"No audits have been held on the new centenals yet this cycle," Maryam says. "I'd have to set my program to run globally."

"Do that," Roz says. "And do it quietly."

"You still think someone within Information is involved?"

Probably, but that's not what's worrying her. "I think they're coming after us."

CHAPTER 35

When she hears footsteps, Mishima opens her eyes in time to see one last close-up of a twisted rope pulling taut on some unseen weight, and then the four screens around her go indigo blank. The dome above is dark, and except for the approaching footsteps, the hall is quiet. It's late, late enough to be after-hours even for these workaholics.

A man walks through the projection to her left, at a nicely calibrated angle that tickles her peripheral vision and forces her to turn her head if she wants to see him well. She does. Middle-aged, coiffed, reasonably fit, hair perfectly black—almost certainly a modification. He's wearing an old-fashioned suit, even to the tie. It's supposed to harken back to a time when China was strong and expanding, but Mishima has always thought it one of the ugliest eras in men's fashion. She doesn't recognize him, which means he's not the premier, vice-premier, not the minister of interior, nor the minister of defense. He has the unmistakable smell of staid bureaucratic government, and he's meant to look powerful.

"I certainly hope you're empowered to negotiate," she says before he stops walking.

There's no laugh, not even a twitch, although Mishima thought it came out pretty well, especially considering she's thirsty, hungry, and had to piss herself a few hours ago.

He waits long enough for her to wonder if he'll answer. "I suppose you are?" He speaks Chinese with an affected burr to recall the previous capital, Beijing, now a micro-democratic patchwork.

"I can show you my diplomatic credentials when you untie me." In point of fact, Mishima could reveal the endorsement—temporarily tattooed on her upper arm with an iridescent ink that appears only under a precise frequency of ultraviolet light—without being released, but no need for him to know that.

"An ambassador?" he says, allowing surprise—or skepticism—into his tone. "Most ambassadors announce themselves."

"Would you have accepted an ambassador from Information at this time?"

He blinks: he didn't expect her to be from Information. "Perhaps," he says, but it's unconvincing. China does not have diplomatic ties with Information, although messages are sometimes passed through 1China.

"We preferred to be as discreet as possible," Mishima offers, thinking it will show common interest.

Instead, his face tightens. "So, it's blackmail? What have you found?"

Mishima shakes her head. "No blackmail. Just a suggestion."

"Go on."

She inhales. This is where she needs to use what she's learned: the hints, slants, nuances in all the narratives she's seen over the past week that tell her what China wants. She lets her eyes unfocus as she builds the story. "China is not so different from Information. A diverse population, experience with autonomous regions"—in the past, and with varying degrees of actual autonomy, but no need to get into that. "Great military power, tremendous access to data." She doesn't think he's swelling, but he is listening. "We are the ultimate judges and admin-

istrators, arbiters and governors, within our own territories."
Pause. "What both Information and China need is greater influence beyond their frontiers. Not the kind of influence that
comes from military expansion, with an unending and costly
burden of maintenance, but the kind that derives from engagement and authority in international events." *Wind it up before
he starts getting antsy.* "The war on your western border is out
of hand." She catches a slight shift at that, a loosening; he would
far rather talk about Kyrgyzstan and Kazakhstan than about
China. "Information is looking for a partner to help end it."

"What are you asking?"

"That you go in intending to end the conflict, not exacerbate it. A respect for the rights and safety of all noncombatants
but especially those in the micro-democratic centenals between
you and the K-stans."

She lets him think about it. The opportunity here should be
obvious to him: neither China nor Information can broker this
alone.

"Information will not use this opportunity to expand its
jurisdiction?" he asks.

"We cannot tell people not to switch to micro-democracy if
they want to. But we will not campaign for it in these areas at
this time. You are likewise expected not to use the negotiations
to expand your borders."

There is another pause. Mishima thinks about the longer-
term aspect of the deal, but she prefers to leave that until later.
He seems to see the sense in her proposal. At last he moves,
stepping toward her, closer, and leaning over her until she can
see the loose skin under his chin, the thickened skin around his
eyes. Definitely modified his hair to black, she thinks. But he's
old enough to have real power.

He releases the catch on her restraints. "I'd like to see your credentials now, I think. And then, assuming everything is in order, we can discuss this somewhere more comfortable."

Voting opens at six A.M., and Ken is in the office with Amran and Minzhe, watching the initial flurry of ballots. The voting slows after seven, but the three of them stay in the heat-shielded office, watching the ballots trickle in and slicing the numbers across various demographics. Amran is tracking requests for technical assistance and deploying her team of stringers to help people connect. There's another rush around eight, but it's briefer, and by ten, Ken is bored. Malakal will be arriving at one with a crow for them to do a quick tour of the eleven DarFur centenals showing the tightest polls, but Ken is antsy now.

"Let's go for a walk," he says.

Amran looks up, eyes wide. "Now?"

"Sure," Ken says. "Why not? We don't have to be here to follow the numbers. Besides, I've never seeing a voting station." In most micro-democratic jurisdictions, people vote from their personal devices, from anywhere and at any time during voting hours. In DarFur, however, handheld ownership is well below universal, and Information has shipped in a number of specially configured handhelds for public voting. With explicit encouragement from the SVAT team, the centenal government added flags and banners to make the polling area more festive.

"All right," Amran says. "Let's go." Her gaze slides toward Minzhe and away again. He doesn't bother looking up; he hasn't left the compound since he got out of jail. As they leave, Ken notices Minzhe amplifying his projections: voting data in one, some slow-moving, dark-palette gameplay in the other.

There are puddles on the sandy ground, so it must have rained earlier in the morning, but the heat has reasserted itself and the sky is cloudless. As they step through the gate, Ken's antennae twitch and he jumps, but it's just bird shit falling from the unsettled flock of storks making a racket in the giant tree.

Ken has been to the market only twice since arriving, but even to him the number of people heading that direction is striking. "Do you think they're all going to vote?" he asks Amran, watching three women walk past in toubs—pink, green, and indigo—that flash as they walk.

"Maybe," Amran says hopefully as they are passed by a group of men in dull-colored trousers and shirts, laughing at something.

The crowd does get thicker as they approach the polling station in front of the centenal hall. Ken is accustomed to population density—he used to live in Tokyo, after all—but as the streets fill in around them, he starts to feel nervous. For one thing, he attracts a lot more attention here; he keeps catching people staring at him. His antennae are jumping constantly, so he turns them off.

"Does this feel okay to you?" he asks Amran. Ken's trying to keep his voice down, and she doesn't seem to hear him, but the way she's glancing around and behind her answers the question for him. They are now as close as they can get to the voting station; Ken can't see it, but he can see the flags and behind them the top of the centenal hall. Someone jostles him, and he looks around, but the man is already looking away. The crowd doesn't look angry but expectant: people are laughing, elbowing each other, or standing with their necks craned toward the center.

"I think we should leave," Amran says.

"Don't we need to document this or something?" Ken asks.

Just then, there's a roar of motion, and they're pushed toward the front. "All right, let's go," he yells, but Amran has already turned and is trying to worm her way out through the pressing bodies. Fortunately, the crowd is not too deep, and after a short struggle, Ken emerges, disheveled but unharmed. "Did you hear that guy calling me 888 scum?" he asks Amran indignantly.

"Look!" Amran says, and Ken turns back to the crowd in time to see the first rock fly through the air.

The more comfortable place to which Mishima and her interlocutor—Wu Jing, special advisor to the premier, according to the confirmed name card he sends her via 见闻网—decamp is a penthouse apartment overlooking the glowing lights of the city. From the glass wall, Mishima looks for the flicker of a refinery fire but can't find one. She was offered a shower and a change of clothes, but she declines; she doesn't want to stay here—or be beholden to Wu—any more than she has to. Besides, it was his tactics that put her in this bedraggled, smelly condition; let him face it.

There is not much left to talk about. Mishima offers the contact details of the people who will set negotiations into motion, as well as those who will give it the sheen of importance by attending. "Of course," she adds, "I will need assurance of my own safe-conduct out of here."

Wu waves his hands negligently. "Of course. You may leave tonight if you wish." A young woman comes in with a tray of tumblers and bottles, and he serves himself and invites Mishima to do the same. "There is one other condition," he adds as she pours.

Mishima gives the servant time to get to the door, close it behind her. "And that is?"

"You must front the negotiations for Information."

For a moment, she is flattered, thinking he's misunderstood. "I can certainly be on the support team, but I'm not at the level to . . ."

He is shaking his head, smiling. "No, you are the lead representative or China won't take part."

The lead representative? "For status reasons, it's important that the lead representative . . ."

"You will be the lead representative, the most visible figure. You!" His forefinger stabs the air, then he leans back again and sips his drink. "You, with your real name, and your real face. Or we don't talk."

And Mishima thought she was going to get out of this unscathed.

B etween the time difference and the long day of voting, Roz doesn't expect to hear about the DarFur election until late at night, and although she has to steel herself from checking in with Ken at several points during the day, she is surprised to get a call from him mid-afternoon.

"Hi!" She walks away from the community meeting Laurent is leading. "How is the election going?"

"Uh, fine. No clear result yet, although Fatima has a slight lead."

"It's early," Roz says after checking that they are only three hours into voting.

"There has been an instance of, um, minor unrest." Ken is not sure how to break this. It's true it's not exactly his fault, but he wishes it hadn't happened on his watch.

"Unrest?"

"Well, kind of a riot."

"A riot?" Roz steps outside the meeting hall. "What caused it?"

"Unclear." Ken squirms. "I can't believe how little Information infrastructure they have here; it's really tough to get solid intel—"

"Ken. What happened?"

"There was a mob-like situation by the centenal hall. At the voting station. There have been some more rumors about 888. In retrospect, I might not have been the best person to send here."

Roz comes down on that instantly. "Ken. You are the best person to be there. I wouldn't have picked you otherwise." Well, best available person, anyway. But it still stands.

"Right," Ken says, only a little happier. "Also . . . I can't be sure this has anything to do with it, but when I went to check on Abdul Gasig the other day, he said something about regretting it if we tried to hurt his chances . . ."

"What?" Roz is trying to keep up. "You went to see Abdul Gasig? And he *threatened* you?"

"Not specifically. I'm not positive it had anything to do with it."

"Can you send me the recording?" Roz does *not* have time for this, but she can't let it go. Was the assassin in front of their noses the whole time? "What happened with the riot?"

"The governor was trying to shut it down and he got a rock in the face—"

"*What?*" Roz is standing up straight now, rigid and sparking, bloody images already forming behind her eyes.

"They were throwing rocks, and one of them hit the governor in the eye. The clinic sent him to Nyala."

"Nyala—the hospital is in—"

"The 888 centenal," Ken finishes with a sigh. Like there weren't enough problems.

Roz doesn't think Minzhe's mother will take it out on the governor personally, but she doesn't actually know Minzhe's mother. "Ken, can you get a guard on him, or surveillance, or something?"

"Already done," Ken says, happy to have gotten something right.

Roz wonders if she can ask, if the question gives her away, or if her voice will give her away, but it turns out she can't not ask. "Is he all right?" His eye. She imagines it smashed, again and again.

"It's not life-threatening," Ken says. "But they aren't sure about his vision."

Something else, Roz tells herself, *cover it up.* "Who's running the centenal now?"

"He hadn't appointed a deputy governor yet, but I was just at the centenal hall, and it looks like the finance manager is keeping things moving. People have quieted down. Most seem pretty upset that he was hurt; he's not unpopular, so no one is making any trouble so far."

"I . . ." She doesn't know *what* to do. "Do you need help? I can try to get back there if I can . . ."

"No, no," Ken says, mortified. "No, it's fine. As I said, everything has calmed down. Besides, what's going on there is so important! DarFur will be fine."

It's not really DarFur that Roz is worried about.

Roz is looking for flights to Nyala before she's even off the call with Ken. Suleyman needs her, and she has to go. If the flights had been bookable, she would have paid before she had time to think about it, but as soon as she decides to throw her career to the winds in a thoughtlessly romantic gesture, it becomes apparent that it is, in fact, impossible to leave the front. There are now only two commercial flights a day out of Urumqi, and they are overbooked for weeks and weeks ahead with desperate asylum seekers. She's stuck here until Information decides to end the deployment or, as is looking more likely by the day, evacuate them.

CHAPTER 36

Roz is never sure how these things happen, but somehow the rumors about negotiations travel the hundreds of kilometers from Xi'an to Urumqi before they make it on to Information. She overhears refugees whispering about talks in the fair in the morning and discounts it, is asked about it by the waitress at her favorite restaurant over lunch and confirms that there is nothing on Information at noon, and sees a news alert at 1:24 P.M. How do people know? How could Information know faster?

She doesn't have time to trace the rumor nor to design algorithms to speed their ingestion. Roz and her team scramble into a frenzy of community discussion and explanations and the construction of a process to decide representation at the talks. The heavy overhang of fear has retreated, but the fighting hasn't stopped yet; mortars pound the mountain range that night.

None of this alleviates Roz's need to get to DarFur; if anything, it exacerbates it. She had a flash of hope that Information would let her leave early, but it's clear that even if the talks go as smoothly as can be imagined, the SVAT's work in Urumqi will remain urgent for at least a week to come. Roz tries getting a ride to the negotiations and leaving from there, but she can't find a good-enough excuse for her presence at the talks to get her travel approved on an official flight. She is beginning to think about hitchhiking down to Kunming to see if she can get a flight out of there when she gets a call from Minzhe.

"I hear you're trying to get to Nyala," he says without preamble.

"How did you—"

"I might not be an 888 spy, but we do have plenty of them."

We, Roz notices. "My mother . . . appreciates how you supported me. There happens to be an 888 crow in Xinjiang that will be leaving for Harare later today. If you would like to be on it, a stop in Nyala can be arranged."

This is not what she does. She doesn't leave her work, not for anything, and especially not an urgent job like this. She's on the front lines of the biggest crisis of the year, maybe the decade. Her team needs her.

But how much of that is hubris or misplaced masochism? They have agents here; they might need every one of them, but it's unlikely that they need her specifically.

But does Suleyman really need her?

She thinks about staying. Staying feels okay.

She tries to imagine not going to Suleyman if he does need her, and has to stop because she can't bear it.

"Thank you!" she whispers.

"It's okay," Minzhe says. "I owed you. And—don't feel too bad." Roz waits, breath held. "This place. It gets to you. It gets into your blood."

Roz exhales. "Thank you," she says again, louder this time. "Minzhe?"

"Yeah?"

"Why are you still there?"

He fidgets. "There's one of the militia members. I think he . . . might have a crush on me. Or maybe not. He . . . took my side when I was arrested."

Roz doesn't know what to say. That certainly puts her own problems in perspective.

Minzhe clears his throat. "It's complicated. Don't worry about it. But I want to clear my name, for him."

"Let me know if I can do anything to help," Roz says.

She can't walk away without a word, especially from a job like this. Better to do it in person, she decides; harder, but it leaves less of a record. Laurent isn't in the apartment, but they are required to keep their location trackers on at all times in emergency or pre-emergency situations. She finds him two streets over in his favorite Sichuan restaurant, slurping down some incredibly spicy tofu. "Hungry?" he asks when he sees her. "Have a seat."

But Roz doesn't. She tells him she has to go, and it's important, and he immediately says, "No problem, go! We'll figure it out."

Roz thanks him, but she knows that he's saying it because that's what a team leader should say. She's sure he's going to make desperate, probably resentful calls for more assistance as soon as she's out of sight. He'd certainly be entitled to that resentment.

She gets her bag—since she never unpacked, there is very little packing to do—and follows Minzhe's coordinates to the crow. They take her past the People's Park and then up the white concrete external staircase of a moderate high-rise. It is windy in the desolate way of this city, and once she gets above the surrounding buildings, the mountains loom, wild and insistently close. The air is blue and heavy with portents. Despite herself, Roz wonders if it's a setup, if Minzhe sent her into danger. There could be anything waiting for her on this rooftop, or nothing. Then she climbs up the last flight and sees the bumpy oblong craft humming there, a Chinese man in the background finishing a smoke.

The biggest hurdle is figuring out where to hold the negotiations. Everyone agrees from the start they will take place in an 888 centenal. Not only are they close enough to China that the Chinese will feel safe, with enough distance from China to be perceived as neutral, but companies in the 888 consortium still sell to both Kazakhstan and Kyrgyzstan, although from what Mishima understands, supply chains are pretty torn up in the former. China initially argues for the 888 centenal in Darjeeling, probably to remind everyone about how their armies briefly overran the area twenty-five years ago, but 888, who spend every election cycle trying to persuade the voters that incident is distant history and their companies had nothing to do with China's military overreach, flatly refuse. Eventually, the parties settle on Pokhara: remote, with facilities to offer the elite from each warring party a pleasant and ego-massaging boondoggle, and suitably neutral.

Vera dug her nails in and screamed for Policy1st to have a seat at the table, and with Veena dropping hints to news compilers, Information finally gave in. The presence of the Mighty Vs means Gerardo is in attendance and Nougaz is not. The other top eight governments howled, naturally, and dropped spitebombs into the plazas and gossip sites wherever they could, until a determination was made that any government with troops committed in Xinjiang should have representation at the talks. The hotels are full, the negotiating tables keep getting longer, and there is a sideshow of intergovernmental elbowing, but there is also a growing sense of critical mass. The largest players in micro-democracy are in the same room for something other than a debate; it might actually lead somewhere. Meanwhile, the Chinese delegates are planning a few extra days to enjoy the hot springs in the Annapurna range, although from what Mishima understands, no hiking will be involved: luxury crows, all the more coveted because of their rarity in China itself, have been hired.

Mishima herself cares little for the surroundings, except to wish she could fade into them. She kept her hair black, hoping for that shred of anonymity, but in every vid she's seen of the conference, she's the one in perfect focus, as if there were a spotlight on her. Every morning, she has to march into the conference room at the head of the Information delegation, even though once they are inside, where the only feeds are closely guarded, Nejime takes the power seat at the table and Mishima hangs in the back. She knows her input would be listened to if she had any, but she's still stunned by this punishment. Besides, there's little doubt as to the outcome of the talks; she's completed the task she was sent there to do.

"Now what?" she asks Nejime, during a rare private moment in the older woman's hotel room. They have been drinking—wine from some experimental Nepali vineyards—and despite the alcohol neutralizer Mishima is as close as she can get to showing how this has affected her.

"We'll see," Nejime says, sounding not the least worried. And why should she be? It's Mishima's life, not hers. "We'll see when this is over."

CHAPTER 37

There is a glassed window in the wall of Suleyman's room at the clinic, and Roz stares through it before going in. He is lying on the bed, and the eye she can see is closed, but it's his injured eye, so she doesn't know if he's asleep or not. Nanobots, programmed in Juba based on the injury report and flown in, are invisibly at work under the translucent bandage, occasional twitches under his swollen eyelid the only sign of their progress. When she finally opens the door, he has to turn his head to see her. His face stays petrified for a moment, and then he holds out his hand.

Roz doesn't remember crossing the room. She is standing beside him, holding his hand in both of hers. She slides down into a chair and looks down at their clasped hands because she can't look into his eyes any longer.

"I thought you weren't going to come," he says.

Roz blinks, bringing up and discarding a quick succession of calendars and maps as she tries to clear away her tears. "It wasn't easy to get back here."

"But you did." He puts his other hand on hers, holds it tight as though he can't believe she's there.

"Are you okay?" She reaches toward his face. "What happened?"

Suleyman shifts on the bed. "I didn't see it coming. I didn't realize people were that upset. You saw the debate; people were very interested. Yes, some were concerned, but the election was channeling that. And then, as the voting was going on, suddenly there was this anger. 'What happened to Al-Jabali?' 'What are you doing to protect us from our enemies?'" He smooths the sheet over his legs. "I was in my office, but I saw the crowd yelling and pushing on Information, and I went out to try to calm them. Obviously," he says, and she sees the tear shimmering in his good eye, "it didn't work. Maybe I was wrong, maybe I should have resigned, or run for head of state myself, maybe—"

"Did you assassinate Al-Jabali or order his assassination?"

His eye flicks up at her, startled into alertness. "No."

"Then you're not to blame for this. I'm not sure what's happening, but it's not because of you."

Suleyman hmphs, and pats her hand, and mutters something that might be *thank you.*

"Wait, I'm not done. Did you know about the plastic guns?"

"Yes."

"You knew they were illegal?"

"Of course. But we needed them."

"Wasn't there any way you could negotiate with the people who were attacking you?"

"With the NomadCowmen, maybe. But there is no way to negotiate with stateless people. They are paid by others to attack us. There is nothing we can offer them."

"Are they really stateless?"

"They are unregistered to any government, or their employers are powerful enough to hide their registration. Or remove it, so that they have no choice but to fight for them."

"Who employs them?"

"Sudan. Or Chad, perhaps. Probably Sudan."

Roz feels like banging her head against a wall. "Sudan doesn't exist anymore, and neither does Chad."

"Maybe not. But there are those who wish they did. Who believe their nations still exist, in their hearts if not on the maps."

"Why didn't you ask Information for help?"

"We weren't sure."

"Weren't sure we would help?"

"Weren't sure what it would cost."

Roz lets her head hang for a moment. "You heard that 888 are being punished for the attack?"

Suleyman nods. "The governor of their Nyala centenal is resigning in the face of the sanctions."

Roz waits. "And?" she prompts him.

"And we hope they won't do it again." He smiles at her, strokes her hand again. "I told you before: I believe you are doing your best. I believe you are our best option. We will try."

He is still using the plural *you,* but Roz's whole body illuminates. She swallows. "So, when can you get out of here?"

"Tomorrow or the next day. Depending . . ." She can feel his good eye traveling her face, her body, which should have given her some warning. "Will you marry me?"

"What?" Roz pulls back, shocked.

"What?" he echoes, his eye now searching her face, his expression a mirror of hers, as astonished that she is surprised as she is that he asked.

"I just came to see if you were okay . . . I'm not *staying* here!" In her panic, Roz is blunter than she might have wanted.

"We don't have to stay here. In fact"—his hand straying toward the bandage—"I'm not sure I have a place here anymore. We can go to . . . wherever you work."

He doesn't even know where she's based! "As it happens, I'm probably on the job market myself," Roz says.

"You gave up your job to come see me?"

He is smiling, as if he's proved something. "I didn't think it through."

"Take your time," Suleyman says, leaning his head back on the pillow.

Roz's comms sound: someone is calling. She doesn't bother to look. No need to answer if she no longer has a job. "We don't even know each other that well."

He opens his good eye to glance at her but doesn't respond.

"Why have you never married?" The question has been pushing to get out of her for weeks.

"Because I didn't want to do it the easy way," he says. "And you?"

Why hasn't she? When she thinks about it, she supposes she had a few opportunities to do it the easy way. There was Demetrius at university; he would have stayed with her forever if she hadn't moved away for work. Landon, at her first posting, seemed committed; she was the one who broke up with him. Guillaume, her most recent serious boyfriend, got as far as proposing two years ago, and that was the end of that. "It never felt right," she says. "It was never enough."

Roz jumps: an alert on her comms, shocking through her nerves. *Urumqi*, she thinks. She left and now something's happened, her team is under fire, or trapped by a mob. *Laurent*, she thinks, with a pounding of guilt. "I have to take this," she tells him, and he says again, "Take your time."

Roz ducks out into the hallway to answer the call. "What happened?"

"I need you to get to Gori as soon as you can." It's Nejime.

Gori? Roz is so surprised, it takes her a moment to place the city. "The Caucasus? But—did something happen in Xinjiang?"

"Besides you leaving? No. Nothing's happened, at least not yet. But I can't afford to move anyone else out, and I need people on the ground with eyes on Russia."

"Russia? Why?"

Nejime sets her mouth. "They see what is happening at these negotiations. They want in. To be honest, that was always the plan: improve treaties with all of the null states, work toward something global. But in what I can only assume is an effort to improve their bargaining position, they are pushing the South Ossetia border."

Roz feels herself twitching into professional mode. "Pushing how?"

"We have previously ignored minor incursions, but over the last few days, they have been essentially moving the border, pushing people out and taking over their land, and last night's case was egregious, five hundred meters."

"What do you expect SVAT to do about that?" Roz asks. "You need military out there." She is looking through the window to Suleyman's room. With his sealed eye facing her, it feels almost like spying on him.

"There will be backup; don't worry," Nejime huffs. "Your-Army. LesPros are strained in Xinjiang."

"It should be the other way around," Roz points out.

"It should," Nejime agrees. "The point is, I want nonmilitary support for our centenals out there."

"To do what?" Roz asks, her voice bitterer than she means it to be. "Convince them it's okay to be annexed?"

"No. To humanize the other. What Information is supposed to do." Nejime sounds weary, but then her voice sharpens again. "And if you don't think that's a worthwhile use of your time, you shouldn't have walked out on the most important conflict in the world."

"I didn't think I was still employed," Roz says after a brief pause. In a way, she wishes she wasn't, wishes she hadn't picked up this call. She can still walk away, but she thinks she may have used up all of her rebellion.

"You had something you needed to do," Nejime says crisply. "But now we need you back. Roz, you haven't taken a personal day in three years. Your timing is sensationally bad, but personal matters rarely take global politics into account. So, you were reassigned for urgent duty in South Ossetia and in the interim saw an opportunity to resolve the situation in DarFur. It is resolved, is it not?"

"It will be," Roz says.

"Good. Your background packet is on the way." Nejime signs off before Roz can reconsider.

She stares in through the window for a moment, then shakes herself and walks inside. This is her life. If he can't deal with it, now is a good time to find out.

"I have to go," she tells him.

"Where?"

"Gori."

He shakes his head. "I'll look it up. And where do you live?"

"Doha." She says it almost reluctantly: Doha seems too easy.

Suleyman considers. "Doha is not far. It is Muslim. I understand something of the culture there. But I have heard"— watching her face carefully—"that they are not always fair toward Africans."

Roz nods. "Yes." She has experienced rudeness, condescension, subtle clues that she doesn't belong. "You will find that anywhere outside of Africa. Sub-Saharan Africa. But I have friends and colleagues I trust." She rubs her forehead. Doha no longer seems easy. "I didn't choose to live in Doha, you know. It was a work assignment. I could ask for a transfer. I could move."

He waves his hand, probably because it hurts too much to shake his head. "Doha is fine, until you're ready to go somewhere else."

Roz tries to picture the sheikh in her apartment and succeeds only in transposing the image of him in Kas, white robes flowing against the background of her bright yellow walls and

NULL STATES · 387

woven hangings, a paper cutout of a prince inserted into her
mundane life. "I don't know."

He takes her hand again. "Don't worry. Go do your job. Just
call me when you get there. Please. I will be waiting to hear your
voice again."

Nejime has prevailed upon the Nyala mini-hub to lend Roz
their crow, so she's able to travel to Gori in reasonable comfort, privacy, and speed, but she has one stop to make on the
way.

Abdul Gasig has been under subtle house arrest since the
election. They couldn't have done anything more stringent
without more evidence, but seeing him in his airy salon, legs
propped up on cushions with a carafe of date juice at hand,
gives Roz flashbacks to standing outside Minzhe's dank cell
and fills her with fury.

It is some consolation that Abdul Gasig starts violently when
she enters. "You've come," he whispers.

Roz strides over and pushes her anger right into his face.
"What did you do?"

Abdul Gasig shrinks, his bravado gone, but he's still ready
to obfuscate. "Nothing, I did nothing, I know nothing . . ."

"I do not have time for this," Roz tells him through clenched
teeth. "I have to go manage Russia now; do you understand?
A great big null state is threatening our borders, and I don't
have any time to waste. You tell me what happened, and you
tell me now."

He doesn't have much resistance left in him. "I never meant
to hurt him," he whispers. Roz almost shakes him. "They approached me last year. Pointed out how my business interests
were less spied-on than most." Roz manages not to roll her eyes

"They asked if I'd like to keep it that way, maybe even get some position in the government."

"And all you had to do . . ." Roz prompts when Abdul Gasig stops, gazing into his regrets. It makes his face look old, and Roz suddenly remembers that he's nearly seventy.

"All I had to do was fiddle with some dials on the governor's tsubame. The energy management settings. I looked it up; there was nothing dangerous about it at all. So I did it." He takes a deep, shuddery breath, like a toddler about to let lose a wail. "How was I supposed to know they intended to kill him in that very tsubame?"

"Who were they?" Roz asks, scenting blood.

He stares up at her, his eyes big behind his dark lenses. "I thought they were you. I thought they were Information."

The night before the talks end, with the K-stans so neatly tied up you could put a bow on them (the war won't end that easily on the ground, Mishima knows; they never do), the second-in-command of the Chinese delegation slides into a seat next to Mishima at the bar. Mishima has been drinking shōchū with her alcohol neutralizer in, pretending it works anyway, and the short Chinese woman buys her another glass.

"We've been watching you," she says, voice low against the chatter of other delegates sitting a few meters away.

"You and the rest of the fucking world."

"You're not a figurehead," the woman purrs. "You have essential skills." A pause while Mishima declines to answer. "We don't see it as a disorder, you know."

Mishima finally turns to look at her, the room swimming as though the alcohol had pickled her brain.

"Your talent. It's something we value very much." The

woman clucks her tongue. "Shocking that your bosses would expose you by suggesting it to us while you were undercover."

Oh yes, Mishima thinks, *Because China is well known for prioritizing the safety of their agents.* But she can't get her tongue to push the words out.

The Chinese woman's face is softened with middle age. Not where people expect to see power, even now. "It's a shame Wu Jing was not more polite, but he was angry. Not many people get as close as you did." She taps in her payment and slides off the stool. "I'm sure we could find a very interesting position for you in our public service. Please keep that in mind, should you ever be in the market for such an opportunity." And then she is gone.

Mishima drinks, uselessly.

Roz puts in a request for an InfoSec team, or, since they're probably still shorthanded, some Information backup to support Ken and Minzhe with the interrogation of Abdul Gasig. She doubts they will learn much, since he swore that he never saw the assassins in person, but maybe they'll identify some useful technical detail. As soon as she is in the air with the course set for Gori, she calls Maria.

"Why didn't you tell me you knew about the guns?" Roz asks.

"Guns?" It isn't that Maria is trying to stall; after a week in Xinjiang, the idea of guns has taken on a whole new meaning, and it takes her a moment to realize what Roz is talking about. "Oh. You mean in DarFur."

"Yes, in DarFur! You saw what happened to Minzhe; why didn't you say something? Not to mention the risk to the rest of us."

Maria speaks carefully, as if she's making an effort to keep

390 · MALKA OLDER

her voice steady. "I reported it to Information, as anyone should have."

"And what about Minzhe?"

"Minzhe?" Again, Maria is at a loss. "Wait—is *that* why they arrested him?"

"They assumed he reported them, because he worked with the militia and had access to the intel."

"Oh, no."

"Yes. How did you know?"

"From some of our surveys."

"You didn't realize that's why Minzhe was in jail?"

"I heard it was for treason. Nobody mentioned the guns! Besides, I made that report ages before he was taken in, at least two weeks. We got the tip when we first arrived."

"Why didn't you tell us?" Roz asks. She remembers the gun she thought she saw in the market, the first day, before Al-Jabali was killed.

"I didn't want to jeopardize our investigation. I didn't think there was any direct danger to us. The guns were for use against outsiders in battle. No one was waving them around threatening us, or anyone else for that matter. I was really conflicted about telling anyone, but in the long run, it's a very dangerous trend. So I reported up the chain the way I was supposed to, and I said very specifically that there was no immediate danger, and no action should be taken until the ongoing mission had been completed."

Roz sighs. "Makes sense. I wonder who fucked it up."

Maria absorbs the profanity, unexpected from Roz, who always seemed fairly buttoned-down as a team leader. "I thought the anonymous-tip function was unbreakable."

"As far as I know, it is. But I was looking through the vids from when Minzhe was arrested. You said you thought you heard shots."

"I was almost sure I did."

"There were no shots there, nothing that even sounded like shots." Maria must have been terrified of those guns.

"I'll call Minzhe," Maria says. "Man. I feel terrible."

"I think he'll be relieved he's not going to lose his job for espionage," Roz says. "Maybe you should call the governor, too."

"You don't want to tell him yourself?"

There's an awkward silence, then Roz brings herself to laugh. "All right, I guess I could. But he should hear it from you." She pauses, but she's really curious. First Minzhe, now Maria. "Were we that obvious?"

"Nah," Maria says. "I doubt it. I'm told I have a good eye for these things. And that eye was turned on Sheikh Suleyman quite often because he is very pleasant to look at."

Roz can feel herself blushing. "Um, yeah." She finds herself thinking of the conversation with Minzhe, his complicated something with an unnamed soldier, maybe or maybe not and definitely not allowed. What right does she have for this to work out? "Can I ask you something?"

"Sure."

"When I left DarFur"—*the first time*, she doesn't say; no need to get into her desertion right now—"the governor said something to me about autonomy, and I didn't understand. Is it—Do people think Information threatens their autonomy? I mean, I can understand privacy as a concern, but autonomy? Governments can do whatever they want with their centenals."

There's a long pause, and when Maria answers, it's with a patient tone, the one Roz uses when she's explaining, say, that being from the Great Lakes region doesn't mean she knows anything about West Africa. "Privacy is *part of* autonomy. Deciding what is reported and how much you spend on reporting it is part of governing."

"Granted," Roz says. "But they didn't say privacy; they . . ."

"Roz. Roz. They know, just as well as you do, that data is power. They've had higher authorities use it against them long before we came on the scene. Why should they trust Information when it tells them all the data will be made public? Why should they trust them not to take punitive action based on that data?"

"So they use the vid money for infrastructure projects." Roz has to admit it is hard to argue with.

"Ballsy, though," Maria comments. "What I'm wondering is how they covered it up so well. Nobody noticed until we were looking really hard for something else."

"Maybe," Roz says. "Or maybe that's exactly what we were looking for."

When Mishima gets home, the Saigon apartment is empty. Ken is in DarFur, filling in for Roz, which seems like a pretty great career move for him. He sounded excited about it. Still, the apartment feels very quiet.

On the way home, Mishima learned that she is now incredibly famous. She is a mystery, a superwoman, a geopolitical powerhouse, at least according to the covers of three vidlet mags she noticed while browsing in the Pokhara airport. The flight attendants' mouths went *O*-shaped when they saw her. There are images of her walking through Xi'an neighborhoods pasted into the vid backgrounds for karaoke songs across Asia, diagrams of her face on the covers of Chinese-language anatomy and drawing textbooks, and her photo on the cover of at least five different, unrelated novels published in the last week. All that in addition to the news coverage of what she actually did.

Glory and fame. And the definitive end of her career in espionage.

She can imagine her old team in Xi'an working their usual overtime to find places to plant her image. She wonders if they think they're doing her a favor, or if they understand it's a punishment. She wonders which they'd prefer.

She tries her usual tactic of narrative immersion, but the stories fall flat. Mishima is relatively well versed in psychology, and she's aware that she's experiencing a minor existential crisis. She has just lost a part of herself: her anonymity. She misses Ken.

A news alert flashes, and Mishima perks up at the idea of something not about herself, but this particular item doesn't help her mood. Halliday has surfaced in Guantanamo. As a tribute to (or, some say, an exploitation of) its carcelous past, a single-centenal government in Guantanamo has turned itself into an open prison for nonviolent international criminals, mostly corrupt or otherwise discredited politicians. They are automatically granted asylum within its borders, where they live in relative comfort and bring in a steady tourist trade of convict-watchers. It's the last part that Mishima likes the least: these narcissistic megalomaniacs should be cut off from any kind of power or attention. People shouldn't be allowed to come stare; that's practically a reward for them. She huffs about that until she notices another alert about herself, a long-form profile titled *The Mystery Woman of the K-stan Negotiations*.

She needs to work. Work and exercise. She puts on some music, loud, a stream of '40s slide that is one of those lapses in taste she doesn't even want Ken to know about, and dives into the first unfinished project she finds: the assassinations.

CHAPTER 38

The Shida Kartli region of what was once Georgia is now a patchwork of Georgian nationalist centenals mixed with a sprinkling of EuropeanUnion and, Roz learns on her way there, one lone outpost of USA!USA!, a tiny government popular mainly in Europe that claims to emulate the culture and values of the former superpower. (No one has ever been able to figure out whether they're being ironic; even the citizens seem confused.)

The bulk of the region has united into what is generally agreed to be one of the most successful conglomerations of centenals in the world. It's particularly feted as an example of a smoothly functioning rural coalition, which is still far less common than urban ones. While it helps that the governments are broadly aligned in terms of foreign policy and political leanings, what really ties them together is the economics of agriculture in the late twenty-first century.

None of this prepares Roz for Shida Kartli's beauty. Maybe it's the contrast with the austerity of the Sahel and the desperate hardscrabble feel of Xinjiang, but the spreading orchards backed with blue, sharp-edged mountains take her breath away. Along the older avenues of Gori, the hard edges of stone buildings are hazed over by pine trees and vined trellises. The food is a welcome change from Darfur: khachipuris and Borjomi water, even for quick working lunches.

And *all* of the lunches are quick working lunches. Though the setting is idyllic, the situation might be even more depressing than in Xinjiang. At least the world is paying attention to the disastrous conflagration of the K-stan war and now even more avidly to the peace negotiations. Here, Roz listens to centenal after centenal explain how Russia pushes the borders in day by day. Tanks and soldiers come and tell people that the line between centenal and nation-state has moved, and therefore it has, whether it moves on the maps or not. Eventually, the maps always catch up. Sometimes, she visits the border itself, where tearful farmers and their sullen children who didn't want to be farmers anyway point out indistinguishable plots of stolen land a kilometer or two away.

Population numbers are changing little, which makes this an almost-invisible problem in terms of centenal elections and demographics: a smaller area with one hundred thousand people is still a centenal. For the people there it's unmissable: the loss of livelihoods and living spaces is putting a burden on social services and the economy. Still, it's the fact that she didn't know this was happening that shocks Roz the most.

As requested, she calls Suleyman when she gets there. Roz can feel her pulse speeding up as she waits for the connection. She's not sure what to say, and she can imagine the long, dry pauses as he searches for something to tell her about lying in a hospital bed and she self-censors the technical details of her job. But his face lights up when he sees her, and Roz can feel the smile catching on her own lips. He tells her she's beautiful, that he misses her, and he wants to know all about this new place she's found herself. She finds she has a lot to say, and he listens. It's easier to call him the next day, and the next. Roz isn't sure whether it's a good sign that their relationship is going so much better now that it's entirely virtual, but she's willing to concede that the circumstances weren't ideal while they were in the same place.

She's still not ready to marry the man.

She also calls Ken. She already knows from the news compilers that Fatima won the election, but they don't give a lot of detail to a tiny election in a remote government, and she wants to know everything.

"It went really well," Ken tells her from Zeinab's, where he and Minzhe have taken to breakfasting every morning. "The voting was smooth, no reports of any problems other than that one riot. Everyone accepted the count. And you know the best thing? Fatima is going to create a deputy head of state position and appoint the runner-up, Commander Hamid from the militia, as deputy governor."

"That setup would have saved some trouble last time," Roz comments. She is still angry at Commander Hamid for the way Minzhe was treated, but she can see the benefits of the arrangement.

"Everyone's pleased," Minzhe puts in over Ken's shoulder. "We're sticking around for a few days to make sure, but honestly, the biggest problem is figuring out the centenal governorship in Kas. You need to convince Suleyman that the riot wasn't targeting him."

"Not my job," Roz says, although it's possible she's already mentioned it to him.

Technically, the single Roma centenal that Roz visits on her third day in the Caucuses is outside the Shida Kartli economic zone consortium, but there have been two Russian incursions there in the last three months. This is the first centenal LomDream has ever won, and they only managed to scrape it out in the last election because their head of state, Lel Jaqeli, is a minor celebrity, having won several singing competitions after retiring from life as a professional football player. Even with his fame, it's remarkable that they were able to win with a platform based on Roma cultural rights, given how much prejudice still exists.

The flight takes half an hour, and she can't call Suleyman because he's having his eye checked, which makes her bored and antsy, so she looks up the record of the election. It's a for-mer Heritage centenal, and the discrediting of the Superma-jority helped LomDream eke out a win.

It's only as she scans through their post-election policies in the few minutes before landing that it hits her: LomDream is a populist minority government coming to power for the first time! And so, when she gets to the centenal hall, her first question is not about exclusion from the Shida Kartli economic con-glomerate or even the Russian incursions but "Tell me about the consultants who have come here to support you."

The young man meeting with her—deputy to the undersec-retary of music, economics, and security, or something of the sort—frowns and pulls away. Another centenal still getting used to having Information deeply involved in all their busi-ness, Roz suspects. "All our consultants have been Information-approved," he says quickly.

Roz reins in her frustration, considers his anxieties and inter-ests, recalibrates her tone. "We're not worried about anything you've done. We are researching possible incidents of . . ." She is tempted to say *fraud* to avoid overreaction but reminds herself that she is committed to transparency. ". . . violence carried out by consultants who apparently had Information validation. Obviously, we'd like to put a stop to that as soon as possible."

"Violence?" He's suspicious still, eyebrows furrowed, arms folded.

"Assassinations," Roz says sweetly. "In fact, the first thing we should do is talk to your head of state's security detail."

The young man laughs. "Security detail? The governor doesn't need bodyguards. He's his own security."

"Then we have to talk with him as soon as possible! Only"—
Roz raises her hand—"tell him not to use any mechanical
vehicle to get here!"

Fortunately, Lel Jaqeli is close by, meeting with constituents
in a hall down the street. The deputy undersecretary refuses to
pull him out of the meeting. Waiting for a head of state brings
exploding tsubame to mind, and Roz spends most of the thirty-
six minutes pacing, but the governor is alive and fit when Roz is
shown into a moderately secure room in the centenal hall for a
meeting with him and his assistant. Neither the assistant undersecretary nor Jaqeli are thrilled to be told that the head of state
should walk everywhere for the foreseeable future, accompanied by at least one security officer. While she was waiting, Roz
prepared a montage of graphic images from the assassinations
that have already occurred, and that quiets them down.

"Now that I've got your attention," Roz says as the assistant blinks up a schedule and starts cutting down travel for the
next week, "what can you tell me about this group?" During
the down time, she was also able to go through the list of consultants that has visited this centenal over the last year. It only
took a few minutes for her to zero in on the likely candidates:
DemoGreat sent no invoice and therefore no Information validation number. Their suspiciously vague expertise in "consumer advocacy promotion guidance" also seems like a clue.

The assistant immediately gets flustered and covers it by
searching through his Information for something, or pretending to, eyes blinking and rolling anywhere but to Roz. Jaqeli is
much better at this game. "Let me think," he says. "There were
so many of them."

"They might not use vehicular homicide this time." Roz
wants to drive home the fact that the assassins are a greater
threat than anything Information will do. "They could use poison, a bomb, sabotage the structural integrity of your home . . ."

Lel makes up his mind. "They're here now. They preferred to make this visit unlisted."

"What? Where?"

"Right now?" Lel blinks a few times, bringing up a schedule. "They should be in the canteen, I suppose." Roz notices him pale, possibly remembering her suggestion of poison.

"What do they look like?" Roz is already signaling for back-up.

"Can you pull up some pictures or vid?" Jaqeli asks his assistant.

"I'm looking, sir. So far, nothing."

"Nothing?"

"We've found that they're very good at avoiding feeds," Roz puts in. "Can you describe them?"

Jaqeli looks up, thinking. "Foreign," he says.

For fuck's sake. "Male?" Roz asks. "How many were there?"

"On the first visit, two males, one female. This time, one of the same men and a new one."

"Let's start with the two who are here now. Tall? Short? Skin color, hair color?" Roz can't believe this guy managed to win a European football championship. How did he even tell the other players apart?

"One is medium height, um, perhaps slightly shorter than I am," says the head of state, who is at least a head taller than Roz. "He could be North African or Middle Eastern or South Asian." Or Latin American, then. Or Roma, but she assumes they would have noticed that. "Light brown skin, dark brown hair and eyes. Not bad-looking, but no vid star, either."

Great. "And the other?" The update comes in: a security team has departed Tbilisi, estimated to arrive in thirty-nine minutes. Roz doesn't want to wait, and she asks that Your-Army reps be scrambled from the border to join her.

"Lighter. Taller. Light brown hair, I guess—or was he

blond?" The assistant shrugs. "He spoke English; I checked because I like to practice, so I had my interpreter off but with subtitles."

"Okay," Roz says, sending on the description to all personnel in the area. She hesitates; she wants to go to the canteen now, avoid any chance of these bastards slipping through their fingers again, but the YourArmy officers won't get here for another eight minutes. "What exactly do these consultants do?"

"What do you mean?" Jaqeli says. "They help us with . . ." He glances up, probably checking the list. "Um, consumer advocacy promotion guidance; that's right."

"Specifically?" Roz prompts.

"It's about helping people navigate advid claims, and so on," the assistant says smoothly. "They did several campaigns in the smaller villages last time they were here."

Roz taps her fingers against her leg, surreptitiously adding the assistant's description to her list of suspects. "Can you send me the list of the villages they worked in?"

"I can't seem to find it in the records," he says when it becomes apparent she's not going to move on until he answers. "I can try to get it to you by this evening."

"Do that!" Roz snaps. "And this visit? Why is it unlisted?" She aims the question between them; Jaqeli is more willing to cooperate, but she's starting to think it's the assistant who knows the details.

"They did good work for us the first time, and so when they mentioned they'd prefer not to list their visit, we thought, why not? I figured it was some tax-evasion thing," Lel confides, growing more expansive as no one assassinates or arrests him.

"Because they did such good work for you on consumer protection?" Roz asks skeptically.

Jaqeli glances at his assistant, and then Roz does too. Without thinking, she snaps her arm out, grabbing the assistant's wrist before he can wiggle out any more of a message.

"You're under preliminary arrest," she tells the assistant, and then speaks to the room, because someone at Information should have noticed the conversation by this point and marked this feed for real-time monitoring. "Shut down his comms. Shut down both of their comms!" She gets the answer into her earpiece within fifteen seconds: "Done."

Roz lets go of the assistant's hand now that he can't type out any warnings. "Where are they?"

He pulls his arm back to slug her and Roz ducks, her hands flying up. She feels the blow slam into the top of her head, and loses her footing, staggering back. Jaqeli catches her, and she shakes him off, furious. "Get after him!" she yells, not at the singing footballer but at the listening support team. Or maybe at herself, because before she knows it, she's out the door, taking off after the sound of footsteps down the hall. "Connect me to the YourArmy team leader!" she yells. Fucking mess of an operation; she should have her own team, with dedicated security, and emergency comms hardwired the way they were in DarFur and Xinjiang.

The centenal hall is an ancient structure, probably soviet or just post-, and it's a monument to the longevity of poor building materials, the endless hall punctuated by ill-fitting doors and hanging cobwebs.

"This is Corporal Sanz-Vidal," comes the voice over her comms, punctuated by deep but even breaths. "I am approximately two minutes from the centenal hall."

"He'll make the door before then," Roz says with some difficulty. She's out of shape, and anger and shock hamper her breathing. Her ears are ringing from the blow. "I'm in pursuit. No way I'll catch him, but I'll try to keep eyes."

Except that she doesn't see him. He must be just ahead of her.

"Maintain distance and use caution," the officer replies. "I'll try to get there sooner."

"How many people do you have? The other two suspects are a higher priority, greater flight risk, and—"

Something flies through a doorway in front of her. Roz stumbles, tries to leap it, gets caught up in the legs of the wooden chair and goes down, landing hard on her hands and knees. The assistant bursts out from the door but can't resist aiming a kick at her ribs before taking off. Roz takes the hit and catches his foot, twisting it hard away from the floor. The man shrieks, hops on his other foot once, twice, and goes down.

"Bastard!" Roz hisses, and pulls herself up until she's sitting on his chest. "*Stupid* bastard!" There was no way she could have caught him if he had kept running. His fear must have made her seem scarier than she is. He beats at her with his hands, but with her full weight on his chest, he can't land a solid blow. Roz thumps him in the head before she realizes what she's doing. It doesn't knock him out, but it does quiet him. "Settle down!" she yells.

"You all right?" Sanz-Vidal is asking.

"I've got him pinned," Roz says, breathless. "Second floor of the centenal hall. You have my location. Listen, I think I can hold him; go after the other two! They may be in the canteen, and they should be considered dangerous and slippery. Anything you want to add?" she asks the man she's sitting on.

"Fucking informant!" he spits.

"Charming," Sanz-Vidal comments. "Almost there. You have any restraints?"

"I wasn't planning on making an arrest," Roz huffs. The assistant is struggling and she is wondering if she should hit him again, but she finds it hard to do out of the heat of battle.

She stomps her boot on his wrist instead. He grunts, but Roz has thrown herself off-balance and he's able to push her off and stumble to his feet. He's barely started to scurry down the hall, though, when a dark-haired woman in a YourArmy uniform barrels up the stairs and slams him to the floor.

She has him trussed in seconds, but Roz is already shaking her arm. "The other two! We've got to get them!"

Sanz-Vidal takes her time standing up and looking Roz over. "There's another team making for the canteen. Let's go see what they found."

The YourArmy team found a handful of surprised diners, fragments of glass, and a canteen manager angry about the theft of two plates, two sets of silverware, and a wine glass. By the time Sanz-Vidal and Roz get there, after leaving the would-be fugitive government aide to stew in the reinforced backseat of the YourArmy scooter and putting a guard on Lel Jaqeli ("Barsali? No! He would never betray me!"), the Info-Sec team has arrived and is running basic forensics.

"Anything?" Roz asks the team lead, Mysoon.

She shakes her head. "We'll get a proper forensics team in here to be sure. We're testing the glass fragments and the wine stain, but I don't think we'll find anything useful."

"And the feeds?"

"Take a look." Mysoon shrugs her a compilation they've already put together, all the feeds showing the canteen and its entrances. Roz watches carefully, feeling an eerie déjà vu to the hours of scanning Kas vids with Maria. She can't quite hold back a shiver as she sees an arm and a bit of hair cross the corner of the vid.

"You see?" Mysoon says, watching her. "They were very careful." The two men have to cross the vidstream eventually—

404 · MALKA OLDER

to get their food and go back to their seats—and their physiques match the description Lel gave, but they cover their faces each time: an arm draped casually across to scratch the opposite shoulder, a hand rubbing the forehead, a scarf pulled over the mouth and nose. Their table is on the edge of the vid, and by pulling their chairs to the farthest extent they eat outside of its range.

"At least we know they're the right guys," Roz says.

Lel Jaqeli insists on throwing a supra for Roz and Corporal Sanz-Vidal to thank them for, as he puts it, saving his life. Roz has her doubts about that, but she needs to talk to the singing footballer anyway. Every time she tries, he laughs and equivocates. She's pretty sure he's terrified of Information retribution for whatever he's done, and while she's already put a travel restriction on him, she's not ready to haul him into a holding cell yet (or, rather, have Mysoon haul him). Given his nerves, a social occasion might be more conducive to good intel. Still, Roz stuffs a chemical analysis sensor in her pocket before the feast, although she feels silly about it.

The supra is held in the open-air section of what Lel refers to as "our best, most wonderful restaurant!" It is far enough on the outskirts of town for a rustic vibe, although a crumbling soviet-era factory across the street mars the pastoral impression. When Roz makes her way to their table tucked under a simple gazebo among beech trees, she finds that Sanz-Vidal is a step ahead of her. "We can't be sure they won't keep trying," she explains as she brushes a chemical analysis sensor along the side of a butter-roasted mushroom cap, then blinks for the results. "No poison," she reports cheerfully, and pops the mushroom in her mouth.

Roz finds herself wishing she had tested all the mushrooms individually.

They go through a lot of eating, drinking, and small talk before Jaqeli will listen to anything serious. Roz tries to take her time, nibbling olives, exclaiming loudly over the deliciousness of the khachipuri (which she hopes will absorb a lot of alcohol), but Lel keeps urging them to greater feats of culinary appreciation. "Have some salad! What did you think of the fish? Try this pomegranate sauce; it's delicious, I promise you!" At least he is eating indiscriminately himself; Roz is a little worried about indigestion but no longer fears Jaqeli is trying to poison them.

It takes an hour and a half, three bottles of wine, and five toasts before they can settle down to business. "Look," Roz says when she finally has his attention. "We're concerned about other governments that may fall prey to this group. Information isn't interested in petty issues right now—stretching the regulations or allowing these consultants to come in unlisted. We just need to know what happened."

"Yes, yes, of course," Jaqeli says. "I'll tell you all about it. Have some more wine. So, yes, this group. They came to us before the election, during the campaign. Said they could help us out. At first, it was the same as the others, you know, 'getting culturally acclimated to Information,' 'how to run a campaign without stretching the truth,' and so on." Roz, taking a small sip of wine, meets Sanz-Vidal's startled gaze over her glass—they are both wondering whether that last one is about how to stretch the truth without getting caught. "But then they get here, and it's different. Did you try the imeruli?"

"Different how?" Roz asks, taking the plate of cheese he's handing her.

Jaqeli squirms again. "You have to understand. We were new to this. Information seemed . . . scary."

"Scary?" Roz repeats. She's focused on Jaqeli, but she has the sense Sanz-Vidal is rolling her eyes, and remembers that she's not Information either.

"Well, it's like you want to know everything. Everything! I mean, once we became a part of the system, it was clearer, there are limits, but even so . . . before that, it was really scary! It was like . . ." For the first time in this monologue, possibly since she's met him, Lel's voice drops. "We imagined it the way they talk about soviet times."

Roz has a sudden flashback of Suleyman, back when he was still largely unknown to her, saying something similar. About Sudan. Something she had done. The restaurant! Calling them on those fake stock photos.

Seeing Roz is distracted, Sanz-Vidal takes over the questioning. "So? What did they offer?"

"They told us they could help us find a way around Information," Jaqeli says. "Not entirely, of course, but a way to carve out some space for ourselves that wouldn't be under such surveillance, such scrutiny."

"What—wait," Roz says, snapping back into the conversation. "Are you talking about feeds?" She messages Maryam silently, asking her to listen in, and opens a visual stream for her.

"Yeah, part of it was the feeds," Jaqeli says. "That actually made a lot of sense. They told us to take some of the money that Information gave us for all that crazy feed infrastructure, and use it instead for some of the things people need."

Roz feels like hitting her head against the table. How could she miss this? Sanz-Vidal is eyeing her with worry, and Roz tries to fix her expression. "And besides the feeds?"

Jaqeli waves his hands around, spilling wine from the glass he's holding. "Something about siphoning off the intel before it gets to Information, I didn't understand, techie stuff. Barsali handled most of that. Barsali! Do you really think he would have let them kill me?"

Roz gives up on messaging secretly and whispers a message to Mysoon to suggest a new angle of questioning for Barsali, with the vid of the last few minutes attached, then another requesting a techie to get as much as they can out of Jaqeli once he's sober. Roz tries to extricate herself from the feast via profuse apologies, and then even more profuse compliments to the food, and then by claiming to be too full to eat another bite. But apparently, dessert is coming, then coffee, and Lel won't hear of her leaving. In desperation, she excuses herself to the bathroom and calls Maryam from there.

"Did you hear that?" she whisper-yells. The bathroom is small, with stained tiles, two derelict-looking stalls, and an open roof that displays a water treatment system bridging over to the men's.

"I think I got most of it," Maryam says.

"It's exactly the same as DarFur, ToujoursTchad—autonomy, the feeds, the trauma from previous authoritarian governments—I can't *believe* I missed this. Of *course* the feeds were what these consultants were offering them."

"I'm not following all of that, habibti, but I'm sure you're right," Maryam says. "To be honest, I'm more worried about the other part."

Roz remembers. "Siphoning off intel before it reaches Information?"

"Yeah. That part."

Roz imagines data being collected and vanishing so completely, they don't even know it's gone. "How could they do that?"

"I have no idea," Maryam answers.

CHAPTER 39

Mishima finds hunting down consultant-assassins an invigorating distraction from fame, China, and sneaky intel leaks. So far, she hasn't managed to pin the assassins down to any particular affiliation, which makes it tricky. She's identified unpaid consultancies with six different centenals, all of which lost a head of state, deputy, or centenal governor after the consultant visit. In each case, the name of the consulting company is different, as are the names of their representatives and their professed specialization. Are they changing their names, or is Mishima uncovering a vast network of covert agents?

There is no trace of any of the companies beyond these single episodes. It's baffling to her that anyone, even a government new to Information access, would hire a company with no references, even one they didn't plan on paying. That brings her to another similarity among the six cases: there was no bidding process or due diligence done on any of the contracts. It's an anomaly: all of these governments had processes for hiring consultants, of varying degrees of stringency.

Conclusion: they already knew these guys.

Time to cross-ref. Mishima goes through every link between the six assassinated leaders over the past year, then two years, then three. It's not hard to imagine there are circumstances under which they would meet, at least virtually if not in person. They were all young, charismatic leaders of movements representing groups that had been beaten down for decades, if not centuries. Not all of the leaders were new to micro-democracy, but they were all representing new governments or at least newly multi-centenal governments. What's baffling is how they managed to communicate without it getting picked up by Information.

She finds isolated links during their campaigns: Al-Jabali met the organizer from Nuwara Eliya at a virtual conference; the Xinjiang leader was a member of the same governor's association as the Honduran. It's possible that contact could have spread this way, word of mouth one by one. It certainly would have been the safest way to avoid detection. But it seems awfully slow and random.

Maybe word of mouth can help her, too. You always miss something doing virtual research. Mishima looks up the Information team that worked with Nuwara Eliya during their transition to micro-democracy, and sends a message to the team lead, asking him to get in touch. There's an update from Roz about the events in South Ossetia, and she adds that to the mix. There is surprisingly little analysis, given that it's from Roz, just the timeline of events in that brush with the assassins. Mishima wonders if she's being careful about what she puts on Information.

With the election over in DarFur—the widow won—Ken is on his way home, and Mishima wants to get her workout in before he arrives. He might be the one who needs pampering this time.

As she skates down the boulevard, building speed, she thinks about how dispersed these assassins seem to be and wonders what they're after. Are they anti–oppressed ethnic groups? Pro–status quo? Trying to create chaos?

Chaos reminds her of Anarchy and some of the other anti-Information, anti-election groups she's monitored in the past. Is that where this is headed?

Or is it something more concerted, and she's just not seeing the pattern? A way for them to seize power?

Which would mean taking power from these governments that are finally getting their first shot.

Or—maybe it's not about those governments. Maybe they're the means, not the end. They are thinking globally. Who has real global power?

There is, of course, another point of contact among all of the victims, one so obvious and ubiquitous that she almost missed it: Information.

She needs to call Roz and talk this through with her.

Mishima catches a movement that feels wrong, too fast or too close, from the doorway up ahead on her right. She crouches, throws her arm up, leans into her speed. If she had been running, the metal bar swinging toward her head probably would have caught her, broken her arm at least, but the skates give her the momentum to slide under it.

She spins around, staying low, with one leg out in case she can catch her assailant with a sweep. But no, he stepped back, and now he's coming after her. He's a large guy, metal pipe swinging in figure eights in front of him. Fancy. Mishima keeps her spin going and takes off away from him; there's no way he can catch her on foot while she's on her skates.

She switches off all comms—a personal rule during battle—and opens a rearview vid from her antennae. He's not even trying to follow her, which probably means—

The other thug steps out in front of her, and Mishima crashes into him. For once, her helmet comes in handy: it detects the obstacle before she does and explodes out of its collar, enveloping her head with its shell and giving more punch to her impact with the big guy's chest. Mishima recovers first, bouncing back before he can grab her. She twitches the emergency gesture to switch her blade resistance, so that she can stand and fight without her feet sliding out from under her, and aims a kick at his knee, but he's already got his balance and is swinging at her. Mishima ducks the hook and gets in a quick jab under the ribs, then pushes away from him. He stumbles with the hit and then roars back at her, fists jabbing.

Mishima isn't normally into flashy kicks, but hey, at least she's wearing a crash helmet. She adjusts the resistance on her left blade to almost nothing and puts an edge on her right as she launches into a spinning reverse roundhouse. It works amazingly well, her twist building some serious speed before her foot rakes across his face. As she spins away—and keeps spinning; this isn't going to be easy to get out of—she sees a massive gash open up on his right cheek.

That's good enough to hold him, she thinks. She adjusts her friction to slow her turn until she can start skating again, lopsided from the dizziness but still putting distance between her and her attacker. She accelerates toward the crossing into the green center line of the boulevard, wondering where the first guy is, and how many more of them there can be, and who—

Her feet suddenly catch under her at maximum resistance and she trips forward, flying headfirst into the airspace above the road. She pulls herself into a tight-curled bullet and hears the deep thrum of a horn sliding by her. She hits the tarmac in a hard, bouncing roll, skimming painfully along the sidewalk and slamming into the corner of a fence post.

Mishima doesn't lose consciousness, but there's a dazed moment of looking up at the sky as though it were her bedroom ceiling, observing from a great distance leaves of a tree and the pointy iron spear of a fence. She thinks she hears music, which alarms her because it seems so improbable. She creaks her head to the side and sees the morning ballroom dancers about half a block down, standing around in clusters, looking toward her.

She hears yelling and remembers, and she's shaking her head and rolling, much more slowly than she'd like, onto her side and then her knees. Her right arm hurts. She pulls her helmet off with her left; it's absorbed all it can, and she needs all her senses. She can see one of the men on the other side of the street, hollering at cars to stop, careening toward her. She starts to get to her feet, then freezes, realizing what happened. They hacked her skates!

Her right arm must be broken, because it isn't where she expects it to be but instead limp at her side, so she shucks off her shoes with her left hand and achieves solid ground just before the first thug—blue shirt, burly, mustached—barrels down on her, brandishing the pipe like a baseball bat.

Fortunately, Mishima always carries her stiletto. Pulling it out with her left, she feels a surge of joy that all that left-handed practice will finally come to good use, and she uses that triumphant swell to fuel the blow as she steps inside his swing and jams the knife up under his sternum.

She doesn't wait to see what happens, jerking her knife back with a twist before the muscles can clench, and turning to stumble toward the dancers. Something is wrong with her left leg, a pulled muscle or a twisted joint. She can stand on it but running is painful. She has probably lost the element of surprise with her knife. Surely one of the dancers will have called emergency services by now?

Mishima backs up against the fence and opens comms, planning to tell Nejime to arrest every Information officer who has worked on the integration of the centenals where assassinations happened, but she is immediately deluged by incoming calls. Six incoming calls at once! Something is going down, but it'll have to wait until she's done with this. She sees him as she slams her comms closed, the first man who stepped to her, balding and with a trim chestnut beard. He's keeping pace with her on the other side of the street. His left hand clapped to a bright red bit of cloth against his face, something metal flashing in his right.

Mishima pings emergency services herself. If this man doesn't need it yet, he will by the time she's through with him. And she wants him alive. She finds a limping rhythm, moving away from the dancers because she doesn't want them caught in the melee. Mishima catches the sound of sirens in the distance, but traffic is slowing to a halt and the thug is already darting through the street. Mishima readies herself but sees the indigo blue of an InfoSec uniform moments before the thug goes down, taken to the ground by a flying tackle.

The indigo figures converge, at least five or six of them. She sighs, and sags against the fence, keeping her eyes open for propriety's sake. *How did they get here so fast?*

"Ma'am?"

Mishima rouses herself to see a vaguely familiar face bending over her.

"Ma'am? Are you all right?"

It's the younger of the ballroom dance teachers, she realizes. Mishima straightens. "I'm fine," she says, dredging up a smile. She tastes blood and quickly closes her lips. "You should . . . Thank you, but you should probably step away in case . . ." *In case there are any more.*

But by then, the InfoSec team has reached her, and she gratefully hands over bystander security to them.

CHAPTER 40

Maryam flies out to Shida Kartli herself. "You're giving me a taste for the field, habibti," she tells Roz when she greets her with bisous. They both know she's there in case their digital communications are being hacked. With a conspiracy this tech-intensive, she can't discount the risk that someone on her team was involved.

They hole up in a pleasant café in the old section of Gori, golden stone walls and a dusting of the season's first snow. Lel is being held for intensive questioning by the InfoSec team, but Roz wanted to debrief away from the Roma centenal anyway, to get distance from anyone else there who might be implicated. She and Maryam get their coffees and talk through the problem in the half-sentences of a long working friendship.

"Is it specific intel or . . ."

"Maybe something broader, but that would mean . . ."

"I've confirmed the ToujoursTchad situation; it's very . . ."

"Do you think it's limited to new centenals?"

"It could be a starting point for . . ."

"Or just more noticeable from our side."

Roz leans back. "We have to assume that it's not just the centenals where assassinations have happened."

Maryam is already nodding. "Those are the places where something went wrong."

"Like in DarFur. Let's say Al-Jabali was shaken by the election blackout, agrees to this mess . . ."

"And then micro-democracy works out okay for him, Information is more supportive than he expects . . ."

"Even without that." Roz feels a pang of guilt. "He hears that there's a team coming to do some audit that he doesn't really understand. He panics."

"Or he has second thoughts. Doubts. He starts to push back."

"Now *they* know the Information team is coming," Roz counters. "And he's vulnerable."

They fall silent, remembering the tsubame explosion.

"So . . ."

"So."

"We have some data to sort through."

"A *lot* of data to sort through." Every centenal on earth is under suspicion.

They have their heads together, refining search criteria and trigger points, when a news alert flashes across Maryam's vision. "What the . . ." She flicks the accompanying vid up into a projection between them—discreet enough to be blocked by their bodies from the few other people in the café—and together they watch Mishima perform some ridiculous kung fu, apparently with a blade strapped to her foot.

"What—*When* is that?" Roz asks. She scrambles to pull it up on her own Information.

"Six minutes ago," Maryam says. "This celebrity news compiler had a trace on her. They picked up live as it was happening and have been running vid nonstop ever since."

"Did anyone get some help out to her?" Roz asks, realizing she's on her feet herself, seven thousand kilometers away.

"Local InfoSec is on it," Maryam says, distracted. She zooms in on the attacker. "Do you think he could be—"

"Not the ones we missed here," Roz says. "Doesn't match

the description. But maybe an accomplice?" She jumps: an urgent call from Mishima herself. "Are you all right? We were just watching—"

"Watching? Did they get it up on the compilers already?"

"Um . . ." Roz meets Maryam's eyes. They can both see Mishima's face through the vid connection, but the projection below them is playing live, showing Mishima standing barefoot on a swath of grass, her arm in a makeshift splint, an Info-Sec team in the background and a small crowd of bystanders observing from a respectful distance. She has no idea the world is following her every move. "Yeah, they've got it. I'm here with Maryam; we were just talking about . . ."

"Right." Mishima snaps back to the problem at hand. "Look, I'm almost sure these assassinations are coming from within Information. I just wrote to Nejime, but you have to follow up with her, make sure they put a lock on everyone who worked with these centenals during the transition."

"On it." Roz nods to Maryam, who is already opening comms. "Shouldn't you be in hospital?"

"The helmet caught most of it, I think. But yeah, I'm going; I just want to make sure everything's taken care of here."

By the time Mishima has finished the debrief with the Info-Sec team ("No, no, let's get it over with now") and cleared admittance and triage at the hospital, Ken has arrived, and they're able to go into the doctor's office together.

"I see you refused nanobots for your arm," the doctor notes, blinking through the file with a moue. "We believe they're safe, but I can understand your concern, given the pregnancy. Well, that means a splint for a few weeks. And I suppose you probably won't want THC, either?" In addition to Free2B's generally pro-weed stance, they have poor relations with most pharmaceutical companies, and other types of pain reliever are expensive. "Is the pain level manageable?"

"Sure, no problem. The baby's fine?" Mishima has already run her internal diagnostics five times, but she wants to hear it from an expert.

"The 'baby' is barely visible without a microscope at this stage, and relatively resilient. I see no impact, physical, chemical, or emotional," the doctor says, blinking through the scans one more time. "You didn't take any injuries directly to your torso, and you seem to have avoided any stress spikes throughout the encounter."

For a brief moment, Mishima feels like the consummate badass she is.

"Of course, part of the reason for that may be your high baseline stress level," the doctor adds. "You should try to relax as much as possible. For the baby."

Back to reality. Through her grimace, Mishima notices Ken's fingers twitching minutely by his side. A message pops up in the corner of her vision:

Nobody's perfect.

Much as she would like to believe she can be the one exception to that rule, Mishima has to smile, and that, she supposes, helps her relax. For the baby.

CHAPTER 41

Mishima wakes late and sore the next morning, stiff from sleeping in a position that won't dislodge her splint, a dull ache in her arm beneath it. Her neck is sore, her hands are bruised, and when she leans her weight gradually on her feet, a spurt of fire shoots up from the edge of her left foot where the nail was ripped out of her little toe in one of the skating maneuvers. At least—she checks again before hobbling to the bathroom—the baby is still there, still as okay as a barely detectable clump of cells can be said to be. Even after running the diagnostic, Mishima lets out a relieved sigh when she pees without blood. Maybe, and she hates to admit this feeling even to herself, but maybe it's for the best that she is now the world's most recognizable spy.

Nejime calls before Ken has woken up from his jet-lagged sleep. Mishima is sitting alone at her workspace, trawling the news compilers idly with a mute on for her own image, when she gets the message to meet her at the Saigon Hub. If Nejime has taken the trouble to come out here in person, it's probably important.

Roz and Maryam spend another day in Shida Kartli, sitting in on Barsali's interrogations and talking to Lel again, but both are eager to get back to Doha. With the K-stan negotiations wrapped up, Roz is able to arrange a handover quickly, and they fly back to Doha together, but Roz stays only long enough to unpack and repack before catching a complicated series of last-minute flights to Kas.

The first thing she sees coming off the plane, after the dusty horizon, is Amran's wide smile. Can she really be that happy to see her? Before she can guess at the answer, her gaze moves on, over Amran's shoulder, and meets Suleyman's. His smile is much smaller, a subtle curve of the lips, but—is it just her or can everyone see it?—his whole face seems to be glowing with happiness, and it fills her. Even the protective screen over his right eye doesn't dim it.

She takes a few steps forward and yanks her eyes away from him so she can greet Amran, but they keep straying back. In the moments when she focuses on her colleague, she can almost see the conclusions forming in Amran's head and building into a crystalline structure of hypothesized plot lines running from this point back into the past and forward with terrifying speed into the future. Roz prepares herself to maintain her equanimity in the face of censure, but when Amran's expression finally settles, it's into an even bigger smile, and it doesn't falter when Roz announces she and the governor are going for coffee.

Even though it's been two days since it happened, Mishima's spinning skate-kick has pride of place on the mural wall. There is a small notation far down one end on the upheaval in Gori, which Suleyman must have requested, because that's an awfully minor and remote story to have made it in otherwise. Most of the wall is devoted to covering and explaining the results of the Pokhara negotiations, with several panels suggesting possible new structures and institutions in world government. Roz sends an image of one particularly prescient panel to Nejime before they settle down at Zeinab's.

Suleyman's hand brushes hers as he serves the coffee, and Roz feels sparks go off in her belly. When he is walking her to the Information compound, where she will be staying, she finds herself tilting slightly in the deep sand, catching herself just before her fingers tangle in his. Roz spends some time with Amran and Halima and Halima's new baby, and the stringers all stop by to greet her. Despite the heat and the weirdness of it all, it's a pleasant afternoon. Then Suleyman comes back. They have dinner at New Waves because Roz surprised herself by missing their chicken taouk, and they laugh louder than two colleagues would. But it is not until after dinner, when he invites her back to his compound, that they are alone in any real sense.

Roz knows she can't stay with him, that it's not even a question, but sitting beside him in the courtyard already feels transgressive. She is simultaneously prickling with the awareness of being alone with him and feeling exposed under the broad sky shading toward evening, only head-height brick walls hiding them from the road. The conversation trips and flags, and then he stands. "Would you?" he asks, gesturing toward one of the huts. Her body blooms as she steps after him into the relative darkness, and he takes her hand and pulls her close. "Now?" he whispers, his breath eager on her cheek. "Now," Roz confirms, and raises her lips to his.

The small Saigon Hub overlooks the river. Mishima has been there once before, stopping in on a courtesy visit when she first moved here, although otherwise she tried to keep her distance. The staff part before her like water, guiding her by their evasion to the inner office where Nejime is waiting.

"How are you feeling?"

"You know," Mishima says, meaning *Pretty awful, but not in any way that matters.*

"You may have noticed," Nejime starts in, "we're carrying out a major operation, detaining anyone who might have had contact with these centenals in the run-up to transition. Mal-

NULL STATES · 421

akal's already been released, by the way. We're convinced he wasn't involved."

Mishima blinks and nods; she had entirely forgotten that he fit the criteria for suspicion. She has been avoiding the whole mess as much as she could.

"Unfortunately," Nejime goes on, "some of the most promising leads have disappeared."

Mishima nods. "They would have known. When the attack on me went wrong . . ."

"That," Nejime agrees, "and we were very close in Shida Kartli as well. The ringleaders have gone to ground." She smiles. "We'll find them. The concern is that this goes far deeper than five assassinations. Roz and Maryam believe that the murders were only the most obvious cases, the cases where something went wrong."

"They could be operating all over the map?" Mishima asks. "To what purpose?"

"They were working on our intel networks," Nejime says. "Diminishing them in some cases and, in others, rerouting them."

"Rerouting them?"

"Diverting the intel to themselves."

Mishima doesn't understand. "Sensitive intel? For blackmail? Or financial gain?"

Nejime shakes her head. "As far as we've been able to ascertain, none of the data we've identified as missing is valuable."

"So what then?"

"We imagine these are the first steps in a larger attempt to gather intel, perhaps for distribution."

"A shadow Information?" Mishima is fascinated by the idea.

"Perhaps. It's the only scenario we've found that matches the pattern." Nejime gives a one-shouldered shrug. "We always thought an opposition would be a good idea," she muses, "but not like this."

Mishima is off on another track. "The Heritage comms pipeline, the Inner Channel." She remembers, too, how Nougaz asked her not to look into it. "That message from Deepal. That could have been from—"

"The point is," Nejime interrupts, "we're losing control. The Heritage secession threat is one sign. This is another. We need to make a major shift. If this gets out of hand, we could lose the whole system."

"What kind of shift?" Mishima's mind is running an old-school documentary montage of fascism: goosesteppers in black and white, a DPRK parade in grainy color, the barred activists of the twenties.

Nejime throws a projection, small but beautifully animated, into the air between them. "We need to rework, or perhaps enhance, the system architecture." Her projection represents microdemocracy as a flat layering of centenals, the governments with the most centenals only slightly taller than those with less, all of them side by side. A thin, intermittent line across the top of the structure represents the Supermajority's extra influence. Information overlays the whole, transparent and scaffold-like. "We need something more." Nejime twitches a finger, and another schema is lowered gracefully over the first. "What we are thinking now, and we are open to suggestions"—she nods her head at Mishima, who is wondering fiercely why they're courting her so hard—"is a kind of council, or senate if you will."

"Mm," says Mishima. The ache in her arm is biting into her concentration. She wonders how painful childbirth really is.

"People imagine that the Supermajority has far greater powers than it actually does. Sometimes, even Supermajority holders imagine that." A complicit smile, meant to be shared. Mishima waits. "It's becoming clear that while actually awarding such powers to a government would risk corruption, there is a need for an entity with the power to manage oversight and ground rules."

"A House of Lords, as it were?" Mishima asks. It's possible she's still a little snappy from the fight yesterday.

Nejime does not appreciate it. "I've been fighting for government rights since before you were born. It's just not working. We need to adjust." She pauses to sigh. "We are still debating the exact composition of this body, but it would be composed of representatives of governments—either as individuals or as blocs. That body would be balanced by specific but very limited powers entrusted to the Supermajority, and, perhaps, an observational role for null states. It would also include representatives of Information, probably in a leadership role."

"Information was never intended to govern," Mishima says.

"Another element of the system that is often forgotten or misinterpreted. A refresh will remind people exactly what it is we're supposed to do."

"Where's the accountability? You'll be open to accusations of being undemocratic." Mishima realizes she's forgotten to say *we* but decides that's okay. Her work status with Information has shifted so frequently over the last few years that she can't even remember what it is right now. She'll happily take the role of an external consultant in this conversation.

"Ah, but these representatives will be elected."

"How?" Mishima asks, still suspicious. There are any number of ways to elect people. With the same number of votes cast for each of a certain number of candidates, the system—representative, direct, party-based, individual, winner-take-all, first-past-the-post, run-offs at certain levels, primaries, secondaries, tertiaries—any of these may give a different result.

"As I said, we're still working out the details," Nejime pauses. "Even so, knowing what we know about campaigning for

424 · MALKA OLDER

election"—a toothy grin—"we'd like to get started as soon as possible. And we'd like to present you for the position of chief Information delegate."

Mishima looks down at her hands, concentrates on the pain in her arm. It's a nagging ache, not too sharp but hard to ignore. She thinks about the pinkish color of the pain, its sawtoothed shape, and when that is clear, she leans on her left foot and feels the flame in her toe, slightly dulled since the morning. Then she looks up again. "Why me?"

"You are competent, committed, and you know the system inside and out. Also, you are now a celebrity. Your spy cover is pretty much blown, I'm afraid, but there are advantages to exposure, and one of those is electability."

If Mishima was famous before, she is now a megastar. At least three different interactives have already incorporated the mechanics of her spinning slice kick, speedblading is the new favorite exercise on the planet, and she has been approached for sponsorship by Nike, the makers of her skates. (Child and youth sizes have been immediately discontinued pending safety upgrades.) Her auburn hair, hidden during the negotiations, has not gone unnoticed: there is extensive use of her image in ads for hair color modification products, both genetic and dye-based, and a new manga series titled "Mishima Kenshin" has been announced, documenting her supposed adventures (Mishima, who has always been something of a Rurouni fan, is secretly pleased about that one).

". . . they may use the killing of that man against you, but the vid makes it very clear that it was self-defense." She realizes Nejime is still talking.

"They?" Mishima asks.

"Well, you won't be running unopposed." She hesitates. "I imagine Nougaz will be interested in the position."

Mishima puts that disturbing news aside. "What exactly

would I be doing? Is this a figurehead position, a repeat of the negotiations? Because you couldn't pay me enough . . ."

"Don't be ridiculous," Nejime snaps. "We have plenty of money-loving celebrities more famous than you we could pick if that were the case. This is going to be a powerful governmental body. More than that, it's going to be defining its own role for at least the next decade." The last words echo uneasily in Mishima's mind, with the response *Will it last for a decade?* but she keeps that to herself, pulls her shoulders back, and tilts her chin up.

"I'll let you know within forty-eight hours."

The first kiss was incredible." Roz and Maryam are on Maryam's terrace, a balcony almost the same square footage as her apartment.

"Who made the first move?"

"He did, I guess. Unless you count me ditching my job in Xinjiang."

Maryam laughs, takes the hookah mouthpiece. "And? After the kiss?"

"Just the kiss," Roz shakes her head slowly. "I couldn't stay alone with him long. It wouldn't be appropriate in DarFur. But . . . maybe next time, he'll come here."

Maryam exhales apple-scented steam, passes the mouthpiece to Roz, arches an eyebrow. "Just one kiss?"

Roz considers as she inhales. "Maybe more than one kiss. But nothing below the neck." She thinks again. "The collarbone. Nothing below the collarbone."

"It sounds good," Maryam says.

"It was good," Roz says, taking one more toke and handing the mouthpiece back. "Really good. But I convinced him not to move here yet."

"He took his job back?" Maryam asks.

"He did. People are relieved, and I think he's happy."

"And when is he coming here?"

Roz can't hide her smile. "Next weekend. That's the plan, anyway. I told him if something comes up, I might have to cancel . . ."

"So, next weekend," Maryam finishes.

"We'll see." Roz shifts in her seat, holds her hand out for the hookah. "It has occurred to me that it's quite possible he's a virgin."

Maryam thinks about that, nods. "Possible, although I see it as unlikely. And if he is?"

"We'll take it slow." She grins. "Or not." Another pause. "We are so different."

"Are you worried about religion?" Maryam asks.

"That, but everything else too. He's barely traveled, never lived anywhere else, we care about different things . . ."

"So, you'll take it slow," Maryam shrugs.

"Or not," Roz mutters. She's already booked her next trip to Kas, at the end of the month. "And you? You seem to be doing better."

Maryam shrugs, her scarf slipping off her shoulder. "You were right. Getting out to the field was just what I needed."

Roz smiles but says nothing, taking her toke. She suspects Sanz-Vidal, but she's not sure. She takes a few puffs and moves on. "Are you still working on the leaked data trails?"

Maryam nods slowly. "It's going to be a while."

"Any sense yet for how big it is?"

"Not sure," Maryam says. "It could be just those centenals, maybe a scattering more."

"Or it could be everywhere," Roz finishes. "Is that even possible? It took Information years to build up this level of infrastructure."

"Technology has improved. Besides, they probably piggy-backed a lot of it. If they did it right, we won't be able to cut them off without cutting ourselves off, too."

Roz looks out past the lights hung around the balcony, into the darkness around them. "What do you think they're planning to do with it—siphon off or take over?"

"Their cover is blown now," Maryam says. "Take over or nothing at this point, I think."

Mishima chose her apartment in Saigon for the direct sunlight, the sizable terrace, and the layout permitting two separate workstations, but also, possibly most of all, for the fact that there was a Japanese bath already installed. Deep enough to sink in to your neck, large enough for two people, temperature-controlled both on-site and remotely. She tells Ken about her meeting with Nejime stretched out in the hot water, hair knotted atop her head, nape resting on the edge of the bath. Ken, whose tolerance for near-boiling immersion is lower, is sitting on the step at the other end, chest deep. Because Mishima is now obsessed with privacy and hasn't had time to put vid-reflecting glass in the windows, the lights are off except for a single candle on the distant sink.

"Wow," Ken says after she's told him everything she can from the meeting. "Are you going to take it?"

Mishima fidgets, causing ripples. "I don't know. It's tempting. It would be different, high stakes, fascinating."

"All the things you love." Ken stretches his hands into the hot water and takes one of her feet. He loves them both, so he reaches at random and ends up with the right.

"Not a bad job for parenthood, probably," Mishima goes on. Ken grins in the darkness. He wasn't about to say it.

"There's something else, though." Mishima hasn't been able

428 · MALKA OLDER

to articulate this to herself yet, but it has been percolating all day, and now, in this dark space, she's ready. "The way she was talking about trying to control the threats to Information, these attempts to drastically change a structure that is still more or less functioning . . . I think Information's system has passed its zenith, as all systems must."

Ken's fingers still on her instep while he digests that. Information has always seemed immutable, inevitable, timeless.

"If that's the case," Mishima goes on, more decisive now that she's past the insight part and on to the doing, "as I see it, we have three choices."

Ken starts rubbing again; he loves her analytical side.

"We can work against this decline and try to make micro-democracy last as long as possible. Two: we can try, either from within or without, to bring about a quick mercy killing, to let the world get on with it and find something new." Option two sounds masochistic to Ken, but he waits. "Or three: focus on the transition to whatever comes next and try to smooth that."

"There's another choice," Ken says after a moment of quiet and lapping water. "Jump ship." He can't see her frown, but he can imagine it. She doesn't disagree immediately, though.

"You know what I've been thinking about?" Mishima says. "That fake job I had for a week in Singapore."

"At Moliner?" Ken releases her right foot and reaches for her left, but she hisses. He forgot about the torn toenail. Chastened, he lets go and takes the right one again.

"Yeah. There were moments when I wanted it to be real. It was so perfect . . ." In all the ways that her perfect life until now has not been. "Fun, funky neighborhood. Fun, funky job. They all probably think it's high-stress, but to me? That would just be chill."

"And you'd be good at it."

"I bet I could get them to make it real. I bet Poppy would take me on."

"Being famous wouldn't hurt there, either," Ken points out.

Mishima lolls, sliding in deeper, up to her chin. "Do you think you'd like that?" she asks, her mouth barely above the water.

Ken shrugs. "I like Singapore all right." Nice though it might be, he's not ready to settle down. He doubts Mishima is either. But if that's what she decides, he'll manage.

"We could try it," she murmurs to the steaming water. "Stop worrying about saving the world."

Ken keeps his counsel, and they are silent for a while, imagining the alternate life.

"If it were to be one of the others, though," Mishima goes on.

Ken goes back over the first three. "You don't think it's a little early to be deciding which one?"

"Maybe," Mishima admits. "I may be exaggerating the demise of the world order." She pokes at him with her left foot, and he takes it again, more carefully this time. "But I will say . . . this job they offered me? It would a good place to be for whichever of those three paths we choose."

Quiet again, in the warmth and the candlelight.

"It could also be fun."

"In a different way."

"Not exactly stress-free, but . . ."

"A different kind of stress."

"You want to do it."

"So do you."

"I guess we're going into politics."

ABOUT THE AUTHOR

MALKA OLDER is a writer, humanitarian worker, and Ph.D. candidate at the Centre de Sociologie des Organisations of Sciences Po, studying governance and disasters. Named Senior Fellow for Technology and Risk at the Carnegie Council for Ethics in International Affairs for 2015, she has more than a decade of experience in humanitarian aid and development, and has responded to complex emergencies and natural disasters in Sri Lanka, Uganda, Darfur, Indonesia, Japan, and Mali. Her debut novel was 2016's *Infomocracy*.